"Forgive me in advance, because _ .... be shouting about my love for *One on One* until my voice gives out. In her stunning debut, Jamie Harrow paints the game of basketball in a way that feels like life and love itself—in moments of struggle and perseverance, in breathtaking joy and heartbreak that gets beautifully repaired. Ben and Annie are so fully explored that they are now real people to me, and their love story unfolds with perfect tension and tenderness. A new all-time favorite."

—Jessica Joyce, *USA Today* bestselling author of
You, with a View

"Jamie Harrow's *One on One* is such a sweet, sexy, and deeply sincere debut. It's a book all about showing up, whether on the basketball court, for the person you love, or for yourself. It made me feel all the expansive heart-thumping feelings—the anticipatory tension of setting up a free throw, the surge of adrenaline from a game-winning buzzer beater, the absolute power of a first kiss when you can tell it means something. I know I'll be thinking about this book for a long time!"

—Alicia Thompson, *USA Today* bestselling author of
The Art of Catching Feelings

"*One on One* showcases the best of what the romance genre has to offer! I cheered for Annie and Ben as they peeled back their layers and allowed themselves to fall, and I was completely in awe of Harrow's ability to balance both humor and hard topics with care. Complete with an enchanting ensemble cast of friends and family, and tension that keeps you on the edge of your seat, this book is an engrossing, propulsive read and an absolutely stunning debut!"

—Naina Kumar, nationally bestselling author of
Say You'll Be Mine

"*One on One* is a perfect balance of the magic and the heart-break that come alongside loving a sport—the way these teams and institutions shape and carry us, the ways they often fail us, and the difficulty of holding both sides at once. With quiet humor, a patient slow burn, and immense tenderness for Annie, Ben, and the team that brings them together, Harrow's debut is a beautiful ode to falling into trust and love in equal measure, and to taking up hard-won space."

—KT Hoffman, author of *The Prospects*

"In her absorbing debut novel, Jamie Harrow has crafted a moving journey about following your dreams, falling in love, and the power of finding your voice. When Annie returns to her alma mater's basketball program as a video producer, it feels like a last resort. What she discovers is an opportunity to rekindle a sweeping romance, redefine her legacy, and rewrite the ending of her own collegiate athletic chapter. As enthralling, captivating, and addicting as the very best basketball games, with sparkling cinematic moments worthy of one of Annie's own electrifying sizzle reels, *One on One* is a total slam dunk. I couldn't put this down!"

—Becky Chalsen, author of *Serendipity*

"Harrow's breathtaking debut delves deep into the raw emotions of grief and the pure beauty of rediscovering joy in an exquisite tale of second chances, featuring an enemies-to-lovers romance."   —*Library Journal* (starred review)

ONE
ON ONE

A Novel

JAMIE HARROW

DUTTON

DUTTON

An imprint of Penguin Random House LLC
penguinrandomhouse.com

DUTTON and the D colophon are registered trademarks of
Penguin Random House LLC.

LIBRARY OF CONGRESS CATALOGING-IN-PUBLICATION DATA
Names: Harrow, Jamie, author.
Title: One on one: a novel / Jamie Harrow.
Description: [New York]: Dutton, 2024.
Identifiers: LCCN 2024012228 (print) | LCCN 2024012229 (ebook) |
ISBN 9780593474822 (paperback) | ISBN 9780593474839 (ebook)
Subjects: LCGFT: Romance fiction. | Novels.
Classification: LCC PS3608.A7838544 O54 2024 (print) |
LCC PS3608.A7838544 (ebook) | DDC 813/.6—dc23/eng/20240325
LC record available at https://lccn.loc.gov/2024012228
LC ebook record available at https://lccn.loc.gov/2024012229

Printed in the United States of America
1st Printing

This is a work of fiction. Names, characters, places, and incidents
either are the product of the author's imagination or are used fictitiously,
and any resemblance to actual persons, living or dead, businesses,
companies, events, or locales is entirely coincidental.

For Jeremy, M., and H.

And for my mom, who drove me everywhere.

ONE ON ONE

ONE

I USED TO BE A SUCKER FOR A CINEMATIC MOMENT.

When the woman with the dark bob and Skechers perches next to me on the bench and says, "It's like something out of a movie," I get it. I understand why she's whipping out her phone, trying to figure out how to take a panoramic photo.

It's one of those perfect October mornings when there's a bite in the air, the kind that always makes my lungs crave more. Everything is dripping with caramelized sunlight. Ardwyn University students stroll through the quad toward a cluster of old stone liberal arts buildings, the field green like tuition dollars and mown with precision. I breathe in the smell of fallen leaves and, inexplicably, apple cider donuts.

"It's something," I mutter in response, eyeing the brochure sticking out of her colorful paisley shoulder bag. *A Bright Future*, it says at the top.

There was a time in my life when I would've eaten this shit up with a spoon. Now, Ardwyn seems suspiciously like

Disney World: too perfect, like it must've been synthesized through a series of focus groups to feel like college, and all these young people in their chunky sweaters are going backstage for a cigarette break as soon as they're out of my field of vision.

"Beautiful day," the woman declares.

My anxious brain does not have the bandwidth for small talk right now. I try to get away with a noncommittal *mm-hmm*, but she snares me with eye contact and sticks out her hand. I shake it a beat too late, offering a perfunctory smile.

She tells me her name, and I forget it immediately.

"I'm Annie," I reply.

"Oh, there they are!" She waves to a man in a windbreaker and a teenager twirling a bucket hat in her hands, both walking toward us from the student center. "My husband and daughter. They went to find a restroom."

I rise. "Let me make room for them to sit with you." I can't stay still, anyway. My jaw aches from clenching, I'm tapping my foot, and I picked the cuticle off my right thumbnail before she sat down.

She protests, but I wave her off. As I back up, a student walking behind me says, "Excuse me," so I step off the path into the dappled shade of a heinously majestic oak tree to let him pass. He's dressed in what must be all the Ardwyn gear his parents bought him at the bookstore on move-in day: Ardwyn hat, Ardwyn lanyard holding his Ardwyn student ID card, Ardwyn Tigers T-shirt featuring the mascot holding a basketball.

At the sight of the basketball, my stomach churns like the quaint old waterwheel behind the library.

Another student pops up in front of me, a perky, red-faced

kid in a polo and khakis. "Hi! Are you here for the tour? It'll be a few more minutes."

For the first time I notice a handful of other families milling around behind the bench. Prospective students and their parents, chatting and waiting and peering around.

"No!" I respond too quickly. "I'm not. I don't. Um, no. Thank you."

I shouldn't be allowed within a ten-foot radius of this tour group. Eight years ago, I graduated and swore I'd never set foot on this campus again. For eight years I kept that promise to myself. Yet now, thanks to wedding-induced nostalgia, *Home Appliance Magazine*, and Ben Fucking Callahan, here I am.

My new friend leans toward me. "I was wondering!" she says. "Are you a graduate student?"

I shake my head. "I . . . work here." The words feel all wrong coming out of my mouth. "Today is my first day." Which is why my eyes snapped open before sunrise and now I'm loitering outside, forty minutes before my first meeting.

"Which department?" she asks. "Madison is debating between biology and computer science."

"I'll actually be working for the basketball team."

Some of the other parents and kids swivel in my direction, and one of them *oohs*.

"So lucky," says a mom in a cable-knit sweater, lifting her sunglasses. "You must be excited to be here."

I'm here because I have no other options. But if I say that, the tour guide will probably haul me off with a hook and lock me in whatever cell they're using to hide the creepy frat boys and the protesters pressuring the school to divest its endowment from fossil fuels.

Her husband sidles up to me, hands on his hips. "Basketball, huh? I'm a big fan."

"Of Ardwyn?"

He laughs like my question is a joke. "No, I'm a Duke guy. Cool job, though. You guys have been so-so the last few years, so keep your expectations low and you'll probably have fun. Shame that old coach of yours didn't stick around. I always said he could've done something special here."

I shrug like I don't know exactly who he's talking about: Coach Brent Maynard, everyone's favorite Ardwyn icon. I swear, if I turn a corner and run into a bronze statue of that man, I will drag the thing to the Schuylkill River and drown it. The tour guide won't be able to stop me.

It's still early, but this is my cue to exit. "It was nice meeting you," I say to the mom on the bench as I make my escape.

She beams. "Have a great first day, Annie!"

I drift down a weathered flagstone path past the dorms, gawking at the scenery. It's familiar and foreign at the same time. I snap a quick photo of the ornate arched entryway of Cloughley Hall, where Cassie and I shared a room our first year, and send it to her. **I can practically smell the mold from here**, I add.

Aww, memories! Cassie responds immediately.

I'm about to drop my phone back into my bottomless pit of a tote bag when it vibrates again. This time, Cassie is calling.

"Hi, Cass."

"Hi! Did you drink the tea this morning?"

Ugh, the tea. It's some kind of calming yet invigorating herbal blend Cassie dropped off at my new apartment last night as a supportive gesture. It could've been worse. I half expected her to show up this morning to escort me to work like it's kindergarten orientation day. Luckily, Ardwyn is on the Main Line, in the idyllic suburbs outside Philadelphia, and Cassie had to be at her office in Center City by eight o'clock.

"I had an Irish coffee instead," I say. "Great for the nerves." Ah, there's the source of the apple cider donut smell: A group of sorority sisters is hawking them at a table in front of the dining hall, with a handmade sign touting a fundraiser for a local animal shelter.

"Yeah?" Cassie asks, like she's pretty sure it's a joke, but not one hundred percent sure. I can picture her face, her tawny brown skin, a wrinkle forming between her eyebrows, her cloud of curly hair falling to the side as she tilts her head in concern.

"I drank the tea," I lie.

"Good," Cassie replies, satisfied. A faint voice filters in from her end of the call. "Hold on a sec," she orders me. "Don't hang up!"

"Is that your boss? I want to talk to him for a minute," I say. "*Give. Cassie. A raise!*" The partners at Cassie's firm call her a "rock star," which basically means they wouldn't be able to function without her but still don't pay her enough.

Cassie stifles a laugh. "Shush!" There's a rustling sound, and then a muffled conversation with some guy on the other side of the glass ceiling.

It's partly her fault I'm here. I was drugged up on sentimentality at her and Eric's wedding this summer. It's not every day your best friends marry each other. As the after-party wound down, the three of us sat around a fire pit in a courtyard full of greenery, perfectly tipsy and content. Eric, an assistant coach at Ardwyn, caught me off guard when he turned serious. "Come back and work for us," he said. "We're shaking things up. Coach wants to revamp the video program."

He made some good arguments. And I was desperate. It had been forty-two days since I'd impulse-quit my latest soul-sucking job, a gig creating instructional content for a refrigerator company, after making *Home Appliance Magazine*'s 35 Under 35 List. Which had been as embarrassing as a Jumbotron proposal from someone you don't want to marry. My health insurance coverage was about to lapse, I was running out of money, and for the first time ever, I was struggling to find work.

Apparently, the Internet knows what it's talking about when it says job-hopping is a "résumé red flag." Despite seven jobs in eight years, I'd always managed to bullshit my way through questions about my history during interviews, until this time. *Flaky?* one HR person scrawled at the top of my résumé, the question legible across the conference table. I didn't get a callback.

Despite all that, I hesitated. Part of me thought I might be better off calling time on my video career and moving on to whatever happens after you accept that you've utterly failed to live up to your potential.

"Sorry, I'm back," Cassie says. "Anyway. How's campus?"

"Weird," I say. "I didn't anticipate how strange it was going to be to come back." My voice gets stuck on the last word, and I clear my throat.

A pause. "Annie. Are you sure this is what you want?"

I grit my teeth. "Do I ever do anything without thinking it all the way through first?"

Cassie says nothing. She's taken enough depositions to know not to answer the question.

I was on the fence when Eric offered me the job, until somewhere in his fervent speech, he mentioned Ben. "He just won a big ESPN award," Eric said offhand. "Young Front Office Leaders, or something."

Ben Callahan, team data whiz. We worked side by side for the Tigers in college, leading the crew of student managers that kept the whole operation running. Until, for me, it all fell apart.

That could've been me. I felt something hot in my chest I didn't recognize, and the words flew out of my mouth: "I'll do it."

Three years of penance, then get the hell out. Three years is long enough, I think, to prove to other employers that I can be reliable. I know I'm lucky to have a friend who can give me this opportunity. And I swear on *Home Appliance Magazine* I'll try my best to build something more permanent once I'm done here.

The peals of the campus church bells ring out from across the quad, snapping me out of my thoughts. It's too loud to talk over the noise, so I say, "Hang on," into the phone and hope Cassie hears it.

While I wait, I finally allow my eyes to settle on the Church. Not to be confused with the actual church with the bells. The Church is the nickname for the Simon B. Curry Arena, where the Tigers play. Towering over the treetops, it's a giant, crumbling pile of red bricks with a pointed roof that makes it look like a cathedral.

I swallow hard. Basketball was my first great love, and nothing else has come close, not even my ex Oliver. I never really played, but I grew up courtside and adored everything about it: squeaking shoes and sweat, the arc of a perfect shot sailing toward its inevitable destination, the camaraderie among the players and staff. The dopamine rush of winning.

I haven't seen Ardwyn play since I graduated, and I haven't watched a basketball game at all since Dad died two years ago.

The bells ring out again and again, marking the time. Then the noise fades, and it's nine o'clock. Time to go.

I let out a theatrical sigh. I pause. And then in my gravest voice, I proclaim, "They toll for me."

Cassie groans. "I knew you were going to say that."

Okay, maybe I'm still a *little* bit of a sucker for a cinematic moment.

ON THE WAY to my introductory meeting in the athletic department office, I pass the gym and library, congratulating myself on remembering where everything is located. But when I reach the building and pull the door handle, it doesn't budge.

A passing student glances at me, and my cheeks heat. I peer through the glass. This door is clearly not the entrance anymore. Inside is nothing but an abandoned vestibule.

Right. Don't mind me. I totally know what I'm doing here.

I wander tentatively for a couple minutes, drawing the attention of a security guard. "They remodeled the building five years ago," he explains. "The back is the front now."

In the interest of laziness, I walk behind the building along a long row of bushes and cut through the grass, instead of going back the way I came. When I emerge on the other side, there's no gap in the landscaping to use as an exit. I squeeze through two massive rhododendrons, batting away branches, and pop out onto the pavement.

A pair of guys stand a few feet in front of me, holding paper coffee cups. "Can you get us tickets to the opener?" one is asking. Their heads swivel toward me simultaneously as their conversation stops. I don't know the first guy, but the other is Ben.

"Annie Radford," he says neutrally, without blinking, as if he's been expecting the shrubbery to spit me out at his feet all morning.

Junior year, when he and I competed for the Philadelphia 76ers internship, I used to say to Cassie: "Ben Fucking Callahan, my nemesis." And then we'd dissolve into a fit of laughter. Not because I wasn't afraid he'd beat me—I was. But because the idea of him being anyone's nemesis was absurd, because Ben is—ugh—a good person.

I'm instantly dizzy at the sight of his face, maybe because it's the first familiar one I've seen since arriving. Or maybe because, *whew,* it's not exactly the same face.

Ben was always good-looking in a wholesome way, if you're into that sort of thing. Earnest brown eyes, white teeth, excellent posture. Six foot two on the roster when he played, which means six feet flat in reality.

I still remember what one of the upperclassmen said during the freshman roast: "Ben Callahan is here tonight, folks. He's accompanied by the little flock of birdies that follow him around chirping wherever he goes because he's such a cutie."

Hilarious, but not applicable anymore. The geometry of his face has evolved, and sparks slingshot through my nervous system at the overall effect of his jawline and cheekbones. A few intriguing fine lines and a darker, magnetic look in his eye, some neatly groomed stubble. His deep brown hair is styled meticulously, like an uptight newscaster's. If you ignore the hair, he's almost . . . is it possible he's . . . hot now? I check for a wedding ring, because I am *extremely* thirty years old. Nope. Surprising.

He's sizing me up too. His eyes scan me rotely from head to toe and back again. His face is impassive, his mouth turned up so tepidly at the corners it doesn't qualify as a smile. These are not his usual facial expressions. Where's the eager grin? The warm hug?

Oops, it's my turn to say something. The silence has gone on too long. "Ben, hi!" Despite my nerves, I force some enthusiasm and a smile that probably looks as stiff as it feels. As I tuck my hair behind my ears, a leaf comes untangled and flutters to the ground. We all pretend not to notice.

I brace myself for a bunch of friendly questions, but Ben offers none, and it takes me a minute to realize why. My entrance interrupted this other guy's request for tickets. That's why Ben is standing there with the burdened expression of someone who's been asked the same question for the millionth time: *Can you hook me up?*

My wrist stings, and I rub it with the opposite hand. My fingers find a scrape that's puffing up around the edges, courtesy of the bushes.

Right. They're probably wondering why I materialized out of the foliage like an overly friendly squirrel. "I got lost," I explain. "The door moved."

Ben glances at the entrance. "Yeah, they did that a long time ago," he says in a flat voice. "You haven't been here in a while."

I'm not standing close enough to speak at a normal conversational volume, so I take two steps forward to avoid having to shout. "How are you?" I ask.

"I'm fine."

"Good, good. I heard about the ESPN award," I say, giving myself an internal pat on the back for being so gracious. Miss Congeniality right here. "That's awesome. Congratulations."

"Thanks." He shifts his coffee cup from one hand to the other, studying the lid. I fidget with the scratch on my wrist. Ticket Guy coughs. Is Ben waiting for him to leave?

But Ticket Guy isn't getting the hint. "How do you two know each other?" he asks politely.

"We go way back," I explain.

"She used to work here," Ben says at the same time.

"I once puked on Ben's shoes on a flight back from Chicago. Worst turbulence I've ever experienced," I say. We were stuck in our seats for another forty-five minutes, which made cleanup tricky. Ben waved off my apologies and spent more time digging around for a water bottle so I could rinse out my mouth than trying to clean himself up. "That kind of bond lasts forever."

It's a joke, but Ben barely raises his eyebrows in acknowledgment, and an awkward silence follows. A prickle of embarrassment runs through me. Am I being overfamiliar here? My four years at Ardwyn were the most significant of my life, and Ben and I spent more time with each other than with our friends and families. But a long time has passed.

I stand there for a minute, trying to gather the composure to say a casual goodbye and walk away looking unperturbed. Or maybe I should take the most direct escape route and withdraw into the bushes. It was more comfortable there anyway.

Ticket Guy beats me to it. "Callahan, I gotta run. We'll catch up later," he says, backing away. He offers me the slightest jerk of his head.

"Sure," Ben says, his tone suddenly cheery. "And the tickets are no problem, as always."

Then we're alone. He looks down at his half-zip and brushes an invisible crumb off the Ardwyn logo. Pulls up the zipper an inch.

I press onward. "Some things don't change."

A line appears on his forehead. "What do you mean?"

"You know." I gesture at Ticket Guy in the distance. "Everybody wanting you to hook them up."

"Ah," he says. "Nah. He's a friend." He clears his throat. "I was sorry to hear about your dad."

"Thanks." Briefly I wonder if all this awkwardness is because he's uncomfortable acknowledging Dad's death. Some people are afraid to say the wrong thing, so they say nothing at all. At least Ben said *something*.

"I'm excited to be back," I say, steering the conversation toward a lighter subject. "Eric says you guys want to focus on video strategy this season."

His nostrils flare a little. "As long as we also focus on playing good basketball." Spotting an older woman wheeling her bike to the rack outside the building, he waves, his face brightening. "Hey, Cindy, nice weekend?"

My stomach sinks, unease curdling inside it. If I didn't

know better, I'd think this was more than aloofness or fumbling for the right thing to say. I'd think Ben was actively unhappy to see me.

That wouldn't make sense. Ben is one of the most considerate people I've ever met. Junior year, when we were stressed over the internship, he was unfailingly kind. There was no secret sabotage, no pistols at dawn. He combed through old game footage with me when I needed help, and asked my opinion sincerely when he wrote up scouting reports.

It was inconvenient. Sometimes I was jealous, because everything came easily to Ben, and he was so close to Coach Maynard. Ben had played basketball. His connection with Maynard was natural and immediate. After two years sitting the Ardwyn bench as a walk-on, he retired and became a manager to prepare for a coaching career, just like Maynard. Forget mothers and babies; there's no bond as powerful as the one between a man and another man who reminds him of himself.

I had to work furiously to get to the same point. I got there eventually—a perfect illustration of *be careful what you wish for*—but it took a lot of effort. I could never hold it against Ben, though, because he was so *nice*.

Unlike now. My patience turns brittle and snaps, and I cross my arms tightly. "Is everything okay?"

He stiffens, caught. A flicker of guilt crosses his face. "Yeah, of course." His tone is suddenly chummier, but it's forced.

I narrow my eyes. "Not feeling well?"

"I'm fine."

"Somebody screwed up your coffee order?"

The cup is halfway to his lips when I ask the question. He takes a long sip. "All good."

"Didn't sleep?"

"I sleep great at night."

I press my lips together. "Well, if it's not you, it must be me, then."

He smooths his hair with one hand, squinting at me, his jaw set stubbornly. "I don't know what you're talking about." His upper lip jerks, like he's trying to force a friendly expression but can't quite bear it. "Anyway, I have to run. Busy day." He starts to walk away but turns back as a gentle breeze sends leaves skittering across the path. Banners stamped with the university crest billow gracefully on the light posts behind him. He raises his cup to me, as if to prove that everything is fine and he's still the nicest guy around. "And hey, it's good to see you. Welcome back." But it doesn't sound welcoming at all.

TWO

WHEN I ENTER THE ATHLETIC DEPARTMENT OFFICE, the front desk is empty. Someone is talking nearby, out of sight, over the drip of the coffee maker and the clinking of spoons.

After a moment, the receptionist appears, mug in hand, walking with the telltale lurch of decades of desk work. She's got short gray hair and an Ardwyn *A* pin on her sweater. I stare at the pin. I can't help it. Eric and I once made a pact to get that exact *A* tattooed on our bodies after I graduated. The official team color, the official font. Mine was going to be on the side of my rib cage. Neither of us ended up doing it.

The receptionist leads me to an empty conference room, instructing me to take a seat in a thin, disinterested voice. I check my phone and find a text from Eric: **HELLO CO-WORKER! Got pulled into another meeting, see ya this afternoon!!**

Awesome. I planned to cling to Eric like a security blanket until I got acclimated, but he's already abandoned me.

Two young women arrive a few minutes later. The first strides in carrying a nylon satchel and an open laptop, sits down, and hunches over the screen. As her auburn hair falls into her line of sight, she absently gathers it on one side and twists it into a long spiral away from her face.

The second ambles into the room like it takes all the effort in the world. Her laptop clatters as she drops it on the table a little too roughly, and she plops into a chair and exhales loudly. She rubs her eyes under her thick glasses. A slouchy beanie droops on her forehead.

"Hi, I'm Jess." Somehow she manages to sigh after every word.

The other woman looks up, fingers hovering above the keyboard. "Wow, missed you there. I'm Taylor. You're Annie?"

I nod. "Nice to meet you."

Taylor smiles and pets her hair spiral. "We're on the media team. We run the athletic department social accounts."

Jess twists around in her chair. "Is there food at this meeting?"

I take out a notebook and pen. Not a bad idea to look like I'm making an effort. "I didn't see any. I don't think I qualify for the continental breakfast treatment."

"Not even fruit salad?" Jess despairs.

"If anything, I'm probably more on the stale-bagel level."

Jess snorts. "The future belongs to those who believe they deserve an omelet bar. Eleanor Roosevelt."

Taylor pounds at the keyboard with a frown. "I told you to eat before we came. You get weird when your blood sugar is low." She presses one final button and turns her full attention to me, her mouth curving upward. "You know, you're a legend around here."

I blink. "Me?" Surely not.

"Don't get too excited. There are only, like, five of us in the department. But we've always wondered who made those old basketball videos. They're so good."

"Really good," Jess adds. "You obviously had a shit camera, but you did awesome work."

"Wow. Thank you," I say, my face growing warm. "It was a shit camera. I think I found it in a closet. Our budget was zero dollars."

Taylor leans forward and rests her chin on her hand. "Did you graduate a semester early? We always wondered why the videos stopped in December instead of at the end of the season."

"Ah." I shift in my seat. "Yeah, I had enough AP credits from high school, so I couldn't justify another semester of tuition." Not the full truth, but I did meet the requirements to claim my diploma—barely—and head for the hills when I needed to, after the holiday tournament in Florida.

Thankfully, Taylor can't ask any follow-up questions, because a broad-chested man in a blazer and khakis enters the room. He has gray side-parted hair that sweeps across his forehead like the bristles of a broom.

"Ted!" Jess and Taylor say at the same time.

"How's everybody doing this morning?" He's got an open face, an unguarded smile. He turns to me. "Ted Horvath, assistant athletics director," he says with a firm handshake. "Welcome back to the Ardwyn Family."

The Ardwyn Family. Three words, an ambush, a homing beacon's signal activating inside me. An expression so familiar, the cadence, each syllable, like sliding into an ancient pair of shoes from the back of the closet, or remembering all the words to a song from long ago. My heart rate kicks up a notch and the faint stirrings of nausea rise in my gut as I note my symptoms from a distance like I'm my own doctor. Diagnosis: severe allergy to school spirit.

The Ardwyn Family is a family whose former patriarch—a coaching prodigy, a campus hero—got away with being a manipulative, power-abusing narcissist. Forgive me if it doesn't warm my heart.

"No breakfast, Ted?" Jess asks.

Taylor hoists her bag onto the table. It lands with a thud. "Jess is hangry," she explains, digging around inside. "Peanut butter or cranberry almond?"

"Peanut butter, please." Jess holds out a hand until Taylor finds a granola bar and passes it to her. "And do you have my laptop charger?"

She does. I fight a smile. It's like a diaper bag. She's probably got her water bottle and wallet and allergy medication too.

"What's 'hangry'?" Ted leans forward on his elbows.

Before anyone can answer, the door opens one last time, and a man walks through it.

"Coach!" Ted bellows.

Taylor's shoulder blades snap together. Jess rips off her hat and slides her granola bar to the side. The energy in the room evaporates, like when a teacher enters an unsupervised classroom full of chattering students.

Assistant head coach Travis Williams is tall, closer to

seven feet than six. I need to get used to that, otherwise it's going to be a long day of noticing everyone's heights. I'm back in basketball, for shit's sake.

Williams is fair-complexioned with fine blond hair, and his skin has the withered texture of an overripe bell pepper. "Morning," he says. His eyes are the darkest part of his face, which gives him a severe look. He doesn't smile, not even in a perfunctory way. Nobody tells him Jess is hangry.

He sits directly across from me at the table and folds his hands. He puts nothing in front of him, not a notebook or cell phone or coffee cup.

Apparently he's the last person we were waiting for, because Ted starts the meeting. Sort of. "So, Annie, how was your move to Ardwyn?"

Williams rubs a hand across his forehead.

"It went pretty smoothly," I say. "It's nice to be back. Although I was sad to see my favorite ice cream place is gone." I hesitate to add more, looking back and forth between Ted and Williams and fiddling with my necklace. Ted clearly loves small talk. Williams seems like a guy who would roll his eyes if you tried to wish him a happy birthday.

It would be nice to know who I'm supposed to try to please here. Jess and Taylor are no help. They're both engrossed in their laptops, and based on the dueling-pianos rhythm of their typing, I'm pretty sure they're messaging each other.

I used to understand the politics of this place, but there's a lot of turnover in college sports, and everything is different now. The year after I quit, Coach Maynard got a new job making big-time public school money at Arizona Tech and took most of his staff with him. His replacement, Coach

Marshall Thomas, brought in his own assistants, including Williams and Eric.

Ted is still going. "Do you have a lot of friends in the area?"

"Um. A few." My hand is on my necklace again. *Stop that*, I chide myself.

"How long has it been since you graduated?"

"Eight years." I force a smile and widen my eyes like I can't believe so much time has passed. Here's an approach to satisfy everyone: I'll answer his questions in as few words as possible, like I'm paying for them by the syllable, but with my friendliest facial expression.

Ted launches into a story about Jess's first day on the job, and that's Williams's breaking point. He shifts in his seat and clears his throat. "I have to leave for the airport in a half hour, so we need to get started."

Recruiting trip? I had him pegged as an Xs and Os coach, not a schmoozer.

He leans forward on his elbows. "Please explain to me why we need someone like you on our team."

Ted laughs, a ho-ho chuckle from deep in his belly. "She just got here, Coach!"

Williams gives him a dead-eyed look.

"Um, I'm not sure I understand what you mean," I say. "Wasn't I hired because you thought you needed someone like me? You, or—someone."

He's silent for a moment. I uncross my legs and recross them in the other direction. Taylor's typing is feverish.

"I'm asking what you do, on a basic level. I don't spend much time on the Internet."

"Oh. Well, I used to do this type of work for the team when I was a student, as Eric probably told you? I'm sure the role will be a little different this time around. But generally, I'll produce videos for social media. Behind-the-scenes stuff, interviews? And hype videos."

"Hype videos," he repeats blankly, his face giving nothing away.

"Like movie trailers, but for basketball games?" I clear my throat, trying to knock the upspeak out of my voice.

Williams makes a steeple with his hands, each fingertip pressed against its counterpart on the other hand. He looks up, talking to the ceiling. "When I heard Coach Thomas was creating a new position for a video person—to me it didn't seem like a good use of our *limited resources*." He emphasizes the last two words carefully, like they have a secret meaning I'm not meant to understand. "I'm old-school, so maybe that makes me biased. But our director of analytics is a modern guy, and he agreed with me. We made our opinions clear to Coach Thomas."

Ted opens his mouth and then thinks better of it.

Williams's eyes drop from the ceiling to me. "But now you're here."

I want to laugh. What an ass. I didn't even seek out this job. Why should I sell him on it? *Talk to the people who did the hiring. Talk to Eric, especially.*

Speaking of Eric, I should've given him a lump of fucking coal as a wedding gift instead of a fancy Dutch oven. He told me Coach Thomas is desperate to top the innovative ways other schools use video. He neglected to mention that others on the coaching staff adamantly disagree.

He's lucky I love him. I bite back a rising wave of sarcasm. I can handle a guy like Williams, because he's like a lot of coaches I've known. He only cares about winning, and he believes that mindset excuses any number of offenses. His belief is reinforced by the fact that thousands of people stand in the background and cheer while he does his job. All I need to do is tell him what he wants to hear.

I paste on a mild smile. "Let me tell you about how video can help with recruiting."

Thirty painful minutes later, I leave the meeting with clammy, shaking hands. *Three years of this.* I have a long way to go. I wish I could say I'm not going to worry about earning anyone's acceptance here, but I don't have that luxury.

After that shit show, I need to hustle over to the Church. I'm supposed to meet Donna the admin to fill out HR paperwork and get my ID card at ten thirty, and I'm cutting it close. By the time I get there, halfway across campus, I'm breathing heavily. Sweat dampens the armpits of the white top I'm wearing under my blazer.

It's a new blazer, in bitchy brick red. I wanted to channel a power suit vibe for my first day—without buying something boring. Mom yanked it from the rack at Aritzia with a gasp. "It's exactly your color."

When we shop, she reminds me that I'm a True Autumn. I have hazel eyes, a dusting of freckles across my nose, and what my grandma used to call "a misleadingly dainty mouth." My wavy brown hair grazes my shoulders, the evidence of last year's Great Christmas Bangs Debacle thankfully just a memory now. The memory involves my sister, Kat, wielding a pair of scissors after too many cranberry mojitos, telling me, "It'll look French!"

I can't blame her. Mom, Kat, and I spent our first Christmas after Dad's heart attack at home, eating the same turkey we always ate, decorating the tree with the ornaments Kat and I made as kids, playing the board games we'd played every holiday for years. We were miserable. Apples to Apples *sucks* when you only have three players. The next Christmas we overcorrected, fleeing all our familiar traditions for a rental in Florida, where we were equally miserable but drunker. Hence the bangs.

According to the rules of seasonal color analysis, I'm not supposed to wear pastels (valid), black (unreasonable), or anything close to Ardwyn Blue (just another sign from the universe). Mom believes self-categorization is the key to self-understanding. She's right about the blazer, though.

There should be music playing, I think as I look up at the Church. The *Jaws* theme, maybe. I could stand outside and reflect on old times and turn this into a whole thing, but there's no way in hell I'm going to be late for Donna.

Okay. I take one deep, fortifying breath. Let's get this over with.

THREE

OTHER THAN ERIC AND BEN, DONNA IS THE ONLY person still around from the old days. In fact, Donna will still be here long after the rest of us have gone to meet our maker, even though she's got twenty-five years on us. Death will be too terrified to ever come for Donna, especially if it tries showing up without making an appointment first.

She's barking into the phone when I approach her desk. "How many times do I have to tell you? No. Solicitors. Don't you dare call again." She hangs up with such force it probably hurts the person on the other end of the line. "Some people need to get their fucking ears cleaned," she mutters. I worship her in a way that makes me understand why some gods find the vengeful approach effective.

Her glower melts into a beatific smile when she sees me. "My beautiful girl." She stands to hug me. Donna is wiry and tanned year-round, with cropped hair dyed a shade of blond that tells people she doesn't give a shit that they can tell the color is fake.

"It's good to see you," I say.

"It's even better to see you. I missed you, I'm thrilled you're back, and that's all the chitchat we have time for, so let's get down to business."

Donna zips through the paperwork and slides it into a folder.

"There's supposed to be a tour, but you don't need it, and I have to go call a booster about his season tickets. He made one of the girls in Development cry, so now I have to return the favor. Your office is over here."

I scamper after Donna as she strides through the lobby toward the quietest section of the office, away from the conference room and the kitchen.

"The bathrooms haven't moved." She gestures down the hallway. "But there are free tampons now."

"How revolutionary," I say.

We turn left. There are only two offices in this stretch of corridor. The one on the left belongs to somebody. There's a coffee cup next to the computer and a cluster of picture frames on the other side of the desk. A bunch of half-deflated birthday balloons droops in the corner.

Donna deposits me in the other office. The desk is empty, but a massive bulletin board fills one wall, covered in old game programs and crumpled tickets. Evidently, the previous occupant was sentimental enough to save everything, but not sentimental enough to take it when they left. On the opposite wall is a row of pennants, one for each of the major Philly professional sports teams.

"Let me know when you take this stuff down and I'll have someone come patch the holes," Donna says. She pauses in the doorway. "Things have changed here. The people in charge are different, and it shows. I never blamed you for leaving for a better opportunity, but I'm glad you're back, and I think you'll be happier now."

"Okay," I say weakly. *She never blamed me for leaving for a better opportunity.* What opportunity? And why would she blame me, unless someone else did?

On her way out, she peeks in the room across the hall. "Not here," she declares loudly. "Wait until he hears about Kyle's latest fuckup. Lord have mercy." And then she's gone.

I need to start churning out a steady stream of preseason content right away. There are people to help with scripts and shooting, but otherwise I'm mostly in charge. Which means I'm the one who has to reach out to Ben for the information I need for my first video, even though I don't know what to make of this morning's conversation.

Monday, 11:47 A.M.
From: Annie
To: Ben

Hi Ben,

I'm looking forward to working with you again! I'm starting a series highlighting Ardwyn's top players at each position over the years, so I'm looking for some old stats.

Attached is a list of what I need. It's pretty straightforward. The video has to be final by Thursday

afternoon, so please send me everything by
Wednesday afternoon.

    Let me know if you have any questions. Thanks!

I sit back in my chair, satisfied. I even forced myself to include the two exclamation points for extra-friendly vibes. Works well with others! Professional, yet feminine!

Next up, a call to IT to figure out why I can't access the video archives yet. I drag a finger down the phone directory Donna gave me, looking for the right name and extension. Eric's name is near the top, with *Assistant Coach* next to it. I run into Ben's a few rows below it, followed by his title: *Director of Analytics.*

The realization cuts like an infomercial knife through a watermelon. What did Williams say at the meeting? *Our director of analytics is a modern guy, and he agreed with me. We made our opinions clear to Coach Thomas.* I assumed Ben was the director of operations. "Director of analytics" wasn't even a position when we were in school. I should've realized Williams was talking about Ben, though. He was a statistics major. As a student manager, he did all the normal stuff: helped break down film, inventoried equipment, did laundry. But he was also constantly waving a piece of paper in front of Coach Maynard's face with some graph or chart he'd compiled when he was supposed to be sleeping, urging him to tweak the lineup or rhapsodizing about offensive efficiency.

I remember one particular rant. "Elliott should never bother practicing that baseline shot again. Every time he does, he's lighting fifteen seconds of his basketball career on fire. He hasn't even tried it in a game all season." He threw his hands up in the air.

Coach Maynard frowned. "That doesn't sound right."

"The numbers aren't *lying*." Like he needed to defend their honor.

It was a late night in the office and I had been listening to the conversation for too long. I tapped a few keys on my laptop and turned it to face Maynard. "Look, Coach, I made a video montage of all the times he's taken that shot in a game this year."

It was a black screen.

Ben and I high-fived. Maynard laughed and shook his head.

Ben argued against my hiring. Williams's opinion doesn't bother me as much because it's not personal. He doesn't know me. But Ben does, and doesn't want me here anyway.

That stings, badly. And it jibes with the way he acted this morning. But why is someone I used to work closely with— so closely that I still remember his Wawa sandwich order— acting this way? I must be missing something.

There's no time for this. If I'm going to convince Coach Thomas that hiring me was the right call while Williams and Ben are whispering in his ear that it was a mistake, I need to focus.

I set off for the storage closet to check out the state-of-the-art equipment Eric promised. The Church, including the office, is long overdue for a remodel. Even when it's clean it seems dusty, and none of the rooms have enough electrical outlets. But the rich wood molding lining the hallways is charming, if battered, and the carpet is plush, although it's faded from its original Ardwyn Blue.

I pass the room where the student managers work and a wave of nostalgia hits me, even though it's barely recognizable without the odor of Monster Energy drinks permeating the air. Shockingly, there's not a *Saturdays Are for the Boys* flag in sight. It's crammed full of desks with backpacks everywhere, and music blares from a laptop, but nobody's there. Practice just started, so they're probably in the gym. I'll introduce myself later.

I pull open the door to the storage closet, step inside the dark space, and stumble backward. A reedy twentysomething with shaggy hair is standing in front of my beautiful new equipment, biting his thumbnail and watching a clip from *Impractical Jokers* on his phone.

"Uh, hi," I say.

"I needed a minute," he says, barely glancing up.

"Come here often?" I quip.

Donna hollers from down the hall. "Kyle! Where the hell did you go?"

He shoots me a pleading look. "Can you shut the door?"

Whatever he did wrong, hiding isn't going to make Donna any less pissed. "It'll get worse the longer you make her wait," I say. It may have been a while since I last worked here, but I still know some things about this place.

THE FIRST THING I want to film is a fake press conference with jokey questions for Coach Thomas. After Kyle reluctantly drags himself out of the closet, I acquaint myself with all the gear at my disposal, set up a camera in the media room, and check the lighting and sound. I'll have only thirty minutes with Thomas tomorrow and it'll be the first time we meet, so it needs to go smoothly.

As the day winds down, I sit at my desk to review the test

footage. A phone call from the payroll department about my direct deposit sidetracks me for a minute, and when I hang up, an unfamiliar voice emanates from my speakers: "Coach Thomas seems cool."

I look at all the open windows spread across my three monitors and then realize where the noise is coming from. After I set up the camera, I left it running while I ran back to my office to grab my phone and got waylaid by Ted Horvath in the hallway for a while. Two of the student managers appear to have parked themselves in front of the camera to eat lunch while I was gone.

One of them speaks. "I guess. At least he's not, like, a sexual predator or something."

Blood whooshes in my ears.

The other one snorts. "Dude, what the fuck?" I don't remember their names, after a day full of introductions. So far, they're White Polo and Blue Monogrammed Vest.

A third person moves into the frame. It's Ben. "Hey, guys, how's it going? Who's setting up for practice tomorrow?"

White Polo raises his hand.

"Who's the new girl?" Blue Monogrammed Vest asks. "With this thing?" He gestures at the camera, oblivious to the fact that it's recording.

White Polo has the answer. "New digital media producer."

I should probably stop playing the video. The lighting and sound are fine. But instead I plug in my headphones and rest my chin on my fist, face too close to the screen.

"I saw her talking to Donna like they knew each other."

"I heard her dad was Bauer's high school coach."

"Holy shit, bro, her dad was Ken Radford? No wonder she got this job."

Ben says nothing. What the fuck? He has a cornucopia of facts to choose from to correct this ridiculousness. Yes, Dad was the winningest high school basketball coach in New Jersey state history. And yes, he was Eric's coach. But these kids know nothing about Dad or me.

They don't know about Dad's dry sense of humor, or his patience, or the way he made his own snack mix when we watched games on TV, mixing up a separate batch for me because I like a higher proportion of pretzels to popcorn. And they don't know that I invented this job. If these beer-me dipshits are longtime Ardwyn fans, they probably got hyped up on my videos when they were guzzling Go-Gurts in middle school.

"Someone said she used to work here. You know her?"

Finally Ben speaks. "She worked here a long time ago for a little while."

"That's a ringing endorsement. How cringeworthy is it going to be? Do I need to unfollow our Instagram account?"

I'd kill to see Ben's face, but his back is to the camera. "That's not the issue. But she doesn't deserve to be here." He pauses. "All I'm going to say is: Get used to it. We're the best we've been in years. Everyone is trying to elbow their way in because of the hype. Hopping on the bandwagon."

The weight of his words drags my jaw down until I'm gaping at the screen. I want to laugh but can't find my breath. I rub my face with my hands and leave them there for a minute, pressing down from my eyebrows to my chin.

"I wish some of that hype translated into a spot in the preseason Top 25," White Polo says.

"That's meaningless," Ben replies. "We'll be ranked when it matters."

"I've literally never heard you talk shit about anyone," Blue Monogrammed Vest says. "She must be a total nightmare."

I rewatch it three times. The first two times to make sure I understand Ben correctly. The third time serves no purpose other than to make my insides feel like they've been jammed into a pot of boiling water with the lid on.

Sitting still and stewing in these feelings seems unhealthy, so I busy myself with the bulletin board, unpinning yellowed game tickets, old rosters, and printouts of news articles about big wins. It doesn't clear my head, but at least it gives me something to do with my hands.

This is worse than I thought this morning. What am I missing? I haven't seen Ben since the fall of senior year, which is an absolute blur. I spent a significant portion of those months in a state of heavy intoxication. I wasn't much better sober, trapped in a haze of preoccupation with the way my love life and job were falling to shreds around me. It's possible I did something grudge-worthy, but nothing stands out in my memory.

My thoughts are interrupted by a giant man with a ginger-brown beard charging through the doorway and squealing, and I instantly feel lighter.

"Annie," Eric sings, pulling me in for a hug. "That shit is so red. You look like the person a senator calls when they need help covering up a felony."

I squeeze him back. It's the latest iteration of a joke he's been telling for over a decade, since we became friends in high school. Eric talking about clothes is like putting a sentence into a translation app, turning it into Hungarian, and then turning it back into English. You can kind of track, technically, where the sentiment came from, but overall it makes no sense.

After detaching myself from him, I smooth the lapel of my blazer. "Thanks, I think."

He's beaming and nearly bouncing around the room, roaming from wall to chair to window. "I'm so glad you're here! I've been counting down the days. Honestly, I was afraid you were going to back out."

"Nope. I'm in it to win it," I say, with an anemic fist pump.

"I'm so happy. And you started on the wildest day. Did you hear what happened? Donna realized our director of operations, Kyle, used last year's schedule to book all our travel for the first half of the season."

I hadn't heard, but it doesn't surprise me that the guy who was unembarrassed to be caught hiding in a closet watching prank videos on his phone would screw up that badly. "That guy is the director of operations? Why? How? He doesn't even seem capable of directing someone to the bathroom."

"His uncle is the university's CFO," Eric says. "He's new. It was a favor." He spots the pile of thumbtacks and team paraphernalia on top of the filing cabinet. "Redecorating already? I love it. Tell me, how great was your first day?"

I let out an uneasy laugh. He genuinely thinks this job is the key to my happiness, not a means to an end, and I'm not ready to crush his spirits. "It was a day, that's for sure. Williams? You could've warned me."

He's plucking items from the upper edge of the bulletin board, where I can't reach, and adding them to the pile. "What do you mean? I thought you'd get along with him. He reminds me of your dad."

"What?" I hiss. "My dad was nice."

"It's not that. It's the tunnel vision." He switches to a robot voice. "Must. Pursue. Victory."

"Eric, that's not even what I'm talking about. There's a weird vibe here. Some people aren't being very welcoming." I don't mention Ben by name. Eric isn't known for his discretion.

He unpins a birthday card. "What? No. Everyone is stressed, but they shouldn't take it out on you."

"Why is everyone stressed?"

He fumbles the pushpin. It disappears, and he drops to his knees to search for it, bumping into the furniture with all his lanky limbs as he crawls around.

"Eric, why is everyone stressed?" I repeat.

He goes still, his upper half hidden under my desk. "Well, funny story. Not 'ha-ha' funny. More 'the universe is chaotic so you just have to laugh' funny. I did plan to talk to you about it. Maybe after work today?" He pops his head out, looking up at me hopefully.

"No," I say, my stomach dipping. "Let's talk about it now."

He climbs into a sitting position, his back against the desk, and covers his eyes with the birthday card. "Promise you won't get mad?"

"Absolutely not." I snatch the card from his hand. "Spill."

His face droops. "There was an internal announcement last week," he says. "The athletic department is planning a budget cut for after this season. A big one. We're the only revenue-generating sport, and we haven't had any standout seasons lately, even though we've been improving every year. Ticket sales are down, donations are shrinking . . ."

A budget cut. Yet here I am, a brand-new employee with

a brand-new salary and a closet full of expensive, brand-new gear. I fight the urge to staple Eric to the bulletin board. "Why didn't you tell me before I took this job?"

"I didn't know!" he says. "It was clear we weren't *thriving*, but I didn't realize it was this bad. We were still spending money, hiring people. When they told us last week, you were already moving into your apartment." He scratches the back of his neck. "Look, nothing is set in stone. The team has a lot of potential. And I think you belong here, and you're going to help bring new energy to this team."

"But if things don't go better this season," I say, realizations piling up in my head, "budget cuts will mean layoffs. And I'm a new hire in a completely nonessential role." Shit. Another six-month stint to add to my résumé. A heavy weight settles on my chest.

"Maybe," Eric admits. "I'm really sorry. But maybe not. We won't get the worst of it, because we're still the only team that has a chance of pulling in significant money. Coach says they're planning to take away one position from our staff, so it looks like we're in it together with everyone else. Other teams will bear the brunt of it."

"That makes me feel much better. Maybe the field hockey team can play without sticks? When I get laid off, I'll help the swimmers look for puddles big enough to practice in once they lose their pool."

"None of it is inevitable," he presses. "We have a whole season to turn things around and the talent to do it. And even if the worst does happen, the sacrificial lamb isn't automatically going to be *you*."

"Are you sure I didn't get hired just so they can fire me when it's time to cut someone?"

"I'm sure," Eric says firmly. "Coach wants you here. He believes you can make a difference. Prove him right."

I pace across the room to my desk, and my eyes land on the staff directory. If I'm not automatically going to be the one laid off, then who else could it be? It won't be a coach, or the strength and conditioning coordinator. They're vital. It definitely won't be Donna. This team needs her more than it needs an actual basketball. Kyle is safe, given his connections.

"Then who . . ." I say, trailing off when I realize my office door is open. I move to shut it to thwart any eavesdroppers, but someone is coming down the hallway. Half-zip, sculpted hair, dark eyes. Crap, it's Ben. I try to avoid eye contact but it's too late, and he stutter-steps awkwardly, like he'd rather keep walking but feels compelled to stop.

"Callahan!" Eric says, hoisting himself off the floor. "Get in here, buddy. Annie and I were talking about her first day back."

He stands in the doorway reluctantly, a somber pout on his unfortunately still-attractive face. Damn, I was hoping it had just been the flattering October sunlight. Life is truly unfair.

He gestures to the room across the hall. "My office is right there."

Ten feet away. I grit my teeth, and he shoves his hands into the pockets of his chinos. "That's so great," I croak. The two of us, stuck together for an entire season.

The two of us.

There it is, the answer to my question slotting into place. If I'm not the one laid off, it'll be Ben. It makes perfect sense. He's nonessential; having a dedicated statistics analyst is a luxury. Even though he's good enough at his job to win an ESPN award, he apparently still hasn't done enough to earn a coaching position, despite the fact that he's been here for a decade.

He needs me to fail because if I don't, he'll be the one who gets fired.

Eric's eyes land on him and then jump back to me, but he doesn't notice the tension. Instead his face lights up with a memory. "Hey, it's Mom and Dad! Remember?"

Mom and Dad, our old nicknames.

It started with one of the younger managers, Spencer. When we heard he was failing Intro to the Humanities, we sat him down in the conference room.

"We know it's hard to balance basketball and school," Ben told him. "We want to help you."

Spencer slouched in his chair. "There's not enough time in the day. How do you do it? Do you even sleep?"

Ben and I exchanged a look. I survived by taking easy classes and contenting myself with average grades. He did it by staying in and studying every night.

"Let's make a plan," I said. "You have a paper due Friday, right?"

Ben opened his laptop and pulled up the calendar he and I shared. "If I put Garrett on laundry . . ."

I leaned in. "You'll have to set up for practice by yourself on Wednesday."

"Maybe Donna can help get the recruiting letters out."

"I'll look over his paper on Thursday night."

"Perfect." Ben input the changes to the calendar. "Oh, Garrett's birthday is on the twelfth."

"I'll make cupcakes."

"You have a test that day. Sociology, right?"

I amended my statement. "I'll beg Cassie to make cupcakes."

Ben closed his laptop and folded his hands. "You're off duty for the rest of the week," he told Spencer. "Take the time to write a good paper."

"Send it to me before you hand it in so I can make sure it doesn't suck," I added.

Spencer hunched forward, his face red. "I feel bad making you go to all this effort for me."

"Ardwyn basketball is a family." I patted his arm. "We look out for each other."

"Thank you," he mumbled.

Spencer showed his gratitude by calling us Mom and Dad behind our backs. It caught on immediately. I know the other managers used to joke about us hooking up too, but it was never like that between us. Ben had a girlfriend, and I was only interested in emotionally unavailable music snobs. We didn't hang out outside work. All we had in common was basketball, and it probably worked better that way.

Jeez. Is this what this whole season is going to be like? It's like somebody's following me around and hitting me repeatedly with old memories like a rusty shovel to the face.

"This is an epic moment. You two, reunited!" Eric mimes taking a photo of us with an imaginary camera. He feeds off an enthusiastic audience, but unfortunately he doesn't require one. "Dad, how does it feel to have Mom back at home?"

Ben flashes a tight smile. "Hm. Wow. I have no idea what I've done to deserve this kind of luck."

I laugh out loud and his eyes pin me down, etching his displeasure into my skin.

My stomach twists. I barely suppress a scowl and turn back to Eric. In my best patronizing parent voice, I say: "Honey, Mom loves you very much. But that doesn't mean Dad and I are getting back together."

FOUR

AFTER A FEW MINUTES OF SMALL TALK IN WHICH Ben and I each manage to converse with Eric without saying a word to each other, Eric heads off to the film room, humming a Harry Styles song off-key. Ben attempts to escape alongside him, already scrolling through his phone. "Hey, Callahan. Wait," I say.

He pivots back slowly and tears his eyes from the screen.

"Help me with these?" I point to the pennants hung high on the wall: one for each of the Eagles, Sixers, Phillies, and Flyers. He won't say no. Ben would help Darth Vader lift a heavy suitcase off a baggage claim carousel.

He eyes the stack of garbage on the filing cabinet. "I hope you're not planning to get rid of that. A lot of it is worth saving."

I open the top drawer and sweep the pile inside. "There. In case the National Archives call."

He shakes his head and reaches up to detach the Eagles pennant.

"I know what you're doing," I say.

"What I'm doing?"

"I know about the budget cuts." I lean back against the desk, crossing my arms. "The layoffs. Or layoff, singular. I get that you're worried about your job, but putting a target on my back to save your own ass isn't cool. I know you and Williams tried to convince Thomas that hiring me was a mistake. And I know you're trying to turn the managers against me before I've even met them. '*She doesn't deserve to be here.*' I have it on tape."

Outrage washes over his face. "Did you use your camera to spy on us? Wiretapping is a federal crime."

Deflection. What a coward. "Some would say that hair gel abuse is also a federal crime, but here we are," I say. "I had no idea you'd stoop so low, Ben. You've changed."

To his credit, he resists touching his hair. Instead, he stares, his eyes boring into me like he's trying to read my DNA. In another context, the intensity in his gaze would be sexier than—nope, not going there. Burning all evidence of that thought in my mental fireplace.

"And you haven't changed at all," he finally says. "You're the same person you were senior year."

I flinch. Oof, that's a sore spot. "I don't know what that's supposed to mean."

He can see that he hurt me, although I can't imagine he understands why. He has the decency to look chagrined. "Look, I didn't mean for it to be like this."

"It doesn't have to be," I say. "I want to keep this job. I'm sure you feel the same. We're in an awkward position, but Eric said it might not even happen. It's not definite yet."

Ben tosses the Phillies pennant onto the filing cabinet.

"Eric is a great guy and his optimism is one of his best qualities, but he doesn't know what he's talking about. Do you think he's read our financial statements?"

"And you have," I say, because of course he has.

He presses his mouth into a flat line. "Things are bad. Millions of dollars bad."

"And that sucks, but it's not my fault!" I say. "Don't take it out on me."

He pulls the Flyers pennant from the wall. "I'm not trying to take it out on you. You clearly didn't know what you were getting into, but you'd be much better off looking for another job. You can't possibly understand the whole situation. You don't know this place anymore. So much has changed since you were last here."

Another poke at the bruise that never fades, and I can barely stand the condescension. But I take comfort in this: If he were confident in his job security, he wouldn't stress about me. He's afraid if we go head-to-head, I'm going to win. After all, there's a precedent for it.

He reaches for the Sixers pennant. "Leave it," I say sharply. "I like that one."

Junior year, when Maynard announced he'd recommended me for the Sixers internship, I was honestly a little surprised. It wasn't until later that I questioned his motives, revisiting the process again and again in my mind until it wrung me dry, trying to gauge whether I deserved it.

I'm pretty sure I did, but Ben deserved it too. And Ben had the kind of life where everything always worked out in his favor. Fancy prep school. The luxury of choosing a college based on where he wanted to play as a walk-on, without having to worry about getting an athletic scholarship. The ability to waltz into a student manager gig after he stopped playing sophomore year, to have Maynard immediately treat him as indispensable.

The head manager job was supposed to be all mine, but when Ben made the switch, Maynard divvied up the responsibilities between the two of us. I was uneasy, because it seemed like he assigned the most important tasks to Ben. *Maynard wouldn't screw me over,* I told myself. He was being considerate. I liked being a manager, but after college I didn't want to work in operations or administration. I wanted to be a videographer, and my reel would be stronger if I had more time to dedicate to that aspect of my job. He was looking out for me, or so I thought.

Ben and I made a great team. And when I got the Sixers internship, he was gracious. But the stakes are higher now. He could lose the job he's clung to for his entire adult life. He must love it, since he hasn't gone elsewhere by now. The stakes are higher for me too, because I don't have anywhere else to go.

Or maybe it has nothing to do with the internship. Maybe he heard I was recently named to *Home Appliance Magazine*'s 35 Under 35 list. That would leave anyone quaking in their team-issued Nikes.

Ben Fucking Callahan, my nemesis. It doesn't sound funny anymore.

- - - - - - - - - - -

THE NEXT MORNING, I reread the email I sent Ben before he insulted me on camera, before I confronted him about it.

Ugh, I was so polite, and he never responded. He can't ice me out. We have jobs to do, and those jobs will involve interacting with each other. But it takes him over twenty-four hours to produce this:

Tuesday, 3:50 P.M.
From: Ben
To: Annie

Stats are on the website

He can't even spare me a period to go along with his assumption that I didn't look in the most obvious place first. This is someone who's supposed to know me.

Tuesday, 3:57 P.M.
From: Annie
To: Ben

Thanks, I did check the website before I emailed you since I like to think I'm not totally incompetent, but it actually didn't have everything I needed. The list I sent you yesterday (reattached here) is everything I couldn't find on the website and need you to send me.
    Let me know if you have any questions.

Then nothing. I finish the parts of the video I can complete without his information and use my notes from Monday's meeting to fill in my calendar while I wait. And wait.

Wednesday, 4:07 P.M.
From: Annie
To: Ben

Hi Ben, just a reminder that as I mentioned in my prior emails, I need those stats (list attached here again) by the end of the day today. Thanks.

My deadline floats by. I write and rewrite my next email. I'd like to talk to him in person, but he's always hurrying in the opposite direction or hiding in his office with the door closed. I try knocking, but he doesn't answer. Once I manage to corner him in the kitchen, but his dark, stony gaze barely settles on me for a millisecond before he says, "Email me," and slips away as I call after him, "I did."

I make a great effort to restrain myself. It's only week one.

Thursday, 9:02 A.M.
From: Annie
To: Ben

Ben—Please forward me the stats I requested ASAP, no later than 5 pm today. The reason I asked for them by yesterday afternoon was that the video needs to be finalized by tonight. Everything is now ready to go except the stats. It's going to be a great video.

I'm sure you are super busy doing many important things, but this video is scheduled to go up by tomorrow morning, so please let me know if there is anything I can do to help get this done.

I'm relieved when his name pops up, until I read the email.

Thursday, 4:55 P.M.
From: Ben
To: Annie

Annie, I've been in meetings all day on some more urgent matters. What specifically are you looking for? Your last email didn't have an attachment.

I drag my hands down my face. It's pretty brazen of him to feign the inability to search his inbox.

Thursday, 4:57 P.M.
From: Annie
To: Ben

Attaching the list again here. Thanks!

Two minutes. Maybe responding so fast makes me look like I have nothing better to do, but I don't care. Personal vendettas aside, I need to finish this video tonight.

But he leaves the office without my noticing. He must've walked the other way down the hall on purpose so I wouldn't stop him, even though it takes twice as long to get to the stairs. This is sabotage, right? He's setting me up to fail.

Time for a different strategy. I pull out the directory so I can figure out Blue Monogrammed Vest's real name.

The next morning:

Friday, 9:04 A.M.
From: Ben
To: Annie

Had to leave early yesterday. Working on this now.

I'm triumphant as I write back.

Friday, 9:42 A.M.
From: Annie
To: Ben

No need, I spoke to Verona last night and he got me
everything pretty quickly so I was able to get it done
in time. The video is up on our social channels now if
you want to see it. Thanks!

Ha. I've thwarted whatever blend of distraction and nonchalance he's using to make my life difficult. I'm not expecting another response from him, but I get one.

Friday, 2:54 P.M.
From: Ben
To: Annie

In the future please make sure any requests go through
me rather than going to Verona. I see a few errors in
the video. It looks like he pulled from the wrong file.

I have to do some deep-breathing exercises and take a quick lap around the building before I write my final email. I write it and then read it and then highlight the first four words, *Per my previous emails,* and change them to all caps—PER MY PREVIOUS EMAILS—turning them red and bold and increasing the font size to 24. I add the words *EAT SHIT* after *EMAILS*, then delete them and change the font back to normal.

Friday, 3:18 P.M.
From: Annie
To: Ben

Per my previous emails, I needed the info by Wednesday afternoon. I gave you an extra 24 hours, which required me to do some scrambling. I had no problem doing this, but it would have been helpful if you could have informed me of your inability to meet the deadline in advance. I had to come up with something by last night and Verona was still in the office, so I asked him.

Please send me the right numbers so I can figure out whether to delete and repost a corrected version.

A stress headache has my head pounding. I can already imagine Coach Thomas breaking the news to me at the end of the season: *It was a tough decision. I'm sure you understand.* And I would understand. Ben is an evil data genius with an eight-year-experience advantage. Our work is so different it can't be compared directly. If I don't excel, if I don't make myself undeniably valuable, they'll choose him by default. Easily.

Mom, Kat, Eric, and Cassie will pity me for getting punched in the gut by this team again. My inbox will sit empty as I send job application after job application out into the void. The remains of my dignity will wither and die, and I'll move back to Mom's house in New Jersey to live the sad little life of a former wunderkind who never amounted to anything.

Oh, god, my life is going to be a Bruce Springsteen song. I need to try harder.

FIVE

ON THE FIRST DAY, GOD CREATED BASKETBALL. AT least that's how the story would be told in my family's house. Tonight feels like evidence that this version of the story is true.

I'm in the chilly underbelly of the Church, trying to stake out a position outside the locker room. It's difficult because the place is buzzing like a hive, and the worker bees are on all kinds of missions. A trainer darts past with a roll of athletic tape. A manager hunts for a missing jersey. Kyle wanders around looking lost, his tie flapping.

The Tip-Off is Ardwyn's version of a preseason pep rally, and it used to be one of my favorite nights of the year. The band and cheerleaders perform. The players are introduced one by one, running onto the court and debuting gloriously elaborate handshakes before playing a fifteen-minute intrasquad scrimmage. To cap off the event, a C-list singer with only one song anyone recognizes—the most star power the school can afford—performs a short set.

Jess is helping me shoot tonight. I already sent her off to the mouth of the tunnel that feeds onto the court. I'm going to get footage of the team walking out of the locker room, and Jess will catch them as they burst onto the court while thousands of fans scream for them, like babies being born into stardom.

"Excuse me," I say to a university administrator who's here to gawk and has parked himself in front of me, but he doesn't hear me. Too tentative. Eight years ago I would've verbally flicked him out of my way without hesitation. I'm out of practice. "I need you to move, please," I say, louder, and he shuffles to the side.

A few minutes ago, I went up to the court to take a peek. When I was a student, the stands would have been packed with families, locals, and other fans. This year, it's half-full, and I know for a fact the ticket office had to hand out free-bies to local middle school teams to fill out the crowd. But the student section is full and rowdy, the kids' buzzes peaking as they take their seats after hustling over from the dorms, swigging the last of the cheap vodka from their water bottles before making their way through the security line. The entire place smells like soft pretzels.

Unlike this part of the building, which has always reeked of floor cleaner and sweat. Someone else fills in the gap created by the administrator, and I groan to myself. I'm briefly distracted by the guy's suit, the way the jacket frames his firm shoulders and the pants hug his ass. It's a nice ass.

And then he turns to the side and—oh, horror of horrors—it's *Ben*. Ben in a suit, like the coaching staff. Everybody dresses up for game days, and this is like a game day.

I can appreciate high-quality tailoring, and that's all this is. Ben got this suit from somebody who knows what they're doing. At least the hair is awful. He always sweeps it back and to the side in the exact same way, like he keeps a photo of the style he wants to achieve next to his bathroom mirror to copy every morning. It's not a look he should be trying to replicate. Excessively tidy, it looks like it was combed with the stick he has up his ass.

Every time a guy gets that haircut, a paid family leave bill dies in Congress, I texted Kat the other day, when she asked me what it was like to see Ben again. It's not a fair joke. He's a registered Democrat; I looked it up the other day while canvassing the Internet for information to hold against him. The search was a bust. The worst thing I found was a Venmo payment for $69.69 from @JimK-Iggles for fantasy football.

I vow to never, ever tell Kat about the way I accidentally checked out Ben's ass.

"Can you make sure the water and Gatorade are set up upstairs?" he asks Verona. When he notices me, his face turns as cold as a beer at the parking lot tailgate before a January night game. He declines to acknowledge my existence and pivots back to face the locker room door.

How did we get here? An ache fills my stomach, but I brush it off. "Callahan, you're in my shot."

"I'm busy."

"All you're doing is standing there."

He waves a piece of paper in his hand. "I need to grab Coach Thomas as soon as they come out. He needs some info about the charity partners for his speech."

A group of alumni wearing VIP badges stops next to us,

reeking of whiskey and laughing too loudly. I ignore them. "Isn't that Kyle's job?" I ask.

"Yes," he says tightly.

If it were anyone other than Ben I'd be sympathetic. Ben bails Kyle out a lot. He also goes out of his way to water Donna's fern when she forgets, give career advice to the managers, and track down the janitor to order candy bars for her daughter's marching band fundraiser. I'd admire his kindness, but I'm the only person exempt from it. Not to mention how his whole golden-boy shtick gives him a leg up with the powers that be.

The boozed-up alumni crowd together to take a photo of themselves with the locker room in the background. The one closest to me takes an oblivious step backward, jostling me with one wild elbow. I backpedal, turning my head to avoid getting whacked in the nose.

"Hey!" Ben barks, swooping in to take the guy by the arm and steer him a few feet away. "Watch where you're going. This space needs to stay clear for employees." He turns to me. "Are you okay?"

This does not count as kindness, for the record. It's basic civil behavior with a sprinkle of showy chivalry.

"Fine," I mumble. "I could've handled that." He retakes his position in the exact spot I need him not to stand. "Please move back a little bit?" I ask. "I need to see them when they walk out, not you."

Ben sighs. "Right, I forgot. The purpose of this entire event is to give you video content."

I step forward so I'm right next to him, my arm nudging his as I try to ensure I have the camera angle I want.

"Are you trying to box me out?" he asks. He doesn't budge. In fact, he leans back into me. I hate the pleasurable zing that shoots through my stomach at the feel of him next to me, warm and solid. I pull away.

Just then the locker room door flies open and the team files out. I'm distracted, still thinking about Ben's proximity, as they walk past us. Thomas leads the way. He's young, only forty-two, and he's the team's first Black head coach. He has a goatee and a quiet intensity, but he's quick to laugh when he's not in coaching mode.

Ben has to lunge forward to shove the page of notes into his hand.

"Smooth," I say.

He sees me fumbling with the camera. "Try pressing the big red button," he responds, and stalks off, closing the top button of his suit jacket.

I miss the first couple players but recover in time to get a good shot. Exhaling, I turn the camera off and grip it tighter to steady myself.

The team huddles up at the entrance to the tunnel. "Everyone in!" someone shouts. One of the seniors grabs every staff member in the vicinity, each person stretching a hand into the center of the circle. He beckons me, and every cell in my body screams *no*. I wave him off.

"Come on, A-Rad!" he says.

The camera is my shield. I point to it. "I have to film."

Coach Thomas says a few words, which I can't hear. When they break from the huddle, Eric heads my way. He stops in front of me, eyeing my outfit. A fuzzy cream sweater and leather A-line skirt.

"Biker sheep," he says. "All good?"

"What am I doing here? Coming back was a terrible idea."

"It was an excellent idea, and the person who suggested it must be an incredibly handsome genius."

"I don't belong here anymore."

He takes me by the shoulders and spins me around to face the tunnel. "Okay, you can quit tomorrow, but don't you at least want to get up there and see how they like it?"

Holy crap, the preseason hype video. I've been so focused on getting shots for my next video I forgot about the one I already made.

My video is kicking off the event. It introduces every player to the fans and sets the tone for the entire season. Tomorrow it will be posted online, but tonight it's just for Ardwyn.

This is my best opportunity to showcase the effect my work can have.

The perfect hype video is a couple minutes long. It splices game highlights with behind-the-scenes footage from the sidelines, the locker room, the team bus, the weight room. The players look like rock stars. Someone well-known, usually a former player or notable alumnus, narrates the video, reading some soaring dramatic copy. And the whole thing is set to an absolute banger of a song.

Speaking of which, I hear the opening notes of the music I selected and jerk my head toward the tunnel. The video starts with an extravagantly beautiful rendition of the intro to Kurtis Blow's "Basketball," played by the first-chair violinist from the university orchestra, before dropping into a heavily censored Lil Baby song. I spent days poring over playlists the athletes sent me, paying attention to what they listen to while lifting weights, before making a choice. Yes, the audience for the video is the fans in the stands. But the team can hear it too. And if it injects them with a bit of extra adrenaline, it's a success.

I scurry through the line of people, weaving around them until I reach the end, at the corner of the court. Creeping out farther, I look up at the crowd in the section closest to me. I already have every frame memorized. I don't need to see the video. I need to see their faces.

It's not like I ask for much. It just needs to leave people breathless, begging for more, hearts thumping, fingertips electrified, screaming their heads off when it stops and the players run onto the court.

In the video, each player does a bit that shows his personality, mixed with highlights from last year. Team captain and super-genius Jamar Gregg-Edwards solves a complicated equation on a whiteboard while dribbling with his free hand. Ever-stoic Luis Rosario walks along the path to the gym and rescues a cat stuck on a tree branch without breaking stride. It's playful, because basketball is supposed to be *fun*, but the clips from last season's most exciting moments keep the energy high. The voiceover is simple, a few lines about the team working hard and getting ready.

My heart is pounding and my chest is vibrating from the bass of the music. The arena is dark except for the illumination of the video. The fans are slack-jawed, their eyes glued to the screen.

Finally the last beat of the song rings out and the narrator, senior guard Anthony Gallimore, speaks the final line: "And so it begins." A spotlight hits the corner of the court a few feet away from me, where the real Anthony Gallimore stands holding a basketball.

The screen goes black. The crowd roars much louder than I expected based on all the empty seats. Nobody in the arena can possibly hear a thing except the sound of their love for this team.

I knew the video was good. I hoped I'd get a reaction that would stick it to Ben and Coach Williams. But what I forgot, and what almost knocks me over, was how the fans' reactions would make me feel. Giddy. Moved. Like I'm part of something big. Better yet, like I have the power to remind all these people they're part of something big too. I swallow hard. I've gone a long time without this feeling.

There's a young woman crying in the third row. She's clinging to her friend, jumping up and down. "I fucking love this school!"

I smile. She's probably drunk, but it still counts.

The team jogs onto the court, following Gallimore, shot through with an extra streak of swagger. A rangy teenager with a high-top fade reaches out to me for a high five as he runs by. Quincy Roberts, freshman phenom.

Quincy is one reason everyone is optimistic this season. He's barely eighteen years old but projected to be a first-round draft pick. This may be his only season of college basketball.

I've known Quincy since he was fourteen. He played for Dad, like Eric did. He was Ken Radford's last superstar. Of all the years to be at Ardwyn, I'm glad I'm here for this one, with him.

His section of the video was all his idea. I just made it happen. In it he's playing a video game, and when the camera pans over to show the screen, he's also in the video game, shooting a three-pointer.

"Hell, yes, A-Rad!" he yells as he passes me, a flash of crisp home whites and warm brown skin. "That was fire." The team is doing a lap around the court, but Quincy doubles back to add: "Your dad would've loved this."

"My dad would've hated this," I reply, and Quincy throws his head back, laughing, as he sprints off to catch up with everyone else. We're both right. Dad only cared about the game, not any of the fuss that surrounds it. But I've always liked both, and the fuss is my job, so Dad would've loved this moment for me.

The crowd is still on their feet. My smile grows and I touch my cheeks with trembling hands, like somebody receiving a marriage proposal. I allow myself to bask in it for a minute before attempting to organize my face into a more stoic expression and heading for the bench with my camera.

Ben is holding a clipboard and raking me over with his eyes. "The video was good," he says begrudgingly. My eyebrows shoot up, and his face turns sour. "But you look like a movie villain who just tasted power for the first time."

It's not a compliment but it feels like one, because it means he's jealous. His spreadsheets have never gotten a standing ovation, even if they are genius. Tonight is a point in my column, and I should be ecstatic. I *am* ecstatic. At the same time, anxiety gnaws at me like a stressed dog chewing its own paw. My relationship with Ben has devolved into something my college self would find unrecognizable. We both have a lot on the line. This would be less stressful if we gave each other a little grace.

Then again, he started it.

I spin slowly in a circle, face lifted toward the fans in the cheap seats who are still on their feet. "Feel that, Callahan?"

"Feel what?"

I hold my arm out. "Goose bumps."

He frowns at me. I smirk at him.

And so it begins.

SIX

THE FRIDAY BEFORE THANKSGIVING WEEK, I MEET
Taylor and Jess at the student center for coffee. Taylor sent
an Outlook invite calling it a "meeting," but we spend the
whole "meeting" talking about Taylor's childhood horse and
Jess's recent breakup with the assistant cheerleading coach.

My cup is nearly empty when I spot game highlights playing on the TV in the corner. The screen shows Coach
Thomas standing stock-still in front of the bench, his face
neutral as he watches Gallimore shoot free throws. It's the
same expression he wears whether we're winning by twenty,
losing by ten, or tied with a minute to go in the second half.

I swallow my last bite of blueberry muffin. "He's the most
composed coach I've ever seen. It's incredible."

"He never moves! He doesn't even put his hands in his
pockets," Jess says.

Taylor motions for me to hand her my plate so she can

add it to the neat stack of trash in front of her. "I heard Brent Maynard was the opposite," she says. "Did he have a temper?"

My fork slides off the plate and clatters to the table. "Um." My mouth is dry. "He used to flail a lot. Sometimes he needed an assistant to hold him back by the jacket so he didn't tackle a referee."

The camera pans out to show the rest of the bench. Every game they sit in the same order: coaches, players, Ben, and a few other staff members. A collared priest sits at the end of the bench like a decorative finial, a reminder from the university that this too is the Lord's house, and the Lord cheers for the Ardwyn Tigers.

Taylor throws away our garbage, and Jess and I follow her outside. It's a crisp, cloudy November day. Ahead of us a professor in rumpled tweed trousers and a pair of students chat in French, walking toward the library. We turn the opposite way, toward the Church.

"Three and oh," Jess says. "Not a bad start."

"And Quincy's already the conference player of the week!" Taylor adds.

The conference anointed Quincy Player of the Week the first chance it got. He played well enough to contend for it, but that's irrelevant. They've been dying to tie his name to theirs since he committed to Ardwyn, for the same reason celebrities end up with a lot of godchildren.

They talk about Quincy a lot on TV. There's a familiar story they like to tell, and they fit him into it, omitting the bits that don't work like the slivers of dough that hang over the edges of a cookie cutter. It's all "instincts" and "natural athleticism." "Knowledge of the game" and "hard work" are nowhere to be found. They throw in the quirky fact of his video game livestream hobby, which they'll surely use against him when he plays poorly ("lack of discipline" and "distracted," not "blowing off steam").

Then their voices get solemn and they use their most practiced newscaster intonations to talk about the Serious Subject of his childhood. There's the "unlikely journey," and his mom's barely criminal record, and they tell and retell this one story about a worn-out pair of sneakers with duct tape patching a hole.

Tragedy porn, but it's okay, everyone, because he's going to be rich soon, as long as he doesn't blow a knee first.

After the season, Quincy will need to decide whether to go pro or return to Ardwyn. His family is pretty grounded, thankfully. But ever since his talent became obvious, there have been plenty of other people hovering around, calling themselves "friends" and "advisors," telling him to hurry up and get to the NBA, where he can make the most money.

For some players that is the right choice, but for many it's not. I'm dying to know which way he's leaning, and hoping he can block out the noise of the hangers-on angling for a slice of the pie. It's only beginning. I can't help worrying about him.

"Annie?" Taylor waves a hand in front of my face. I must've zoned out completely, because we've already arrived at the building.

"Hm? Sorry." I shake my head.

"I asked if you want to come down to the court with us while we take pictures of the mascot with a guy in a turkey costume."

I take out my ID to scan us into the building. "As much as

I'd love to see that magic moment, I need to do some editing before this video goes up."

"You're hard-core," Jess says. "It's already great. I don't know what more you can do."

But I'm itching to get back to my computer. It needs to be better than great. It needs to capture the way things feel right now: the team starting on a hot streak, the air in the arena vibrating with promise. I want to keep cranking up our follower count. I want to remind Coach Thomas why he hired me. I want the people in the finance office to get the message that they need to slow down, wait to make any final decisions, because big things are happening here.

Taylor and Jess stop in front of the stairwell. "Same time next week?" Taylor asks.

"Yes," I say quickly, already looking forward to it. As a rule, I try to avoid real friendship with coworkers. But a weekly coffee break is harmless, and other than Eric and Cassie, all my friends and family are back in New Jersey. My social life has been dead since I got here.

I could try dating, but I don't have the energy for my usual diet of uninspiring three-month relationships and mediocre hookups. It's been a long time since my last breakup with Oliver, but I still feel like I need to ascend to the next plane of adulthood before I'm ready for something serious, and I have no clue how to get there.

Taylor and Jess head to the court, and I climb the stairs to the office. When I turn down the corridor, a familiar dark-haired jerk with a tragically well-sculpted ass hovers suspiciously at the other end, wearing yet another uninspired half-zip. When he sees me coming, he darts back into his office and slams the door.

He was standing near the thermostat.

"No fucking way," I growl.

I should've known. My office is freezing. I learned quickly to wear layers and keep a blanket on the back of my chair. Earlier in the week I tried bringing in a space heater, but Donna sent it packing—something about the fire inspector. I adjust the temperature several times a day but still have a tab on my browser open to an Amazon search for fingerless gloves.

Every time I turn the heat up, somebody else turns it back down. At first I thought it was a maintenance person. But of course it's Ben. He's the only one who sits as close to the thermostat as I do, and the only one irritated by my very presence in the building.

I check the temperature. Sixty-two degrees. "Son of a *bitch*."

He's trying to refrigerate me into quitting. Well, the joke's on him, because now I'm a seething volcano. I charge into the kitchen, fling open the fridge, and grab his string cheese. He brings one every day for his afternoon snack. Well, not today, mister. I don't even peel it, just eat it in three bites like a monster.

We've mostly attempted to avoid each other in a way that looks effortless but requires a lot of choreography. One morning I pretended not to see him behind me as I walked into the building and let the door slam in his face. Another time he noticed me struggling to replace the water cooler in the kitchen and walked right past instead of offering to help.

He's terrible at being mean, even when he wants to be, which is why when we're face-to-face he mostly looks constipated. I don't think anyone has noticed the tension, but who knows what he's saying behind my back? In a weak moment last week, I signed him up for a contest on a sketchy website, a chance to win a free trip to Antigua that undoubtedly doesn't exist. It took only twenty-four hours for the scammers to sell his cell phone number to a million telemarketers.

I felt a twinge of guilt when I heard the incessant buzzing of his phone and his nonstop grumbling about it. And the string cheese incident is a little embarrassing. I should be focused on work, and I am about ninety-eight percent of the time. I make no excuses for the other two percent. There is a petty beast inside me, and sometimes she needs to let off steam.

That night, Ben is working late, as usual. I've been doing the same, needing the extra hours to experiment and fine-tune and perfect. I can't see him, but it's easy to tell what he's doing after everyone else goes home and the building gets quiet.

Tonight, he's mostly been sitting at his computer, typing. Occasionally a desk drawer opens and closes. The tip of his tongue is probably sticking out of the side of his mouth a little bit. It always happens when he's concentrating deeply. It's extremely dorky and not at all attractive, so I have to check to see if he's doing it every time I walk past. Every so often a ball thwacks against the backboard of the miniature hoop on his door.

I tune him out when he takes a phone call, walking somebody through a calculus problem. If I remember correctly from college, he has a much younger sister.

My coffee date with Taylor and Jess has me thinking. I need to get out more, to take a break from fixating on my work problems. I curl up in my desk chair, sitting on one foot and hugging the opposite knee, and pick up the phone to call my own sister.

"I'm at the end of a climb," Kat says when she answers, panting heavily.

"Don't slack off on my account," I reply. "I'll be quick."

Kat spends a lot of time on her stationary bike. The athlete of the family, she played college basketball herself and still sticks to an intense workout regimen, on top of her job and her hobby posting hair tutorials online.

"You and Mom should visit tomorrow," I say. "We can go shopping. And you should stay with me for the night after Mom leaves. You can take the train home." When I was in college, we went to the King of Prussia Mall every time Mom and Kat visited.

She's only listening halfway, and her voice is strained as she huffs out her words. "That . . . sounds like a lot of public transportation . . . just to spend a night sitting . . . on . . . your . . . couch."

I straighten a row of pens on my desk. "What if we go out?"

Kat releases a big breath and her voice regulates, climb complete. "Out, out? Like to a bar, at night?" Now she's paying attention.

"Sure."

"You never want to go out with me."

"I never had to go out with you when we lived together because you brought a bar's worth of people to our apartment. Now I live by myself. I'm bored all the time."

"Are you depressed?"

"No. Come on, it'll be fun. I'll buy you a cheesesteak on the way home."

"Fine, but to be honest, you had me at 'out.'"

I hang up and log off my computer. A Friday night alone won't be so bad now that I've got plans for Saturday. Tonight I'll go to the gym, take a hot shower, yell at strangers online about climate change, and watch ASMR videos in bed until I doze off and drop my phone on my face.

I toss my phone into my tote bag and scan the room to make sure I'm not forgetting anything.

"Her offensive rating was incredible the year they won the conference."

Ben's voice startles me. I forgot he was there. Is he still on the phone? No, he must be talking to me, because Kat's offensive rating *was* incredible the year her college team won the Big Ten.

I try to remember what else I said to Kat. "Are you obsessed with my sister? She posted a super cute topknot tutorial yesterday, in case you haven't checked it out yet."

I don't really think he's obsessed, even though Kat's college basketball career ended four years ago. This is just how he is. People used to quiz him on obscure, decades-old basketball statistics like it was a party trick. It was sort of cute.

"You're bored here?" The words are soaked in disgust.

I rub my forehead with the heels of my palms. "No. I can probably get you a lock of her hair this weekend, if you want it. She has beautiful hair."

He releases a high-and-mighty sigh, as if he's the only adult in the building. It's impossible to resist antagonizing him further.

I spin from side to side in my chair. "More of a toenail clippings guy? I'll see what I can do."

A stifled choking sound escapes his mouth. It might be a

laugh. He's probably covering his mouth, trying to stuff it back in. He clears his throat. "Pretty sure you said you were bored all the time. Sorry to hear we're not keeping you entertained here."

"Thanks for eavesdropping. I'd have been less bored this week if *someone* didn't leave me off the email chain about happy hour last night."

I was home cooking a single chicken breast when Eric texted me from the bar asking why I wasn't there. The chicken was curling at the edges like it was frowning at me. If Ben did it to hurt my feelings, it worked. I ended up taking a long, brooding walk around campus in the dark, listening to the old emo music I used to play in high school when I sulked about boys.

I wouldn't have gone to a work happy hour, anyway. Like I didn't go to bowling night or the Phillies game outing. Regardless, being excluded sucks. It reminds me of the times Maynard's assistant coaches let Ben sit in on meetings because they all *happened* to be yakking about Deflategate or whatever outside the conference room beforehand. He'd come back with a rueful grimace and a message they'd asked him to pass along, like he was my boss.

"I didn't—" I hear Ben's mouse clicking as he checks whether I'm right, or pretends to. He's probably tapping random icons on his desktop. Maybe karma will intervene and he'll accidentally delete something important. "Oh. I did. Sorry about that. I didn't do it on purpose."

"Sure." I pick at my cuticle. The cold, dry air has been rough on my hands.

"I swear. Donna was supposed to add you to the staff

contact group in Outlook. She must've forgotten. But I should've double-checked."

Of course he manages to pin it on someone else while acting like he's accepting responsibility. "Bold move, blaming Donna. You better hope she doesn't find out you threw her under the bus."

He doesn't say anything for a minute, but then: "The Devil Wears Prardwyn."

A smile blooms on my face and I leap up, I can't help it, and cross the hall to his doorway. "You remember that?"

I once used cinema classic *The Devil Wears Prada* as inspiration for a preseason spoof video. Donna played the terrifying boss, ordering Maynard to style a team uniform with accessories and bring her coffee while dribbling a basketball down the hallway. He was always game for my most ridiculous ideas, and Donna was delighted to have the opportunity to shine.

Back then, nobody in the athletic department paid attention to the weird little videos being posted by the basketball team. I could never get away with making anything like that today.

He assesses me with wary eyes. "Hard to forget the humiliation of my walk down the runway." That's right. There was a fashion show montage, and I conscripted some of the players.

I press my lips together to restrain a smile. It's flattering, I can't deny it. Almost—touching? It's annoying, actually, because it means the bar is so low it's in hell. All he's said is he remembers something I made once. He didn't even say it was good.

"I have a question for you," he says cautiously.

I brace myself. *He knows about the string cheese. He can smell my shame.*

"Did you spend the *entire morning* showing Lufton how you edit hype videos?"

Not the question I expected. But instead of relief, irritation spikes inside me. The *nerve* he has. Like I needed to clear it with him first. That's not how this works. But heaven forbid I interact with the student managers, and they (gasp!) grow to like me. "Yeah," I say. "He's been asking me about it for weeks. But I promise, he still loves you more than me."

His forehead wrinkles. "Uh, okay. I wanted to say . . . that was cool. You made his day."

I'm dumbfounded. "Thanks," I say slowly. "These kids work hard and don't get paid. I want them to learn something."

He rubs his chin. "I want that too." He's looking at me thoughtfully, his expression less guarded than usual, and I let him. We used to be those kids. We *should* agree on this. We should agree on a lot of things.

The faint smell of his soap lingers in the air. Sometimes he goes to the gym around five, showers, and comes back to the office to do more work. It's a nice, clean scent, I'll admit it. Everything smells good after spending half the day in an old gym surrounded by sweaty athletes.

I resist the impulse to step farther into his office. Even being this close gives me an electric-fence feeling. The boundary is invisible, but it's there. My eyes land on a framed photo on his desk in the spouse-and-kids spot, a college-age Ben standing at center court with Maynard. It looks like senior night. I wasn't there, so I can't say for sure.

My tongue is stuck in my throat. "Nice picture," I can't help saying, as I fold my arms and squeeze them against my body.

"Thanks."

"Do you still talk to him?"

His eyes flick to mine. "You don't?"

"I don't know why I would."

He sits back in his chair, the wheels rolling a little. He makes a self-chastising face, like he shouldn't have asked. We both look at the photo. "I talk to him pretty regularly," he says. "See him every summer. He still has the beach house in Bethany. Does a big Memorial Day weekend thing every year."

A shiver runs through me. "You still *see* him?" I ask. "You talk *regularly*? Like, how often?"

He gives me a baffled look. "I don't know, every few weeks? We text, mostly."

"Every few *weeks*?" The pitch of my voice rises.

"Yeah, that's too much," Ben says dryly. "It's not like I owe my entire career to him or anything."

I shouldn't be surprised by this, by Ben's unwavering loyalty. The night Maynard invited us to dinner at his house to tell us we were candidates for the Sixers internship, Ben headed for the kitchen after our plates were cleared and picked up a sponge. "Wow, playing dirty," I teased.

A wounded huff escaped his mouth and his cheeks turned pink. "I always help Kelly with the dishes!" Like dinner with the Maynards was a regular thing, like he was part of the family.

Maynard was ordinary-looking, a little nerdy, with an unremarkable face. He wore his blazers too big, like a child.

But he walked in a beam of light. When he entered a room, people looked at him, sensing that he was somebody, even if they didn't know who. And the light landed on you if you got close enough. When he talked to you, even in a crowded gym, it was like you were the only other person there.

"You really think you owe him everything?"

He shrugs. "I do, yeah."

"He helped you get your foot in the door. That was a long time ago. Pretty sure at this point the only person you have to thank for the fact that you're in here playing with numbers on a Friday night is you."

He shakes his head. "I don't get it. Is it that hard to be grateful for the opportunities he gave you?"

My face goes hot and cold at the same time, and my hand flies to my necklace, coiling it between my fingers. I'm going to have to allow Ben to add this to the list of things he's holding against me, because I can't pretend to have fond feelings for Maynard.

We're never going to resolve our differences. We can't have this conversation without dredging up the past, and that's a risk I can't take, because the past is full of dangerous land mines.

Time is so thin here. My college years feel so close. The same plaques rest undisturbed in the same places on the same walls; they've been here all along, even when I wasn't. The sound of Donna's voice carrying down the hall, the work getting under my skin, the way the autumn air hits me when I leave the building at night. It's as if I could reach out and slip through whatever separates now from then with almost no effort at all. Sometimes it seems like I am doing that, like now, in this conversation. The earlier part, the friendly bit between Ben and me, that's the kind of thing that happened back then. The second part, about the photo on the desk, reminds me there's pain here, and where to find it.

The pain is in my memories of the man who treated me like a daughter for three years, and then spent the fourth sending me creepy text messages and propositioning me in hotel rooms.

Ben wants to talk about opportunities? Maynard gave me the opportunity to develop my skills, to begin building a career, to make connections in our field. And then he attempted to give me the opportunity to sleep with him.

Behind Ben I see the two of us reflected on the window. Me, casual in the doorway in a long open sweater, him, slouching unarmed in his chair. We look like two people making small talk. We could be talking about Thanksgiving dinner, or how early it gets dark now. But not about this. Any second now the girl in the window is going to laugh, teeth gleaming on the glass.

SEVEN

THE MALL IS ALREADY DECORATED FOR CHRISTMAS. Faux white trees covered in lights sit at regular intervals in squat planters, and a giant wreath is suspended from the ceiling above the escalators like a guillotine ready to fall. Santa is doing his thing in front of an ornate red carousel, a bloated line of families winding infinitely into the distance. The children are restless and sugar-high, dressed for photos, and the parents sag under the long wait.

The guy walking in front of Kat stops dead in his tracks, looking lost. She rolls her eyes and dodges him. "The whole point of coming here the weekend before Thanksgiving was to avoid the holiday shoppers."

"Are you sure you don't want me to pick you up tomorrow?" Mom asks Kat. "I don't mind."

Of course she doesn't, because driving is how Mom shows her love. In first grade, I listed it as her job on one of those cutesy Mother's Day questionnaires: "driver." She did the school drop-off and pickup every day. She shuttled Kat and me to and from basketball and film club, respectively. We sat in the car in the drive-thru line, picking up dinner. We gave rides to Dad's players, going far out of the way to bring them home in the dark, idling at the curb until they got inside. Kat and I stayed in the back seat while Mom showed her clients empty houses for sale. "We're going for a ride," she'd say, and she'd be wearing shoes that clicked and Clinique Happy, and that was how we knew we needed to bring toys, we'd be waiting awhile.

To this day Mom loves nothing more than to chauffeur somebody from point A to point B.

"I'll be fine, Mom," Kat says. "It's the train and a Lyft."

"*Two* trains! Two trains and a Lyft." She cannot fathom this, why an adult woman would take two trains and a Lyft when she could force her mother to drive three hours round trip instead. "At least let me pick you up from the station."

We sit down for lunch in a tall-backed booth at a loud restaurant with artificial columns and a menu as thick as a brick. We talk about work, about the team's schedule and Donna's phone conversations, about Quincy's draft prospects. I walk them through my last hype video, even though they've already seen it.

Kat looks at me funny. "You *like* it."

"Of course she likes it," Mom says.

My stomach dips. "'Of course'?" I rip off a piece of bread from the basket and busy myself with the olive oil. "I didn't know this was an 'of course' situation. What's everyone getting to eat?"

I can't stop to think about whether I like it. I need to con-centrate on why I'm here: to put in enough time to give my-self options.

Kat doesn't give up. "Dad would be thrilled."

It's weird to have basketball again but not Dad. I can't separate the two in my memories. I spent my childhood fol-lowing him around from practices to games to team spa-ghetti dinners. I was eager to be a part of this thing that had such a hold on him, and I quickly came to love it as much as he did. I helped out his team in high school and worked all his camps during the summers. Even in college, when we were apart, we debriefed over the phone after every game.

I glare at Kat. "If you make me cry in a knockoff Cheese-cake Factory, I will suffocate you with this loaf of bread."

She rolls her eyes. "What about Ben? How's the Great Pennsylvanian Basketball Showdown going?"

I take a long sip of water from a glass as big as a jug. "I can't tell who's winning, but there'll be no sportsmanship trophies. Yesterday we managed to have a normal conversa-tion for three whole minutes, and that's the best it's been all season. But then it went sideways. I don't think we're ever going to see eye to eye."

Mom looks up from her menu. "When's his birthday?"

Kat and I make knowing eye contact across the table. "I don't know, Mom. I don't believe in that stuff anyway." But wait. I do know the answer, roughly. "There were birthday balloons in his office when I first started," I admit.

Mom pauses to estimate the date. She makes an unread-able humming noise and looks back at her menu.

"What?" I ask reluctantly.

"I thought you didn't believe in it."

"Well, it can't hurt to know."

Mom takes off her reading glasses and sets them on the table. "It's interesting, that's all. You're opposite signs. Lots of potential for conflict, but you could also balance each other out. It would help to know his rising sign."

"Hang on, let me text him to ask what time he was born." I mime typing on my phone.

Mom sighs. "Look, Annie, if he's treating you badly, it says more about him than it does about you."

"Have you tried to make peace with him?" Kat asks.

Kat has the sometimes-annoying mindset of someone who was exceptional at something from a young age. She sees a straight line from every problem to its solution. As a former standout athlete, she saw her hard work produce success. Cause and effect. Do the thing that makes rational sense, and your desired result will follow. News flash, it doesn't work that way for everyone.

Kat squeezes a lemon wedge and plunks it into her glass. She will never understand.

"Restaurant lemons are filthy, didn't you know that?" I say.

She takes a deep, pointed sip.

"It's not that simple," I go on. "Even putting aside the fact that we're competing for one job—which is a big thing to put aside—we have fundamentally different views on certain important subjects."

Kat freezes in the middle of turning the page of her menu. "*Oh,*" she says knowingly. "Is it chemtrails?"

"What? No."

"Is he a crypto bro? A Cowboys fan? Oh, is he really into green juice?"

"No, no, and no, but thanks for playing," I say. "It's about . . . someone else." I turn to the sandwich options.

Kat's eyebrows hit the ceiling. "Coach Fuckwaffle?"

I nod wordlessly, not looking up, and Mom makes a sympathetic noise. "Ben doesn't know, does he?"

"No," I say. "And he never will."

CASSIE AND ERIC stop by my place before Kat and I go out. My apartment is exactly as beige and run-down as you'd expect based on the cheap rent and grainy video tour I took before signing the lease. I outfitted most of it with flat-pack basics and a hodgepodge of hand-me-down furniture Mom was thrilled to give away.

Cassie lies on the couch, ensconced in a fleece blanket, pretending she's not falling asleep. Eric sprawls on the floor. The TV is on in the background so we can follow the scores of tonight's games.

I lug my floor-length mirror out to the living room so I can do my makeup. While I sit on an ottoman, tapping iridescent powder onto the tops of my cheekbones with my ring finger, Kat hovers over my shoulder, curling my hair and her own balayaged surfer-girl waves between sips of whiskey and Coke.

"I keep writing 'generous gift,'" Eric says, biting a pen. "What's a polite way to describe cash without using the word 'cash'?" He's got a pile of cards next to him and a list of names.

I blend my powder. "Why can't you reuse 'generous gift'? Do you think people are going to compare thank-you notes?"

"I'm trying to make them unique and heartfelt! But I'm struggling for material."

"Let me see." I stretch to grab a card from the pile. "'Dear Jackie, Thank you for attending our wedding. We greatly appreciate your generous gift and are so glad we got to celebrate with you. I have fond memories of the king-size candy bars you used to give out on Halloween.'"

Kat laughs. "That's the best you can do? Who's Jackie?"

"My parents' neighbor. The only other relevant memory I have is about the tight leggings her ex-husband used to wear when he power-walked around the neighborhood."

"Super relevant and a great visual," I say. "You should've gone with that one."

"I should've kept them short," he moans. "But it's too late now."

I pick up an eyeliner pencil. "Cassie, you're awfully quiet on this one."

"I don't care what they say as long as they get done." Her voice is gritty with fatigue. She's in the middle of a big case at work, something about predatory lending. There's a saying lawyers have about their work, according to Cassie: *It's like a pie-eating contest where the prize is more pie.* Cassie is neck-deep in pie these days. "I did the shower thank-yous," she adds. "I cede all control here."

Kat pats her back pocket but comes up empty. "Hey, what time is it?"

I tap the screen of my phone, balanced on my knee. "Nine thirty."

"Good, plenty of time."

"Why do people wait so late to go out?" Cassie asks. "You

can have just as much fun at eight as you can at eleven. I think it's because *other* people wait so late to go out. What if everyone agreed to go out three hours earlier? If the cool people sign up for that, everyone else will follow, and they'll all be better rested."

I look at her in the mirror. She's got the blanket tucked under her heels and pulled up to her chin. "Broker the treaty, Cass. I'm sure there's a Nobel Prize in it for you."

Kat ruffles her hand through a section of curls. "Speaking on behalf of cool people everywhere—"

"Didn't know they hired outsiders," Eric interjects with so much glee he practically high-fives himself.

"—if we had to go out at eight, we wouldn't have time to sit around with our friends beforehand, and that's the best part."

"If you went out at eight, maybe I'd go with you," Cassie says. This is obviously false, and the rest of us laugh.

Eric sits up on his elbows. "How about this sick fuck?" On the TV is a news report with a photo of a sneaker company executive recently outed as a serial sexual harasser. A journalist with red lipstick and glasses—Lily Sachdev, according to the chyron—discusses the story. It's muted because of the music, but the story has been all over the news, so it's easy to get the gist. A ghostly, anxious voice continues to sing a pop song from Kat's portable speaker, and we stare at the TV.

"Horrible," Cassie murmurs eventually. I examine my dash of eyeliner. It's wobbly, so I wipe it off and start again.

Kat releases a lock of my hair from the curling iron and cups it in her palm until it cools. "Do you think anything will happen to him?"

I draw another line, smoother this time. "Not as long as he's making people money."

"I don't know." Cassie's arms have emerged from her cocoon, and she runs a thoughtful finger along her lip. "This feels different."

"If anything, he'll get fired because that one guy said he paid bribes to high school athletes, not because of what he did to any of the women," I say. This subject is killing my buzz. "Hey, did you see Eric's profile?"

I'm working on a set of videos about each member of the operations staff. I started with Coach Thomas, always an easy interview. Eric, born to be the center of attention, was a breeze.

Cassie pulls herself upright. "I loved it. They're all so good. Whose is next?"

"Williams. I've been putting his off. And, ah, I still have to do Ben Callahan." If he ever agrees to sit down with me for an interview. I've been trying to schedule it for days.

"Oh, I like Ben! I'm glad he gets to be a part of this even though he's not officially a coach."

Kat's arm is suspended in the air, a can of some noxious hair product in her hand. She gives me a questioning look in the mirror. I cut it down with sharp eyes and a half shake of my head.

"Are you guys friends with him?" Kat asks. "I don't remember him much from when you were in college."

Eric gives up on the thank-you notes and rolls onto his back, propping his head up with a pillow. "We played together for a couple years and then he was a manager with Annie, but we weren't super close then. We're buddies now.

We've been working together for a long time. He's a good dude."

Ben never went out in college. If we had a free night, he studied or visited his family. The only time I ever saw him at a party was when he rolled up in a glossy black Range Rover to pick up a couple teammates, his girlfriend in the passenger seat wearing a white sweater and Tiffany pearl stud earrings. He didn't even get out of the car. I stood in the grass barefoot, weaving drunk, fighting to keep my balance. "Need a ride?" he called out.

I didn't want to go yet. I had no idea where my shoes were. He passed me a water bottle through the window.

"Thank you, sir," I remember saying, doffing an invisible cap. It would've been nice if my brain could've blotted out that part of the memory.

His girlfriend leaned over to whisper something to him, her inky ponytail swinging forward.

I chugged the water and some trickled down my chin. I wiped my mouth. "You can go. I'm all good."

He opened his door. "I don't mind. Do you want me to help you find your shoes?"

The ground was damp and my feet were cold. I don't remember if I was going to say yes or no to his question, because at that moment Eric ran outside singing a Mika song in a terrible falsetto and flung me over his shoulder, Cassie trailing not far behind.

I don't want to be plagued by memories of college or Ben tonight, so I hop up from the ottoman. "I have to get my lip stuff from my room." The words come out tighter than I'd like.

I pass through my bedroom to the tiny room on the other

side, my favorite space in the apartment. The property manager failed to show it to me on my video tour, probably because it scared other potential tenants away, but I think it's glorious. Its floor is old synthetic grass, the belligerent color of a sea of plastic leprechaun hats in a bar on St. Patrick's Day. There's a big window and a hideous stained-glass ceiling fan. On the wall—possibly since 1992—is a framed still of Marisa Tomei as Mona Lisa Vito in *My Cousin Vinny*, wearing a skintight floral jumpsuit. Now my most treasured possession, obviously.

I head to the windowsill, which I've loaded with so many scented candles it looks like an altar. I pick one up and inhale pink peppercorn and tangerine.

Eric and Cassie know that Ben and I are in precarious positions, but they don't know how ugly it is. I don't want to tell them. I'm already the messy friend, the chaotic, unsettled one. It's easier to ration out the details of the dysfunction in my life than share everything all the time. They don't intend to patronize me, but it's impossible for them to empathize completely. They listen to my tales of disaster, of bad first dates and gaps in health insurance coverage between jobs, and make compassionate noises in all the right places, and they mean it, they really do. Then, they get in the car together and probably say things like *Poor Annie, I worry about her* and *Thank god we're not single.*

When I return to the living room, Eric has moved to the couch, Cassie's blanket in a ball beside him. Kat is on the ottoman turning her waves into an elaborate fishtail braid.

"Where'd Cassie go?"

"More tea," Eric says.

"What is this?" Cassie calls out from the kitchen.

I poke my head in. "What's what?"

Cassie holds up a lidded glass container. She shakes it, an accusation. "This is lasagna."

"You can have it, if you're hungry." My voice is high and soft, projecting innocence.

"You don't make lasagna for fun."

"I was craving pasta."

"You only make lasagna when something is *wrong*."

Well. Yes, that's mostly true. Sometimes I get this feeling like I'm the little ball in that screensaver, the one that bounces off the four sides of the screen again and again for all of eternity. When that happens, I make lasagna from scratch. The noodles, the Bolognese sauce, the béchamel, all the cranking and stirring and layering. It settles me.

Eric appears behind me. "You made lasagna? Why, what's going on?"

I groan. "Nothing is going on. I wanted lasagna, so I made it."

Eric pauses to consider. "That doesn't sound like you."

"Like I said, you're welcome to have some. But only because it's delicious, and not for any weird emotional reasons." I drop it in the microwave carelessly, so it lands with a clatter, and stab at the buttons.

Kat is watching us expectantly when we file back into the living room with plates of lasagna no one said they wanted.

"I think she's doing well," she says brightly.

I set my plate on the coffee table and flop onto the couch. "You guys let me know when you're done assessing my well-being. I'll wait."

"What? You are. You've been different, in a good way.

Honestly, you're kind of glowing. I can tell you're excited about work."

It's an echo of what Kat said at lunch. A seed of agitation burrows into my gut. "Um, no. I glow because of *Selena Gomez*. Rare Beauty highlighter."

"Not every facet of the job, obviously. But the way you talk about what you're doing? And the videos themselves, you can see it. You like your work."

"I didn't realize you were already drunk."

"So you don't like work?" Cassie leans forward. Lawyers.

"I didn't say that." I hack at my lasagna with my fork, taking a big sloppy bite. "Work is fine. But it's not making me glow."

Later, when we say good night to Eric and Cassie, the kneading, insistent nub of unease in my stomach is still there. All of it bothers me: Cassie's concern, Kat's eagerness to draw rosy conclusions. Everyone trying to push me toward deciding whether I'm satisfied or dissatisfied and what to do about it, like my life is a problem to be hashed out and solved in a group project. Yes, making videos about basketball is nice, but so was the cafeteria at my last job, and the technology budget at the one before that. It's not as straightforward as they make it seem. If the work makes me glow (which it doesn't), it makes my decision to stay far away from here for the last eight years pretty fucking tragic (which it wasn't). And it'll make it hurt a lot more if I'm not invited back next year.

Kat and I clomp down the stairs in impractical boots to find our Lyft. The driver misses the building and waits for us a block up the street. The buildings are shadows and floating yellow squares, and the sky is open, and we're going somewhere warm to be surrounded by new people. Only then does the bad feeling loosen and slip away into the blue-black night. I'm left with the taste of wine, wide breaths of cold air, and the sharp giddy sound of Kat cackling in the dark.

EIGHT

A FEW WEEKS LATER, I STAND IN THE OFFICE kitchen, surveying the options. Chocolate-covered pretzels. Chocolate-covered strawberries. Chocolate-covered almonds.

Figure out the first shot of the video, and the rest will fall into place.

I chew my lip. Weren't there muffins here an hour ago? The platter is still there, but it's clean except for a few telltale crumbs. It's almost Christmas, which means daily deliveries of gifts to Coach Thomas from friends and supporters. Gold, frankincense, and Harry & David pears.

What about starting with the empty court . . . Meh, uninspired.

Maybe a pretzel? But it's only nine fifteen in the morning, and I've already eaten three.

What if . . . No, too similar to last week's video. How about . . . Not practical. It'll never be done in time.

I mosey over to the bathroom and examine my eyebrows in the mirror. Is the one on the left thicker than the one on the right? I've never noticed before.

Maybe I'm going about it all wrong. Maybe I should end *with a shot of the empty court.*

Hm. Better.

I meander back toward my office, stopping in the hallway to chat with Betsy from Compliance about her son's wisdom tooth surgery. Eric appears as soon as Betsy walks away. "Hey, Annie, is that video for the recruits ready yet? I want to send it out tonight."

It is, thankfully. Unlike the next hype video, which is still working itself out in my head. "All done," I say. "I'll send it to you when I'm back at my desk."

He raises his eyebrows. "And when will that be? Ten?" His tone is playful, but he's not wrong. It's all part of my process. Also, I have a process now. This job requires actual creativity. I let things percolate in my brain in the morning, sometimes wandering the building while I think. I get them done later, usually at night. I do my best work then, when the office is quiet and few people are around.

"Very funny."

"It's usually closer to ten thirty." Ben's disembodied voice comes from his office. My non-identical eyebrows contract. Eric is my friend, and he's allowed to joke about my work habits. But Ben is not invited to this bantering session.

How does he know my routine, anyway? I tuck my hair behind my ears. "Got my schedule memorized, Callahan?" To Eric: "Let's get away from the heckler."

"You're talking right outside my door," Ben protests.

Okay, fair. I shoot him daggers anyway, but he's already

focused on his computer again, the tip of his tongue poking through at the corner of his mouth. Eric follows me into my office.

"I'm coming over tonight to keep Cass company while she packs," I say, leaning over my computer to drag the file into an email and send it to Eric.

Cassie's big case settled, so she's going to New Orleans for ten days to see her family. Eric will join her for forty-eight hours, flying down on Christmas Eve. I'll be at my parents' house in New Jersey, submerged in Dad's old leather couch with the cupholders, watching games with Kat and reading Mom the instructions for her AncestryDNA kit. Holidays still don't feel right without Dad, and they probably never will. We need to accept that instead of trying to fight it.

Eric points at me with both hands. "That reminds me, Cassie's already thinking ahead to when she gets back. *The Beach House* starts in January. You should come watch at our house."

"You guys are obsessed, huh?" I take a big sip from my new water bottle. It has lines marking how much I'm supposed to drink each hour. I used to be good about staying hydrated, but lately I keep forgetting.

"Have you ever seen it?"

I wrinkle my nose. "I've seen the commercials."

He makes a *pssh* sound and picks up a mass of fleece from the back of the chair facing my desk. He holds it up and turns it in different directions, trying to figure out which end is up. I have a lot of fleece in my office, but this item is reserved for the coldest days. The thermostat war is still ongoing.

"Is the actual show drastically different than the commercials?" I ask.

He ignores the question. That's a no. "We do a fantasy league with some friends. You pick different contestants each episode and get points when they kiss or go skinny-dipping or fight. It gets competitive. Is this a dress?"

"It's a wearable blanket."

"Looks like a dress."

"I bought it at the grocery store. Nothing sold at Giant legally qualifies as clothing."

Before he can say the words "meat dress," my phone buzzes.

Quincy: can you come to my room

Quincy: 911

I squint, rereading the messages. Uh-oh. I hope he's not upset about the assholes online who've been calling him "soft" since he tweaked his ankle during our last game. In high school he injured the same ligaments—badly. Losing him would be disastrous, so he's sitting out tomorrow as a precaution and will have plenty of time to recover over the nine-day holiday break.

I kick Eric out of my office and hustle over to Quincy's dorm. It's easy enough to find. His RA must be a Cricut fanatic, since each door in the hallway is marked with an elaborate sign listing its residents' names atop a cartoon stack of books. Someone scrawled a lazy sketch of a penis on the *I* in *Quincy* with a Sharpie.

"That was fast," he says when he opens the door, dressed in sweatpants and a hoodie. A mountain of similar sweatpants and hoodies sits on the floor behind him. His roommate, another freshman basketball player, is nowhere to be found.

"What's wrong?"

His face is grim. "Follow me. We need to go to the basement."

"I'm not totally opposed to helping you dispose of a body," I say, "but it depends on the circumstances of the murder."

We take the elevator because of his ankle, emerging into a musty corridor and then entering a fluorescent-lit room. There's no body, and, in fact, nothing worthy of a 911 text at all. Just a basket full of sweaty clothes and an unopened bottle of Tide.

"Oh, hell no," I say. "You did *not* summon me here to do your laundry."

A guilty chuckle escapes his mouth. "It's not like that! I summoned you here so you can teach *me* how to do laundry."

I sniff the clothes from a safe distance. The smell is . . . ripe. "How have you survived all semester without learning how to wash your clothes?"

"I have an NIL deal with Tommy John, so I get a lot of free underwear." He looks away, sheepish. "And, uh, Andreatti's girlfriend and her roommates usually do it for us. But they went home for Christmas already."

"Wow. Laundry service *and* you literally get paid to put on your underpants in the morning? I'd say the life of a college athlete is all glamour, but I saw the Sharpie dick on the door of the cinder block closet you live in."

"I think they let stuff grow in the showers to keep us humble." He opens the detergent and pours it into the washing machine. And keeps pouring.

"Stop!" I cry. "That's more than enough."

"I don't use the whole thing?" His expression is guileless. Jesus, I think he's serious.

After an introductory lesson in measuring by the capful and choosing a water temperature, I hop onto an empty dryer while Quincy sorts his clothes according to my instructions.

"An NIL deal for undies," I muse. The NCAA rules changed a few years ago, so now players can profit off their name, image, and likeness without losing eligibility. It's only right, given how much money the schools, sponsors, and advertisers make off them. "Are you leaning toward declaring for the draft?"

He shrugs, pulling the whites out of the pile. "I've been talking to a few agents. They think it's a good idea. If I go pro after this year, I'll maximize my earning potential."

"What does Coach Thomas think?" I don't know the right path for Quincy, but he's so young. It would be a tough decision for anyone. I'm sure he's considering every factor like a weight on the scale: the way college ball is honing his game, the risk to his body, the value of a degree as a backup plan. And money, like gravity, pulling each side up or down.

"Of course he thinks I should stay," Quincy scoffs. "It's better for the team if I do."

"Put everyone else's opinions aside. What do *you* want to do?" I ask.

He stares pensively at the T-shirt in his hands. "I don't know. It doesn't matter. It's not up to me."

- - - - - - - - - - - -

THAT NIGHT, WHEN the hallway is dark except for rectangles of light thrown onto the carpet from Ben's office and mine, a young woman walks past my door.

I pull off my headphones and toss them onto the desk in a dramatic gesture visible to no one. *Come on.* It's the third time this week. The girl is a student. Her ID dangles around her neck, and she has a part-time job in the academic support office, tutoring athletes.

When she visits Ben in his office it's always at night, and they always close the door. Their voices are muffled, and sometimes they laugh. She stays for thirty minutes or so.

I don't know what's happening. Nobody's moaning or anything, but it seems inappropriate. This girl is young and a student, and Ben is senior to her, if only in an indirect way. She tutors basketball players. In theory he has the power to say something to somebody that might affect her future employment prospects. I never would've picked him out as someone who would exploit a nineteen-year-old, but the ones people don't expect are often the most dangerous. Except maybe the ones people call dangerous repeatedly for years to no effect.

Enough is enough. I have a legitimate need to speak to Ben tonight, anyway. I get up and approach his office, hovering for a moment with my ear turned toward the door. They're talking, but I can't discern anything specific.

I brace myself and open the door without knocking. I'm not sure what I expected to see. Skin, maybe. Or Ben giving the girl a back rub while commanding her in a whisper: "Write Andreatti's history essay."

Andreatti is on the cusp of academic ineligibility. He really does need to nail his history essay.

Instead, Ben is sitting in his desk chair and the girl is across from him. There is an unbreachable barrier of computing devices between them, her laptop and his desktop and somebody's tablet and a literal calculator, plus the desk itself. She's got an open notebook in her lap. Nobody is giving anyone a back rub. Relief floods my body.

Ben and the girl turn to me in unison. His hands still on his keyboard, he tilts his head, face blank. The girl smiles, not knowing this isn't normal.

"What are you doing?" he asks.

"Sorry, I didn't realize you were with someone," I say breezily. "I need to talk to you."

"I'm busy." His palm falls open toward the girl.

I take it as an invitation. "Hi, I'm Annie." I reach out my hand.

"I'm Kendall. I love your videos!" Her handshake is like a newborn baby's, her voice bashful as she delivers the compliment. Up close she has round adolescent cheeks full of potential and a constellation of pimples on her chin.

Gosh, I used to be that young. When I was her age, I thought thirty-year-olds were people who had just finished the decade where they made all their important life decisions and were now embarking on a lifetime of living with the consequences.

I'm still not sure that perception was wrong.

"Thanks. Is this a personal meeting?" I ask.

"Uh," Kendall says, turning back to Ben. I want him to be the one to answer, but he's glowering at me silently, his eyes like the stubborn coals at the end of a campfire.

"Because I need to talk to you. About work."

He doesn't say anything. Under the fluorescent lights of his office, I'm starting to feel obvious. My face is hot. I ate a wrap for dinner and forgot to check my teeth in the mirror after, so I slide my tongue across my top teeth. Maybe I should withdraw into the dark hallway like a ghost.

Kendall is not the type of person to allow a silence to linger. "He's helping me with a project for one of my classes. It's about free lunch for low-income students."

"What?" This makes no sense. Ben doesn't know anything about free lunch for low-income students. "Students who play basketball?"

Finally Ben speaks, his voice resigned. "Her topic is related to my master's thesis."

"I can email you. I don't want to keep you from your work," Kendall says to him. Her laptop clicks as she shuts it.

While she gathers her things, I say, "Next time you can keep the door open. I'm the only other one here, don't worry about disturbing me."

I wait until I can no longer hear Kendall's keys jangling down the hallway before I speak again. "You went to grad school?"

He rubs his face and puts the calculator in a drawer. "I did a master's in applied statistics here. I was a grad assistant for a year before I started this job." His stubble is verging on scruffy for once, and he has purple-gray hollows under his eyes.

"Ah." It makes sense. After I left, Coach Maynard stuck around for one more year. If a spot for a grad assistant coach was available, Ben was the obvious choice.

Ben must really love numbers, or Ardwyn, or both. A grad assistant position is a temporary gig, but it could've put him on track to a more permanent coaching job somewhere by now. As director of analytics, he's not a coach, and that's not just semantics. There are a lot of things he can't do in his current position, according to the NCAA: give instruction or feedback to the players, help with recruiting. Things he'd be good at, that I'd have thought he wanted to do.

Right now, though, it looks like what he wants is to throw me out of his office. "Why did you do that? My door was shut for a reason. You can't barge in."

"It's nice that you're helping her, but this is work-related."

"And did you know I wasn't doing work when you busted in here without knocking, or did you not care?"

"But you weren't doing work."

He gives his monitor a dark longing look, like he'd rather jump into it and tuck himself into cell A1 of a spreadsheet, any spreadsheet, even one full of circular references and formula errors, if the alternative is sitting here talking to me. "What do you want?"

"We need to do the interview. For your profile." Not my primary motivation for barging in, but it is true. "It was supposed to go up a week ago, I keep having to come up with new excuses, and we can't put it off any longer. Let's film it tonight."

"I'm busy." It's the third time he's given me this excuse. "I need to finish some lineup analysis."

Bullshit. He doesn't need to do that tonight. Tomorrow's lineup is set, and then we have the long break.

"Yeah, well, I have work to do too. This interview. It's part of my job, and this series was Coach Thomas's idea in the first place, so it's part of your job too."

"Annie. Not tonight."

Case closed, apparently. His voice sounds particularly

firm when he says it. I wish I could teleport to the green room at my apartment and lie on the turf, talking to Mona Lisa Vito while the ceiling fan spins. *Mona Lisa,* I'd say. *Can you believe he said that? In that voice.* Mona Lisa would shake her head. She'd get it right away. *The voice of the patriarchy,* she'd say. Maybe not in those exact words, but the sentiment would come through.

I haven't been able to get him to cooperate by being polite, and I haven't been able to get him to cooperate by being assertive. Probably I could get my way by crying, or not even a full cry, just blinking wet eyes and a shaky voice, but I'm tired and righteous and I can't afford the tears. I'm an hour behind on my water bottle.

I retreat, like I did the last two times I tried to get his interview done. Back to my cryogenic chamber, where the chill hits me harder than usual after all the stress-induced sweating I did in Ben's office.

Before I round the corner of the desk, I spin back to grab my wearable blanket. And to add injury to insult, my elbow smashes into the filing cabinet.

"Fuck," I hiss, but it comes out as unintelligible air. I screw up my face and my fists as the pain radiates everywhere. Now my eyes are actually watering. Something inside me snaps, and I hear Dad's voice in my head: *Don't be afraid to take up space in the paint.*

It's something he used to say all the time when I started out at Ardwyn as a tentative, intimidated freshman, unsure how to make myself valuable to the team. *He takes up space in the paint* is normally a charitable way of talking about a player the size of a sequoia who doesn't do much other than get in the other team's way. But it's not a complete knock. Standing there, ensuring that others need to factor in your presence, is important.

Don't make yourself small, that's what Dad meant.

I don't know if anything I'm doing at Ardwyn this year is making a difference. But at least I can make sure Ben understands that I'm here, and I'm not going away, at least not yet.

"Look, I know you think your job is way more important than my job." I wheel around, ranting before I'm even back in his doorway. "You won't let me forget it, that you don't have time for me, that my work is insignificant and I don't deserve to be here, that you matter more than I do. This didn't have to be a fucking competition. You don't have to sabotage me. You're being a jerk. I don't know how you became this person, but you need to get your head out of your ass, because I'm sick of it."

He looks stunned. "I'm—"

"No." I hold up a finger. "Whatever you're about to say, I don't want to hear it. Just no. Meet me on the court at seven. We're doing the interview then." I turn on my heel without waiting for an answer.

Back at my desk, my computer pings with a new message. An icon with Ben's face and name appears. A first for us.

Ben: Sorry. I'll see you at 7.

NINE

I GO DOWN TO THE COURT TO SET UP AND DISTANCE myself from Ben. My fingertips are still tingling from the adrenaline rush of unleashing my frustration, but now my stomach is roiling too. My outburst was pure emotion. I didn't think about the mechanics of how I would manage filming afterward. It's not ideal for rapport building to berate someone immediately before you interview them.

This video series was Coach Thomas's idea. He likes seeing his people get recognition, and he's sought me out to comment on each profile I've done so far. This is important to him. I can't allow it to suck.

Ben shows up five minutes early with the demeanor of a pallbearer. He's changed his shirt, combed his hair, and found a razor to clean up his stubble.

"Thanks for coming," I say tentatively.

He sits in the obvious spot, the single illuminated chair in the vast darkness, surrounded by thousands of empty seats.

I check the microphone and make a few adjustments to the camera. When I step into the light to turn his chair by a few degrees, we make miserable eye contact. There's nothing else to look at in this lighting, unless you want to stare into the void. We're like a pair of kidneys on an operating table.

Up close, his immovable stone eyes are laced with seams of gold, a detail I've never noticed before. My heart does a traitorous pancake flip.

Christ.

He swallows audibly. "Again, I'm sorry."

"We're doing it now, no harm done." I steadfastly avoid eye contact, studying the rest of him to make sure he's camera-ready. One side of his collar needs to be straightened. "Can I?" I point.

He nods.

I fix it gingerly with my fingertips and back away. "All done."

He shifts in his seat and rubs his arm. "Should I have done anything to prepare? I don't want to look like an idiot."

"It won't be that bad." It's a lie. If he looks this wretched in the video, people will think he's a hostage, and all the incoming recruits will decommit. "I'm not a journalist. I'll ask easy questions. And besides, I can edit it however I need to later."

"Is that supposed to be comforting?"

"I'm planning to use the puppy filter, but if you act like a diva, I've got two words for you. *Talking. Potato.*"

He laughs a little. *More of that.* I need him to loosen up.

"Hey, what if we play a game?" I say.

"What kind of game?"

"I'll shoot free throws. If I make a shot, I get to ask you a

question. If I miss, you can ask me a question. You can col-
lect embarrassing information to use against me in the future."

Nothing truly embarrassing, obviously, but enough for
him to relax and give me decent footage to work with.

He considers. "How old were you when you stopped playing basketball?"

"I did one year of rec. Third grade. I got stuffed by Emily
Chou in the first quarter of our first game and cried. I told
everyone I had to go to the bathroom and hid in the stall the
rest of the game. My parents made me stick it out until the
season was over."

He snorts, then pauses, probably trying to calculate the
average free throw percentage of an unathletic string cheese
thief who's been retired from the sport for twenty years.
"Okay, fine."

I find a ball. After dragging a spare light over so I can see,
I take a few clumsy dribbles and pass the ball back and forth
from one hand to the other, familiarizing myself with the
weight of it. I can feel him watching me, but I don't look at
him. I look at the basket.

It's been a long time since I've done this. My first attempt
is off, but it takes a lucky clanging bounce off the rim before
dropping through the net like a fingertip against silk. An un-
sportsmanlike yelp escapes my mouth, and he grabs his head
with both hands. "That was a hideous shot. That shouldn't
even count."

I can feel how wide my grin is, all teeth, gloating. "Sportsmanship, Callahan. Don't be a sore loser." I clear my throat
and modulate my voice, assuming a more professional tone.
"Now, what's your role with the team? And with each

question, restate it so I can cut my voice out. It won't feel natural at first, but it'll sound more natural."

"Nothing about this feels natural," he mutters.

I make a get-on-with-it motion with my hands.

He exhales and looks at the camera. His face slides into a neutral expression. I'd prefer something a bit warmer, but I'll take what I can get. "My role is to compile and analyze data about our team and our opponents, to make recommendations to improve the team's performance."

"Good." I kick off my ankle boots before returning to the free throw line. They have a heel, and I have no interest in making this game harder than it needs to be.

The second shot falls straight through the hoop, barely touching the net.

I raise my arms in triumph. "You can't tell me that one wasn't pretty."

He shakes his head. "Somehow I've been conned."

I ask him about easy topics: his favorite basketball memory, a fun fact about Coach Thomas, what superpower he'd want to have on the court. Eventually I overshoot one, and the ball hits the back of the rim and sails out of bounds.

"Finally." He crosses his arms. "Okay, please tell me why a third-grade basketball dropout is shooting eighty percent from the free throw line?"

"Because beating you is great motivation."

"Just in this game, or is that your general life strategy?"

I pretend to chuck the ball at him. "My dad always worked late during the season. And my mom was never a disciplinarian, so she did the whole 'Wait till your father gets home' thing. My dad parented like he coached. He didn't know how to do it any other way. When he walked in the door and my mom asked him to deal with me, he took me out to the driveway until I made twenty-five in a row."

We'd stand in front of the garage in the dark, the floodlights illuminating the hoop, me huffing about how unfair Mom was being or how misunderstood I felt. It wasn't the same for Kat. She and Dad butted heads, and Mom was the one she turned to. With me, Dad would listen quietly as I ranted and missed shots until he figured out what I needed: tough love to help me pull my head out of my ass, or a chance to vent. Sometimes it was enough to spend twenty minutes *not* talking about whatever was upsetting me, so we reviewed proper free throw mechanics instead.

I look down at the ball in my hands, my heart heavy. "He could never resist correcting my form."

"Well, you're pretty good at free throws. You must've gotten in trouble a lot."

A laugh bubbles out of me, catching me by surprise. "Look who's suddenly full of jokes," I say. I make another shot. "Who's your role model and why?"

"My role model is, um"—he hesitates for a millisecond, his eyes flicking over to me—"My role model is Brent Maynard, my coach when I played here at Ardwyn. He's a basketball genius and an incredible person. He taught me so much about the game and also gave me a lot of guidance and support off the court. He's like family." He takes a breath as if preparing to say more.

I study my list of questions, trying to maintain a look of clinical detachment, but my chest is tight and my heartbeat has reached my skull, where it's pounding aggressively. "Okay, that's enough, it'll be clear to everyone that you want to marry him." I'm going to cut this whole answer anyway.

I miss the next shot. He hums contemplatively and asks, "What's your most embarrassing basketball-related story?"

Thank god for a chance to change the subject. "I once got ejected from one of my dad's games," I offer.

He barks out a laugh. "No way. Why?"

"There was a guy sitting behind me, mouthing off." I jog over to retrieve the ball. "Calling my dad overrated, accusing him of recruiting violations—total bullshit. I know criticism comes with the territory, but the guy got personal. And he kept yapping about how we should run a full-court press. He had no idea what he was talking about."

"So you did what?" Ben asks.

"I corrected his misconceptions." I shrug. "And I told him his mustache was ugly. In what some might call an 'elevated voice.' Some did call it that, in fact. The referees. They said I was causing a disturbance and had security remove me. The other team's student section booed me on my way out."

Ben's posture is loose as he rests his elbows on his knees and shakes his head. He's amused enough to forget the camera for now. "Fans are brutal. It must've been hard when you were in high school, with your dad having a high-profile coaching job. Hearing people pick apart his decisions."

"Sure," I chirp. "But this was three years ago." Dad's final season, not that any of us knew at the time. His last game was a completely unremarkable state quarterfinal loss with no fanfare. It's not fair that he didn't get to retire properly.

Another surprised laugh from Ben. "You're not actually embarrassed by this story, are you?"

"Not at all." I square up for my next shot, which drops neatly through the basket. Only a few questions left. "What do you love about working for Ardwyn basketball?"

He pulls on the cuff of his shirt. "What do I *love*? Um." His eyes defocus, and he slips away somewhere in his head. Somewhere heavy. He's no longer thinking about basketball, he's about to give an on-screen confession to a cold-case murder. "Pass," he finally says.

"What? Isn't that an easy question?"

He rubs the back of his neck. "Kind of defeats the purpose of passing if you have to explain yourself."

"There are so many things you can say. The people, the history, whatever. The 'Ardwyn Family,' everyone always likes that one."

"I'm getting tired." His voice is gravelly.

I step closer. "Me too, but we're almost done. Come on, this should be easy for you. The only person who's worked here longer than you is Donna. You bleed Ardwyn Blue."

"Jesus Christ. Can you turn the camera off? I want to say something."

His expression is raw and I want to stop him, say *Never mind,* but I don't. Instead I press the button.

When he speaks, he does so with jagged stops and starts, pausing to select his words with care. "The main reason I've been avoiding this interview is I've been dreading talking about my job on camera. Sorry I made you think it was personal. I know you and I haven't been . . ." He stops and shakes his head. "I'm so frustrated right now, and I've been taking it out on you, and that's not fair. I'm sick of fighting for my job, but that's not even the most important part. I'm disgusted with how badly this school has screwed up its finances."

"What do you mean?" I ask.

He works his jaw. "They're not just going after the department with a scalpel; they're using a bludgeon too. Entire sports will be cut. My sister is supposed to come here next year for gymnastics. Competing for Ardwyn has been her dream since she was little, since we started taking her to meets here because I got free tickets. It's an expensive sport for the school and it brings in no revenue, so it's probably going to be gone.

"At the same time, I'm here burning out, and I may have nothing to show for it in four months. I've been here for, what, a third of my life? I'm still in the same role. The numbers guy. Do you remember when we were in school, and we did anything that had to get done, even if it wasn't our job?"

I nod silently, my chest tight. I once did Coach Maynard's annual ethics training for him, sitting through an online seminar, answering the multiple-choice questions when they popped up. I picked out his wife's birthday present three years in a row.

Ben continues. "Well, I still do that. Kyle is in over his head as director of operations, so I do half of his job during all the free time I *don't* have. Do you know what he did a couple months ago? He booked all of our travel for the first half of the season using last year's calendar. Hotels, meals, flights. Guess who had to clean that up? Me."

Kyle screwing up the travel schedule—I knew about that. But nobody told me Ben was the one who fixed it.

"It's thankless, and I'm tired and angry," he says. "I don't have it in me to talk about how much I love being part of the 'Ardwyn Family' right now."

Silence. He's done.

"I'm sorry to hear that," I hear myself say. I can't wrap my head around this information. Ben is a believer. He would wear Ardwyn Blue even if he were a True Autumn. (He's not. It looks great on him.) But if even he's jaded enough to use air quotes around "Ardwyn Family," there's no hope for anyone else.

"Yeah, so. Should we finish?" His mouth is a flattened coin.

There are a few more questions I'm supposed to ask, but the interview feels over. "I have what I need," I say. "Let's get out of here." I turn off the camera and start unplugging things. Neither of us speaks. I take my time wrapping an extension cord into the neatest possible coil, detaching the microphone and breaking down its stand, trying to process what Ben said.

His behavior makes more sense now. It's not an excuse, but it's something, and it's a relief to learn it hasn't *all* been personal. He's under a lot of pressure. His sister's future hanging in the balance, plus his own. He sounds as drained as I feel when I think about what's at stake for me.

He sits for a while, apparently not ready to move. When he stands, he reaches for the chair. "Where do you want this?"

"I'll do it. It's my job," I say, waving him off. "It's late. Go. Thanks for doing this." He doesn't move as I nestle the camera in its case, and I'm not sure whether I want him to say something more or leave.

The latches are loud when I click them shut. By the time I look up, he's gone, and I'm surprised to find myself disappointed.

Say something more, I will him, too late.

- - - - - - - - - - - -

THE LATEST SEASON of the hottest nonsense on television begins the first Monday in January. Eric and Cassie live farther from campus than I do. It's a short drive or a long walk. I never remember the door code, so I slip into the building behind a guy carrying a bag of groceries and take the stairs to the third floor.

The layered sounds of multiple conversations happening in the same room float down the hall as I approach their condo. Uh-oh. When Eric invited me over to watch *The Beach House,* I assumed it would be just the three of us. Not a party.

I look down at my stretched-out leggings and pull up the waistband, which droops again immediately. A few stray stubby bits poke out of the bun piled on my head, and my sweater is a muddled taupe anti-color. I adjust the neckline so my necklace is visible, dangling over my collarbone, and drag a finger under each eye to wipe away any black smudges. A classic schlump-to-slob transition.

The door is unlocked. I kick my sneakers off and leave them next to the mat. To my relief, the first people I see are Cassie's law school friends, standing in the kitchen.

I join the circle. "The last time I saw you guys, we were all wearing the same dress."

"Annie!" Jade hugs me first, then Talia and Grace. One of them pours me a glass of wine and they ask me about the move and the new job. I haven't seen them since the wedding.

"What happened with the guy?" I ask Grace.

"I DM'd the other girl. She asked me for screenshots of the texts but as far as I know they're still together."

I make a disgusted noise.

I ask Jade about her mom's health and chat with Talia about her Etsy shop. I've only met them a handful of times, but there's an accelerated familiarity there, the kind that applies to close friends of close friends. Cassie talked about them for years before I met them, so I've always known about their jobs and personalities and love lives, the same way I know about the characters on the teenage murder show Kat talks about even though I've never seen it. And then I did meet Jade and Talia and Grace, and drank a lot of tequila with them at Cassie's bachelorette party, and boom. Bonded.

I take one of the blank brackets from the pile on the counter. "I'm guessing I need to fill this out."

"Oh, yes." Jade hands me a pen. "Eric's orders. Episode one for now. We'll do the rest after tonight."

"Was I supposed to do research?" I eye the names running down each side of the page.

"We have a printout of their headshots here. For the first episode you'll have to go purely on looks."

The structure of the show is only vaguely familiar to me. There's a romantic element, where people have to couple up to stick around, but there's also a monetary prize at the end. I pick a few people from the photos based on gut instinct and fill in the rest of the names at random. When I'm finished, I make my way over to Eric, who's standing by himself, studying everyone's brackets.

He takes in my outfit. "Did you just get out of ballet practice?"

I roll my eyes and hand him my bracket.

He appraises it with interest, running his finger down each column. "Lots of people picking Jasmine," he says. "We've got ourselves a front-runner."

"Well, yeah. It's because of her face."

There's a group of guys on the other side of the pass-through. I recognize them, other athletic department employees who aren't exactly in my orbit. One of the academic advisors, a guy from the development team, the football facilities coordinator.

I introduce myself. They're friendly enough, and they talk to me for a bit, but after a few minutes they fall back into the conversation they were having before, about people I don't know doing things they haven't explained to me.

I'm considering returning to the kitchen when I see the dog. A Lab mix, curled up into a U-shape on the floor.

I crouch down. The dog sniffs my hand, and I scratch it behind the ears. It groans and leans into my palm.

"What's your name?" I murmur. Eric and Cassie don't have any pets.

I look up to ask someone about the dog. That's when I see Ben, sitting on the couch next to Cassie. They're laughing and he's slouching back against a pillow, one foot on the opposite knee. His hair is damp and undone, sticking up in every direction.

My stomach tightens. How am I supposed to interact with him after our conversation before the holidays? Fighting, playing that game, laughing. Me needling him, him sharing something deeply personal with me. I haven't even concluded whether the whole thing went well or poorly.

"Annie! I didn't know you were here." Cassie hops up.

I climb off the floor to hug her. "I was saying hi to everyone. How was New Orleans?"

Cassie tells me about her time at home, the family parties, the attempts at warding off questions from aunts and uncles about her plans for her uterus. She brought back andouille sausage in her suitcase, which means there's a tall pot of gumbo on the stove. She looks rested, like she might make it through the entire episode tonight without passing out in a chair.

"I didn't realize this was an actual party," I say.

"Did we not tell you that? Sorry, I thought you knew. We've been doing this for a few years now."

"Whose dog is that? I love him. Her?"

"Ben's," Cassie says. She leans over the coffee table and picks up a near-empty bowl of tortilla chip crumbs. "She's a girl. Right?"

Ben nods. "Sasha," he tells Cassie, and not me.

The show is about to start, so Cassie takes the bowl to the kitchen to refill it. I beg her for a chore to do, but she waves me off.

There's only one place to go now. I perch on the end of the couch, ready to jump up if somebody needs help opening a bottle or making guacamole or scrubbing a toilet. I glance at Ben but he's looking at his phone. Back to the cold shoulder, then?

He's wearing fitted sweatpants with a thin, worn-in gray T-shirt that stretches over his biceps. Next to his socked feet sits a pair of pristine sneakers that have a name I can't remember and a stock price on those niche websites for diehards. Of course. He probably gets a new pair every time they get scuffed. Minutes pass and his face is still in his phone, his fingers tapping away at the screen.

I look at the dog longingly, wishing I could give her a belly rub. Maybe get some more hand nuzzles. I haven't had substantial physical contact with any living creature since before I moved. How long will I have to sit here in silence before Ben will initiate a conversation? Maybe I'll try waiting it out.

I last eight seconds. "I didn't know people were allowed to wear those shoes. I thought they were for decoration."

His head snaps up, and he slides his phone into his pocket. "They're shoes. They're for feet." He gestures at the TV. "I didn't know you watched *The Beach House*."

"This is my first time. Big fan?"

He lets his head loll back against the couch and narrows his eyes. "Eric and I started the fantasy league together. I don't care if you make fun of us for it."

"Sure," I say. "Because people who don't care always make a point to tell you they don't care. Isn't making fun of the show the point, anyway?"

He tilts his head back and forth. "It is and it isn't. Wait and see." He hesitates, and then adds, "Please don't ruin this for me."

He doesn't say it in a nasty way. He says it like he understands I might not be able to help it, and it would be a big favor to him if I resisted the impulse. This pleases and confuses me.

"You really like it?"

"It's my favorite thing."

I can't tell if he's serious. It's the messy hair. It's throwing me off completely. All of his usual expressions look different with that hair. How am I supposed to—it's so *distracting,* it's like—and why can't I stop *looking* at it?

He's looking at me too. At the necklace dangling over my clavicle. I graze it with my fingertips self-consciously, my face growing inexplicably warm. It's nothing unusual-looking, just a thin gold bar with a tiny diamond, my birthstone.

He turns his head away quickly, toward the TV. People are starting to squeeze onto the couch and pull over the counter stools and sprawl out on the floor. Time for the show.

TEN

BY THE END OF THE EPISODE I THINK I GET IT, AND that Ben was being sincere about it being his favorite thing. They do make fun of it. Everyone laughs during the argument about the stolen guacamole during the nacho tower challenge. The hottest commodity on the beach appears to be a guy named Logan, an "entrepreneur." He grew up in New Jersey, which garners a whoop from Eric. Somebody points out that his signature move is stroking the knuckles of each woman when he's sitting alone with them. One of the other contestants, Cole, likes to talk about how long his parents have been married, and he repeats it enough times that the whole party starts saying "thirty-seven" in a chorus as he winds up to do it again.

They don't only make fun of it, though. There is a sincere and heated debate about which contestants are the best matches for each other, like they can't help but go along with the premise. I even find myself taking sides and making a mental note of a few people I want to choose for next week's bracket. Later I point out that the margarita in Felicia's glass rises and falls to different levels every other shot, and everyone *oohs*. "The editing," Talia says. "First what she did in the diving contest, and now this? She's going to be the villain."

I learn it doesn't matter if we stop paying attention to talk about something else for five minutes. This happens frequently. All the important parts are recapped before and after each commercial break anyway. And even the important parts are not that important.

What I get about this whole thing by the end of the episode is that the show is a necessary part of it, for the commenting and opining, but the real point is that it gives everyone a reason to get together for two hours on Monday nights in the dead of winter.

Cassie's friends leave as soon as the show is over, because the billable hour tires them out too. The athletic department guys are getting their coats. Cassie gathers dishes and hands them to Eric, who loads the dishwasher. Ben puts the empty beer bottles in a paper grocery bag for the recycling.

I begin dragging the stools back to the counter. "Do you watch it for the love stories? Like, do you believe any of these couples will stay together?"

Cassie picks up empty gumbo bowls from the coffee table and passes them to Eric. She shrugs. "I'm optimistic. I always like to see it work out."

Eric pulls her into his chest and kisses the top of her head. "My wife is a sucker. How many of the couples are still together? One?"

"One," Ben confirms. "Three final couples per season—it has about a seven percent success rate."

Cassie blinks at Eric, and a placid smile appears on her face. Placid like a lake full of alligators.

Eric and Cassie balance each other. He shows his love by giving people a hard time; she is sweet and sincere. He is all boundless energy and hyper extroversion, and she is still and steady. Most of the time. But every so often . . .

"Ben, how many years has this show been on? Five?" Cassie asks.

"Something like that."

Cassie steps closer to Eric and strokes his face. "My dear husband." He leans into her hand. "How many championships have the Knicks won in the last five years? No, the last twenty years?"

Eric's mouth drops. He puts a hand to his heart like he's been stabbed. Ben snorts.

Nobody needs to answer the question, but I do it anyway. "That'd be a solid zero."

Cassie takes Eric's hand and squeezes it. "And you still cheer for them. Does that make you a sucker?"

He sighs. "Yes, it does."

Ben is really laughing now, holding his stomach with one hand. Maybe he's never seen this side of Cassie. She gives Eric shit so sparingly it's magic when she does. Ben leans back and his shirt rides up, exposing a strip of his toned stomach, a smattering of hair visible at the center. He pushes an unruly wave off his face and lets out a happy sigh.

I can't take my eyes off him. After the past couple months, I don't understand how this version of him can exist, the one who lounges on a couch and brings a dog to a party and appreciates a genuinely funny burn. The one who looks like this.

There were girls in my freshman dorm who had crushes on Ben in college, but his Stepford prom king thing never did it for me. Now that I think about it, though, there were a few occasions like this one, when he wasn't completely composed, when I thought: *Oh, I get it.* A couple times when he was a player and got worked up over a bad call. And once when a few of us were stuck in the office at midnight, so we rewatched that old "Boom goes the dynamite" video, and he laughed so hard he cried. It wasn't a big deal, though. It didn't make me feel unsettled, like I feel now.

Cassie turns on Ben next. "I don't know what you think is so funny. You're a Sixers fan."

Now it's my turn to laugh.

THIS NIGHT SHOULD not end with Ben and me walking home together, but it does. It happens so fast. I'm digging in my bag for my keys when Eric reminds Cassie he drove Ben here from the auto shop, where he left his car to be serviced.

Cassie turns to me. "Don't you live in the same neighborhood?"

"I walked here." My response is too fast, an attempt to preempt a request for a ride home.

The problem is that at the same time, Ben says, "I wanted to walk Sasha home anyway."

Cassie narrows her eyes at me, probably because I have never walked here before in my life.

"I like walking in this weather. It's refreshing." It's not, but it's what comes out of my mouth. Today is as frigid as any other day in the big gray blur of January. Even as I'm saying it, I try to gauge how weird it would be if I told them

Never mind, I just remembered I did drive. It would be very weird.

Cassie's nod is like the bang of a judge's gavel. "You can walk back together, then."

I press my lips together hard. In fifteen seconds and with one little lie I've bumbled my way into a long cold walk with Ben, plus the logistical challenge of figuring out how to get my car back before work tomorrow.

We don't talk on the stairs or as we weave through the parking lot. I try not to look at my car. Thankfully, it's far away, in the last spot. I zip my coat all the way to the top and flick up my hood. This warms my ears and comes with the added bonus of blocking me from seeing Ben in my peripheral vision.

We aren't even at the corner and my face is already numb in the razor-blade wind. This is a peaceful residential neighborhood, with a few apartment buildings and lots of charming old homes. Mature trees line the street, their bare branches towering overhead. At this hour, in this part of town, few cars are on the road.

Ben says something but my hood muffles the sound. "What?" I have to turn my head and shoulders toward him to see his face.

He clears his throat. "Sorry if I was weird in there," he repeats. "After the night of the interview—well, I didn't mean to say all that. Feels a little awkward."

Didn't mean to say all that *to me*. I'm not supposed to be his confidante. And fair enough, because I'd be mortified if I spewed my private feelings all over him. Showed him my vulnerabilities, so he could judge me and use them as ammunition.

Except I have no urge to judge him for what he said. It revealed him to be a living, breathing human. My instinct is to empathize with him, but I'm not sure whether to fight it. "No worries," I say lightly.

We walk on the quiet side street in silence for a few minutes until he breaks it. "So tell me what you thought of the show. If you hated it completely."

"Why do you assume I hated it?"

He shrugs audibly, the waterproof material of his coat scratching against itself.

"It wasn't good—"

"In your opinion."

I hold up a hand. "Let me finish. And not in my opinion. Objectively. It's objectively not a good show. But it doesn't matter, it was fun."

He blows into his fist to warm it. "Really?" He sounds pleased. "I thought you'd be too cool for it. That you'd only be into, like, *cinema*." He gives the last word a pompous inflection.

"Ah, yes," I say. "Me, the esteemed creator of The Devil Wears Prardwyn." He laughs. "The person who spent a half hour today filming Gallimore trying to juggle blindfolded. Don't fence me in, Callahan."

He ponders my words. "Wouldn't I be fencing you out?"

Sasha stops to sniff a mailbox, and I shuffle from foot to foot to generate body heat. "No, you're fencing me in. With, like, *cinema*." I mimic his intonation.

He groans. "This conversation is terrible. Should we try again?"

"At your own risk."

"So you had fun, and you're going to come next week?"

I am. I am, because doing it once has shown me that I need it. I need this, I need *Beach House* Mondays, because I am so fucking alone. This is my first time living by myself. I've always had Kat or other roommates, and my parents nearby, and friends in my hometown. That's how I got away with hating all my jobs. *An otherwise full life,* I always told my parents, like a well-coping widow.

I'm not equipped to go home and sit by myself in an apartment every night. I have Cassie and Eric, but they're both busy, so I often make excuses not to hang out so they get more alone time. Mom and Kat's visits have become less frequent since I've settled in. I have coffee with Taylor and Jess once a week, and go to the gym, and spend Friday nights at the mall buying, like, one shirt that I end up returning the following Friday night. I find it comforting, being surrounded by noise and other people, even if those people are strangers. Like I can absorb a social life by osmosis. This, an actual social life, is better.

"I have to, if I want to win the fantasy league," I say.

He switches the leash to his other hand and blows into his fist before sticking it into his pocket to thaw. "Bold words for the new kid. Who's your pick for the money so far?"

"I've narrowed it down to two contenders."

"Which two?"

We reach Ardwyn Avenue, the main road. I glance both ways before crossing, and Sasha's collar jingles as Ben follows. "Well, first, Jasmine."

"Obvious choice," he says.

"But still likely." There's more activity in this part of town: students walking home from the library, a movie letting out at the tiny independent theater. The used bookstore and quirky boutiques are closed, but the bars are open, with bored-looking bouncers checking for fake IDs outside.

"And second?"

I push my hood back because it's getting annoying, turning back and forth to look at him. "Brianne."

"Which one is that?"

"The one with the short hair."

"Hm. You seem confident." He doesn't look sold.

"I am." I debate whether to explain. "Jasmine and Brianne got different music than everyone else when their boats came in. I'm thinking they're going to be battling it out for Logan. We saw the entire exchange he had with each of them at happy hour. They weren't just part of the montage. They both seem to be solid in the challenges. And in the preview at the end of the episode, you could see them both multiple times, in different locations, wearing different outfits."

"Ugh," he says, but a smile plays at his lips. "You're cheating, Radford."

"How?"

He shakes his head. "You're using your video editing knowledge for an unfair advantage."

"What rule does that violate? I assume you have a written rulebook. I'd expect nothing less from you."

He's behind me now, Sasha dragging him toward a streetlight so she can sniff it. "No, it just violates the entire spirit of the game."

I break into a grin and spin to face him. "Oh, the spirit of the game? You know you've already lost when you start referring to the 'spirit of the game.'"

That gets a chuckle out of him. "I asked you not to ruin this for me."

"I'm making it better for you," I protest. "You can use my observations to make your picks. Only for this week, because I'm nice."

"Are you?" He studies me. "On principle I now feel obligated not to pick Jasmine or Brianne."

"Do your principles usually lead you to crushing defeat?"

He laughs again, his face glowing orange under the streetlight like a friendly demon.

This conversation is going too well. It's going so well that I have to ruin it.

"I wish you would've been honest with me from the beginning." The words gush out on a single breath. "I wish we could've agreed that we were in a shitty situation, but we weren't going to take it out on each other. I think we should try to do that now."

My statement is ill-timed, because Sasha still isn't moving forward, so we don't even have the walking as a distraction. We're stuck standing there. She takes a few steps to the left, into the grassy area near the curb, and squats. It's silent except for the sound of her peeing.

Ben looks down, scuffing one shoe slowly, dragging a pebble along the sidewalk with his foot. "I don't know if I can."

Hot frustration builds in my head like an unopened soda bottle rolling around in the trunk of a car. "Why not? I can't figure you out. We used to work *together*! Mom and Dad, right? Will you just admit that even though you want everyone to think you're so nice and charming, you're really a petty asshole like the rest of us? Even on day one, you couldn't stand to look at me. You told Verona and Lufton I didn't deserve to be here. That I was a bandwagoner. What did I ever do to you?"

He gives Sasha a tortured look, a call for help, like maybe she'll chase a squirrel and they'll have to run. But Sasha is an elderly tyrant who walks with slow, arthritic steps and digs her heels in whenever she wants. He's going to have to answer the question.

"I can't possibly trust you," he finally says. "I thought that would be obvious."

"Why would that be obvious?"

He raises his eyebrows. I raise mine, or try to, but it's so frigid I'm not sure if my facial muscles are doing anything. In my pockets, my fingernails stamp half moons into my palms.

"You want me to—okay." He clears his throat. "Annie, you *left*. Senior year, middle of the season, after the team lost five games in a row. Right when it was becoming clear that we weren't going to be any good. You say we were Mom and Dad? Well, you walked out on our family. I know this is a cutthroat line of work, but personally that's not how I operate, and I didn't think it was how you operated either."

A group of students walks toward us on their way to one of the bars, the guys in nearly identical puffer vests and the girls coatless, huddled together against the wind. He pauses as they pass, rubbing his face. When they're out of earshot, he continues.

"Nobody knew how to do your job. When you left, it all fell on me. I tried to make a video once. It took four hours and was eight seconds long. That all sucked, but it wasn't the worst part. The worst part was that I thought we were a team. I spent three and a half years in awe of you, did you know that?"

I should shake my head, but I'm too stunned to move. The

part about us being a team makes sense. I felt the same way. I can believe he respected me. I can believe he liked working with me. But *awe* is a big word.

"I still remember the first time I saw you. This girl in a blue dress with matching sneakers, marching onto the court with a camera and bossing around the starters with complete confidence, this look in her eye like she had a vision in her head and she was going to make it happen. Which you did, of course. All those years I felt lucky to work with you. I thought we were *friends*." His voice turns rough. "We spent more time with each other than we did with anyone else in our lives. And you left and never looked back, never answered any of my texts. Just moved on, like it never mattered."

When he's finished, he brings his hand to his mouth and squeezes his bottom lip between his fingers.

My throat seizes up. "We were never friends," I manage.

He stares at me in disbelief. "Okay," he says, like it's not true. Like he's humoring me.

"I mean it," I snap. "We didn't hang out outside of basketball. We didn't know each other that well. We weren't friends."

If we were, maybe I could've asked him for help.

If we were, maybe it would've made a difference.

Eric was one year older, so he was gone by senior year. I thought I was close with lots of other people who were part of the program. But when I needed someone on my side, I was alone.

"Fine." He shakes his head. "Regardless, I never would've done that to you. I wouldn't have left before the end of the season, even for a good opportunity. I wouldn't have abandoned you to pick up the pieces. Call that whatever you want."

A car turns the corner, headlights curving on the asphalt. A sharp thread of anger laces itself through me, pulls tight, ties a knot. A hot squeezing sensation grips my head.

We have to wait for the light to change. I'm shaking like I'm about to blast off. "I don't even know where to start with how fucking off-base that is," I spit.

"Jeez, Radford." He reaches out as if to steady me.

"No. Stop. You think I left for another *opportunity*?"

"Um. Well. It was a long time ago. I think Coach Maynard told me you found a full-time job and were going to graduate early so you could take it?"

There must be flames flickering in my eyeballs now. I can't swallow. "He said that was why I left?"

"Yeah?" Ben says warily. "You wanted more eyes on your work and we weren't going to make the tournament . . . You got a job offer and . . . It was never clear to me whether it was at another school, or in the NBA, or what. He didn't know."

He didn't know because the job offer didn't exist. "I didn't leave because we were bad or for another job. He and I didn't see eye to eye on a lot of things, and I was going through personal shit. Even when they sucked, I loved that team more than anything. But I couldn't do it anymore. That was it, okay?" My voice cracks.

He doesn't say anything. He looks pensive, clearly shifting around the building blocks in his head, the ones he's used to construct his assumptions about me and our shared history, testing to see whether the foundation still holds up the house. His face says he's unsure.

"Okay?" I repeat.

He nods.

I read the street sign in front of us. Somehow we're almost at my apartment, although hardly anything about the route we walked through downtown registered in my mind. Ben follows a few feet behind as I turn the corner.

He breaks the silence. "There must've been a misunderstanding, because Coach wouldn't have said that if he didn't think it was true." He says this slowly, puzzling it out as he goes.

"You have a lot of faith in him."

"Well, yeah, I do."

I bite my lip hard, like it might prevent me from saying anything else. But I have to say something. Not about what happened to me. I have no interest in going anywhere near that subject with him, but I'm not the only one who got hurt. "You know he made Phil Coleman play on an injured heel, and that's how he ruptured his Achilles?"

He doesn't comment on the sudden change in subject, but it surprises him. "Uh. That's not how I remember it."

"He should've gone pro."

"He was cleared to play."

"He told him he didn't feel ready."

"Coach wouldn't do that."

He really believes it. We've reached my building, so I stop walking. I can hear my own agitated breathing. "You make a lot of wrong assumptions about people," I say. "I don't think you're going to win the *Beach House* bracket."

There were points in this conversation when, if we had stopped talking, we might have ended our walk with some kind of peace. But no, we kept going, to the ugly tender spot at the heart of it all. There is no treaty, no resolution. There's no anything. Ben stands there for a minute, his face resigned, and then Sasha pulls him away, and I wait until they're out of sight before I summon a Lyft to pick me up and take me to my car.

ELEVEN

MY JOB IS EASIER WHEN WE PLAY WELL, SO JANUARY is a challenging month. In the first two weeks of the year, the team serves up two steaming losses and two anemic wins. Our opponents roll over us in the paint, and we look lost on offense, clanging desperate three-pointers off the rim. There's no rhythm, no magic. Even Eric looks subdued on the sidelines.

Quincy misses an easy layup and the ESPN broadcast catches him yelling something profane at himself. At home somewhere, a parent covers a kid's ears and writes an angry letter.

January taunts me: *Now show me what you can do with that.* The day after the first loss, I put together a "happy birthday" highlight reel for a former Ardwyn power forward who now plays professionally in Montenegro. It's all I've got because there's nothing worth posting about the game. Even the cheerleaders' halftime dance was out of sync.

We go all the way to Omaha and lose again. After the game, I wait down the hall from the locker room so I can follow the team back to the bus. The postgame debrief is taking longer than usual. I'm cold, grumpy, and aching for my own bed, a thousand miles away.

Tonight, the budget cuts feel hopelessly unavoidable.

Someone flings open the door to the pressroom, a guy talking to somebody else over his shoulder. "See you tomorrow. Rise and grind, bro!" I spin around to face the wall.

"Mizzz Radford," he says in a singsong voice, like the little brother I never had and don't want.

JJ Jones works for ESPN and covers some of Ardwyn's games. He has low straight eyebrows and a big chin, and he dresses like his mother bought his wardrobe with the proceeds of his father's Ponzi scheme. He believes himself to be everyone's best friend and vice versa, and without prompting he spits out phrases that belong on a free poster that comes with a two-pack of hypermasculine deodorant.

"Tough game," he says. "That lineup isn't working for you."

"I think we're all aware." I offer a perfunctory smile to punctuate the conversation.

"Can't be fun going all the way to Nebraska to lose. Cornhusker State! Omaha, man."

"Definitely not." I look at the locker room door, willing it to open.

"Gotta get right back into it at practice tomorrow. Hey, let me tell you something Chuck once said to me."

He shifts from foot to foot, watching me. Probably aware that I'm looking to escape. Now that I've met JJ a handful of times, I can see the eagerness for validation below the surface. "By Chuck, I mean Charles Barkley," he clarifies.

I sigh. "What did Charles Barkley say?"

He relaxes and grins. "Earn it and learn it. Earn it. And. Learn it." And then he's gone, someone else catching his eye like a piece of glitter.

PRACTICE BACK AT home the next day is light. I'm not filming, but I watch the last fifteen minutes anyway, trying to discern the mood. It's not great. Quincy is still in a funk and everyone else is feeling it. Coach Thomas is as composed as ever, but he must be frustrated.

Afterward, Quincy sits on the bench and pulls the hem of his shirt up over his head to cover his face. He should go back to his dorm room and play video games until he can't see straight. I almost pull him aside to suggest it, but then Thomas sits down next to him, speaking in hushed, calm tones through the fabric of his shirt for a long time. Team captain Jamar Gregg-Edwards joins them, putting an arm around Quincy and guiding him toward the locker room.

That night I work on a hype video for next week. It needs to be good. We're playing Blake, our conference rival, and a fourth loss in one month would be demoralizing.

We saw a modest increase in our social media following and engagement levels at the beginning of the season, when I started making videos. Same with ticket sales. Recently, though, everything has plateaued. So far, I have no tangible evidence that I'm making an impact. That I deserve to stick around. If our lackluster gameplay continues, I'm doomed. I need to find a way to drum up enthusiasm no matter how we're playing. And now that I've gotten to know these players, I'm convinced they *deserve* more enthusiasm and support.

The irony of *this* being my job is not lost on me. That I, more than anyone else, am responsible for selling Ardwyn basketball to the world. But I've allowed myself to forget that. If I try to tell the story of this team, these individuals, it's not so bad.

I start with a song they've been listening to a lot when they stretch at the beginning of practice. I pull clips from previous games against Blake, recent ones plus old fuzzy ones transferred from VHS tapes. The voice-over came in a few hours ago, from an Ardwyn alumnus who won a Tony a few years ago.

When I put a video together, I can physically feel when it's good. Some part of me recognizes that what I've got on my computer matches what I've got in my head. My chest burns and my hands tingle. It's addictive; it's what I chase every time, the closest thing I've ever felt to a religious experience. It's happening now.

I'm watching it all the way through again when someone taps my shoulder. I whip my head around and swivel in my chair.

It's Quincy, standing above me in sweat-soaked practice clothes. "What are you doing here?" I ask, sliding off my headphones.

"*A*-Rad. *A-Rad*." He laughs, and there's beer on his breath. "I'm so glad you're here. I need your help."

"What's wrong?" I humor him. If he's too drunk to operate the DoorDash app on his own, I'm adding a side of fries to his order for my troubles.

He heads toward the free chair opposite my desk. No—hobbles toward it. "Ouch. Fuck."

The air in my lungs ceases to exist. "You hurt yourself?"

He drops into the chair with an *oof* and rests his gym bag on the floor. "I don't know what to do. I had a bad practice and needed to clear my head. I didn't mean for this to happen."

I lean forward. Oh, shit. He's sitting with one foot flat and the other sticking up, heel grazing the floor, trying to keep his weight off it. He makes a tentative attempt to flex it and winces. It's the bad ankle, the one he tweaked last month, the one he injured in high school.

"What happened?" I ask.

"Nothing good," he singsongs.

"Wow, okay." I cross the room to grab the water bottle he always keeps in the outside pocket of his bag.

It's then that I see the skateboard. A ringing sound fills my ears.

I uncap the bottle and hand it to him. "Drink. How did you hurt yourself?"

He rubs his mouth. "It's a complicated story."

"Always a great start."

He lets out a heavy breath as he shifts in the chair, struggling to get comfortable. "I went to a party. I shouldn't have, but I was in a bad mood, and I thought it would help. I drank a lot, and then I had this idea . . . When I want to get my mind off things, I imagine the shots I'd take in the NBA dunk contest for fun. Sometimes I need that reminder that this is a game, you know? When everyone online is telling me I suck. Did you see the comments on that video the other night?"

"Never read the comments," I urge.

"I'm not amazing on a skateboard, but I'm all right. I thought I could skate to the basket, jump up, and dunk it. So I went to the gym."

He must regret it now, but there's still a hint of childlike amusement in his voice as he imagines the shot. He's young, so young. He's a kid who loves to play. But he's also a man for whom massive expectations have been set. The great hope of Ardwyn, the next big NBA star, the pride of his community, his family's future. How could anyone be equipped for that responsibility? And with the media, fans, and critics watching, waiting for something to happen. They want to be entertained, by either transcendent performance or calamitous failure. They don't really care which.

If this gets out, the pundits will sink their teeth in and let his blood drip down their chins. It will fit their laziest narrative: He's reckless, all physical talent and no brains. Can an NBA team trust him? Does he even take this seriously? It could affect his draft slot, cost him unfathomable amounts of money. Salaries are high no matter what, but the average NBA career lasts fewer than five years. There are no guarantees.

Dad was one of Quincy's first mentors, teaching him the fundamentals of the game, helping him focus as the hype about his future ratcheted up. Dad is gone, but I'm here.

The question comes like a train charging in at top speed from the part of my brain where all my most reckless thoughts originate: Why does anyone need to know?

He's a good kid. He needs more time to adjust, mature. Who would it hurt, if the press never found out?

But that means no one here can find out either.

Ben. Shit. The realization crashes into me, that he's still here. Close enough that every morning, I know whether he's starting the day with iced coffee or hot, because when it's iced I can hear the cubes rattling in his cup. In an instant I'm at the door, closing it as delicately as I can so he doesn't hear it click shut.

"Why did you come to me?" I ask Quincy.

He shrugs like the answer is obvious. "I couldn't go to anyone else. I trust you. You have hours of tape of that mustache I was trying to grow when I was fifteen and you've never shown anyone."

I offer a weak smile. "I'm saving it for a special occasion."

"I don't know what to do. I screwed up, and now it's only going to make things worse," he says. And then more carefully: "Are there cameras in the practice gym?"

Our eyes meet. I'm relieved that he said it out loud before I did. "I don't know. I don't think so."

We sit in silence. I cover my nose and mouth with my hands and let out a slow breath through them, trying to regain control of my heartbeat.

He trusts me. That's what he said. He's watching me expectantly, waiting for me to tell him the plan with more patience than most people would have while their throbbing ankle goes untreated.

"Here's what we're going to do," I say, standing, because he's in pain and we need to decide on something. "You're going to sober up. We're going to call the trainer and tell him you were shooting around, as you regularly do, and your ankle gave out. If there's any hint of suspicion from anyone, I was there, grabbing a jacket I left this morning. I saw the whole thing happen. I'll go over in a few minutes and make sure there are no cameras. Stay here and wait for me and keep drinking water. I'm going to put this skateboard some-where." My car would be best. Quincy isn't even supposed to own a skateboard.

"Okay," he says.

I give him a sharp nod, like a confident decision maker might do. Then I quietly open the door and shut it be-hind me.

When I turn around, Ben is standing in the dark hallway with his arms crossed.

I jump back. "Jesus. What are you doing?" I don't know why I ask. The fact that he's standing here like this means Quincy and I were, in fact, talking louder than an iced cof-fee, and therefore, we're screwed. I bring my arm around my back to hide the skateboard anyway.

"You cannot be serious right now," he hisses. "You should've called the trainer as soon as he told you he was hurt. Instead you're, what? Creeping around, hiding evidence?"

I drag him by the wrist into his office and shut the door. "Okay, Callahan. Calm down. Think about it. What good is going to come of this if people find out? You know the press is going to jump on him. And you know how stressed he's been. He made a mistake."

He plants his hands on the desk, spring-loaded with ten-sion, the sharp outline of his forearm muscles straining. "Don't you think he needs to take responsibility for his mis-takes? Learn from them? Seriously, have you never seen what being coddled does to an athlete? He needs to deal with the consequences here."

Only a golden boy like Ben, who's never been treated un-
fairly in his life, could be that sanctimonious.

He takes out his cell phone. "I'm going to call Coach
Thomas."

"Wait," I say, lunging forward and plucking it from his
hands. "Let's talk about this first."

"Hey," he protests. "Give that back." And because I am
twelve, I hide it behind my back and raise my chin.

"Ugh," he says, and moves toward me, reaching one arm
behind me and hunting for the phone. He tries not to touch
me at first, plucking hesitantly at the space behind me instead. "Radford—what are you—come on—"

Fighting fair is overrated. I swivel from side to side so he
can't reach. With each twist he gets closer, until he's near
enough that I inhale a concentrated lungful of his addictive
soapy smell. I press one shoulder against his torso and angle
the rest of my body away, buying myself enough time and
distance to slip the phone into my back pocket.

I remember too late that these pants don't have pockets.
Fuck the patriarchy.

Now my face is buried in his warm chest. My body is im-
possibly contorted, legs in one direction, shoulders in the
other, and I lose my balance. Before I topple over, he anchors
one hand on my hip, and I squeak in surprise. His grip is
careful, but firmer and more confident than I ever would've
expected from a Goody-Two-shoes like him, and everything
goes fuzzy except that exact spot on my body. The warmth
of his palm, the grasp of his fingers, all imprinting on my
brain, distracting me.

Focus. To get the leverage I need to push off, I lean into his hand instead of away from it. Until his other hand catches my other hip, and then he's turning me around, his hand closing around mine on the phone. He's going to wrestle it from me.

I drop it.

The phone hits the floor. The element of surprise is on my side, so I react faster. I pick it up and shove it down my shirt, into the left cup of my bra, and give him a triumphant look that says *I dare you.*

He does not accept the challenge. My pulse skitters uneasily around my chest like a handful of party poppers thrown on the sidewalk. He gives me a long, dark look and exhales a frustrated breath.

"Listen," I say. "You know how it'll be if the press finds out. Bullshit. Racist bullshit. They'll say he's not smart, that it's a sign of his character. That he can't be trusted with his own talent. If he were white, they'd say he has some maturing to do. Don't you agree with that?"

He exhales again and his shoulders drop. "Yes, of course I do, and it's not fair at all—"

"Then why subject him to it? He may be seriously injured, don't you think that's bad enough? Don't you think he'll learn his lesson from that?"

"Yeah, but there's an entire injury protocol we're supposed to follow that I don't even fully understand, and I doubt you do either—insurance hoops to jump through, reporting requirements. Lying about it could make this worse in the end if people find out."

Ben sits down in his chair and hunches forward, eyes closed, probably envisioning the fifty-seventh page of some handbook I never read. We're on two different existential planes, shouting into two different voids. "Why the hell are we talking about insurance?" I cry.

"Are we supposed to keep it from Coach Thomas? You think he wouldn't want to know?"

I roll my eyes. "He has to say he wants to know about things like this, but I bet he'd rather not." This is starting to slip out of my control. I sit in the chair across from him and lean forward with my elbows on the desk, mimicking his posture. My eyes are level with his. "Look, you don't have to be a part of this. I'm not asking you to lie, I'm just asking you to pretend you weren't here."

He buries his hands in his hair and squeezes like he's going to rip it out. "Is there a difference? What's going to happen if he finds out? We could both get fired. That would help with the budget. Maybe Kyle will get a raise."

I should care about my job security. It's what we've been fighting over for months, and I'm screwed if we get caught. But I can't sit back and watch Quincy suffer.

"I don't care if I get fired," I say.

A bitter look crosses his face. "That's great for you, but I can't afford to be unemployed."

"Neither can I! But it's not the most important consideration right now."

"Family money, then?" he asks knowingly. "Must be nice."

"Ha. No. My dad didn't exactly rake it in coaching and teaching," I say. "You're one to talk, anyway. Isn't your family loaded?"

He laughs at that. "I came here on an academic scholarship. I grew up with nothing."

I have nothing to say to this. It's entirely at odds with everything I thought I knew about him. He went to an expensive private high school, and his girlfriend wore those big pearl stud earrings. He was Main Line wealthy. Wasn't he? Everything in his life came easy to him, that's what I always thought.

"What about the Range Rover?" I ask weakly.

"The what?"

"Didn't you use to drive one, sometimes . . . ?" My voice trails off.

"I can't believe you remember that." He shakes his head. "It was my ex-girlfriend's."

Processing this information is like watching a familiar scene from a new camera angle. He must've been on scholarship at his high school too, a place where anyone could meet a girl who wore expensive jewelry and had a fancy car.

And at college, so many differences flatten out into nothing temporarily. Everyone lives in the same dorm rooms and eats in the same dining halls and drinks the same cheap beer. Everyone on the basketball team is issued the same logoed sportswear. If you don't look too hard, it's easy not to notice who came from less.

Which maybe proves his point about my privilege.

My mouth opens and freezes that way, because I don't know what to say. He presses further. "If your family isn't well-off, how can you be so cavalier about keeping a good job? I'm guessing you have no student loans?"

Another blow to my sense of moral superiority. My face heats, throbbing with embarrassment at the depth of my ignorance. "I did have help with school," I admit. "But it's not how it sounds." My parents were middle-class. They put aside everything they could for our educations, driving modest cars and keeping their old '80s kitchen long after most of their friends had renovated. Still, I was going to be stuck with a pile of student debt, but then multiple schools offered Kat basketball scholarships. Her half got reallocated to me, with a cheerfully morbid promise from my mother: "Kat gets a little extra in the will!"

Annoyingly, that means I have my sister to thank for my financial freedom.

"I'm sure." His voice is cold.

I wince. *Cavalier,* he called me. A perfect word for my attitude toward all the jobs I've had until now. They never made me happy, and I didn't want to be happy making videos about dishwashers or debit cards anyway, and I was too afraid to do the one thing I found fulfilling. So I quit, and quit, and quit. And it's true, my financial situation enabled me to make those choices. "Sorry, you're right. I shouldn't have assumed. And I wasn't thinking about what would happen if we got caught. I'm afraid this is going to break him."

I can hear him swallow. "He was crying after practice today," he says.

"Yeah."

He puts his head in his hands and groans. Looks back up at me, blinking, worn out. Opens his mouth to speak, and then groans again.

Finally he sighs and sits back in his chair. The wheels squeak. "I don't think there are cameras in the practice gym. But there are cameras outside the practice gym, and records of who swipes into the building. You can't say you were there."

"Do we need to worry about that? The FBI isn't going to investigate."

"Probably not, but it's, like, a four-million-dollar ankle. So who knows?"

He's giving in. The tension keeping my shoulders stiff and my fists balled subsides, but I try not to move. I don't want to do anything that might cause him to change his mind.

"I was in the weight room earlier," he says. "There'll be a record of me swiping into the building. If anyone questions anything, Quincy should say I heard it happen."

"No, come on. That's not—I don't want you to have to do that."

He shakes his head. "You're right about the pressure. It's a lot for him. It would be a lot for anyone, let alone an eighteen-year-old."

He's playing you, a voice whispers in my ear. *He'll let it happen, rat you out, and boom, you're done.* But he sounds sincere. And I know he cares about these kids. I have to trust him.

It'll be fine. It has to be. "Are you sure?" I ask.

"No. But I don't see any other way."

I swallow. "Thank you." My voice is shaky with relief as I reach into my bra for his phone. His eyes dart to my hand and then away. Which is good, because I need to wipe the boob sweat off the screen before I hand it back to him.

- - - - - - - - - - -

BEN AND I give Quincy a slice of reheated pizza and a half hour to sober up before making sure he stays upright as he limps to the training room. Then we retreat to Ben's office. The plan is in motion, and there's no going back now.

Ben shuts the door and begins pacing along an invisible path from wall to wall behind his desk. I wander the rest of the room unfocused and impatient, half looking at the pictures on the walls the same way I look at the diagrams of the female reproductive system hanging in the gynecologist's office while I wait for my Pap smear.

"I'm freaking out." I peel off my outermost layer, a thick, bottle-green sweater, and roll up the sleeves on my striped button-down. "It's making me sweat. I can't even think straight."

"You're sweating because it's hot in here." He diverts from his path to unlock the window and crank it open.

I cross the room and rest my forehead against the screen, closing my eyes to savor the bracing air. "Yeah, it is hot in here. I thought it was just me."

He snorts.

"I didn't mean it like that." I turn around and lift my ponytail to cool the back of my neck. His eyes follow my hands. If I concentrate on how refreshing the cold air feels, maybe I'll forget about the vision in my head: the trainer declaring Quincy's injury serious, season-ending. A rare type of ankle break he's only seen at the X Games, one caused exclusively by falls from wheeled objects.

"What did you expect?" he asks. "You crank the heat up to seventy-five degrees every day." He picks up a rubber ball and tosses it one-handed through the miniature basketball hoop hanging from the back of the door.

Only because you turn it down to sixty-two, I almost say. Actually, sixty-two sounds pretty good right now.

"Oh," I say. "Oh! Your office is hot." Every time I've gone

to his office and left feeling overheated—I thought it was because he made me angry. But it was because of the *temperature.*

He doesn't turn the heat down to spite me, after all.

"Yes," he says slowly, picking up the ball.

"My office is cold." I resist the urge to shake him by the shoulders. "Freezing, actually. That's why I turn the heat up."

"What? Oh, that explains the cape."

"What ca—No, that's a blanket."

"It has a hood."

"It's a wearable blanket. Shut up. You're as bad as Eric."

A smile spreads across his face, and it's contagious. He has a nice smile. I can admit that now. It's sweet and boyish but the corners are lazy, turning up a beat after the rest. "I thought you were messing with the thermostat to torture me. I thought you stole my string cheese too."

He tosses me the ball and I catch it. "I don't even like string cheese." It's the truth. Part of the truth, because I don't care much for rubbery mozzarella, but I ate his anyway. Not that he needs to know that.

Ben shakes his head like he doesn't believe me but also doesn't mind.

This is what it feels like to get along with each other. For the first time, I think, *Too bad we can't both stay.* "What would it take to avoid the budget cuts completely?"

His response is immediate. "A national championship."

I laugh, but he doesn't. "You're serious?"

Winning a national championship is about more than skill and strategy. It's also about luck. Who gets the most advantageous matchups, who gets hot at the right time, who gets one favorable call in one close game. That's why it's difficult for even the best teams to do.

I step away from the window. "Let's go win a national championship, then." I chuck the ball toward the basket, and it bounces off the rim twice before going in.

Like I said, it's about luck. But *somebody* gets to be the lucky one. Why not us?

TWELVE

AT NINE O'CLOCK THE NEXT MORNING, A MAINTE-
nance worker appears in my office to inspect the air vents.
Ben must've called them first thing. A strange light feeling
bubbles inside me.

An hour later, word arrives: Quincy's injury is a sprain.
An ankle sprain is one of the most common injuries in the
sport, and so far nobody's asked too many questions about
how it happened. Quincy gets a lecture on pushing himself
too hard outside official team practices, a sympathetic pat on
the back, and he's off to the land of rest and ice and physical
therapy for two weeks. He'll miss four games. It could be
worse, but four more losses would make it impossible to win
the regular-season conference title.

On the bright side, Quincy's spirits improve immediately
after the first couple days of respite from the spotlight. He
has a concrete, achievable task to focus on: recovery. He has
breathing room.

"Tell Mom not to worry. He's handling it well." Mom always had a soft spot for Quincy. I'm on the phone with Kat on Sunday night, padding barefoot into the green room with an insulated tumbler full of Cassie's favorite bedtime tea. A pink glow fills the space, thanks to the strawberry-shaped string lights I hung from the ceiling.

"You must be relieved it didn't blow up in your face."

"Well, yeah. I was pretty nervous at first. I'd have been fine lying, I'm a good liar. My accomplice was the bigger concern."

"You don't think he's going to have a crisis of conscience and come clean, do you?"

The morning after, Ben did look a little pale when Coach Williams stopped by to talk about what happened, but he managed to keep it together. "I don't see why he would. We're in the clear. And it's obvious we did the right thing."

"Obvious to you. You better make sure it's obvious to him. What if he confesses to the team chaplain? 'Bless me, Father, for I have sinned'? Which one is it, bearing false witness against your neighbor?"

I set my tumbler on the floor and light a candle, which perfumes the air with citrus and jasmine. "I don't think he's that Catholic. And the priest isn't allowed to tell anyway."

"I don't remember the rules. I haven't gone to confession since grammar school."

There's only one seating option in the room, a monstrous, sagging purple beanbag chair. When I moved, I snagged it from my parents' basement, where Kat and I hung out with our friends in high school. Part of my virginity is somewhere in this chair, deep in the mountain of beans, never to be found. It's so big it's unsafe to sit in without someone else present to haul you out. I flop onto it anyway.

"Neither have I. In fifth grade I told Father John I used curse words, and he said God was going to cut my tongue off if I didn't stop. After that, I told Mom I was never going again. I still think of him sometimes when I use the word 'fuck.'"

Kat laughs. A seed of worry plants itself inside me, and I can't shake it. Ben seems sincere in his concern for Quincy. He has no reason not to stick to the plan unless he wants to screw me over, which I don't think he does anymore.

But maybe I'm thinking too much like myself. At heart, Ben is a rule follower. Under stress, isn't he always going to revert to that behavior? At the same time, my biggest take-away from that night was that a lot of my assumptions about him are wrong.

"Oh, two things before I forget," Kat says. "One, Mom wants you to help her figure out how to do her family tree on that ancestry website."

I groan. If my remorseless abuse of obscenities lands me a spot in hell, I'm going to be assigned to whichever circle in-volves an eternity of teaching my mother how to use a com-puter.

"Don't complain," Kat chides me. "You're lucky you weren't around for Sunday dinner. She made me take the Myers-Briggs test with her. It was ninety-three questions."

"Okay, fine, I'll text her when we hang up. Next item?"

"You know my friend Noah? He and his boyfriend are getting married in November, and they want to know if you'll do the video."

"Oh." I loosen the lid on my tumbler, then tighten it

again. Sometimes I do wedding videos for extra cash, a few times a year. But November is too far away. From now until March the calendar is all blue dots on game days, and it doesn't go beyond that. Plus, I may not even be around next fall, especially with Quincy on the bench. "Well, I have to see. It's early."

"To book wedding stuff? It's less than a year away. That's not early."

"I don't know my schedule for the fall yet. If they want something set in stone now I can recommend a couple people who do it full time."

"Okay, thanks. You probably won't be able to do it anyway, since Ardwyn has a lot of Saturday games." Kat tries to sneak the last part in, her tone casual.

"Very cute."

"What?" Kat feigns innocence. "Are they switching to Fridays next season?"

"I can't take on any wedding jobs when I don't know where I'm going to be after this spring."

"I know exactly where you're going to be. The same place you are now."

I look at Mona Lisa Vito for help. Maybe it's the way the light flickers when the ceiling fan spins, but I could swear she shrugs. "Do you know if Father John is still around? I'd like to find out how many Hail Marys I have to say to arrange for God to cut your tongue off."

THE NEXT MORNING, I get to work early and wait for Ben. I give him enough time to get his coffee and read through his emails before sending him a message.

Annie: how are you doing?

His response takes a few minutes. *Ben is typing* . . . it reads, and across the hall I hear the clacking of keys, ninety words a minute, a stream of consciousness. Then it stops, and starts again, and stops. He must be writing a novel.

But no. Instead, I get:

Ben: Fine

I sigh.

Annie: you sure?

More typing, vigorous tapping at the keys, like the sound of *Riverdance.* Then silence.

Ben: Yes

I shift in my seat. Ugh. This is dire.

Annie: . . . okay good talk!

I exit the chat window and check the scores of last night's games. By the time I'm done, he's messaged me again.

Ben: Completely unrelated but did Cassie ever tell you about the case where she spent two months reviewing employee chat records exactly like this one, looking for evidence and weeding out all the conversations about office romances/personal drama/evil bosses?

So strange to think about how it feels like a private
conversation but it's not at all.

Paranoid much? Not a strong sign that he's coping well.
Lying doesn't come naturally to him. In a way this is my
fault, so I have to indulge him.

Annie: ah gotcha

Annie: and yes, I am her best friend thus I know all her
interesting anecdotes. if I recall correctly some of the
office romance talk was pretty spicy

Ben: Anyway, maybe we should walk home from the
Beach House party tonight and catch up?

Annie: WOW sounds like something somebody in an
office romance would say

Annie: I accept your invitation (note to lawyers:
PLATONICALLY). I swear this is the truth, the whole
truth, and nothing but the truth, amen

Ben: Sorry to disappoint with the lack of spice. Please
resume searching for crimes.

He hasn't assuaged my concerns, but I'm smiling anyway.

- - - - - - - - - - -

THE EPISODE STARTS with a dance contest, with the
winner determined by heart rate monitors. Whichever con-

testant gets the others' blood pumping fastest earns a couples massage. It ends with Felicia abandoning Cole in the rainforest after he calls her annoying during a scavenger hunt. I definitely lose some brain cells watching, but it's worth it.

When it's time to go, I put on my new coat, an oversized parka with insulated pockets and a giant hood that cinches tight with long drawstrings. Yesterday's snow melted this afternoon and is starting to refreeze. An ice-and-salt crust sits on the sidewalk like patches of bread crumbs, so I've also resorted to a pair of practical waterproof boots.

"Those are nice!" Eric says as he watches me tug them on. "Where'd you get them? Do they make them in men's?"

Now I need to burn them, but I can't do it yet. I need to walk home with Ben first.

"So," I begin as we set off. The piles of plowed snow lining the road are already turning gray. The first house after Cassie and Eric's condo building has a lopsided snowman in the yard, one stick arm jutting upward as if to wave at us. Ben too is wearing boots this time, instead of fussy sneakers. And he doesn't have Sasha today.

"So," he repeats.

"Are you cracking under the weight of our deception?"

He breathes out a puff of laughter and it hangs in the air like a cloud. "No, I'm good. Are you?"

"I'm fine. You don't go to confession, do you?"

He squints down at me. "Like, at church? No. Why?"

"No reason, just wondering. What other kind of confession is there?"

"I don't know, the way you said it made me think you were talking about a workout class or something."

I snort. "A workout class called Confession? What the hell are you talking about?"

"I don't know! Sometimes I see you leaving the classes at the gym. They always have new ones, I can't keep track."

I hold up my fists in a fighting stance. "I do boxing classes. It helps with my inner rage."

He cocks his head skeptically. "Does it?"

I pretend to hit him with a jab. Confession, the Workout. Hm. Groups of people lunging to the beat of techno hymns, repeating chants about sin and forgiveness. "I think you've stumbled upon something genius. We're going to be so rich."

We both smile. It's silent and still out here. Usually there's at least one person walking a dog in this neighborhood, but not tonight. Somebody in one of the old stone houses on this block has a fire going, and the air smells like woodsmoke.

"So I don't have to worry about you telling everybody the truth, then?" I ask.

His face grows sober. "I wouldn't do that to Quincy, or to you. We made our decision. And I think it was the right one. He seems like he's handling things well."

"I think so too," I say. "I'm hoping it's like hitting the reset button. I want to see him come back strong."

"If he's at the top of his game, we can hang with any team in the country."

We turn the corner onto an even quieter side street, narrow and poorly lit, the sidewalks only half cleared of snow. I dodge an icy spot by stepping onto the frozen grass. "Why are we walking when you don't even have Sasha?"

"Didn't you say you like to walk in this weather?"

"Right." Is that what I said that first week? I remember fumbling for an excuse but not coming up with such a terrible one. Nobody likes to walk in this weather. "Where is Sasha, anyway?"

Somehow he looks steady, picking his way through the slippery spots with ease as I struggle. He glances at me. "This sidewalk is a mess. I think it'll get better when we get to the corner. Do you need help?"

I'm walking like a penguin, taking short steps with my arms out for balance. "I got it, thanks."

"Sasha's my mom's dog, not mine. She has horrible separation anxiety when she's alone. She howls and chews on her paw until it bleeds." He pauses, waiting for me to catch up. "My mom works nights, and my sister is usually home, but gymnastics sometimes runs late on Mondays. She loves that dog. I don't want her to worry while she's at her workouts."

"That's very—" A layer of black ice materializes under my feet, and my treads find nothing to grip. My leg slides out from underneath me and my body jerks forward. I reach out, and one hand hits the cold, rough sidewalk, but Ben catches me around the waist before the rest of my body crashes into the ground and hoists me back to my feet.

"—on-brand for you," I finish. "Thanks."

He doesn't let go right away. "You okay?" he asks first. The words brush my temple, his face close to mine. My balance isn't coming back to me yet, so I sway toward him.

"I'm fine," I say faintly. "Oh. I'm bleeding."

The hand I used to break my fall is wet and stinging. I squint at it in the dark.

"Let me see." He cradles my hand in his and uses his

phone to get a better look. It's not that bad. The source of the blood is an inch-long shallow scrape, but most of the wetness is melted ice from where I touched the ground. He traces a path alongside the scrape with his thumb and I shiver.

Human contact. It's been a while. First his hands on me when we fought over his phone, and now this. My body has completely forgotten how to keep its cool.

"Will I live?" I joke in a scratchy voice.

"We should clean it," he says.

"Do you have a Band-Aid?"

He's still holding my hand. "A Band-Aid?" he repeats. "Do I seem like someone who carries around a first aid kit?"

"Kind of!" I say. "It's not a weird question. I asked for a Band-Aid, not a condom."

"A *condom*?" He drops my hand.

"I need Taylor," I continue, sighing. "She'd have both."

"Dare I ask what the condom is for?"

"Well, Callahan, when two people love each other very much . . ."

"You can't be nice to me for five minutes after I stop you from falling on your face?"

"I can't hear you," I say, pretending to sway unsteadily. "Everything's fuzzy. I think I'm bleeding out. You'll have to go on without me."

"Okay," he says. "Bye."

I walked right into that one.

HE'S RIGHT ABOUT the sidewalks being clearer on the main road. Thanks to the weather, the bars are dead. Most of them have closed early, stools stacked upside down on the bar tops, barely visible as shadowy outlines in the dim lighting.

"You said your mom works nights, right?" I ask. "What does she do?"

"She's a nurse," Ben says. "She went back and got her degree a few years ago."

"That's great," I say. There's no mention of a dad. There never has been, has there? He's not in any of the photos in Ben's office, and I can't remember ever seeing him at a game with the rest of his family.

"Before that she was all over the place, jobwise," Ben adds. "Mainly waiting tables."

Oof. Ben and his sister were raised on restaurant tips, likely by a single mom, and last week I asked him to jeopardize the one stable job he's had in his whole life like it was nothing. After months of trying to make sure he gets laid off instead of me. While his sister's gymnastics scholarship hangs in the balance. The reminder of my misconceptions plucks some internal guitar string inside me, and embarrassment reverberates throughout my body.

"I've been meaning to talk to you about something else," he says in a tentative voice. We're between streetlights, so his face is all shadows. "I spoke to Phil Coleman."

I wince. "Let's not do this." We've been doing so well. Cooperating, being friendly. It's all I need from him to get through the rest of this year until our fates are decided. I don't need to convert Ben. He can go on believing what he wants about Coach Maynard; it doesn't matter. We don't have to talk about it, not if it's going to ruin this. It's better if we don't.

"No, I need to. Phil told me Coach used to tell him that the longer he sat out, the more likely it was that someone else would take his spot in the lineup. That athletes need to push themselves and sometimes that means playing through pain. That he was letting everyone else down by focusing on himself instead of the team. He thinks he pressured the doctor to clear him early."

I focus on the cracks in the sidewalk and wonder how many I can step over while maintaining my normal stride. "It was awful." One. Two. Three.

"You were right, and I'm sorry I didn't believe you. I can't stop thinking about it, honestly. It's so different from the way I remembered it, and it scares me a little, that my perception was so wrong."

Three cracks seem to be the maximum. "He has a way of showing different sides of himself to different people based on what he needs. It's one reason he's so good at his job."

"I know we don't see eye to eye on Coach, so I don't want to dwell on this. But I've always had the utmost respect for him. He gave me so much, and I've always wanted to be like him. To be able to lead a team, to support kids who need it, the way he did for me. But it makes me sick, what happened to Phil. I don't know what to do."

I stop counting and look at his face. It's gentle, contrite, vulnerable, anxious. But I don't know what that last part means. There's nothing he can do about it now. He can't go back in time and fix Phil's Achilles.

We pass a house that still has its Christmas decorations up, red and green lights flashing in a neat row of evergreen bushes. "Don't try to be like him. You're better than that." I need to leave it there, because this conversation is fragile, capable of disintegrating with the slightest clumsy touch. "Why are you still at Ardwyn, anyway? You want to coach."

"I've always wanted to coach," he says, with a sad smile. "I didn't realize it would take so long."

"There are schools other than Ardwyn, you know. I know we were brainwashed to think otherwise. But I'm sure you can get a coaching job somewhere. I think you'd be great at it."

"Wow, that's two nice things you've said to me in the last ten minutes."

I poke him in the shoulder. "Don't expect a third."

We wait for the light to change. His nose is pink from the cold. His hair is so much better like this, messy.

"I probably will leave eventually. When the right position opens up. My plan has always been to stay until my sister graduates, so I can look out for her while she's here. Go to her meets when they don't conflict with our games. Assuming there is a gymnastics program next year, of course. When I leave, I'm sure I'll have to leave Philly, and I won't be able to do any of that from a distance."

"But that's four more years, and you've already outgrown your job," I protest.

He shakes his head. "It has to be the right time," he says firmly. "Can I ask what brought you back here?"

I purse my lips. "I heard from somebody else on the bandwagon that the team was supposed to be good this year," I deadpan.

He nudges me with an elbow. "Really, though."

"Turns out when you develop a pattern of bouncing around

every eighteen months, potential employers question whether you're worth the investment," I say. "Eric helped me out. If I can't make this work for a few years, I don't know if I'll ever get hired anywhere again."

I can feel him looking at me, and I don't know what he sees. His competition. My desperation.

My apartment building comes into view. The strawberry string lights are twinkling in the green room.

"I still don't understand why you left basketball—"

"Speaking of jumping on the bandwagon," I cut him off, opening my bag and picking through it to find my keys, "I saw your bracket tonight. I didn't realize you hopped on the Brianne train. I'm going to take full credit for that."

He laughs. "Nope. She's been a beast in the challenges so far. And she has a lot of chemistry with Logan. Did you notice they have the whole witty banter thing going?"

I want to make fun of him, but it wouldn't be fair because yes, I did notice. "She makes him seem slightly less boring."

"He's not like that with anyone else. That's why I'm picking her."

"Okay, we can go with that answer."

"It's the truth!"

We stop at the short brick walkway leading to my front steps. "We better quit while we're ahead. Congratulations to us. We made it through an entire conversation without arguing." I raise my hand for a high five.

He obliges. But then he surprises me by tugging on my hand and pulling me in for a hug. Two people hugging with our heavy winter coats between us is a bit pointless, since it feels more like wrestling a down comforter into the duvet cover than an actual human embrace. But for a moment my face settles in the warm crook of his neck and he cups the back of my head with his hand—and, god help me, I'm starved for affection, because I think about it all the way up the stairs.

THIRTEEN

WE LOSE TO BLAKE. THERE'S STILL A LONG WAY TO go, but I can't help but worry about the bar for saving the athletic department—*a national championship*—and after the way we played today, it feels impossible to reach. After the game, I find an empty seat on the bus and slouch against the window, staring up at the concrete façade of the unfamiliar arena. My phone buzzes with texts from Taylor and Jess back at home, brainstorming for content now that we don't have anything celebratory to post.

> **Taylor: what else do we have?**

> **Taylor: wtf. there aren't even any alumni birthdays this week! I checked all the rosters going back thirty years**

> **Taylor: cute baby dancing in Ardwyn gear?**

Jess: no

Taylor: favorite team sneaker post w/ a poll??

Jess: no

Taylor: history of the soft pretzel????

Jess: hmm, maybe

I put my phone away. While the bus idles, waiting for the team to come out, one of the student managers walks down the aisle passing out sandwiches wrapped in wax paper for the ride to the Indianapolis airport. The clunky mechanics of the door sound as it opens, and Ben jogs up the steps, weaving through the people standing in the aisle, looking for a seat. His suit jacket is off, his shirt rumpled, and his tie loose. He slides in next to me and grabs a sandwich from the box in one motion.

He's never sat next to me on the bus before. *"Friends!"* I want to shout, with jazz hands. It's a universal fact that regardless of age, everyone reverts to middle school behavior on a group bus ride. The players always elbow each other out of the way to claim the last row, and Coach Thomas and Coach Williams once bickered about rights to the window seat all the way down the Blue Route.

Ben is holding a bag of chips. "Where did you get those?" I ask. I lean over him to pick a sandwich, bracing myself on his shoulder.

"You have to know the right people."

I sit back and put the sandwich on my lap. "I know you, does that count?"

He opens the bag and turns it toward me. "Only one?" I ask. Grumbling something indecipherable, he hands me the bag and leans into the aisle.

"Psst, Verona." He snaps his fingers. Another bag flies toward him from a few rows ahead and he catches it with one hand.

"Never would've pegged him as your dealer," I say, crunching on a chip. "That fleece vest helps him slide under the radar."

My phone buzzes again in my bag, and I sigh. It's time to put Taylor out of her misery. An idea is brewing in my head. Fragments for now. That's how it always starts, with one image, or a specific line from a song. This time it's a voice.

We've been going to ridiculous lengths on social media to distract from our inability to win a game, and it's never going to work. I've tried getting people to watch my videos despite the fact that we're losing. It's time to try getting them to watch *because* we're losing.

Dad was never afraid of losing during the regular season. When his most-hyped team ever fell in double overtime, ending a fifteen-game winning streak, he said, "Eh. They needed it. They'll come to practice hungry tomorrow."

I turn to Ben. "Callahan, do you know Keith Wesley?" Keith Wesley played for Ardwyn in the eighties. His Wikipedia article is three paragraphs long and talks mainly about one thing: the infamous free throw he missed that lost the team a double-overtime tournament heartbreaker in a year they were supposed to win everything. I hadn't yet been born when it happened, but repeated YouTube views have stamped it in my brain. The shot went up, and the ball took one full rotation around the entire rim, hung still for a moment, and fell the wrong way to the floor.

Ben is unwrapping his sandwich. He pauses. "Believe it or not, he does our alumni community service event every year. Why do you ask?"

"He's still involved with the program? That's even better. I want to talk to him about doing a voice-over this week."

"I have so many questions, I don't even know where to start." His knees nudge my thigh as he turns to face me, his mouth tilting into a curious smile. His shirtsleeves are rolled up. Does he normally wear his sleeves rolled up? My proximity to him is forcing me to pay attention to his forearms. They're nicely toned, thanks to years of dribbling basketballs and opening jars for little old ladies, probably.

It feels like a private place, the bus's leather seat for two. Long and narrow and walled in by the tall back of the row ahead, drawing us closer, making me forget we're not alone. It's having a strange effect on me, warming my face and weighing down my blood, forcing my heart to beat harder. What the hell? This must be why Mom always insisted on driving me to and from school when I was a teenager. Dangerous things could happen here.

But I can't dwell on this, and Ben doesn't have time to ask any of his questions. A funereal hush overtakes the bus, which can only mean that the team has arrived.

"Look," I say, pointing out the window.

Ben leans over, his shoulder pressing into mine, his breath skating over my ear as he laughs a little. "Not what I was expecting."

They're walking out of the building together, athletes

first, coaches behind them. Usually after a loss they're subdued, wearing their headphones like a shield and not making
eye contact with anyone, hence the respectful silence from
everyone else. Not today, though. Their heads are up. Anthony Gallimore is singing to himself and no one is com-
plaining about it. A couple of the guys are dancing along.
Even Luis Rosario is bopping his head, and he's typically as
stoic as they come.

Ben hasn't moved, and I'm hyperaware of every place our
bodies are touching. My breathing is too shallow. He's close
enough to notice, if he's paying attention. That would be
humiliating.

Intimacy is a basic human need for most people, and the
last time I touched a man was the night of Cassie's bachelorette party last summer, when I shared one lackluster dirty
dance with a stranger. Sex? I still had bangs when my most
recent relationship petered out, nine months and three hair-
cuts ago.

Ben is not inspiring this reaction. Being close to any reasonably attractive man would do it. Lufton isn't terrible-looking,
so he could probably get my pulse racing right now.

Okay, definitely not. But only because that's a bad example.

The players board the bus single file. "What do you think
that's about?" I ask, turning to look at Ben.

He's closer than I realized, even. His lips are parted
slightly. "I don't know," he says in a quiet, hypnotizing voice.

Eric sits down in front of me, snapping me out of my daze.
I lean forward and tap him on the shoulder. "Why are they
all in good moods?" I whisper.

He tilts his head to whisper back. "I'm not sure. JGE

kicked all the coaches out of the locker room before they came out. The players were in there for twenty minutes. I'm guessing he gave them a pep talk."

Jamar Gregg-Edwards plays a background role on the court, but he's not striving for a career in professional basketball. He might be the smartest person I've ever met. Engineering major, president of the Black Student Union. Next year he's off to England for a prestigious fellowship to study water treatment. He's this team's rock.

When we get back to campus, I set up a meeting with Keith Wesley for later in the week. He's gracious and open and spends an hour in front of the camera, talking about adversity and self-doubt and his baby granddaughter.

I begin the video with a soundbite from a twentieth-century philosopher, because nothing sends the message that something serious is coming quite like the authoritative voice of an old British man. "There is no chemical element on this planet as sturdy as the mettle of mankind," he says, over the clip of Keith Wesley's missed shot.

Then I show Keith Wesley now, grayer and softer, thumbing through yellowed newspaper clippings, running his hands over old trophies, and studying the "Ardwyn Basketball: 1987 Sweet Sixteen" banner hanging in the arena lobby.

"I failed in the most significant moment of my basketball career," he says. "We lost the biggest game I'd ever played in. Do I wish we won? Of course. I'm an athlete. But I learned a lot from that game, and I'm grateful for that. I learned how supportive my teammates and friends and family were. I learned that life went on, and so did basketball, and so could I."

I try to get Quincy to tell me about JGE's speech in the

locker room, hoping to work some of the themes into the video, but despite my wheedling, he refuses to say a word. No one knows what he said, and the players seem to have sworn themselves to secrecy. Regardless, whatever JGE said, it works. We win the next three games, even without Quincy playing. And then we win the next four after he returns.

The fans can feel the momentum shift. It's obvious in the sellout crowds, in the comment section, in the follower counts. My video about losing gets more views than anything I've ever made. I wake up the morning after it's posted to a text from Cassie, the earliest of early risers: **LEBRON SHARED YOUR VIDEO!!!**

"What do we do, after?" Keith Wesley says as the video ends on a shot of the players walking into the practice gym for an early workout while the sun rises over the building. "We show up."

"LET'S RUN TIGER and then we're done," Coach Thomas calls out at practice, hands cupped around his mouth.

Gallimore swings around to look at him. "Already?"

"We're wrapping up early today. Everyone needs a break." What he means is: It's Valentine's Day. And on this one night, everyone with a partner needs to shower that person with love, affection, and assistance with household chores to compensate for the fact that they'll be almost completely absent for the next four to seven weeks until the season is over.

Before I head back upstairs, Coach Williams flags me down.

"My son showed me Instagram last night," he says, the

unpracticed syllables of the word *Instagram* coming out of his mouth stilted, his dark eyes boring into me. "He said Jalen Austin left a comment on one of our videos." Jalen Austin is a junior in high school, one of the top shooting guard prospects in the country.

I saw the comment too. "Beast mode, fire emoji," I say, the corners of my mouth twitching as I fight to keep a straight face.

"Beast mode, fire emoji," he repeats, with gravity. He nods, I nod back. It's the closest he's ever going to get to saying he was wrong about me. I won. Pride bursts inside me like a champagne spray. I don't need his approval, but it still feels good.

Back in the office, the sounds of everything shutting down start before it's even dark outside: the chorus of goodbyes, the flick of light switches, the loud metallic *click* of the stairwell door.

Donna pauses in the hallway on her way out, hand on hip. "Plans tonight, Ben?"

"Nah," Ben says. "Plenty to do here."

"I'm not saying you need a girlfriend, but at minimum you need a life."

I laugh to myself, and Donna whirls around. "I assume you have something exciting going on this evening?"

"I do."

"Really?" She sounds skeptical.

"My dad's old assistants are in town to see a big high school game. We're meeting for dinner after." I've been checking the clock, leg bouncing with anticipation. Paul and Big Ed are like uncles to me. When they told me they'd be in the area, I jumped at the chance to see them. The game should be over around the time I finish work for the night, so they're going to pick me up straight from campus.

Donna taps a long nail on her chin. "Cute, but that doesn't count."

I could swear I hear Ben snort from across the hall.

There's something about this place that makes it impossible for me to keep my distance. I've had more personal conversations here in the last four months than I had at my previous workplaces combined in the last eight years. "Can't you be nice? I'm single on Valentine's Day. Maybe I'm wallowing."

"You? Nah." Whatever that's supposed to mean, it doesn't sound good. She jerks her head toward Ben's office. "Him, though? Maybe."

"Ouch," Ben says. He sounds more entertained than offended, but there's a kernel of truth in Donna's analysis. Ben is sincere, responsible, clean. He was made to be somebody's boyfriend.

Four hours pass at an excruciatingly slow pace, the ounces on my water bottle dropping away like the tide going out. At nine o'clock, I check the score for the thirtieth time. The game is going into triple overtime, and it's time to accept that Paul and Big Ed are bailing. On the bright side, I am fully hydrated.

Rain check, Paul texts a few minutes after I see the score. **Getting late. Have to see the end of this one.**

And, yeah, it's triple overtime. It would be unreasonable to expect them to leave before the end. They're like Dad, and it would've been physically impossible for anyone to drag him out of his seat to make an early exit from a game like this one.

It would've been nice, that's all. Dad, Paul, and Big Ed used to go to this frozen-in-1974 Italian restaurant near the high school after every home game to debrief over bar pies. As a kid I always begged to tag along, and Dad let me. We'd stay out way past my bedtime, and they'd strategize and reminisce about the old days, and I'd soak it all in while mainlining Shirley Temples. Sometimes I'd fall asleep on the faux leather cushion of the booth and Dad would have to carry me to the car.

They'll make up for tonight some other time, so it doesn't make sense that I've got a lump in my throat that I'm trying to swallow, or a knuckle pressed up against the outer corner of each eye. I was looking forward to spending time with them, that's all. And I'm exhausted. I'll get over it by tomorrow.

What I wouldn't be able to get over is letting Ben see me cry in the office on Valentine's Day. If I pack up my stuff quietly enough and take the stairs, I can slip out without saying good night.

When he appears in the doorway, I have one arm in a camel wool coat, my tote slung in the crook of my other elbow. "Hey," he says in a gentle voice. He looks at my jacket and then my face. I busy myself with my bag, digging around the bottom so my head is nearly inside it.

"You heading out too?" My voice is overly chipper, but I've been caught. I'm sure my eyes are puffy, my cheeks blotchy. There's no hiding.

He shoves his hands into his pockets and rocks back on

his heels, studying me carefully. "I saw people talking about the game online. Sounds epic."

"Yeah, I told the guys not to worry about dinner. It's too good to miss."

Peeking up from the jumble of lip balm tubes and loose change, I see him nod slowly, working his jaw back and forth. Uh-oh. I thought he was letting me off the hook, but the longer he stands there the more likely it is he's going to try to say something nice—

"Come on. Let's go out to dinner."

I withdraw my face from my bag. "Like, me and you? Together?"

My mind flashes to the night Quincy hurt his ankle, to Ben's hand on my hip when we fought over his phone. Goddamn. That memory invades my thoughts at the most inconvenient times. Despite the completely nonsexual context, my legs go liquid when I think about it, which is too often. I could sketch the exact position of his palm and each fingertip from memory. His grip was steady. Decisive. Purposeful.

If I dwell on it too much, I short-circuit.

He rolls his eyes. "Yes, me and you. We both need to eat. It won't be that different from every other night. We'll just be sitting in the same room for once."

That's true. Recently, he's started poking his head in to ask if I want anything when he orders food. We eat at our own desks and talk about basketball from across the hall.

But this feels different. It's not about convenience, or passing the time while taking a break. This is intentional. I should probably decline, because my body and mind will end up more confused than they already are.

Except I want to go. The idea of retreating to my apartment is too depressing to contemplate, and being around Ben is easy. He's good company.

I'll build a fortress of sarcasm to protect myself, like I always do. It'll be fine.

"You want to have dinner with me *tonight*?" I ask.

"Don't overthink it," he grumbles.

I clasp my hands to my chest and bite my lip. "On Valentine's Day?"

He sighs and runs a hand through his hair. He went to the gym and showered earlier in the evening, so it's his post-work mass of chaos. "I mean, technically, yes, I guess that's what I'm proposing."

I step toward him, offering my best Disney princess smile. "Wait, now you're proposing? This is moving a little fast, but I'll be honest, it just depends on the ring." I wiggle my left hand in front of his face.

"You know what, I changed my mind. I think I'd rather eat a frozen burrito in my office and spend the rest of the night trying to convince my Facebook friends from middle school that vaccines are safe."

He grabs the hand I'm waving in his face and squeezes once before batting it away. Probably a pity squeeze, but a warm one all the same. A long-dormant, hungry ache rises in my chest, like something buoyant I've been holding underwater, fighting to reach the surface. *Down, girl*, I order.

I turn off the light and give him one extremely nonchalant pat on the chest. "Too late, technical Valentine. Let's go."

FOURTEEN

WE CHOOSE A CASUAL PLACE THAT'S NOT CATERING to the date-night crowd and sit at the bar, watching the Kansas–West Virginia game. The lively restaurant makes it easy for me to brush off what I felt at the office. It's not too dim, it smells like burgers, and a rowdy group of senior citizens are throwing back margaritas at the table behind us.

During a time-out, I notice that one of the other televisions is showing a preview of the next episode of *The Beach House*. I tap Ben's arm. "Look."

Next week, Brianne wins a sandcastle contest, earning her a visit from her loved ones. Somehow this leads to Logan being grilled by her father while hooked up to a polygraph machine.

"What makes you think you'll know which of these girls is right for you in the next two weeks?" the father asks Logan, his mouth a stern line beneath his thick mustache.

I throw up my hands. "Finally, a voice of reason."

Ben's mouth curves up at the corner indulgently and he shakes his head. "You're lucky Cassie isn't here to eviscerate your favorite crappy sports team when you talk like that."

"I'm a bandwagon fan, remember? I only cheer for winners." I pop a fry into my mouth and chew, enjoying the look of suffering on his face as he forces himself to absorb the jab. "Seriously, though, do you think any of these people will stay together?"

"Stay together? Who knows. Do I think they can fall in love? Yeah, maybe."

"Logan's told four of the women he's falling in love with them. *Four.*" I slap the bar with my hand four times. "I don't even love four pizza places in the entire state of New Jersey, and I *love* pizza. He loves more women than I love pizzas. That's not love, it's bullshit."

"I love more than four pizza places."

"You're from Pennsylvania. Stay in your own lane."

"You're missing a key nuance here," Ben says, shaking his head. "I'll excuse it since this is the first time you've watched the show."

"What's that?"

"He's told them all he's *falling for them.* Not that he's falling in love, or that he loves them. Huge difference on this show."

He grabs a napkin and a pen from his bag and begins to outline.

"There's a prescribed path of escalation in feelings that everyone on this show follows. It's crucial that the contestants confess which step they're at as we get closer to the end."

He slides the napkin toward me, and his elbow presses against mine. *I could see myself falling for her,* I read.

"That's step one. Followed by 'I'm starting to fall,' then 'I'm falling,' then 'I've fallen.' Only after that does the L-word come into play. 'I'm falling in love,' 'I'm in love.' We usually don't see a straight-up 'I love you' until the finale."

I must care about this show even less than I thought, because I'm paying more attention to Ben's elbow than to his explanation. There's something distracting about the warmth of it, the pressure of it against mine. The slight tickle from the hair on his arm and the firmness of the muscles, the way he doesn't seem inclined to move away.

I try to sneak a look at him, but he's looking at me too. His dark eyes glitter intimately, like we're sharing a secret. Maybe he can tell I'm flustered.

I swallow hard. "This show is bizarre."

"You don't believe they can fall in love in eight weeks?"

"I absolutely believe they can fall in some version of love in eight weeks. But it doesn't matter."

"What do you mean?"

"It's fantasy-land love. It's too tied in to the experience they're having with the island and all the filming and over-the-top romantic dates for anybody to know if it can last. That's why the proposal is bullshit. They won't have a clue whether it can really work out until after the show is over."

"That's actually less cynical of an argument than I was expecting from you."

"From me?" I rake my fork through my Caesar salad and cut a piece of chicken into a careful square. The word stings, *cynical*. It's rooted in a perception of me that I intentionally perpetuate. It's the same one that led to Donna's comment earlier, which didn't bug me at all, but it bothers me coming from Ben. "I consider myself an expert on this topic. Remember senior year?"

He looks at me blankly. He must remember. It was the most obvious thing in the world. I disappeared to the bathroom for long periods to cry. I sat at my computer ignoring my work, typing long messages and ignoring everyone around me. I missed deadlines and came in late. I felt like I was walking around with a sign stuck to my back that read, WARNING: EMOTIONAL MELTDOWN IN PROGRESS.

But it's clear he's being honest. He doesn't remember, he's not pretending for my sake. I exhale. "That's a good thing, I guess. I thought everyone knew about my hot mess of a love life then."

He goes still. "What happened?"

"Nothing. Don't worry about it."

"Radford, tell me," he wheedles.

"No," I say, failing to suppress a nervous smile.

He smiles back. "Come on, it's Valentine's Day. In the grand spirit of the holiday, tell me about your hot mess of a love life."

I let out a theatrical groan. This is dangerous territory, senior year. It's all mixed up in other subjects I can't discuss with him. But I need to prove him wrong about me being a stone-cold cynic. *How close can I get?* How close, to the touchiest subject, without someone getting hurt?

I drain my water glass and order a beer. After the bartender sets it in front of me on a cardboard coaster, I begin. "The summer after junior year, after my Sixers internship ended, I did a summer session in Italy. I had always wanted to go there, and I was so jealous of my friends who did full semesters abroad."

He nods. He couldn't study abroad either. Given its status as a winter sport, basketball monopolized the entire school year.

"I'd never had any sort of emotionally intense relationship before." I make a self-mocking face. "But my first week there, I met a guy."

"Name?"

"Oliver." It's weird to say his name out loud. I haven't, in the longest time. I don't miss him, but I used to spend a lot of time dwelling on our history. Before I came back to Ardwyn and this job consumed so much space in my mind.

"He wasn't Italian. He was British, living in Florence. We met at a park where I was taking pictures. Imagine a movie montage and you're pretty much there. We clicked right away. We'd take these long walks on cobblestone streets and talk for hours. It was Florence. You don't have to try to make it romantic; it just is. We found a twenty-five-dollar flight to Paris on a weird budget airline with hot pink planes and spent a weekend there. Eating pastries in the Tuileries and talking about our hopes and dreams."

I stir the ice in my empty water glass with the straw and sneak a look at him. He's watching me, listening, with a careful expression.

"I wasn't naïve," I continue. "I knew it couldn't be a long-term thing, and I was fine with that. But then he told me he loved me. And he asked me to be his girlfriend. He said we would find a way to make it work."

Ben chews his lip.

"At that point I let myself fall pretty hard. He said those things even though he didn't need to, so I trusted that he meant them. I imagined a future with him. He Skyped my sister with me. We were talking about him visiting me at Ardwyn around Halloween. I even started looking into whether I could get a job working for a pro team in Europe after graduation."

I shake my head. "I'm sure you can see where this is going."

His voice is gentle. "Tell me."

"A week after I got home in August, he broke up with me. Via video chat. I remember the connection was bad so the screen kept freezing and catching my ugly-cry face."

"He's the worst," Ben says.

I feel a smile unfurl on my face. "I don't think he meant to hurt me. He was just reckless with my feelings. He got caught up in it like I did. It wasn't until the fantasy was over that reality hit and he realized it would never work. And he was right; I understood that eventually. But it was my first heartbreak—my only heartbreak—and I didn't cope well. I didn't sleep, I drank a lot. Slacked off in my classes, couldn't focus at work. So, yeah. I don't doubt that they fall into something on this show. Maybe even love. But I think that's the easy part."

He's quiet for a moment, spinning his pint glass in his hand.

"I never noticed," he finally says. "That you were having a hard time."

I shrug. "You and I weren't close outside work. I'm glad you didn't notice."

"I'm not." He presses his mouth shut, a contemplative half smile. "Maybe we weren't best friends, but I wish—" He runs a hand through his hair. "I don't know."

There was one night, a random sweaty Wednesday at one

of the bars near campus. I was in the bathroom with Cassie, blubbering over Oliver and rubbing the melted mascara from under my eyes, when I got a text message from Maynard that made me leave my phone next to the sink and make a beeline for the bar. I took three shots in a row, bam, bam, bam. Then I tried to convince the band to play "Since U Been Gone," waving my middle finger at them when they politely declined. Finally, I grabbed a baseball cap off the head of a complete stranger and kissed him next to the old arcade game in the back.

"You never went to the bars," I say. "Believe me, you would've noticed if you'd seen me out."

His face is serious. He traces a line in the condensation on his glass with his finger. "I had my own stuff going on that year."

"Like what?"

He hesitates in a way that makes me shift on my barstool, turning toward him. "Do you remember Hailey?"

Hailey. His high school sweetheart. A perfect heart-shaped face and shiny hair, those big luminous pearl earrings. She went to some other college—in Baltimore, maybe? She came to a lot of games and smiled at everyone, wearing little jeans and neat button-down shirts. She was lovely.

I give a casual shrug. "I think so. Vaguely."

"That fall she told me she wasn't sure if she wanted to be in a relationship anymore."

"What do you mean? She dumped you?"

"Not exactly," he says. "I wish she had. I think she wanted to, but she felt guilty about it. I was there a lot when her dad was sick a few years before. We spent all of senior year in a cycle where she'd tell me she didn't know what she wanted, and I'd try to convince her we could make things better, and she'd go along with it for a while. Then the whole thing would start again. But it got uglier every time."

It's hard to imagine. "You guys seemed . . . perfect." There is a one hundred percent chance they were voted Cutest Couple for their high school yearbook superlatives.

He shrugs. "We both grew up in college. But we grew up differently."

"When did it end?"

"Not until right before graduation. She drove up here from Ocean City in the middle of the night during her Senior Week. She showed up at my apartment crying. Told me she'd hooked up with some guy from her marketing class. She left his hotel room and came straight home to tell me."

Sweet young Ben, the boy with the flock of chirping birdies, betrayed and heartbroken. My chest almost collapses from the pressure at the thought of it. "Oh, Callahan. Fuck that."

"At least she told me."

"So that was it, then?"

"That was it. I had been desperate to make it work before that, but not after she cheated. I think she did it so I'd have to break up with her. Subconsciously. She'd spent an entire year trying to end things. I just wouldn't listen."

"She could've ended things herself instead of making you do it."

"Yeah. She could have."

We fall silent. The door to the kitchen opens and a server appears with a tray, the sound of the sizzling grill filtering in until it swings shut again.

"Whatever happened to her?"

"She married the guy she cheated with. She sends me Christmas cards. I have no hard feelings."

I flick my straw wrapper at him. "Of course you don't. That's so you. You were together for, what, five years?"

"Seven."

"Jeez. So that's why you never fell in love with me." Flippantly, for the record. I say it flippantly.

From the corner of my eye I see his head jerk toward me. A curious look passes over his face. I glue my eyes to the bartender as he mixes a drink. Gin and tonic, fascinating.

"I never had a problem staying faithful," he says slowly. "That doesn't mean I never noticed when someone was objectively beautiful. I have *eyes*."

"Ah," I manage to get out, trying to ignore the flicker of heat in my belly as the bartender adds a lime wedge. "Someone beautiful, like . . . Jasmine." I gesture at the television that played the *Beach House* commercial. To say anything more would be fishing for something dangerous.

A beat passes. The bartender drops a cocktail straw into the glass and takes it to a customer at the other end of the bar. "Sure," Ben says. "Like Jasmine." He turns back to his chicken sandwich. "What about Oliver? Please tell me he showed up at your door months later and you slammed it in his face?"

My shoulders relax. "Well," I say. "This is where the story gets funny, I think." I press my palms against my cheeks.

"Oh, god," he says, and steals one of my french fries. "Hit me."

"He called me months later, after graduation. And I picked up so I could hang up on him, which felt good."

"Nice."

"But then he emailed me to tell me he had moved to Boston and he wanted me to move there too."

Ben's eyes pop out in horror. "Radford, no."

"Oh, yes. I did it. It was after I—after I left here. I got an internship up there and used it as an excuse to go, and then once I got there we were on and off for a couple months and then he freaked out and told me he didn't want to get married—"

"You wanted to get married?"

"Hell, no. I said fuck-all about getting married. I was, what, twenty-two? It was all in his head. But naturally I had to stay in Boston for three more freaking months to prove a point."

"Naturally. And that was it?"

The coaster under my beer is getting soggy. I fold the corner over with my thumb and press it down. "Well."

His head falls back and he groans. "Damn you, Oliver." He breathes in sharply. "Wait, tell me it's over now? I can't handle it if it's not."

"No spoilers," I chide. "A year after that, he moved to New York and asked if we could be friends, and of course he started telling me I was the one that got away."

"And then you told him off?" At this point he looks distraught.

I could cut to the end of the story, but now that he's emotionally invested it's more fun to draw it out. It would be more effective if I could keep a straight face, but I can't.

Mom used to tell me: *You'll laugh about this someday.* Also: *Please, no more Geminis for you.* I couldn't fathom laughing about it then. But now, with all the feelings long since vacuumed out, the bitterness swept from the corners, all that's left are the bones of the story and people that seem like characters written by someone else, even me. So yeah, now it's funny.

"No." It comes out on a laugh like the tiny shriek of air being let out of a balloon. "We got back together for a few more months, and then he decided he was homesick and wanted to go back to England. He asked me to go with him."

He looks ready to fall off his barstool. "Please, please tell me you didn't move to England."

I settle down and sip my beer, allowing the dramatic tension to build. After dabbing the corners of my eyes with a napkin, I shake my head. "I didn't move to England. He'd already decided he was going, and I was tired of all the emotional turmoil. We didn't know how to be in a relationship with each other. We fell in love the first time because we were running around drinking wine in the fucking hills of Tuscany. But that was all we had, and we spent the rest of the time trying to get that feeling back. Finally I ended it, and he left."

"For good?"

"For good. And I'm not a morally superior human like you. We don't talk, and we certainly don't exchange Christmas cards."

"Never send him a Christmas card," Ben implores me. "If he sees the return address he'll show up at your door."

"To bring this back to *The Beach House*—"

"Oh, I forgot there was an actual point to this story."

I backhand his arm lightly. "The point is I think it's a mistake to ascribe grand emotional significance to a relationship that develops in a fantasy world. But also, no judgment if you have to make the mistake three times before learning your lesson."

After dinner, he drives me back to campus. My car is the last one in the parking lot. After I unbuckle my seat belt, he leans over to give me a hug. It's long enough that I take in his clean soapy smell for two full breaths. Long enough that he drags his thumb down the side of my neck in a way that feels deliberate. His stubble grazes my cheekbone as he pulls away.

This is now the second time we've hugged. It's apparently a thing we do now. I'm not sure of the parameters.

"Before you go," he says, his voice a little rough. I stop with my fingers wrapped around the door handle. "I'm sorry your dad's friends didn't make it tonight. They missed out."

He's looking at me in a soft way that makes the car feel too small, like I'm sitting too still, like I need to get out and start moving. I look back at him. *How close can I get?* I pull the door handle. "Thanks," I say. "And Happy Valentine's Day. Technically."

FIFTEEN

"HEY, WE HAVE TO SHOW YOU—OH, SHE'S BUSY."

I peer around my computer monitors to see Ben in the doorway, with Eric behind him. "What's up?"

"How do you know she's busy?" Eric asks, nudging his way past Ben into my office. "It's not even nine thirty." He tosses an apple from hand to hand.

"Yeah, how?" I'm poring over clips from the last game, my screen full of tiny thumbnails like pieces of confetti. It's my procrastination-slash-brainstorming hour, so they were as likely to find me in the middle of a deep dive on Mindy Kaling's relationship with B. J. Novak as they were to find me working.

"Your hair," Ben says without guile. "When you're working, you always put it in a ponytail."

Eric crunches down on his apple.

I touch my hair, *no, don't touch the hair,* and my face flushes.

It's clear when he realizes this wasn't a normal thing to say. In one squirming motion he ducks his chin, rubs the back of his neck, and directs his gaze to the hallway, where nothing at all is happening. Eric watches him with a confounded squint, slowly chewing.

I've never thanked a piece of fruit before, but I'd kiss the waxy skin of this Granny Smith if I could. I don't want to hear whatever Eric would say if his mouth weren't full. He's as subtle as a leopard print faux fur coat.

Once in high school, Shane Kowalski walked into a party while the perfect song from the *Gossip Girl* soundtrack was playing, and I tried to perch on the arm of the couch and throw my head back, a glamorous curve in my wrist as I held a red plastic cup. Eric looked at me then much like he's looking at Ben now. "Why are you laughing like that?" he bellowed. "Are you having a neck spasm?"

I clear my throat. "What did you guys want to show me?"

Ben whips out his phone, and the Joint Task Force for Changing the Fucking Subject is all systems go. "Logan's Instagram post," he says, pulling up a photo of a sunrise with a cryptic, long-winded caption.

We're fortunate it's a *Beach House* thing, because Eric has an elaborate theory about the sun and Jasmine's tattoo and whether Logan's typos are a mistake or a code. I nod and make thoughtful noises at regular intervals, hoping I'm pulling off a reasonable impersonation of someone who's listening.

I shouldn't be surprised by Ben's observation about my ponytail. It feels intimate, but isn't it just factual? Does noticing things necessarily constitute an act of tenderness? I'd be able to tell if he was working. He does that thing with his tongue, and he gets too close to the computer screen and coaxes his spreadsheets in a whisper, his mouth tracing words and numbers, soft and nearly silent.

We walk straight into each other's offices now when we want to talk. No more knocking on an open door or asking if the other is busy. I show him half-finished videos and hover over his shoulder while he watches. He makes impassioned arguments in favor of certain player rotations and offensive schemes, test runs for conversations with Coach Thomas.

We don't talk about the budget cuts. That's a problem for our future selves.

The texting starts when Blake loses to the worst team in the conference. Within the first four messages we're off the subject of basketball and onto political corruption and the gymnastics meet that comes on after the game.

Annie: should we watch and discuss

Ben: Obviously. Who you got?

Annie: gotta be LSU. they're wearing bedazzled tiger stripes. you should take inspo from this look for our next game

Ben: I need to save my leotards for off days. They're hand wash only.

Annie: i'm confused about how the scoring system works

Ben: Don't bait me into talking about this unless you're free for the next four hours.

Annie: aww did you memorize the rule book because of your sister?

Ben: Memorize it? I send a letter every year listing all the ways they need to fix it.

The following night a notorious member of the House of Representatives goes viral for stating that he doesn't "believe in all that." "All that" being the entire field of mathematics, because data shows that immigration has a positive impact on the economy. Ben sends me the video one minute after I see it myself.

Annie: lol numbers aren't real

Ben: 😖

Ben: Am I real?

Annie: not in the 5th congressional district of arkansas

Within a couple days the new-message notifications with his name on them cease to surprise me. The texting becomes part of the natural fabric of my evenings and days off. We don't talk about it at work, which gives it a clandestine aura.

It's not that we're discussing anything exceptionally intimate: mainly TV and Sasha, the news and our families. It's the fact of the conversations themselves that makes them impossible to acknowledge, that we're having them at home when we could wait eight hours until we see each other again.

The texting changes the way we communicate with each other, each time more familiar, more comfortable. Sometimes in person the morning after a long chat, we try to talk the way we did the day before, and it doesn't feel right. We need to recalibrate the way we interact face-to-face to match the way we interact through our phones. Or maybe we don't need to. We could maintain two parallel relationships, but that's not what we do.

One day I poke my head into Ben's office. "Is three minutes too long for this video?" I ask. "I should cap it at two and a half, right?"

"Do what you want," he says with a slow, private smile. "Numbers aren't real."

That night after my shower, I'm standing in the bathroom, squeezing some of the moisture out of my hair with a towel. I grab my blow dryer from the cabinet under the sink and check my phone before I plug it in, recoiling when I see what's waiting for me. It's one long message, longer than the entire screen. To reach the top I have to scroll up.

Before I start reading, I can already tell this is something he drafted with painstaking effort. He read it and revised it and reread it. He might even have put it together in his notes app to make sure he didn't accidentally send it before it was done. My chest burns with anxious dread. Nothing good can come of a message like this.

I've been wanting to talk to you about
something. It never seems like the right time
but now that we've become friends (I hope?) I
think I should be honest with you, so here goes.

I told you once that I'm waiting for the right
time to leave Ardwyn. The truth is, I've always
planned to go coach with Maynard at Arizona
Tech someday. The timing isn't set in stone and
he doesn't have an opening right now, but
we've talked about it for years. Obviously, the
stuff we talked about with Phil Coleman is
weighing on me, and I'm still not sure what to
do about that. But I owe it to Coach to give it a
chance, see how he runs the program, and try
to be a positive influence. I know you have a
different opinion of him than I do and I respect
that. But I don't think you can possibly
understand how much he's done for me and my
family. I've looked up to him for my entire adult
life. He taught me what it means to be a leader.
I need to give it a shot.

Anyway, this may seem sudden, but I want to be
honest with you and it was starting to feel weird
that I hadn't said anything.

I put the hair dryer on the counter and go to the green
room. After lighting a candle, I nestle myself in the cocoon
of the beanbag, watching the tiny flame in the windowsill
stretch and ripple. The faint sound of the television seeps in

from the apartment downstairs. Sporadic whistles and the fervent shouty voice of a commentator, a basketball game, probably the big Duke-UNC one.

The lump in my throat is so solid it's painful. It's been easy for Ben and me to pretend Maynard isn't a sticking point, because neither of us brings him up anymore. But now it's not just a source of conflict between the two of us. It *matters*. The idea of my *friend* (one I occasionally thirst after, but a friend all the same) working side by side with Maynard is sickening enough, but it's worse than that. There's no way Maynard has changed his behavior since leaving Ardwyn. If Ben joins his team, he'll be part of a culture that enables Maynard to hurt people.

I can't let that happen.

I lie there for a long time, until the fabric beneath my head is damp from my hair. Eventually my left butt cheek falls asleep, so I climb out of the chair and sit on the floor. The turf scratches the backs of my bare thighs. I pick up my phone.

"Hey," Kat says when she answers. Music blares in the background.

"Hey. Are you out?" My voice is high and wobbly.

"Nope." The music turns off. "What's wrong?"

I tell her everything, and Kat doesn't speak until I'm done. "Okay, there's a lot to unpack here. Did you know they were that close?"

"I knew he still idolized him. I knew they kept in touch. I didn't know he was going to move across the country someday to be his right-hand man."

"It's ridiculously naïve of him to think he can go into a situation like that and fix any ethical fuckery that's going on.

Maybe he's just saying he wants to be a positive influence to make himself feel better about his decision."

I comb the turf with anxious fingers. "I don't think he would do that. He sincerely believes the Phil Coleman thing was an isolated incident, or that worst-case scenario, he can stop Maynard from doing anything similar again."

Kat snorts. "Which is absurd because he was so oblivious to Fuckwaffle's bullshit he didn't even know what happened to Phil, and he was *there*."

"That's how it works," I say. "Maynard shows people only what he wants them to see to get what he wants from them. And it's easy for him to take advantage of his power because everyone else feels easily replaceable."

The structure of the college sports industry breeds abuse. To outsiders, it's glamorous, and those in charge capitalize on that. A large number of people clamor for a small number of junior positions, eager to get a foot in the door, even for low or no pay. They put up with lots of things they shouldn't because they're lucky to be there, or so everyone says. They can't demand better treatment because a thousand other people not demanding better treatment would happily take their places tomorrow. Those who attain the highest positions are paid fuck-you money and worshipped like gods. The environment in many programs oozes toxic masculinity: glorifying toughness, celebrating dominance, literal and figurative locker room talk. Those who embrace it often rise to the top.

"What are you going to do?" Kat asks.

I squeeze the damp ends of my hair. "Nothing yet. But after the season is over, if we're still friends . . . I'll tell him. Maybe not everything, but enough."

Kat exhales. "Wow."

"Yeah."

Only a handful of people know what Maynard did, how he drove me away from Ardwyn and basketball altogether. My family, Eric, Cassie, and Oliver—that's it. I haven't told anyone else, but this isn't a difficult decision. It will be a difficult conversation, however. *I've looked up to him for my entire adult life,* Ben said. *He taught me what it means to be a leader.*

It might break him.

"Okay, so one more thing," Kat says. "And this is important. You know that what you're doing with him is flirting, right? Like, you said 'friends' but that's not exactly what's happening here."

"Kat. Stop."

"Annie. The Rold Gold."

I made a big mistake recently, telling her Ben gives me the little bags of pretzels that come with his student center café lunch combo. "It's like when a penguin brings another penguin little pebbles because he wants to mate," she cooed.

I don't want to hear that again, so I hug my knees and grumble, "Yes, fine, I'm aware we're flirting."

"Really? Damn, I was hoping we could do that thing where you deny it and then eventually I'm proven right and I get to gloat about it."

"You must've forgotten that I'm older and wiser than you. I'm incredibly self-aware."

"What about him, is he aware you're flirting?"

"I haven't asked." I'm pretty sure he is, except when I'm certain he isn't.

"Wiseass. But no one has made a move?"

"Ugh," I groan. "Nothing is going to happen."

"Oh, I get it. *This* is the part where you deny it, and then eventually I'll be proven right and get to gloat about it. Do you mind repeating what you said in writing for my file?"

Kat's wrong. Nothing is going to happen, because I'm going to make sure of it. Flirting is one thing. In fact, I'd forgotten the thrilling, addictive pleasure of good banter. I can't remember the last time I felt it. I couldn't stop even if I wanted to. *How close can I get,* as close as I want, and no further. But I'll keep it from escalating, because I'm not a fool. There are too many complicating factors, a weight that can't be supported, that will bring the whole thing down.

After I hang up I look at the message again. A sick feeling floods my body anew, and my fingers are bloodless as I type a response.

Annie: thanks for letting me know.

Annie: now where's my sasha pic, I know you were with her today

SIXTEEN

ON *BEACH HOUSE* MONDAY, I ARRIVE EARLY TO catch up with Cassie before Eric gets home.

"Third place is pretty impressive considering I'm the only one who's never watched the show before." I blow on my tea and sink into the couch cushions.

"Very impressive," Cassie says from the bedroom, where she's changing out of her work clothes. When she returns to the living room, she's wearing leggings and a hooded sweatshirt, fuzzy socks on her feet. "I'm going to check on the food."

"What are we having?" I ask. "Can I help?" A lid clinks as Cassie sets it on the counter.

"Oh, *no*."

I set down my mug on a coaster and crane my neck to look. "Not done? Can you turn it up to high?" I'm only vaguely familiar with the settings of a slow cooker, not being the kind of person who has the eight hours of foresight necessary to use one.

Cassie pops her head around the corner, one hand pressed against her forehead, the other brandishing a pair of tongs. "I must've forgotten to turn it on this morning! I was on the phone with one of the junior associates on my new case while I was getting everything ready and I was so distracted. It's been sitting here all day at room temperature."

I make a sympathetic noise. "That sucks. Should we order takeout?"

Something visibly cracks inside Cassie, and her shoulders sag. "All I want is to cook for my friends once a week. Is that so much to ask? I don't think so." She waves the tongs like an angry fencer. "This is my one thing. My. One. Thing. The one thing I do just because I want to. Because I like to have one nice evening cooking something delicious and watching my favorite show with the people I care about. And I'm so tired and busy all the time I can't even do it right."

Her voice wobbles, and she blinks rapidly, her eyes shining with tears. This obviously isn't just about tonight's dinner. Something is wrong, has been wrong for some time, and I missed it. Dammit. I've been so preoccupied with my own life I missed the warning signs.

I jump up and cross the room, squeezing Cassie's shoulder and gently sliding the tongs from her grasp before they slip from her hand and fly through a window. "Hey, hey. No. First of all, you're an amazing human being. Second of all, forget the takeout. We have"—I check my phone—"ninety minutes. You have me, I'll be your sous chef, we'll throw something together. Ninety minutes, it's doable, right?"

"Okay." Cassie nods, inhaling and exhaling in a controlled manner. "You're right. We'll make—let's see." She returns to the kitchen, opening cabinets and peering into the fridge. "Wait, how about your lasagna? That's good for a group."

"Uh." There's not enough time to make pasta from scratch, so we'll have to use store-bought noodles. I let out a tortured gurgle and cover it with a cough. Cassie is a better cook than I am in general, but I only have the one good dish in my repertoire, so I'm normally precious about it. But I'm not about to tell Cassie no. I grit my teeth. "Sounds great. Can I borrow your car to run home? I have frozen Bolognese we can use."

Later, when we're working together to assemble the layers in two glass baking dishes, I glance up at her. "You okay?"

Cassie methodically pats the sauce into the corners of the pan with the back of a spoon. When she speaks her voice is quiet. "Just stressed. I'm not good at turning things down at work. New cases, more mentoring, pro bono stuff. I always say yes." She looks up. "I don't know if I've ever told you this, but sometimes when I'm overwhelmed I think, 'What would Annie do?' You're good at setting boundaries. It doesn't work for me."

Here Lies Annie Radford: She Knew How to Say No to Life. It's not even true anymore. If only Cassie knew how bad I've been at setting boundaries lately. "Please. You don't want to channel anything I do." I wipe a splash of sauce from the counter. "It sounds like something needs to change. At least you love what you do, right? That's why you keep taking on more. I think you'll be better at the parts of your job that you love most if you can find a way to say no to the parts that are bullshit."

Cassie shakes her head. "Half the reason they want me

there is to deal with the bullshit. I thought you of all people would be telling me to quit."

Ouch. That feels like a slap, but Cassie has no way of knowing it. It's like Donna dismissing any possibility of me being emotionally vulnerable, like Ben calling me cynical. I've insisted to everyone for so long that I'm a certain type of person and now I'm disappointed to learn they've all believed me.

I smile through it. "If you want to quit, I would support you. Not financially, I mean, I don't make that much money. But emotionally."

We finish our work in silence and Cassie slides the pans into the oven. "I'm glad you came early to hang out tonight. I've been so jealous that Eric gets to see you more than I do."

"I know. The whole reason I moved out here was so I could spend your first year of marriage with you guys, like you always dreamed. But I see way too much of Eric and not enough of you."

Cassie folds a dish towel into a neat rectangle. "I don't even know what's going on in your life. Anything exciting other than work?"

"Nope," I say with an affected shrug. "Just basketball." It's not a lie, exactly. So why do I feel a twinge of guilt saying it? Either way, there's no way I can talk about Ben to Cassie, not with her sense of caution and rationality. Not right now.

Cassie goes to the living room to fluff the throw pillows. I stay in the kitchen, scrubbing the dishes with a concentrated vigor, until the skin on my hands is pink and soggy.

- - - - - - - - - - -

IN THE MIDDLE of the episode, Eric checks his phone and announces that Blake lost another game, which means

Ardwyn has clinched the regular-season conference title. Everyone whistles and applauds loud enough for the neighbors to hear, even Cassie's friends, who don't follow basketball at all.

Ben and I are silly and hyper on the walk home, immune to the cold, spinning imagined scenarios about different people's reactions to the news. Ben thinks Coach Williams probably grunted and gave his son a lecture on how the only title that matters is the national championship. I prefer to envision a secret second world for him, one in which he gathered his family around to celebrate with ice cream sundaes. Ted Horvath is already on a conference call with the fundraising team, telling them about his kitchen renovation, and Donna's popping lozenges to prepare for the onslaught of well-wishing callers she's going to have to yell at tomorrow.

"Look," Ben says, waggling his phone at me. "Williams is already messaging us with a lecture."

"While he finishes his banana split, I bet," I say, peering at the screen. There's a long block of text about heads staying down, long roads ahead, and keeping a foot on the gas.

I'm reading it out loud when a notification pops up, a familiar icon in marigold and white. A dating app. "Oh!" I avert my eyes and thrust the phone back at him. "Sorry."

He looks at the screen and slides the notification away. His face is completely unself-conscious, as if it were a notification from the Weather Channel about tomorrow's chance of precipitation. Embarrassment pours over me like cold water. The possibility that Ben was seeing other people never once crossed my mind. But of course he is. He's trying to find a girlfriend or get laid like most single people, not obsess over innocent text message exchanges and incidental physical contact with his coworker.

He glances at me as if to continue our conversation, but something must show on my face. He freezes, his expression turning distressed. "Sorry," he repeats after me, and I don't know why either of us is apologizing.

"No need." I give what I hope is a cool shrug. It's not like I want to be his girlfriend. I like him too much to ruin things with a feeble attempt at dating one month before one of us is probably forced to leave this place. Not to mention the Maynard-shaped grenade buried in the space between us.

I won't make the same mistake I made with Oliver. There was a moment one night on his balcony in Florence. We were drinking Sangiovese, watching the sun set over a sea of terracotta roof tiles and talking about our childhoods, when I thought, *It can't get better than this.* And I was right. If we'd allowed it to be the dreamy summer fling it always should've been, I could've avoided a lot of heartache. I might've looked back fondly on it as a youthful adventure.

This is a wonderful surprise of a friendship in the middle of a wonderful surprise of a basketball season. That's enough. When it's over, we can both walk away intact.

But if somebody gets to be so blasé about it, why is it him?

His dark eyes are fixed on me. "I thought you read it. It's telling me it's been a while since I logged in. I don't really date during basketball season."

Oh. I attempt a detached nod as the tense knot inside me unwinds.

"Maybe that sounds bad. Our schedule is just too hectic to meet someone and start a relationship. I don't bother with these apps between October and March."

A six-month window to meet someone, otherwise it's *better luck next year*? "Well, that's a little depressing."

"You're dating right now?" A stricken look passes over his face that I enjoy more than I'd like to admit.

"Obviously not. I'm stuck with you eighty-seven hours a day. No time for swiping."

His phone buzzes, and he looks at the screen. "I have to get this," he says. There's nowhere for him to go for privacy, so we continue walking together while he talks and I pretend I can't hear his mom's voice coming through the phone.

The call is apparently one he's been expecting, about a big meeting at the high school today. Ben's sister, Natalie, was accused of sharing an essay with another student, a boy, who copied it word for word. Amateur. They got caught, and the school threatened to sanction them for honor code violations and notify their colleges. Ultimately, they let Natalie go with a warning and a community service project.

Ben keeps asking questions about proof. *Maybe she didn't give him the essay. Maybe he took it from her backpack without her knowing. How do they know? She's a good kid, she wouldn't do that.* His mom sounds a little scatterbrained. She doesn't know anything about proof, didn't ask. It's not until the end of the call that she mentions that Ben's sister confessed to her crime.

Ben sputters a bit. It's so like him, to assume the absolute best of someone he loves. To give her the benefit of the doubt at everyone else's expense. His sister probably is a good kid, a good kid whose teenage brain said yes when a cute boy asked to see her homework.

When he hangs up, it's clear he needs to simmer in his thoughts, so I let him. We're on Ardwyn Avenue now.

Through the window of a bar, a television plays the Blake highlights while clusters of students chat over bottled beer and do a blunted, sober-ish version of dancing. Just a little sway; it's only ten thirty.

"My mom had me young," he finally says. "My dad was in and out of our lives for a long time. Sometimes for years. I've had to look after Natalie for as long as I can remember, and I'm glad to do it, don't get me wrong."

I don't say anything, just look up at him and listen.

"Lately I've been wondering if leaving Ardwyn even if Natalie goes to school here wouldn't be the worst thing. For me, and for her. But now, after this? She's not ready to be on her own. How can I leave?"

"Callahan." I squeeze his arm. "She'll figure it out. You've stayed in a job that doesn't make you happy for a long time, just for her, when you could be doing what you want instead. It's so sweet it makes me want to puke. But it's time."

He nudges me with his elbow. "You're saying that because I'm the competition."

"I'm saying it because you taught Lufton to be proficient in Excel without banging your head against the wall, and he's an English major. There are kids out there who need a good coach, and they deserve someone like you." *As long as they don't go to Arizona Tech.*

His cheeks turn pink. "Work has been okay lately, though."

Yes, it has. "The team is really fucking good. That always helps."

He laughs.

This is not a one-off. It's a personality trait. He's doing the same thing with Maynard, putting him on a pedestal, brushing aside his own concerns because of some sense of ancient obligation. Does he even want to live in Arizona? He's so loyal he chains himself to people. He'd keep himself chained to them even if they were sinking to the bottom of the ocean.

We're coming up on my building. Here on the side street the night is empty, stripped bare now that the snow has melted. Everything is flat: the dormant grass, the sidewalks clear and dry, the street dead of traffic. The knobs and points of tree branches provide the only punctuation in the cloudless sky. The moon is nearly full, so the whole wide unbroken scene is silver-lit as if from within.

"Do you want to know what your problem is?" I ask.

"Go ahead, tell me."

He stops walking. I whirl around and we're face to face.

This is not a position I'm used to being in with Ben. Usually there are walls and hallways between us, or phone screens, or at least a desk. Sometimes we're next to each other, sitting on the bus or the plane or watching *The Beach House* or walking. But now he's standing in front of me. His body, my body.

His arms are crossed and his eyes sparkle, like he's humoring me. I smile, like I'm only needling him, even though I mean what I'm about to say.

"You spend so much time worrying about what you're supposed to do for other people. About what you owe them. Don't you ever do anything for yourself? Just because you want to? Turn off that brain of yours and tell me, without thinking. What would you do right now if you could do anything you wanted?"

He looks at me. I expect him to throw his hands up or shrug or make a joke about going to Wawa. Anything but answer the question. Instead something dangerous flickers in his eyes, an intention manifesting that makes me want to run. Toward him or away from him, I'm not sure.

When he moves, I'm disoriented at first. Because all he does is lift his hands to my collar and pinch the drawstrings of my coat between his thumbs and forefingers.

I fall completely still. *How close can I get?* This is not what I meant to incite with my rant. Or maybe it was. Understanding my own objectives is not my strong suit. Either way, it's the perfect distance, the last acceptable distance. Nothing has happened, but almost. Almost.

"Radford." His voice is low and unsteady as his fingers move down the drawstrings. When they reach the end, he'll be able to grab the little knots and tug me closer, too close, and then something will actually happen. It's like watching the wick of a cartoon bomb burn down to an explosion, except the bomb is a sex bomb.

He's watching his hands and I am too, and I'm not making any sort of decision, only listening to his breathing and smelling his soap and the cold and feeling the closeness of him. My heart is thwacking away at my breastbone. He has nice thumbnails, I notice, and just before he reaches the knots I turn my head slightly, out toward the road. Just my chin, just a couple inches. A car glides by lazily, kicking up some slush.

"I should get inside," I say to the car.

He backs off immediately. *Don't go,* I want to say. He rubs a hand over his remorseful mouth.

"Sorry."

"For what?" I try.

He shakes his head. "You don't have to do that."

"Nothing happened."

"It won't happen again. I thought—I misinterpreted things. But that's on me. The last thing I want is to make you uncomfortable."

"You didn't," I say, supremely uncomfortable, but not the way he thinks. "Okay, well, good night!" I don't look at his face or wait for him to reply. I turn on my heel and flee into the building, flying up the stairs until I'm sure he can't see me anymore through the glass. The whole way up I skim one palm along the handrail. I squeeze the knots on the drawstrings tight in the other fist.

SEVENTEEN

HINDSIGHT IS A SMUG ASSHOLE. WHEN I STUMBLE into my apartment in a daze, I can't even make it to the green room. I get as far as the bedroom and fall face-first onto the mattress without taking off my coat. Hindsight is sitting in the dark corner, studying its nails with a condescending smirk, until it deigns to turn to me and say in a prim voice: *I was wondering when you'd get here. Was it not glaringly obvious this would happen?*

It is now. It wasn't thirty minutes ago. It would've been nice to get a warning in advance.

Hindsight sniffs. *Not my thing. You're looking for my cousin, foresight.*

Yeah. I've been looking for foresight my whole life.

If I'm honest with myself, I didn't need foresight this time. I had Kat, and I didn't listen. I knew what Ben and I were doing, I knew what direction it was going. It was escalating, but I enjoyed it too much and didn't put a stop to it in time. I played a game of chicken and crashed.

And here is what I learned from the experience: I wanted it to happen. For the first time in a long time, I *wanted* something. Not out of fear, or self-protection, or to avoid something else. I wanted it badly, for its own sake.

That almost-kiss felt like a boat engine revving in my body, my blood beginning to thrum like the surrounding water, brought to life by the energy of it. Who knew I was still capable of feeling that way about a guy?

But I didn't go through with it. That's worthy of a pat on the back. I vowed not to repeat the Oliver mistake, and I didn't cave.

There were other good reasons not to do it. The job, for one. Plus, we haven't cleared the air about Maynard, and I'm not ready for that conversation. Barely five minutes ago, Ben and I couldn't stand each other, and imagining his reaction makes me sweat.

But none of that is fair. Neither of us signed up for the pressure we're under at work. And Maynard is supposed to be gone, no longer a factor in my life, my decisions, my anything. Definitely not here, right in between Ben and me.

If it weren't for him—well, I can't even think about what I'd be doing right now. Tonight would be different. Everything would be different.

And what about Oliver? *It can't get better than this,* that's what I'm supposed to remember, but it doesn't feel true. Kissing Ben would've made this night way, way better. My mistake with Oliver wasn't getting physical. It was believing him when he said we had a future together. A celebratory make-out session after winning the conference title wouldn't have hurt anyone. We can kiss without falling in love. All we have to do is not make promises.

I sit up and turn on a lamp. It's just me in the room. No imaginary friends or enemies here, telling me what I can or should do, or how it's going to go wrong. Fuck all those ghosts.

I'm going to do what I want. I'm going to kiss Ben Callahan.

EIGHTEEN

THE NEXT MORNING I GET TO WORK EARLY, NERVES
burning like acid in my gut. I'm not exactly sure how to do
this. Last night I thought about texting him to ask for a do-
over, but hiding behind my phone seemed like a cop-out.

I sit at my desk and jiggle my leg. Open my email, close it.
I realize I didn't actually look at my inbox and open it again.
Adrenaline has me jumping out of my seat every time I hear
someone walking by or opening a door or talking down the
hall. *Calm calm calm,* I type over and over again in a blank
Word document.

Slipping on my headphones, I nestle into the protective
shell of my semicircle of computer monitors. This is good.
Now I can't possibly hear him arrive, so I'll be less skittish. I
pull up a half-complete video I've been working on and,
well, to say I "watch it" wouldn't be accurate, but at least I
aim my eyes at the screen. Seven excruciating minutes pass.

I barely hear him over the music, or maybe I sense him

knocking on the door. Either way, he's standing there in an Ardwyn crewneck sweater over an oxford shirt and fitted gray trousers, his cheeks wind-reddened. My body jerks upright and I slide my chair abruptly to see around the monitors, forgetting my headphones. They tumble from my shoulders down the back of my chair.

"Um. What did you say? Sorry." I comb my fingers through my hair to untangle the wire.

His face is circumspect. "I said good morning."

"Oh! Well, hi." I'm already out of breath.

He opens his mouth like he's going to say something else, then decides against it.

"Can we"—I start, then lower my voice—"can we talk?"

He glances into the hallway. "Now?"

"Yes. Please." Eight thirty in the morning in the office is not the ideal time or setting for this conversation, but I can't bear it hanging over my head any longer.

He nods reluctantly and closes the door. "I want to apologize again—"

"Stop."

His mouth twitches once and he lowers his eyes.

"You have nothing to be sorry for, but I have something I need to say."

He winces. "If you don't want an apology, I'd rather not relive that excruciating moment again, thanks." He shoves his hands into his pockets. "I meant what I said last night. I'm not going to make this awkward. I'm glad we're friends."

"*I'm* going to make this awkward," I say. "I'm trying to tell you—I didn't stop you because I didn't want it to happen." I bite my lip. "I want it to happen."

Our eyes lock and a thrill charges screaming through my

chest as I watch him reach a sonnet-worthy conclusion: *It's on*. I give him an opening to respond. "Go on," he says slowly.

"I stopped you because—I'm bad at this."

"Kissing?"

I roll my eyes. "Normally I'm an impulsive person. But I overthought it. You caught me off-guard, and I panicked."

"I don't know whether to be relieved or insulted that how I've been feeling wasn't the most obvious thing in the world."

I swivel back and forth in my chair. "I'd be happy to critique your game later. But for now I just want to say that if you want to try again sometime, I promise I won't run the other way."

He laughs. "Oh, no. No. That's not how this is going to work." He puts a hand to his heart. "My pride is wounded. You're going to have to be the one to make a move on me."

"Wow. You're going to milk it, are you?" I fold my arms. "Okay, that seems fair."

"And not now. Not here. Unlike you, I like surprises."

"You want me to surprise you?"

He grabs the door handle, his dark eyes hot and playful. "Sweep me off my feet, Radford. I deserve it."

- - - - - - - - - - - -

IT'S NOT GOING to happen this evening because it's the last home game of the season. Senior Night, when JGE and Gallimore and a couple of the student managers are honored during halftime. There are no postseason home games, so it's the last time they'll ever play on this court.

There are flowers and a nice little speech from Coach Thomas. Proud families and friends stand courtside. We win by a large margin, and Thomas pulls both seniors out with five minutes to go so they can receive one last standing ovation from the crowd. I get great footage during the postgame press conference, where both seniors get teary-eyed talking about the end of their college careers. I can't imagine the team without them, but in a few months JGE will start his fellowship and Gallimore will likely be playing in Europe.

It's my lucky night. JJ Jones sidles up to me as everyone trickles out afterward. He's wearing no socks but like, seven shirts, their varying necklines and collars arranged in elaborate layers around his neck like the plumage of a showy bird.

"Champion vibes," he proclaims. "You guys seem unstoppable."

"Still a long way to go." I shrug and busy myself with my camera case. Eric walks toward me from the front of the room, but when he sees JJ he freezes. *Rescue me,* I plead with his eyes.

"And you. Everyone is talking about you. Even my boss's boss wanted to know who's making Ardwyn's hype videos this season. And he's big-time. He was like, 'JJ, who's making Ardwyn's hype videos this season?' And I told him, 'Oh, it's my buddy, this girl Annie Radford.' And he was like, 'Wow, next level.' And he's right."

"Thanks, JJ." I give him a guilty smile. It is a nice story, if you ignore the delivery and only pay attention to the content.

"Annie, I need to talk to you," Eric finally cuts in. "I heard what he said." He lowers his voice as we walk away. "He may be a doofus, but he knows what he's talking about. You've impressed all of college basketball. I told you that you belong here."

He did, about a million times. On multiple occasions over

the years. When he offered me the job. When I took it, when I got here, when I doubted my decision. He's never stopped telling me. And for the first time, I'm starting to think he may be right.

I HAVE THE barest sketch of a plan for the next day. After work, I'll invite Ben out to dinner, and I'll jump him on the walk to the employee parking lot. No need to overcomplicate things.

I spend more time trying to choose an outfit than anything. I want to wear something that doesn't scream "I'm here to see a man about a kiss" but does kind of whisper it. It also has to be something that won't draw attention at work. The last thing I need is anyone asking whether I have a date.

I end up in a maroon dress with a bow at the neck, black tights, and loafers, and the only thing Eric says about it is "Is that ribbon holding your head on?" which is the best I could've hoped for.

My mistake is not telling Ben the plan. I'm trying to be cool and mysterious, because he wants to be surprised, after all. But then he screws the whole thing up by leaving work at five o'clock.

"Do you know if he's coming back?" I ask, leaning casually on the reception desk as Donna packs up for the night. "I need his help with something."

Donna shoots my elbows a suspicious look. "Who? I'm not a mind reader."

Smooth. Subtle. "Sorry! I meant Ben."

"I don't think so. He said he was going home."

Home? Since when does he go home at five? I resist the urge to laugh. He must be doing this to mess with me.

Okay, change of plans. I go to the bathroom, dab my shiny forehead with a tissue, and apply a coat of mascara and a swipe of tinted lip balm. I don't have his exact address, but I can figure it out. He's mentioned the street, and I know what his car looks like. It only takes a few minutes of driving up and down the block in a slightly sketchy fashion before I find it parked in the driveway of a duplex.

I park on the street. The lights are off in the downstairs apartment, so I take a gamble on the upstairs. It's quiet, so every step on the sidewalk is as loud as a car engine backfiring. He probably already hears me coming. I step onto the small porch, comb my fingers through my hair, and ring the bell.

There's a brief silence, and then somebody comes hurtling down the stairs, hollering, "I got it!" The voice sounds female. Shit, this must not be Ben's apartment after all. The girl flings the door open. "Hi."

She's a teenager, with long dark curly hair poking out of the hood of an oversized sweatshirt. "Sorry," I say, making a guilty face. "I think I have the wrong place."

"Is it the food?" A fiftyish woman with a short version of the same dark hair appears at the top of the stairs, peering down at us. A crooked tiara sits on her head.

"No, she's lost," the girl says.

"Who are you looking for?" the woman asks. "Maybe Ben knows them." She pokes her head around the corner, out of sight. "Ben!" she yells.

Oh, no.

A dog barks. "Sasha, calm down," the woman says.

"I'll just go," I mumble, trying to slink away into the darkness.

"Radford?" Too late.

I close my eyes, freezing with my back to Ben and his entire fucking family.

"Heeey." I turn around, offering one sheepish wave with my palm open, like I'm wiping a window.

"You know her?" his mom asks. I don't hear his response. "Well, come in, hon, it's cold out there!"

I trudge up the steps behind his sister, staring at my feet. When I reach the top, I look everywhere else to avoid meeting his eye. His apartment is clean and comfortable-looking. Extremely coordinated, like he bought everything from the same page of the furniture catalog. Matchy-matchy is not my taste, but it makes perfect sense for him. A blown-sugar balloon inflates in my chest, pink and fragile and unfamiliar, and I fight the strange urge to bundle him in bubble wrap so no one can ever hurt him. He's got a few throw pillows and a basket full of blankets, all in the prescribed blue and taupe color palette. On the small round dining table are two wrapped gifts and a cake with candles in it.

Oh, no.

"So, Annie, to what do we owe the pleasure?" his mom, Lisa, asks after we get through introductions.

Ben feigns confusion. "Yeah, Radford, to what do we owe the pleasure?"

I finally meet his eyes. He's failing to repress a smile, reveling in my discomfort. I attempt to glare at him in a way that his mom won't notice.

"Just came by for that work thing," I say. Sasha bumps her nose against my hand, demanding to be petted.

"What work thing?"

"You know," I say casually, scratching Sasha behind her ears. "That one we were working on?"

"Can you be more specific?"

His sister snickers, one of those cutting teenage laughs that makes you realize you're acutely transparent.

"You have to stay for dinner," Lisa urges. "We ordered plenty of food and we'd love to have you join us."

"Thank you so much, but I don't want to intrude," I say. "Ben and I can talk about work tomorrow. I'll leave you to your family dinner."

"Nonsense! It's my birthday, and I want you to stay."

"I really—"

"Don't you dare say no to me on my birthday." She motions for me to hand her my coat.

I scan Ben's face, hunting for any sign of dismay, but he looks completely at ease. And annoyingly entertained. He gives me a reassuring nod.

"Okay," I say weakly. "And happy birthday."

Lisa barrels on. "I didn't know you were a girl, and such a pretty one! Radford—Jesus, Ben, why do you call her that? All this time I thought she was a guy."

"Talking to your mom about me a lot?" I whisper, elbowing him gently as we follow Lisa into the living room. He leans into it for a second, the side of his body pressed against the side of mine, his eyes hot and knowing.

More of that, please.

"Had to warn her about the stalker who was planning to crash her family birthday dinner," he says.

When the Vietnamese food arrives, Ben moves the gifts and cake to the kitchen counter so we can sit around the table. Lisa spreads the containers out in the middle and Ben asks Natalie to set the table.

We talk about our favorite places to eat nearby and the town down the shore where Lisa used to take Ben and Natalie when they were young. Ben's mom is a die-hard Bruce Springsteen fan and, well, I'm from New Jersey, so we've both been to multiple concerts.

They ask about my work. Natalie doesn't care about basketball but wants to know the wildest thing I've ever seen doing wedding videography. The answer is a fistfight between the groom and his own father, and Lisa and Natalie want every detail, but they've seen worse on their favorite television shows. "Never been married but haven't met a wedding-themed reality show I didn't like," Lisa declares.

Ben uses the word *home* in a sentence and the letter *o* goes in a direction I've never heard coming out of his mouth. Lisa's strong Philly accent clearly rubs off on him when he's around her. Natalie gives Ben the play-by-play of her most recent gymnastics meet, and he asks thoughtful questions about the recent changes to her beam routine.

I excuse myself to go to the bathroom, where I retie the loose bow at the neck of my dress and check my teeth for food. Nothing about this night is going how I expected. But it's nice to meet Ben's family, see who he is around them. They're friendly. Laid-back. Despite the circumstances of my arrival, his mom isn't overtly sizing me up as a potential love interest for her son. She doesn't seem like that kind of mom, anyway. Maybe it's her age, since she had Ben so young. She talks to her kids like friends and equals, with no attempt at asserting authority.

When I open the bathroom door I hear Lisa: "When should we do the financial aid paperwork?"

"Another night," he says. "Soon, I promise."

"I don't know how to answer the child support question. And do you have a copy of my tax return? Because I can't find it anywhere."

"I have a copy. I'll look at whatever you need help with before I leave for New York."

I clear my throat before walking back into the room.

"Annie, I didn't know whether to clear your plate. Are you done with your food?" Lisa asks.

"I can get it," I say, and bring it to the kitchen.

"Having a good time?" Ben appears behind me with the last of the dishes as I'm scraping my plate into the trash. He touches my lower back as he passes me on his way to the dishwasher, the lightest brush of his hand, and my entire body lights up like a neon sign.

After Lisa blows out the candles and Ben passes around pieces of the cake Natalie baked, the conversation turns to Natalie's college plans.

"I'm still trying to figure out where to go if the gymnastics program gets cut," she says, picking off a blue sprinkle and frowning at it. "Ardwyn was by far the best school that recruited me. And my favorite. I think I'm just going to hope for the best for now."

"Natalie and Ben are different," Lisa explains. "Ben always knew what he wanted to study, always had a plan. Nat isn't like that."

"I don't even know what I want to major in," Natalie says. "Sometimes I think history and then sometimes I think political science and, I don't know, what about business? It stresses me out because once I pick one, all the other options go away. And what if I pick wrong?"

"You probably will pick wrong at some point," I say. "I've picked wrong a bunch of times. Having a brother like yours might make you think it's not normal, but trust me, it is."

"Yeah?"

"Even after college. In school I had a job working in basketball, which was exactly what I thought I wanted to do." I chance a look at Ben. He's watching me with a circumspect expression. "It didn't work out. So after graduation I got an unpaid internship working for a local news station. But there was no way it was going to turn into something paid. I did another internship in Boston, and then I went back to New Jersey and worked a bunch of different places. A company that made garage storage systems, a credit union, an appliance company. It's normal to bounce around, although I don't recommend doing it as much as I did. And if you don't like the first thing you do, or the second, that's okay."

"You never even tried to get another job in basketball after you left here?" Ben asks, puzzled. "I didn't know that."

"Natalie, don't forget, Ben had Coach Maynard to guide him every step of the way, which was lucky," Lisa says. I push frosting around my plate, piling it all together and then spreading it into a flat layer. "Not everyone has a mentor like that. Such a wonderful man."

"I hope he has a spot for you someday so I can visit you in Arizona," Natalie says. "I've never seen a cactus in real life."

A bitter taste floods my mouth, and I fix my gaze on my plate. Ben pushes his chair back and clears his throat. "Should we do presents?"

"And then we're watching *Married at First Sight*," Lisa declares, adjusting her tiara. "Birthday girl's choice, and I don't want any complaints."

That's my cue. Intruding on dinner was bad enough, but squeezing onto the couch for gifts and family TV time surpasses the permissible limits of awkwardness. I'm never going to hear the end of this from Ben as it is, and now I need an entirely new plan for making my move. Ideally one that doesn't involve a cousin's baby's christening or a grandparent's funeral.

After making my excuses, I pet Sasha one last time and cross the room to fetch my coat from the armchair in the corner. I don't notice Ben trailing behind me until he grabs the back of my dress by the waistband and gives it a gentle tug. "I'll walk you to your car," he murmurs into my ear.

My pulse quickens, and anticipation builds low in my abdomen.

I pause by the stairs to say goodbye to Lisa and Natalie, so Ben walks down first. As I follow him, we don't speak. Instead I think about his hand on my hip the night we fought for his phone, and his fingertips on my back tonight in the kitchen. About him handling Natalie's financial aid paperwork. About the way his bedroom smelled when I walked past it on the way to the bathroom: nothing fancy, just clean laundry and his usual soap.

It's my favorite smell these days. It's been my favorite smell for longer than I'd like to admit.

Ben opens the door to the bracing night air. One small light glows on the porch, illuminating his messy hair and catching his face in side profile. His jaw is tense. He can't be mad I came here tonight, can he? My palms are starting to sweat, so I rub them on my coat. "I'm over there," I say, nodding toward my car, parked in front of the house next door.

He doesn't head for the car, though. He turns abruptly and now I can see his whole face, his dark eyes, and *oh,* he's not mad. The way he's looking at me, an unadulterated *I want,* the first time he's ever looked at me openly that way—well. It's rare and powerful, that kind of look.

His fingertips catch my waist and he backs me slowly against the door, his mouth grazing my cheekbone. The world tips over and I grab him by the shoulders, dragging him down toward me. The force of my reaction makes him stumble, but then he's holding me steady and our mouths connect.

We spent some time joking about kissing, but holy hell, there is nothing funny about this kiss. It's frantic and intense, all messy lips and swooping tongues and hot, unsteady breaths. He ducks his head to kiss my jaw and pulls aside the fussy bow at the collar of my dress. My head does not fall off, but it feels like it might when his stubble scrapes my neck. "Oh," I gasp, a little surprised at the effect it has on me. I dig my nails into his firm shoulders and our mouths meet again, deeper and more thorough this time. He tastes faintly of Funfetti.

My voice is faint when we break apart again. "I was supposed to sweep you off your feet. Now that's twice you've made a move and none for me."

"Numbers aren't real, Radford," he says, out of breath. He presses his lips to my temple. "Besides, the second we were alone I couldn't think straight."

I feel slightly drunk on the walk to the car even though I haven't had any alcohol. We kiss again on the street, and he makes a rumbling sound into the thin skin of my collarbone as he pulls me close, close enough for me to feel his phone vibrate in his pocket.

It isn't until after I slide into the driver's seat with my head spinning, and get a solid night of sleep, and walk into work the following morning with a sickeningly perky bounce in my step, that he enters my office with a sheepish smile and shows me the message that made his phone buzz.

Natalie: asshat your blinds are open and this is NOT the show mom and I are trying to watch!!!

NINETEEN

A STILETTO POKES OUT FROM FOLDS OF PALM-PRINT silk and finds the ground.

"Here we go," Eric says, rubbing his hands together. There have already been two proposals, both of which were accepted. But Jasmine won the fan vote, Logan won the contestant vote, and Brianne won the most challenges, so the outcome of their love triangle will determine who wins the money.

Or something. I'm still not exactly sure how this show works.

Everyone leans toward the television. The lights are off for once, to enhance the atmosphere. The camera pans up, revealing a woman with short hair. Brianne. A mix of groans and cheers rings out.

"Damn," I say. "He's making a big mistake."

Ben looks up at me from his spot on the floor with a self-satisfied smirk. "And this means I'm going to beat you."

"I'm sorry, I didn't hear what you said. I'm busy watching the show," I say, pretending to be transfixed by Logan's breakup speech to Brianne, which mostly involves a lot of talking about how difficult the decision was for him. I kick Ben lightly and he catches my foot, rubbing the side of my ankle with his thumb.

He continues to do this through the rest of the speech, and Brianne's tearful departure, and Jasmine's arrival in a coral jumpsuit. No one notices. Their eyes are suctioned to the screen.

"Jasmine," Logan says, his forehead slick with sweat, his cheeks red. The lack of shade is not doing him any favors. "I sent Brianne home because she and I aren't right for each other."

Jasmine smiles, a display of physical perfection.

"But—and it's so hard for me to say this—you and I aren't right for each other either."

A collective gasp sucks all the oxygen out of the room. Cassie brings her fingertips to her temples. Eric's jaw is hanging. I dig my nails into Ben's shoulder. Our rapt attention dissolves into debate. Why did he do that? Is he allowed to do that? And who wins the money now?

"Guess this means I beat you after all," I gloat to Ben after the final points are tallied.

On the walk home, he kisses me under streetlights and then again in front of my building. He doesn't ask to come up. He's letting me take the lead, thanks to my initial skittishness. I don't invite him in either. There's been a fair amount of kissing the past few days, but like tonight, all of it has occurred outdoors and in a vertical fashion. It's enough, or at least that's what I keep telling myself. Obviously, I want more. But I want more the same way I used to want another drink at the bar at one in the morning. More isn't always better.

I can't allow this thing to pick up too much speed, or I won't be able to control it. If we keep doing this and only this, no one will get hurt.

"Okay," he says, detaching his mouth from mine before burying his face in my hair. "I better go, before—"

I skim my teeth along his earlobe. What? It's right there, I can't help it.

He chokes out a muffled, frustrated laugh. "Radford. What are you doing to me?"

I duck under his arm and step away. "See you tomorrow!"

- - - - - - - - - - - -

THE NEXT DAY I'm in the weight room, weaving my way through the jungle gym maze of machinery, past the long dumbbell rack toward the treadmills at the back. I find JGE where I expect him, jogging at a modest pace on the last machine in the corner.

"Mind if I film for a minute?" I ask, raising my camera. "I'm doing a 'day in the life of Ardwyn basketball' thing."

"No problem." He's not winded at all. Running before a road trip is part of his routine because his legs get restless on the bus, and we leave tonight for the conference tournament in New York.

"What about me?"

I turn around to find Quincy on the floor, stretching out one long leg and grasping his shoe. "I already got you this morning."

"Yeah, eating," he scoffs. "You get this guy running, and me stuffing my face?"

"You were showing the world what a nutritionist-approved breakfast for athletes looks like," I protest.

"I'm messing with you. I have to go shower anyway." Quincy hops to his feet. "Podcast club tonight?"

"Yup," JGE says from the treadmill.

"What's that about?" I ask after Quincy leaves.

"Quincy and I have been listening to podcasts and talking about them. Like a book club," he explains. "We did a whole series about leadership skills. For tonight, we listened to this fascinating deep dive into the NBA's collective bargaining agreement. He's trying to convince me to do this one about the history of Super Mario next. Not so substantive, but at least he's exploring his interests."

"That's great," I say. "He's doing well, don't you think?" Quincy has been seeing a sports psychologist since he came back from injury, learning how to tune out the hype and concentrate on basketball. I'm glad he's been connecting more with JGE too. He's got his head on straight, and his focus on long-term goals is a good counterpoint to all the voices urging Quincy to cash in as fast as possible.

After I get my shot of JGE, I leave the weight room and cut through the practice gym. It should be dark and empty, but instead there's a group of sweaty men milling around, sucking on water bottles. Eric is one of them.

"What are you doing here?" he asks, rubbing his face with a towel.

"I was filming in the weight room. The 'day in the life' video."

He spreads his arms out. Dark, wet rings saturate the underarms of his T-shirt. "Want to film us?"

I shudder. "You look like you need a shower. I'm trying to attract views, not scare people away."

"The Internet's loss." He shrugs, moseying off toward the locker room. "We just finished anyway. And I am going to shower."

I look around. There are a couple guys from the athletic department, an assistant football coach, and a few others I don't know. This is the usual pickup group that plays together every week. Which means—

"Hey," Ben says behind me.

I turn around and swallow hard. He's wearing gym shorts, his hair is the best kind of disaster, and he's shirtless and covered in a sheen of sweat. I've never seen this much of him. He has a former athlete's body, like a stick of butter that's barely softened, which is a compliment. No marble six-pack or anything, but strong and toned.

Unlike Eric, I would be glad to get this on camera, for purely selfish reasons. The idea of sharing this image with the Internet gives rise to an instinctive sense of possession. *Mine.*

"What are you doing?" I ask faintly. The answer is obvious, but I can't string together enough words to say anything intelligent.

He takes a sip from a bottle of Gatorade. "We wanted to get in a game before we leave for New York."

A bead of sweat runs down his neck and lands in the hollow at the base of his throat. My entire body is scorching hot. "I didn't know you played shirts versus skins."

His mouth curls into a smile. "Sorry to disappoint, but we

have pinnies." He holds up an old mesh practice jersey with peeling lettering.

"I'm not disappointed. I've seen all I need to see."

Something ignites in his eyes that makes my head feel heavy and woozy, like I'm swimming deep underwater. He holds the pinny to his heart. "I'm feeling a little objectified. Are you trying to objectify me?"

Not now. Maybe later. My eyes dart back and forth, trying to gauge whether anyone is paying attention to us. "In your dreams."

"Yeah," he says in a low voice.

"Yeah," I repeat. We stare at each other for what could be ten seconds or ten minutes, until one of the other guys yells to Ben from across the gym to ask if he's ready to go.

Ben breaks eye contact. "Yeah, one sec," he responds. "Gotta run."

"Goodbye, then," I say to his chest with a forlorn sigh.

He laughs and scrubs his hair with one hand.

"Hey, Callahan?" I call as he heads for the exit, pulling a sweatshirt out of his bag. "You should leave your hair like that all the time."

- - - - - - - - - - - -

A CONVOY OF buses ferries the team to a hotel in Midtown. We're technically "in New York," but we're shuttling back and forth between the hotel for meals and sleep and Madison Square Garden for practice and media events, and the only time I stand under the weak blue March sky is when I find fifteen minutes for a brief escape to pick up coffee.

A ninety-four-by-fifty-foot basketball court stands between Ben and me everywhere we go. When we're at the arena, we're both working. Sometimes he's there and I'm back at the hotel, editing in a conference room reserved for the media team.

Everyone sits down to eat together for breakfast and dinner—the signature Ardwyn Family way—but we congregate with our own departments, so Ben is across the room. Something in my body pings his location at all times, so I know when he's standing at the buffet or sitting at his table. The media team is traveling with us for the rest of the season, so I'm sharing a room with Jess. Ben is stuck with Kyle, like always. The most we get is a few clandestine kisses behind a giant potted palm in a quiet corner of the lobby.

Working on-site during a tournament is different from working in the office. At home the pace isn't so brutal, and I know what's on the schedule next. There's planning involved. But here, there are no days off between games, so it's a constant scramble. We win our first game on Thursday, but have to wait until almost midnight to learn who we'll be playing on Friday. Then on Friday, we play the late game, giving us less than twenty-four hours' rest before Saturday's finals.

It's exhausting but freeing, in a way. I sit down at the table in the windowless conference room, and one part of my brain turns off and another part turns on. Hours later I emerge as if from a cave, with a finished product I don't quite remember making.

That's why when Cassie shows up on Saturday morning, I'm surprised.

"You're early," I say, tearing my eyes from the screen.

Cassie looks perplexed. "I'm an hour late. It's eleven thirty."

"No way." I check the time. Wasn't it just six in the morning? There's a crumpled ball of tinfoil next to me. Right, at some point Ben brought me a bagel. I thought that was a dream, but apparently not. Wasn't Taylor just in here with her laptop? Or was that three hours ago?

"You look like you need sustenance," Cassie says. She's right. The bagel was a lifetime ago. The video is done anyway. I played with sound in this one; it's all heavy bass and menacing synths, and I tried to sync the punchiest parts of the music with visuals of lockers slamming shut, our cheerleaders' crisp arm movements, and a particularly epic blocked shot. I want people to *feel* the intensity of this one, the way it feels more intense for the team now that the postseason is here. For the last hour, I've been watching it back and tinkering with little details. At this point, I can't make it better but can definitely make it worse, so I send it to Taylor and stretch my arms above my head.

We pick up smoothies and set off on a walk. There's not enough time to go far, so we stay in Midtown and wind our way through the streets around Rockefeller Center, past tourists taking photos and shoppers scanning window displays insisting that SPRING IS HERE! Most days in March, the daffodil-printed dresses and pastel-colored chocolate boxes behind the glass would be lies, but today is one of those warm, sunny days when Mother Nature throws us a bone to tide us over until the real end of winter.

"How's work?" I ask, shrugging off my coat and tying it around my waist.

Cassie takes a long sip of her smoothie. "That's why I was late. The managing partner asked me to join the DEI committee and my first meeting is on Monday, so I was prepping some stuff."

My heart sinks. This is the opposite of what Cassie was supposed to be doing. "You joined a new committee? What happened to saying no?"

She winces. "I know, but it's important. How could I say no to promoting diversity within the firm? I did tell him something has to give in another area in order for me to do this."

I make an effort not to sound too skeptical. "And what did he say?"

"He said we'd figure it out." She sees the look on my face and sighs. "I know. I know that means nothing."

We walk in silence for a block, past big glass office buildings and a chain steakhouse, until Cassie says, "I'm thinking of leaving and starting my own practice."

"Seriously?" I stop dead in the middle of the sidewalk and have to apologize to the people behind us. "That's amazing!"

Cassie shrugs, trying to downplay it, but her smile is hopeful. "It's going to take me a while to figure out the details. But I know I'd be able to handle cases on my own. And this way I can manage my own workload."

"You don't have to convince me. I'm already in full support."

"I just feel guilty. The partners I work with have invested a lot in my career development. I think they'll be shocked."

"You can't think about that. You have to put yourself first."

Cassie's mouth pinches. "I know, but it's not that simple. I've worked at my firm forever. I'm close to these people."

I make a *hmm* sound. I don't know what to say. All of this used to seem simple. I do believe Cassie should put herself ahead of her law firm, but I also used to believe in keeping my distance from my colleagues and not getting emotionally attached to work.

A stream of people exits the subway, and Cassie maneuvers around them. "What about you? What's new?"

I take a deep breath. It's become exhausting, keeping quiet about this thing that occupies so much of my thoughts. Also, Ben and I aren't being sneaky enough. Potted plants don't provide great cover. Someone is going to see something, if they haven't already, and Cassie needs to hear it from me.

I stir my smoothie with the straw. "Promise you won't freak out."

A look of dread crosses Cassie's face. "What is it?"

"It's not a big deal, I swear."

"Okay, so tell me."

"Something . . . is happening . . . between Ben and me."

"Something?" Now Cassie is the one stopping in the middle of the sidewalk. "Oh. Oh, Annie."

Her eyes are so wide I can see straight into her brain, where two trains of thought are at war. One side says *I think your wedding dress should be a sheath with a low back* and *Let's go on weekly double dates for the rest of our lives.* The other side knows what all my relationships since Oliver have been like: brief, nonserious, and underwhelming.

"He's pretty great," I say.

"Yeah." She nods vigorously. "Yeah, of course he is. On one hand, it makes complete sense. You guys complement each other. But on the other hand, I don't want to see either of you get hurt. He's different from anyone else you've ever dated. More . . . sincere."

"We're not dating," I say reflexively. "It's casual. It can't become more than that."

Cassie steers me off the sidewalk toward a large fountain at the base of a skyscraper. We sit on the edge, surrounded by office workers on their lunch breaks. "Tell me why," she says, "because to me this sounds like you self-sabotaging."

I give her a sharp look. "I'm not self-sabotaging. I'm realistic. One of us is probably about to get laid off, and that's going to cause a lot of resentment."

"Not if you care about each other."

I barrel on. "And it means one of us will probably be moving away."

"That's not ideal, but it doesn't automatically mean—"

"And whether it's him or me, at some point in the next few years, guess where he's planning to go coach? Arizona Tech."

Cassie stops, and her shoulders slump. "Oh, goodness." She studies my face. "You haven't told him, then."

I squint, watching the cars stuck in traffic. "Nope. I think I'm going to, though. After the season is over."

"*Wow.* You must really like him."

"Sure," I concede. "But I'm not going to tell him as a way of, like, furthering our relationship. I'm going to tell him because he's a good friend—"

Cassie rears back. "Good friend? Get out of here."

"—who is probably going to be working and living somewhere different than me no matter what, which is good and fine, and I'm not about to have a *good friend* going to work at Arizona Fucking Tech. That's all." I shake my head. "Basketball season is . . . all-consuming. When I'm in it, it becomes my whole world. That's the best thing about it, but it's also the most dangerous. I spend all day in this magical bubble with a hot guy, so is it any surprise that we want to make out with each other sometimes? Winning makes people horny. That's just science. When it's over and we're not working together anymore, we'll be friends."

I rise to my feet. Ominous rainclouds are rolling in, and I'm aching for a power nap before tonight's game.

A skeptical expression crosses Cassie's face, but she can't argue with the facts. Her bottom lip pokes out. "It makes me sad if you guys are a good match and this is all you get."

"This" gets one step closer to ending that night, when we lose a tight one in the tournament finals. We've beaten Saint Mark's twice this season, but they play a tough, physical game, and our guys are exhausted.

There's no time to reflect, because March Madness is here. It's time to find out if we can pull off the near-impossible.

TWENTY

"WHY AREN'T YOU WEARING THE SHIRT?"

Donna stands in front of me, chin jutting, gesturing at my torso with one scalpel-like fingernail. Damn. She must've sensed me violating the rules from across the room, like a shark smelling a paper cut.

I attempt a wide-eyed look of spacey innocence. "I lost it."

Donna turns her attention to my bag on the floor. A puddle of blue cotton spills out the top.

"It doesn't fit," I try.

"We have extras in every size."

"I'm allergic to cotton. I'm too cold for short sleeves. This is my lucky sweater?"

Donna skewers me with a ferocious stare.

I groan. "I'm the one behind the camera. No one will see that I'm not wearing the shirt."

"That's a crock of shit. You're not behind the other camera." Donna points.

I don't have to look. Donna is right. It's Selection Sunday, and in twenty minutes the championship seedings and matchups will be announced live on television. The network likes to show the reactions of a handful of teams, and this is Ardwyn's lucky year. There's a camera bigger and fancier than mine twenty feet away.

It's a good thing. The athletes get the attention they deserve, and more eyes on them means more money in the bank.

Somebody has decided that everyone at the watch party—the team and staff, their families, the university bigwigs—needs to wear the same blue T-shirt with the school logo. They've set up chairs and a projector in the lobby of the Church, and boosters sit at cocktail tables with white tablecloths on the mezzanine above. A ceiling-scraping DNA double helix of balloons flanks each side of the double doors. The only people exempt from the T-shirt requirement are the cheerleaders, who are in uniform. Even the mascot is wearing a custom-sized version.

For the record, I am sort of dressed on-theme. My jeans are blue enough to count, and my cream sweater has gray varsity stripes on the sleeves. I've made it through this entire season without wearing team gear, and I hadn't intended to break the streak now. But if Donna murders me, I'll never get to eat one of the hot pretzels from the table in the back, so I pass my camera to Jess and head to the bathroom to change.

I'm queasy, looking at the shirt while I'm locked in the stall. I used to own a ton of Ardwyn clothing. The first week of senior year, I lived in a T-shirt like this one, only older and rattier. Oliver had dumped me (for the first time) a few days before, and I spent most of that week marathoning *Black Mirror*, lying on the futon with a cup of sangria on the floor next to me, drinking from a swirly straw I got at the dollar store. I had it angled just right, so I could reach my drink without lifting my head. I was wallowing, and it was ugly.

One night Cassie and my other roommates dragged me out to a bar in Philly. It was super swanky, with velvet booths and dim lighting and bronze wallpaper. A bar for grown-ups.

We had each other and fancy cocktails, and at first it was fun, but then I got drunk and weepy. I fell off my barstool, and the bartender kept trying to give me water. I had deleted Oliver's number from my phone, so I was trying to type it from memory, even though I couldn't see straight, while my friends figured out how to get me home. They didn't think I'd be able to handle the train, and Cassie was worried I'd puke in a cab. And then Maynard just . . . appeared.

He'd been having dinner with friends in the other room and saw us at the bar. It was obvious I was a mess, so he offered us a ride home. Apparently, my response was, "Do you have a puke bucket?" I was too drunk to be embarrassed. Most of the ride was a blur of Cassie trying to make polite conversation and Maynard playing an O.A.R. album. I had to pee badly the whole way.

At one point I said, "Boys suck." He was nice about it. He said something that seemed fatherly, something like, "They do, they're boneheads. Whoever he is, he doesn't deserve you."

That's all that happened that night. But it feels like that's where it started. Maybe I'm wrong, maybe it would've happened anyway. I don't know.

Pushing aside my unease, I remove my sweater and slip

the shirt over my head. As I exit the bathroom I studiously avoid looking at my reflection in the mirror.

I make it back in time to film Coach Thomas addressing the crowd. Jess is shooting on her phone, and Taylor is posting the best clips right away.

"Get a shot of those kids dancing with Gallimore," Taylor says after the speech.

"I've got it under control," Jess replies.

Taylor cranes her neck. "Oh my god, they brought in Miss Mary." Miss Mary is a one-hundred-year-old fan who attends every home game. "She's talking to Coach Thomas! She brought him a scarf in our colors! It looks hand-knit! Jess, get over there. *Jess!*"

Jess sighs. She stands up, takes her time re-tucking her T-shirt, and crosses the room.

"Did you get it?" Taylor asks when she returns.

Jess taps on her phone. "Relax, I—oops, it didn't record."

"What?" Taylor screeches. A vein bulges on her forehead. She wraps her own ponytail around her fist tightly. "Were you distracted by Maura staring at you? Because she's being extremely unprofessional and she treated you terribly."

Interesting. I scan the crowd for Maura, the assistant cheerleading coach and Jess's ex.

"Easy. I'm messing with you." Jess flashes her phone screen at her. "I got it. I wish you could've seen your face." She shakes her head. "Your freckles are ridiculous when your face turns red."

Taylor's mouth opens and closes.

Very interesting.

I check the time. The broadcast should start any minute. Taylor buries herself in her laptop while Jess scrolls through

Instagram. I spot Cassie, seated at a table with the other coaches' wives and their kids. Williams's wife is next to her, taking a photo of him with their sons. Surprisingly, she is an absolute delight, friendly to everyone and so perky she's practically carbonated.

"This is hilarious," Jess says, forcing me to stop leaning sideways in an attempt to catch a glimpse of Williams smiling for the photo. "There's a whole thread of comments on our last video asking who the hot guy with the wild hair is on the bench."

"What?" I snap a little too loudly. Ben is sitting next to Eric, talking and making animated gestures toward his tablet. In New York he gave up his Work Hair for good and started wearing it unstyled, the way I like it, even during games. I thought it was cute, that he listened to what I said. But now I've sicced the horny people of the Internet on him? The price may be too steep. "Let me see that."

Jess leans away from me, still reading. "'Sex on a stick,' one of them says!"

"We should delete those comments." I turn to Taylor for help. "That's not appropriate. Think of the children."

The clock on the projector screen hits zero, cutting off all conversation. A hush descends on the crowd.

The South region is announced first, and our name isn't called. The East region is up next.

"The number four seed in the East region is the Ardwyn Tigers. And they'll be facing off against the thirteen-seed Monmouth Hawks, champions of the Colonial Athletic Association."

I knew it was coming, but it still delivers an electric shiver all the way down my spine.

The congregation rises, possessed by one spirit. People cheer, pom-poms shimmy, more balloons drop from the heavens. Coach Thomas stands off to the side, letting the athletes savor the spotlight. All he does is nod once. In the words of JJ Jones: "That dude is so chill he'll give you brain freeze."

The players have thirty minutes to celebrate, and then they'll be whisked off to learn about their opponent. I make my way through the crowd with my camera. I catch JGE squeezing his mother, lifting her off the ground as her feet wiggle. When he puts her down, he reaches out to me for a fist bump. Gallimore and Andreatti hit one of the big blue balloons back and forth like a volleyball, arms swooping and wrists flicking. When they spot me, they bat it at me and shout my name in unison. Quincy makes the rounds, high-fiving all the little kids, meeting the looks of wonder on their upturned faces with a joyful grin from above. And when he stops in front of me, he wraps his arms around me in a big hug.

When I film, they're supposed to pretend I'm not here. I'm going to have to do a lot of editing.

Meanwhile, Ben hunches over his tablet, shutting out the world. I don't have to see his screen to know what he's doing. He probably pulled up Monmouth's stats the second the announcer uttered their name, trying to see how much of their code he can crack before everybody sits down in the film room.

I'm multitasking, one eye on the camera and the chaos, the other on the rest of the bracket still being populated on the big screen. There's one other name I'm waiting to hear. Waiting to see it filled in on one of the sixty-four lines, waiting to find out how far it is from Ardwyn's, how long and how much it would take for the two to meet.

Finally it comes: "The number one seed in the West? The Rattlers of Arizona Tech." I whip my head around. The West. The opposite side of the bracket. The only way we'll play Maynard's team is if we both make the finals. It's only then I notice the tension in my shoulders, which are somewhere up near my ears. My body relaxes like one of those encapsulated toys that unfurls when you drop it in water.

I lower the camera. I have what I need. Ben looks at me with an indecipherable expression, and I smile at him. I squeeze through the masses to the back of the room, but the pretzel tray is already empty. Damn.

On the way back I run into Verona and Lufton, in the middle of a debate about the competence of the selection committee, and they pause to ask my opinion. Then Eric grabs Quincy and me so Cassie can take a photo of us together. Eric wants to send it to Mom.

"Why do you look weird? Are you sick?" Eric squints at his phone, looking at the photo.

I have no idea what he's talking about. Maybe my hair is flat? When I lean over to look, my first impression is that it's my head on someone else's body. "Oh." I laugh. "I never wear blue. It's not my color."

A hand touches my waist. "You always look good," Ben says in my ear. He pulls me in for a quick hug, the kind nobody will question tonight unless they're already suspicious. Cassie clocks it but doesn't say a word.

"For me?" Eric asks, pointing at Ben's hand.

He's holding a soft pretzel. "Absolutely not," he says, and hands it to me.

Be still my heart.

"I'm heading upstairs," he tells me.

"You have fifteen more minutes to party," I tease. I'm surprised he's lasted this long.

"Come say goodbye before you leave," he says, giving me an extremely unprofessional look, and strides off.

The party stretches on long after the team goes upstairs. Everyone is excited and loose and silly. The people with the checkbooks like to hang, drinking serviceable wine from the ticket booth masquerading as a bar. I sit at a table with Cassie and Taylor and Jess, and other people who come and go. Williams's wife wanders by, tipsy, and tells a story about the time her husband caught their oldest son sneaking out of the house. She has me in tears.

"And to top it all off," she says, gesticulating with one hand, "since he climbed out the window, every time we dropped him off or picked him up somewhere for the next month, Travis made him use the car window to get in and out. Even when his friends were watching!"

This is a perfect night, the kind you miss before it's over. There's a lot to take in. I'm brimming with it all, like a plant gorged on sunlight: elation and relief and an unexpected sentimentality. I've had nights like this before. I've had nights like this before in this building. But those are wrecked in my mind and this one is solid and warm, like bread tucked fresh into a crisp paper bag.

I made an assumption when I came back here. I convinced myself this job was going to be as shitty as any other, and three years here would be like a punishment. That I didn't lose anything valuable by leaving here the first time.

But it's not as shitty as every other job. The institution of

Ardwyn University, my employer—I'm indifferent about that, after everything I went through. But the work, and the people? They don't suck at all. In fact, they're great.

I've spent the last eight years steadfastly choosing jobs that did suck over this. I lost eight good years by leaving. Maynard took them from me.

I don't know what to do with this realization. I'd like to say Dad would have the perfect advice if he were here, but it's not true. This was the one subject area where he struggled to understand what I needed. He tried, but he couldn't comprehend why I didn't lick my wounds and bounce back stronger, like a player after an injury. "Try again somewhere else," he urged me for years. "Don't let your talent go to waste." I felt like a failure for not being strong enough. I think he felt like a failure for not protecting me, for introducing me to this industry, for not knowing Maynard's true nature despite being well-connected. Eventually, we stopped talking about it.

Tonight isn't for reflecting on painful things, though. Tonight is for celebrating.

Eventually people say their goodbyes, and the few conversations still going rattle in the big empty room. Cassie slips away to head home, but the rest of the group decides to head to a bar. I run upstairs to leave Ben a note telling him I'm gone. I could text him, but I want to include a drawing of Williams in the driver's seat while his son's legs hang out the car window.

It must be later than I thought, because Ben is back at his desk, not at the team meeting. He's in deep concentration, working his bottom lip between his teeth. I wait a moment— yup, there goes the tongue, sticking out of the corner of his mouth. An internal pom-pom shakes in my stomach.

"Hey," I say breathlessly, hanging onto either side of the doorframe and leaning into the room.

"Hey," he repeats. "Are you drunk?"

"What? No. Why?"

He shakes his head. "You just look really happy."

I am really happy. Being here makes me happy. Being with you makes me happy.

"Tell me about the meeting," I say.

He's almost vibrating as it spills out of him: his analysis so far and the strategies they're putting together. The defensive matchups, the other team's playing style. He's completely unself-conscious as he rambles on. His hair is everywhere, one piece arcing over his forehead, and his face shines.

"Everything we've worked for is happening," he says. "Tonight is a good night."

It's how I feel too. And the longer I stand here, the fainter my plan of going to the bar with Taylor and Jess becomes in my mind. And what replaces it is this thought: The kissing is not enough.

It can't hurt, to celebrate together. We deserve this. At most, there are three weeks left. And there's his mouth, and his hair, and the way he looked at me earlier. The sweat in the hollow of his throat after his pickup game. That first kiss. I'm harboring so much tonight, everything I've absorbed, and I want to turn it outward. Toward him.

I pull my keys out of my bag. "Are you almost done working?"

"Yeah, I've got nothing left. I can't look at a screen anymore. I was going to see if you wanted me to walk you to your car. You heading out now?"

I fidget with the metal in my hand, prying the metal loops

of the key ring open with the tip of my thumbnail. "Yeah, I'm ready to go," I say. "Come home with me."

We exchange looks, asking questions and answering them wordlessly. His eyes do this hot hypnotic thing that grabs me by the solar plexus. And then he practically hurdles the desk, grabs my hand, and pulls me down the hall.

TWENTY-ONE

AT MY APARTMENT, I PACE FROM ROOM TO ROOM, trying to burn off the restless churning sensation in my stomach. I move my night guard from the bedside table to a bathroom drawer and stuff the explosion of dirty clothes back into my half-unpacked suitcase. I debate lighting a candle and decide against it. It's what I would ordinarily do when I get home, but he doesn't know that. He'll think I'm trying to set some type of mood, and I'm definitely not.

Light on in the living room, off in the bedroom, on in the green room. Or on in the bedroom too? No, off. This place could use a dimmer switch. I curse myself for leaving my nice table lamp at Kat's apartment.

Ben drove to his place to drop some things off or pick some things up—I honestly didn't pay much attention to what he said—giving me time to get home and get ready, or at least freak out.

My Ardwyn T-shirt is making me itch, so I whip it off, but

I don't know what to wear instead. I play musical chairs with my wardrobe, changing into and out of things until the buzzer rings, and I'm left with the thin tank top I wore underneath my clothes all day and a pair of cotton sleep shorts. There's not enough time to think about what this outfit says. He's here.

I buzz him in and hover by the door. A minute later he knocks, two quick raps. I fling the door open.

"Hey," he says, in a voice that's just for me. His smile is easy, but his eyes are like firewood, glowing hot and nearly crackling. He's changed too, into a soft black hoodie. Unlike me, however, he has the advantage of wearing pants. I tug my shorts down an inch to cover more of my thighs, which exposes a strip of my stomach, and then pull them back up.

"Want a tour?" I ask in a chirpy voice that doesn't sound like mine, setting off briskly down the hallway without checking to make sure he's following. "It'll only take five minutes."

"I'd love one," he says with breezy enthusiasm, as if it's the main reason he came over.

I walk him around the living room and the kitchen and point to the bathroom. It's the most unremarkable apartment ever to exist, so there's not much to say, but I show off my pictureless white walls and generic furniture with the enraptured focus of a tour guide at the Uffizi. Anything to avoid looking at him.

The bedroom is next. Why did I leave the light off again? He's right behind me as we enter the room, colliding with my back when I stop abruptly to step around the suitcase on the floor. I speed past the bed like the bogeyman is underneath.

"Wow," he says, awed, in the green room.

"This is the best part, obviously." My voice almost sounds normal, the ridiculous floor and goofy purple beanbag helping to slow my heart rate. "I always wonder if this used to be somebody's sex cave. Also, I'd like to introduce you to Mona Lisa Vito. We spend a lot of quality time together."

His laugh is relaxed. Contented. I wring my hands. "I guess it's only a three-minute tour," I say.

He's watching me carefully. "You seem nervous."

"Me? No."

He ambles over to the window, where the candles are shoved together in a jumble. "We can watch TV. Or go to sleep, if you want." He picks one up and sniffs it. "Or I can go, if you've changed your mind." Okay, his nonchalance is starting to grate.

"I'm not nervous. Maybe you're nervous," I say in a tone that belongs on the playground, snatching the candle from his hand and setting it back on the windowsill.

"I am a little nervous," he admits. And that's my absolute limit. This is supposed to be *fun*. It doesn't have some grand significance. Nobody should be nervous.

I pounce on him, throwing my arms around his neck. I kiss him hard, like I did the first time outside his apartment, moving my lips against his urgently, with quick passes of my tongue. And for a little while he matches me in a perfect rhythm, and it's so good, even though it doesn't settle me.

He pulls away and presses his forehead against mine. "Hey," he says, reaching up to take my shaking hands. "It's just me." And he takes my chaos and meets it with his own intent focus and transforms it into something better. *I've got you*, he says without words. When my teeth click against his, he soothes me with soft lips. When I retreat, searching his face, he murmurs, "Come here," in a hoarse voice and reassures me with a dizzying bite of my bottom lip. He holds the side of my face with his hand, his thumb brushing my cheek, and I press closer, our lips barely grazing each other.

No. These are all snapshots from the wrong mood board. Tonight is supposed to be celebratory. We're supposed to be flooded with the elixir of athletic triumph, on a breakneck, hasty sexual victory lap. My legs should be around his waist and he should be pinning me against the wall. Something should be knocked off a table, smashing on the floor. There should be noisemakers, and sparklers crackling. It's not supposed to be deliberate and tender, with shuddering and whispers and protracted gazes.

I throw myself onto the beanbag and thread my hands together behind my head. It's so worn out and shapeless that when I lie back I'm almost flat on the floor. "Take off your shirt," I command.

He raises his eyebrows and his mouth does that slow, lazy curl up at the corners.

I flick my hand upward, urging him on. "Come on. I'm a visual person."

He slides his T-shirt over his head and my heart almost gives out. I saw this very torso less than a week ago, but the effect is more powerful now that I'm about to touch it.

"Good, me too," I say breathlessly, peeling off my tank top and chucking it across the room. His eyes skate over my plain black bra, and his Adam's apple bobs like it's genuflecting.

He's watching me with a perceptive look like he's about to say something, and he sees my bravado and what's underneath, so I reach for him. Then I remember: This chair is burdened with history. Shane Kowalski, junior prom, a lot of fumbling and poking in not quite the right places. "No!" I say sharply, stopping in my tracks. "Wait."

"Okay," he says, bewildered.

I grab a throw blanket, spread it across the chair like a bedsheet, and tug him down on top of me. It's an awkward position, lying together on this old lump of beans, but he gives in to my chosen vibe. My bra comes off and his hands and lips are there. My mouth goes slack, and he presses up against my thigh and it's getting harder to think straight, and I love Mona Lisa but I don't want to be making eye contact with her right now, so I look away from the wall and shift positions. The floor is hard underneath me, my ass and his weight compressing the chair. "It keeps deflating," I say.

He drags himself upward, his hair tickling my throat, and meets my eyes. "Not the words I imagined you saying when I fantasized about this."

I yank him down to press his mouth against mine again, but he's smiling so my lips connect with his teeth.

"I meant the chair," I say, but he's already pulling me up. "You fantasized about this?"

He drags his knuckle across the bare skin above the waistband of my shorts. I make a throaty noise and close my eyes.

"Bed?" he suggests.

"Floor," I counter.

He follows me down, lying over me. I pull on his belt loops until his hips press against mine, his knees between my legs. He grabs my waist tightly as I touch the fly of his pants. "Okay?" I ask.

He squeezes me tighter and makes an affirmative noise.

I try to undo the button but my hands aren't working properly. "Can you?" I ask, and he helps me work his pants off. I wrap my ankles around the backs of his legs and he slides his hands around to grip my ass. A groan escapes his mouth, and he kisses me thoroughly. There's so little between us now, just my threadbare shorts and our underwear, and the rhythm we find arching into each other is addictive. I can almost quiet my mind enough to do this with him for hours, maybe forever. Almost. It's just . . .

"Are you comfortable?" I whisper after several minutes.

"I don't think this floor is meant for kneeling," he says. "Tomorrow when I ask the trainer how to treat my turf burn, he's going to have a lot of questions."

"What are you going to tell him?" I press harder against him, rocking.

His lips part and his eyes flutter closed. "Who?"

"The trainer."

"Why are we talking about the trainer?"

I laugh at that. I don't recall ever laughing before while dry-humping, and I never would've thought it would be so nice, but it is, and he's laughing too.

He sits back on his heels abruptly, touching my ankle and brushing little circles around the bone on the outside with his thumb. "Hey. Are you sure you want this? All I want is to spend time with you."

He can tell I'm still nervous. Of course he can. The realization lands heavy on my chest like the palm of a reassuring hand, and the mood board slips away. "No," I say forcefully. I'm reluctant to talk about anything going on in my head, but it's imperative that he understand. "I want you so much— so much it scares me. Don't you want me?"

"Annie." His voice catches. "All I think about is how much I want you."

My throat isn't working. It's stopped up with something, possibly the chemicals they used to make this floor so green thirty years ago. They're probably illegal now. I finally manage to say, "All you think about? What about basketball?"

"What's basketball?"

"What about reality TV and standard deviations? What about Wawa subs?"

"Wawa *hoagies*," he says. "And no. Just you."

I reach out to pull him back toward me fiercely, but he catches my hand. He places the most delicate kiss on my palm, and then another on the inside of my wrist. I shiver.

"Let me?" he asks.

I nod. Okay. I haven't been fooling anyone but myself.

"I think about your mouth," he murmurs into my wrist. He releases my hand, leans in to whisper in my ear, his lips grazing my cheek. "Your body. This necklace." He dips his head and drags his teeth along the chain, the sensation overloading my circuits, my brain function flickering in and out. "Sometimes I catch myself staring right here, and I can't look away." He slides back up to my other ear. "I think about how much you make me laugh. I think about that terrifying look you get in your eyes when you're determined to get something you want."

"I want you," I say, dizzy.

"Yeah," he says. "Sometimes you look at me like that. And I can barely handle it. I'd give you anything you wanted when you look at me like that." He plants a hand on his knee and stands. "This room has never been, and never will be, anyone's sex cave." He nods at the doorway. "Bed."

The word shimmers in the air like the haze above hot pavement. "Bossy," I say.

"Bed, please," he amends.

"I liked it."

He squeezes my hips and presses a kiss to my shoulder as he follows me into the bedroom. I sit on the edge of the bed while he closes the door partway. His pants and shirt are in the green room, so he's in his boxer briefs. Most of his face is shadows, but I can make out his chest rising and falling and the intensity of his eyes on me. His mouth is red and wet, like he's been eating cherries. The perfect amount of light filters in from the green room, and at the optimal angle. I couldn't have lit the scene better myself.

"So beautiful," he says, which is exactly what I was thinking.

He sits next to me, takes my face in his hands, and kisses me once, softly. When he pulls away I let him guide me onto my back, and his hot eyes scrape me clean of all my armor. No worries about what my facial expression reveals about me, about what this tenderness means. Just me, melting into the mattress, and him.

He moves next to me, propping himself up on one elbow, the strong curve of his shoulder outlined in the dim light. With one hand he traces my body. Up my arm, leaving a trail of goose bumps in his wake. Across my collarbone, along my cheek and through my hair, his thumb stroking the base of my skull with the perfect amount of pressure. Down, skating across the underside of my breasts. Then he adds his mouth, leaving a trail of delicate kisses along the path from one hip bone to the other. Takes a detour to drop a single kiss on the freckle to the left of my belly button. He runs a hand lightly over my shorts and down my thigh, squeezes one knee gently and lifts it up, so my foot is flat on the bed. Shifting, he drops his mouth to the inside of my ankle and up my shin.

It's all gauzelike strokes from intent fingers and focused, worshipful kisses. His hands and lips are causing a chemical transformation of every inch of skin they touch. They must be. Electrons are moving, atoms shifting. New molecules form in the wake of his mouth, his fingertips. It's no longer the same old skin and maybe never will be again. Not after being treated as reverently as this.

Ben Callahan takes care of his people. I've known that for a while. And for the first time I'm realizing I might be one of them. A strange fluttering starts in my chest and expands outward, until it reaches my toes and leaves my head spinning.

He touches the hem of my shorts and studies my face. "Can I take these off?"

I'm practically a puddle at this point, but I manage to lift my hips. "Yes, please," I say in a scratchy voice, my throat full of anticipation.

My shorts and underwear come off and then his hand is between my legs. A greedy noise I don't recognize comes out of my mouth. My hand flies up to his shoulder and squeezes, my nails digging in.

He slides down my body, and my knees fall open. He looks up at me through his eyelashes and, well, it's a staggering image. This is why good lighting was invented. "Yeah?" he asks.

I nod, and his breath and the ghost of his stubble skim my thigh. My fingers slide into his hair and I drag the tips along his scalp. *Mine.* The word lights up in some primal part of my brain like marquee letters, travels down to my fingertips like an electric current.

And then his mouth is on me, and there are no words in my brain at all.

He's doing the most wonderfully obscene things in the sweetest way, erasing the entire concept of time from my blissfully blank mind. Minutes or hours or days pass—numbers aren't real—and it's all so overwhelming I grab at his shoulders, trying to pull him up, and rasp, "Ben, I need you here," and he obliges. He's there with me, his eyes soft, and all I want is to be as close to him as I can get.

This is not just for fun. I don't know what it is. But it's bigger than that.

"You sure?" he asks, running a finger across my bottom lip.

"So sure."

I help slide his boxer briefs off and then he's gone for a minute. It's like losing gravity. How quickly can you get addicted to the feeling of another person's body? A wrapper tears and then he's back, stroking my hair and kissing me. I direct him and he presses forward. The most perfect stretch overwhelms me, and we let out simultaneous shaky groans.

He whispers nice things about my body and the way I feel and that's all great, but the best part is when he says, "*Fuck, Annie*," because it's so not him. Take that, Father John. He presses his fingertips between us, against me. His motions get frantic and his skin is so hot and he's finally, finally starting to lose control.

That's what does it for me. "Ben." His name slips out and he brings his mouth down to mine. Not to kiss, neither of us can manage that. Instead he just inhales my panting breaths and that one final cry, like he's trying to consume what's happening to me. And that takes him over the edge too.

Afterward, we take turns using the bathroom and sprawl out limp on the bed, one of his legs tossed over mine. I push strands of sweaty hair off his face with one finger, and he strokes the spot on my neck reddened by the friction of his stubble on my skin.

"Your thighs are still shaking," he murmurs lazily.

"Your fault," I slur.

Ben has sex like he plays basketball, which is absurd but also makes complete sense. He was a point guard, so he's always been good at setting the tempo on the court. An excellent communicator. Vocal at the right times. He pays close attention to other players' body language, quickly discerning how to read them. He's a good teammate, selfless, patient, happy to make an assist rather than score himself. An excellent judge of when to attack the basket and when to step back and create space. Effective at creating pressure in passing lanes on defense—okay, maybe that one's not so relevant.

"Stay with me," he says, his voice low and sleepy.

"We're in my apartment. I don't plan on leaving."

He shakes his head. "That was not a complete thought. I'm not at my most coherent right now."

"You're welcome," I say.

He runs his thumb up and down the side of my neck. "Stay with me in the hotel. In Boston," he says, shy and eager at the same time. "One of Kyle's fraternity brothers lives there, so he's staying with him."

"Okay," I say.

"Yeah?"

I nod.

He pulls me in close and I rest my head on his chest. "You're incredible," he says.

There are a lot of things I want to tell him but they won't budge from my throat. I do my best, whispering into his skin. "The pervs on Instagram were right about you."

TWENTY-TWO

BITS OF THE CHARLES RIVER ARE VISIBLE THROUGH the window of the hotel room, but the main thing to see is the Zakim Bridge. Its cables and pylons rise like the great geometry lesson in the sky, like a supersized string instrument on steroids.

"Like two giant concrete Spider-Men shooting webs from their wrists. That's what I always used to think," I say, rolling over in bed. It's Wednesday, and we're in Boston. The first round of the tournament—tomorrow's game and, if we win, Saturday's game too—is down the street at the Garden.

The pulsing glow of the muted TV lights Ben's face. He closes one eye and lifts a strained brow. "I think I can see it. You have quite the imagination."

"I told you the other day, I'm a visual person."

He nods toward the window. "Did you live near here?"

"Across the river and west. In Cambridge." I often forget that this is a place I once lived, because it doesn't feel like home. In my memory that time is more like a series of scenes from a movie I remember, not my actual life. Long cold walks to the T with my headphones on, a drunken fight with Oliver outside a restaurant in Inman Square, an office where nerdy bros played pranks on one another. I can't summon the faces or names of any of those former coworkers.

Version 2.0 of my relationship with Oliver was all-consuming, sucking up all my energy so I had nothing left for anything else. When he wasn't with me, I was worrying about our relationship or missing him or analyzing his text messages. I began to fade out of my own life. I thought—so, so wrongly—that it was a sign, that if I spent so much time stressing and crying and he spent so much time sulking and withdrawing and then showing up at my door in the middle of the night, it meant the relationship was worth fighting for. Because we did fight over it, over and over and over again. I measured its value in quantity of emotion.

Version 1.0 of the relationship had been costly for me, and I couldn't bear the idea that it was all for nothing. Senior year, everything with Maynard, wouldn't have gone the way it did if our breakup hadn't wrecked me.

After the night Maynard drove me home from the bar, he started texting me. I have the screenshots saved in a Google Drive folder. Cassie was a lawyer-in-training even back then. "You don't have to do anything with them," she urged me months later, after I finally told her what happened. "But keep them, just in case."

I opened the folder for the first time the other day. The first few messages were things like **You doing okay? I'm always here if you need advice.** My reaction at the time was

Wow, he's such a great coach. Not just taking care of his players, but also checking in on *me* about parts of my life completely unrelated to basketball. I felt like he cared.

It changed so gradually. **I'm up late reviewing scouting reports. Please tell me you're out at the bars like a senior should be, not moping around over that guy?** Or: **After my first heartbreak I moved into the gym and didn't come out until I had abs that looked like they were drawn on with a marker. You do spin classes, right? If you want to come into the office later on Fridays to catch an extra class, go ahead.**

Each time he got more personal than the last, but not so much more that I could even point to what made it different. Nothing that seemed inappropriate, exactly. I didn't feel uncomfortable about it in the beginning. Not until October.

What are you dressed as for Halloween? he asked, at 11:07 P.M. He only ever messaged me at night. **You're a beautiful girl (I bet I sound old saying that) so I'm sure you look great no matter what. Don't forget to post pictures on Facebook so your ex can eat his heart out.**

Then, at two in the morning, when I was sitting on the living room floor with my friends eating chicken fingers, dressed as a bumblebee: **Will you send me a costume picture too?** And a minute later: **Are you dating anyone?**

I was wasted, but for the first time, an alarm went off in the back of my mind. Yet I told myself maybe it was a clumsy way of trying to play matchmaker, because he was always talking about his younger cousin from Maryland. Or maybe he was clueless about how his texts came across because he was older. Or he was trying to be cool and supportive but didn't know how. Telling someone they're beautiful doesn't have to be anything more than a neutral observation. Plus, what an obvious cliché—the college coach creeping on a student?

I know it wasn't my fault. But it's hard not to think I might've been able to keep his behavior from escalating if I had been thinking more clearly, if I hadn't been such a heart-broken wreck. That can never happen again. It's why I've only dated guys I'm certain will never breach my defenses. Guys who'll never cause me to lose control of myself, who will never turn me into a mess. Which often means choosing guys I don't like much.

Ben's not like the guys I normally date. But he's not like Oliver either. Being with him makes the rest of my life sharper, not blurrier. Maybe it's me. Maybe I'm mature enough now for something real, and I didn't realize it. Maybe it's the fact that I know there's an expiration date. Or maybe it's him, us, together.

I'm not going to dwell on this, not right now.

Sneaking into Ben's room undetected took a bit of spy craft. We're staying on different floors, and he's near the coaches. There was a hooded sweatshirt involved, and an empty manila folder with a ready excuse in case of emer-gency. He stood sentry in the doorway, peeking toward the elevators, and I looked around corners before speed-walking down the hall. Neither of us is all that worried, but it does add to the thrill.

My phone vibrates on the nightstand. I reach over to feel around for it. "It's my dad's friend Big Ed," I say. "All week he's been texting me everything he knows about Monmouth. A lot of their players are in-state, so he's coached against them."

"That's adorable. What's he saying?"

I read it. "'Greer's right-hand dribble is weak. Always prefers to drive left. Force him to go right.'"

"Hmm," Ben says thoughtfully. He falls silent. I assume he's thinking about basketball, but then he turns toward me. "What was he like?" he asks, propping himself up on one elbow. He rests his other arm on my waist, his fingertips tracing patterns on my lower back. He smells like his own soap, not the generic hotel stuff.

"My dad?"

His patient, discerning gaze is fixed on my face. His eyes look black in the weak light of the TV. I pause to consider all the ways I could answer this question.

"He had the best sense of humor," I start. "He always kept a straight face when he told a joke. If you didn't know him well, you'd wonder if he was being serious or not. You had to earn the ability to recognize his humor. But when he thought someone else was funny, he couldn't hide it—he'd laugh until his eyes watered. I loved that about him, that he broke for other people but not himself. He was a good listener. He had excellent taste in TV and movies and terrible taste in music. How can a person's favorite show be *Friday Night Lights* while his favorite musical group is the Bee Gees? It's unnatural."

Ben laughs and lifts the thin gold chain of my necklace. He runs it back and forth between his fingers, thinking. "You must miss him."

"So much," I say. "When I had to learn the states and their capitals in grammar school, he volunteered to teach me. This was a lifetime first. He never helped me with my homework. He came up with all these word associations using the mascots of each state school. And on top of memorizing the states, capitals, and mascots, he made me memorize which ones were good at basketball."

"Did it work?"

"Short-term? I did okay on the test. Long-term? I can tell you the University of Maine is the Black Bears, but I don't have a freaking clue what the capital is."

He smiles, a sweet, contemplative one, like he's imagining me as a kid. "So it was all basketball, all the time."

"Yes. For sure. He came to Career Day in fifth grade and brought everyone autographed cards from some of his former players who made it to the NBA. He missed my cousins' weddings because of his coaching obligations." I swallow. "Not just my cousins' weddings. I don't know why I said it like that. He missed a lot of my milestones too—holiday concerts and winter formal photos and honor roll breakfasts."

Ben tilts his head. "I'm sure that wasn't always easy for you."

I frown. "It was fine. I understood. I loved basketball too. In high school I started making videos for his team, so we spent a lot of time together."

"That's great," Ben says. "But it's okay if it wasn't always fine."

I shrug. "When I was a toddler, he brought me to a summer league game at the outdoor courts and left me there. Totally forgot I was with him, got swept up in a conversation with a friend of his, and they decided to go to another game. One of the refs had to lift me up and yell to him as he was pulling out of the parking lot, 'You forgot something!'"

I don't know why I'm telling him this. I don't even remember it happening. I've just heard the story a million times, a funny anecdote about his one-track mind.

Ben doesn't laugh. "You're allowed to remember everything," he says. "Even the parts that weren't good. You can miss him and love him and still wish certain things were different. It's not a betrayal to remember him as imperfect."

I huff out a laugh. "Yeah. I wish he were a little less dead, for example."

He covers his face with his hands, his shoulders shaking.

"Sometimes I wonder what our relationship would've been like if I hadn't been interested in basketball," I venture, rolling the corner of the sheet between my fingers. "Would he have made an effort to connect with me if I were obsessed with synchronized swimming or playing the oboe? I'm afraid he died disappointed in me. I gave up on the dream we both had for my future. I was working at an appliance company. He never knew I came back to Ardwyn."

"Annie," Ben says. "He wasn't disappointed in you."

"Please don't say anything nice," I plead. "I don't want to cry right now."

"He couldn't have been disappointed in you," he insists, pulling me close. He whispers in my ear: "You're an excellent free throw shooter."

I kick him lightly in the shin, even though it was the perfect thing to say. Turning from my side to my stomach, I nudge him down so he's lying on his back and tuck myself into his chest.

I know him pretty well by now. Well enough to read his face in the dark. But I don't know everything. There are some things I've wondered but hesitated to ask. "Tell me about your dad," I say.

His face doesn't change at all. He expected the question, maybe even wanted me to ask. I rake a reassuring hand through his hair.

He stares at the ceiling for a long time. I'll wait all night for him to be ready, if that's what he needs. In the near-quiet of the hotel, muffled voices float in from a nearby room over the footsteps and jostling sounds of somebody dragging a heavy suitcase down the hall. Finally, in a resigned voice, he says, "Not all parents have redeeming qualities."

It all spills out of him so calmly while he rubs the nape of my neck. The worst bedtime story anyone's ever told me.

"My parents started dating when my mom was a senior in high school," he begins. "My dad was a couple years older. They were together for about a year, and then she got pregnant. He stuck around until I was six months old and then . . ." He shakes his head. "He said he was going to stay with his brother in Raleigh for a bit, to see if it was a better fit. My mom thought he meant for all of us. She didn't realize he'd left us until a few months later.

"Eventually he did come back. It was like that for years, him bouncing in and out of our lives. Usually when he wore out his welcome somewhere else or got lonely. We were like a friend's couch he crashed on whenever he felt like it. We moved a lot because my mom had trouble paying the rent, the bills. It was hard for her to turn him away, especially when he had a job."

The shame of my old assumptions about him, that he was a spoiled brat who was used to having everything go his way, corrodes a hole in my lungs. "I'm sure it was hard for her," I say. "And it must've been confusing for you."

A minuscule nod. His hand drops a few inches, and he

kneads gentle circles around my shoulder blades with his knuckles. "I dreaded him coming around, because I spent the whole time waiting for him to leave again. Every day was like the last day of a vacation. When you can't enjoy yourself, because you know it's almost over? Each time he'd fixate on some father-son bonding activity that he'd talk about and talk about but never actually do with me. The zoo was a big one. Phillies games. One time it was building the Lego pirate ship. I swear, he saw a commercial for that thing with a dad and a kid, and he liked the idea of being that kind of parent. But he could never bring himself to sit down and put together all one thousand pieces with me. I learned early not to expect him to keep his promises."

I wrap my ankle around his. "What was it like when he was gone?"

"Rough on my mom. She sees the best in people, so it blindsided her every time. She tried so hard to act like everything was fine. I think she hoped I'd be less upset if she hid that she was upset, but it made it worse." He swallows audibly. "I was confused about why he was there one day and gone the next, and I had no framework for processing it. I thought since she wouldn't talk to me about it, it must've been something awful. And it must've had something to do with me."

When I was ten, Dad's team had a rough season. They lost so many games he almost got fired. I knew my parents were stressed, but nobody explained why. Tension filled the house like pollution. I convinced myself they were getting a divorce.

When adults refuse to talk, kids fill in the blanks with something scary. And a missing dad is a pretty big blank.

Ben continues. "Sometimes he'd be gone for weeks or months. Other times it was years. The last time, Mom got pregnant with Natalie. It's weird to think about it, but at that point she was the exact same age I am now. And she was responsible for two kids with no help."

I press my lips to his chest, feeling his heart beat against them.

"After that, I told her I didn't want him around. I made a PowerPoint presentation to plead my case."

A load-bearing wall in my chest cavity crumbles. "*No,*" I say, my head snapping up. "Ben." I tighten my arms around him. "Were there slide transitions?"

"Twelve-year-old me would never have expected a Power-Point to be taken seriously without slide transitions," he says. "Clip art too."

It's so him and so heartbreakingly vulnerable that I have to close my eyes. Ben learned too young that there are people who chip away at your limits to see how much room they can make for themselves. How much of you they can get without giving anything up. It's them or you. You have to choose. I had to learn this lesson too, but not until later.

"I don't know exactly what happened after that," he says. "My mom didn't tell me back then, and she either doesn't want to rehash it now or has blocked the details out of her memory. But I haven't seen or talked to my dad since."

I place a whisper of a kiss on his cheek. "Thank you for telling me," I say. "You don't know where he is?"

His chin pokes out. "I don't know and I don't care."

It explains a lot. The unwavering loyalty to the people he loves, because that's all he ever wanted, and he knows what it's like not to have it. The trust he places in the people who've given him loyalty in return. This is why he won't give up on Maynard. Maynard chose him, mentored him, took care of him. Did everything his father didn't.

My throat burns and I let out a shaky breath.

"Hey, I don't want to make you upset," he says, trying to turn my face up to his. I bury it in his chest instead. "We're all good now, and we have been for a long time. Though I sometimes feel bad for Natalie. Guilty. My mom and I know the alternative—him being around—is worse. She has to take us at our word on that."

I sit up straight. "No," I say with force. "You should not feel guilty. Your sister has you. And between you and your mom, that's all she needs."

He looks at me, his mouth rippling, turning down and then up into a faint smile. I've affected him, somehow. It can't be what I said, because it felt so inane.

We've spent several thousand hours of our lives together. Yet I'm just beginning to understand him. "I didn't actually know you at all in college," I say.

His hand catches my waist. "Do you know me now?"

I nod.

"Good." The faint smile again. "Do you think this ever could've happened back then?"

"Us?" I try to imagine it. Ben, the Disney prince, and me, the main character in a music video directed by an overdramatic teenager. "I wasn't adult enough to date an actual adult. I would've ruined it."

"I can't imagine it either. Which is wild because it feels so inevitable now. Even if it weren't for Hailey, I never would've been able to wrap my head around the possibility back then. You scared me. You were fearless and funny and confident and so smart. I wouldn't have known how to handle you."

I try to ignore how moved I am by the compliments. "You wouldn't have survived it. Cause of death: girlfriend picking a fight because we didn't fight enough. An actual thing I would've done at the time." My face ignites when I realize I used the word *girlfriend,* even though it was in the context of the eight-year-old relationship we never had. I'm sure he notices, but he lets it go.

Instead, he whispers, "I like you so much."

The words land like a Taylor Swift key change, and my heart grows a pair of wings. But my brain immediately hits the panic button. Like the sprinklers above us might start spraying at any second. My whole body does this wiggle like I've just felt a spider crawling down my back, and I cough.

I recover enough to take one of his hands. I turn it upright and trace the lines with my finger. "Ben," I say. "Please, can we not say things like that until the season is over?"

He looked so comfortable and open a minute ago, re-clined unself-consciously like someone in a painting who knows he's being studied and depicted on canvas but doesn't mind. Now he sits up against the headboard. "What do you mean?"

"We're in a fantasy world right now. This is a once-in-a-lifetime season. We're traveling nonstop, with nothing else except us and the best basketball this team has ever played. Right now we don't have to worry about anything outside our little snow globe. We've never gone to the grocery store together or spent an hour trying to decide what to have for dinner on the third boring Friday night in a row. We can pretend the budget cuts aren't coming, that things aren't about to change. It's not real. It's like *The Beach House*."

"I always knew I hated that show," he says. "Hm." It's a contemplative noise, and he goes silent, thinking. "Wait, so does that make me Logan? Is this the hammock room? There should be some melted chocolate somewhere around here . . ."

It coaxes a smile out of me.

He squeezes my knee. "It's like Italy, you mean, right? Oliver said nice things in the snow globe and then as soon as you went back to normal life, it didn't work out."

I nod, my mouth dry like paper.

"Your fear is, what? That I'll say nice things and you won't be able to believe me?"

"No," I say. I swallow thickly. "I'm afraid you'll say nice things and I *will* believe you. You can't trust anything you think you feel right now. Not until things are back to normal and we know what's going to happen."

He might think we can rise above the fallout once Coach Thomas chooses between us, if it comes to that, but I'm more skeptical. Regardless, he doesn't do any of the things Oliver would have done. He doesn't sigh and get moody and passive-aggressive. He doesn't argue about why my feelings are wrong. He just sits there with his hand on my knee, thinks about it for a minute, and says, "Okay."

It feels too easy. "Okay?"

"If this is what you need, sure. Until the season is over, right?"

"It might be over tomorrow," I offer.

He arches an eyebrow. Yes, it's March Madness. Anyone can beat anyone on a given day. *That's why they play the game,* Dad always says.

We both know the season won't be over tomorrow.

I amend my statement: "Not until the last piece of confetti hits the ground after the ticker tape parade."

Then he can tell me anything he wants. And I'll do the same.

TWENTY-THREE

SOMETIMES A TEAM COMES OUT FLAT. FLAT MEANS all the hunger vaporizes somewhere between the locker room and the court, and everybody plays like they have cement blocks for feet, glue for brains, and no heart whatsoever. This can happen even when the game is important. Even when the team is good and its opponent is much weaker—maybe especially then.

This is how the Monmouth game starts, our team playing sloppy and listless through an excruciating first half. It's the most delicate thing. It can be over, just like that.

Luckily, it's not. At halftime we find whatever we were missing, and after that we play loose and fiery, building an unassailable lead that holds firm through the final buzzer. In the second round we'll play Indiana.

I stay up late Thursday night working on the hype video, until my body tells me to stop with a tension headache like a thumbprint burrowing between my eyebrows straight into my skull. Ben stays up even later. He studies film until it's so late I don't remember him slipping into bed next to me, just find him curled around me the next morning.

The pundits are hyped for the matchup, because Ardwyn and Indiana both experienced championship glory decades ago, grew accustomed to the lifestyle, and have won a big fat nothing ever since. The parallels have people salivating. But the buildup promptly deflates, because we run right over the Hoosiers.

It's an early game and the flight back to Philly takes only ninety minutes, so we're home in time for dinner. I go to my apartment to do laundry and pick up clean clothes before heading to Ben's. When I check the scores, I see that Arizona Tech has moved on to the Sweet Sixteen too.

Taylor calls to talk about the voice-over for next week's hype video. Lately celebrities have been reaching out to us to ask for the gig instead of the other way around, and it's way better than making lists of people to beg. Last week we had Pink, a Bucks County native. For the next game, we've locked down the Phillies' star first baseman.

During the dryer cycle, I wait in the laundry room and text Kat about the games, the videos, the flight. And the nights in the hotel, within reason.

> **Annie: and on top of all that . . . he told me he LIKES me**
>
> **Kat: No fucking way. You and Rold Gold are hooking up and spending every night together and baring your souls, and you're trying to tell me he likes you? Sounds like a bit of a stretch**

Annie: hate you

Annie: anyway I made him agree not to discuss such unseemly matters as "feelings" and "the relationship" until the season is over. no point in getting attached if this is just march madness-induced infatuation

Kat: So you're going to *continue* hooking up and spending every night together and baring your souls but since you're not talking about it, you won't get attached?

Kat: That sounds like a thing that's going to work. For sure

Kat: In other news, the day has finally come, batten down the hatches: mom bought a book about enneagram types

- - - - - - - - - - - -

PRACTICE IS LIGHT on Monday. I sit in the second row with Taylor and Jess, my feet propped up on the chair in front of me. The players are warmed up and waiting for Coach Thomas. Unfortunately, he's at the other end of the court, deep in conversation with Ted Horvath. Every once in a while he tries to retreat, only to get sucked back in for another round of semi-relevant chatter and hearty laughs.

Quincy stands near half-court, lunging sideways to stretch his inner thighs. "That Horvath dude is always smiling."

"It's creepy," Andreatti says.

Gallimore pops up from the floor, where he was half-heartedly touching his toes. He looks from side to side like an overexcited long-necked bird. "Hey, what three words do you think you could say to him that would wipe the smile off his face the fastest?"

A wave of muffled laughter ripples over the court.

"'Season-ending surgery,'" one of the sophomores offers.

"Not if it was your surgery," says Gallimore. "I bet he doesn't even know your name."

A chorus of *ohs* rings out. "How about this one?" Quincy says, snickering to himself. "'Country club closed.'"

Gallimore grins. "Now where'll he get his lobster rolls?"

"'Notice of allegations,'" Lufton offers from the sidelines. "I'd be shitting my pants too if the NCAA came knocking."

Jess mimics the quavery voice of Ted's assistant. "'Lily Sachdev called.'"

Quincy claps three times, delighted. "We've got the Instagram crew joining in!"

"Please do not ever joke about Lily Sachdev," Taylor says, shuddering.

"Who's Lily Sachdev?" Andreatti asks.

"A journalist who writes about sleazeballs in sports," Taylor says. "Team owners groping cheerleaders and stuff. And she did that one NFL concussion story, about the cover-up. If I ever see your name in a Lily Sachdev story, Andreatti, I will hunt you down."

Andreatti looks terrified. Of Taylor, not of Lily Sachdev.

Then strong-and-silent Rosario clears his throat. Heads turn. "'Taking a knee,'" he says solemnly, the first words I've ever heard him utter. I'm astonished. He talks like a baritone saxophone. He was born to narrate a hype video. Everyone knows, intuitively, not to make a big deal of his speaking, in case it discourages him from ever repeating the behavior.

Quincy nods coolly, like it's normal for Rosario to participate. "That's a good one, man." Then people toss out their own answers all at once.

"'Amtrak quiet car.'"

"'Low ticket sales.'"

"'Can't talk, busy.'"

JGE shakes his head. "You guys need to think bigger." He holds up his hand and lifts one finger with each word. "'Protected. Concerted. Activity.'"

I snort, then quickly google the phrase, because I only have the faintest idea of what he's talking about. Something smart. About . . . unionization?

Gallimore blinks. "I'll be honest, I have no idea what the hell that means, but thanks for playing."

Quincy turns to JGE for an explanation. "Protected concerted activity?" he repeats.

He says it loud enough that Ted stops talking to Thomas mid-sentence and gives them a deer-in-headlights look, and everyone dissolves into laughter again.

ON MONDAY NIGHT, Ben roasts a chicken. It's a ridiculous thing to do since we're both exhausted, but he swears he's dying for a home-cooked meal and wants to go all out. It's been nearly a week of hotel food and takeout, and after we head to Atlanta tomorrow morning it'll be more of the same.

With the chicken he makes potatoes with rosemary and honey-glazed carrots, and while he cooks, I nurse a glass of wine. It's all so domestic that if I'm not careful with the wine, I'm going to wake up tomorrow with a Dyson vacuum and a butter dish that says *butter* on the side in a whimsical font.

We sit at the table. It's late March now, and the sun is just starting to sink below the horizon. The sky out the window is blazing like a bonfire with streaks of orange and yellow, and the light turns Ben's skin golden. He's wearing a worn-in gray T-shirt and his feet are bare. When he scratches the side of his neck below his ear, my eyes follow his fingertips. I know what the skin there feels like against my mouth. And if it's not fresh enough in my memory, I'll have the opportunity to re-educate myself later.

"You're smiling," he notes.

I wipe my mouth with a napkin. "Because this is delicious. I wouldn't even have known where to start with a whole freaking chicken."

"I can follow a recipe, that's all." His forehead wrinkles. "But I thought you were into cooking. The lasagna?"

When did he—oh, that night Cassie and I made it for the *Beach House* party. I set down the napkin and cover his hand with mine. "Good news and bad news about that," I say, squeezing. "Bad news first. Lasagna is the only good thing I make, so if you're only hanging out with me for the food, you're going to be extremely disappointed."

He signals to an imaginary server. "Check, please."

"Don't you want to hear the good news first?" I ask, leaning forward. "That was emergency lasagna. We made it last minute. The real thing is a hundred times better. And it takes, like, eight fucking hours."

"And how might one get the opportunity to try the real thing? To confirm that it is, in fact, better than the emergency lasagna."

I pick up my utensils. "Unfortunately for you, I only make it when I'm super stressed or upset about something. On a related note"—I pause to sever a carrot—"I made it a lot during the first half of this season. This guy at work was being extremely unpleasant. Big-time lasagna material."

"I'm sorry to hear that. Sounds like a jerk. But, um, since you made so much of it, did you happen to freeze any?"

I chuck a sliver of potato at him.

While I clean up in the kitchen, Ben cracks open his laptop. His dishcloths are the same blue and taupe colors as his living room décor. I still can't get over the excessive matching, simultaneously precious and dorky; I want to razz him about it but also go to war with anyone else who tries to do the same.

"Their ball control is solid," Ben says when I turn off the faucet. He's talking about our next opponent, Tennessee. "I can't get over this assist-to-turnover ratio. It's just . . ." He trails off with an aching sigh.

"Turning you on a little?" I finish the sentence.

"Absolutely. It's over one point six."

I start the dishwasher. "Now I know what kind of dirty talk you like."

His eyes flick to mine over the top of the computer. "Pretty sure you've already got a handle on that."

My cheeks grow warm and I press my hands to them. He

laughs at my sudden shyness and then he's closing the laptop and dragging me out of the kitchen and I'm following him to his bedroom. The whole way there I chant, "One point six, one point six," until I'm lying over him on the blue comforter, his hair dark against the taupe pillowcase under his head.

After, when he's in the bathroom, I ask, "When you're a coach, are you going to miss analytics?"

He climbs back into bed. "All coaches have different strengths. It'll always be a tool I use, but I can't wait to do other stuff too. Work directly with the players, especially. I want to do for them what my coaches did for me. Hopefully in four years."

"You don't have to wait four years." I intertwine my cold feet with his warm ones. "You can do it next season."

He nudges me with his toes. "Still trying to get rid of me. Ruthless as ever." Turning to face me, he plants his elbow on his pillow. "A while ago you told me you came back to Ardwyn because you had no choice, but it seems like you're happy here now. Aren't you?"

I scoff, but it's weak. "I guess," I admit. Out loud, for the first time. He smiles, satisfied, as if I said *Absolutely, yes, with all my heart*. In a way it feels like I did.

But then his brow furrows. "I still don't understand why you stopped working in basketball to begin with."

I pause, swallow. "I always liked the actual work, but there were other aspects of the job I couldn't handle. The whole swearing-your-undying-loyalty, taking-the-blood-oath, loving-the-team-like-your-own-mother thing. This isn't a family, no matter how many times people say it is. It's a business. And college sports are a mess."

"How do you mean?" he asks.

"Where do I start?" I shake my head. "Shitty medical coverage for athletes, including football players who get whacked repeatedly in the cranium. Racial disparities in graduation rates. With NIL, I'm glad they get paid now, but it's total chaos. There's so much money and power on the line. It's hard for things to change."

Senior year, when the season started, Maynard asked me to sit in his hotel room and take notes while he watched film on road trips. He made the request in front of other people, certain coaches and staff members he was close to. They didn't say a word, so how could it be inappropriate? Who would allow it to happen if it was inappropriate? Those people looked the other way for him. I saw their presence as a sign of my safety, but they were there to keep *him* safe. Their careers depended on him.

He didn't do anything weird the first couple times. Never said anything he wasn't supposed to, just watched film and told me what to write down. There were always snacks.

Sometime in mid-November he was on the phone when I knocked on the door. He let me in, pointed to the couch, and walked into the bedroom. He left the door open a crack, so I couldn't avoid hearing his end of the conversation. "I don't know what to tell you," he was saying. "It's already stressful. Please don't make it worse."

When he walked back into the room he said, "Sorry about that. Kelly doesn't want to go to this hospital banquet." He let out a big, dramatic sigh. "I should bring you," he said, "but everyone would say you're too young for me." And then he laughed, like of course it was a joke.

I said, "I hope everything is okay." What I meant was: *I*

want you to be happy with your wife, because if you're happy with your wife then this is probably all in my head. He was giving me this look, and I was so uncomfortable, so I put my head down and pretended to start taking notes, even though he hadn't started the tape yet. He said, "Ah, married life," and left it at that.

A few nights later, when I came into the room, he sat down on the couch and immediately said, "Sorry I'm in a mood." I hadn't been there long enough to notice his mood. Then he said, "Kelly is pissed at me again for missing a family thing last night. I've been coaching for fifteen years, you know? She knew what she signed up for." His arm was over the back of the couch, behind me but not touching me.

I said, "Sorry to hear that." I was sweating. I couldn't stop thinking about his arm. I was wearing the biggest, baggiest Ardwyn sweatshirt I could find, like that would protect me.

He looked down at his wedding ring, twisted it. "She doesn't understand me. You'd be out recruiting with me." And then he laughed again. There was always a laugh, for plausible deniability.

Later that week, I got another middle-of-the-night text: **I hope I'm not scaring you off marriage with my venting. Just make sure you're compatible with whichever lucky guy you end up with. You need to be on the same page about careers, family, sex. Unfortunately, Kelly and I are having issues with all three.**

I felt sick when I read it. At that point I couldn't pretend he wasn't being inappropriate, but I convinced myself I could keep it under control. I told myself he had a crush, he was lonely, he had marital problems. Maybe a midlife crisis. He knew my dad, recruited his players—why would he jeopardize that by making a move on *me*? If I found the perfect balance of acting like everything was normal, laughing off the flirtatious stuff without engaging with it, but not being so direct that I hurt his ego, he would stop. It was like walking a tightrope. I spent a half hour coming up with a response to each of his texts. I used to cry before going to his room. I figured eventually, he would get that I wasn't interested and give up, and it wouldn't affect my job.

But I was wrong about my disinterest and discomfort warding him off, because he never cared about whether I was interested. And I was wrong about him not making a move. It wasn't a game I could win by saying all the right things and using denial and deflection as weapons. I thought I had agency, and I thought he had character. I was wrong about both.

I can't tell Ben any of this yet. I don't know how he's going to react, and there's no need to drop the bomb right now, before the season is over. "Do you want to know what's fucked up?" I say instead. "I still love it. I feel so strongly that all those things are wrong, and I complain about them anonymously on the Internet, but I still love college basketball. Does that make me a huge hypocrite?"

He strokes my hair, thinking. "Every industry, every business, every institution has its issues. But you have to work somewhere, so work in the place where you get to do the thing you love. And if you're here, you can make it better, even in small ways."

"I don't know if I believe that," I say. "Sometimes the only way to make something better is to blow it up."

"True." He shrugs. "But I don't know how to blow anything up. I just want to be good at what I do and make a difference that way."

"You're going to be a great coach," I say.

He squeezes my waist. "Don't you ever regret leaving? After college?"

I flop onto my back and look up at the ceiling. I can barely make out the shape of the fan. My eyes are heavy, and it's getting late. There are some things you can only say in the dark.

"It's complicated," I start. "On one hand, no. But at the same time, I keep thinking about my best video."

"Which one? The one with Keith Wesley?"

I smile. He has a favorite. He didn't even have to think about it.

"No. I don't know. See, that's the problem." I lay my forearm across my eyes.

Eight years is a long time.

I don't know if I want to continue, but the words claw their way up my throat anyway, my voice jagged with the scratches they leave behind. "I've realized lately that I haven't actually lived my life in a long time, and it's made me wonder what I've missed. Sorry, this is really heavy."

"You can be anything you want with me," he says. "But please never be sorry."

I nod. Swallow. "What if," I hazard, "I never made my best video? What if I never did my best work? What if it's something I would've done five years ago, and never did, and never will? That probably sounds like nonsense. And it doesn't matter anyway, I'm not curing rare childhood diseases—"

"Annie." He sounds surprised. Concerned. Maybe because of what I said, maybe because of the vulnerability in it. "You haven't made your best video yet. Even if you count all the ones you never made." He punches out the words with force, like he wants me to understand how sure he is.

"How do you know?" My voice is small. I hate that it is.

"Because I know this team, and next week—I don't care, I'm saying it—we'll be playing for a national championship. And I know you. You're going to turn it into magic."

TWENTY-FOUR

"SO MUCH FOR TENNESSEE'S SWEET ASSIST-TO-turnover ratio." I pat Ben on the back. Ardwyn blew that stat to pieces in our rout of the Volunteers. I'm lucky to have spotted him when I made my way back to the court after packing my camera away. The band is blasting the fight song, and people—players, staff, media, VIPs, security—are moving in every direction. I grab his shoulder and pull him down so I can shout in his ear. "How will you cope?"

"I'll manage," he says with a smile. "Elite Eight is a decent consolation prize."

Elite Eight. That means we're three wins away from pulling it all off: winning a title, making history, and saving the athletic department and our jobs.

Looking around, it's mind-boggling. At this stage of the tournament the games are in football arenas with basketball courts plunked in the middle. It's like playing on the moon, plus spectators. Coach Thomas and Quincy are at center

court, doing a post-victory interview with the sideline reporter. Taylor appears in front of me like a type-A mirage,
squeezing through the throng, saying something I can't hear.

"What?" I yell.

"I said, 'There you are!'" Taylor yells back.

When the music stops, it gets quiet fast. Even the chatter
of the remaining fans hanging back in the stadium isn't
enough to fill the vast space. It's quiet enough for me to hear
JJ Jones behind me, telling someone that Arizona Tech is
trouncing St. Mary's.

"What's the score?" Ben asks, turning around.

"Can you imagine if we make the finals and play them?"
Taylor asks with wide gleeful eyes.

I grimace. "Let's not get ahead of ourselves."

"Think about the hype video. The story writes itself. All
that history, Maynard coaching here—coaching one of our
coaches—and leaving to go to Arizona Tech? Then having
to face us in the finals?"

"Ben too," I say.

"What?"

"He wasn't just Eric's coach. He coached Ben too."

"What's that?" Ben reappears at my side.

"Brent Maynard," Taylor says. "We're going to have so
much content if we play them."

Ben rakes a hand through his hair. "Let's not get ahead of
ourselves."

Taylor ignores that statement for the second time. "I forgot you were here at the same time as him, Annie," she says.
"Are you friendly with him? I wonder if we could do some
cross-promotion, something we could post on both our
channels if we both make the finals."

"Absolutely not," I spit.

"Taylor, please," Ben says. "Don't plan that far ahead. You'll jinx it."

He's not superstitious.

"We don't talk," I tell Taylor. The last thing I need is for her to put something into motion that I won't be able to stop. I need to squash it before I end up in a room with him. "Let me be perfectly clear: There's not a chance in hell we'll be filming anything with him."

"Maybe you guys should talk about this somewhere else." Ben looks around to gauge whether anyone is listening. JJ Jones is still standing behind him, but he's engrossed in his phone. His belt is embroidered with little chipmunks holding tennis rackets.

"Hey, Annie?" he asks distractedly, looking up. "You got time to grab coffee tomorrow?"

"Hey, now," says Ben.

"Um," I say.

"I want to interview you. For a story. We're working on a piece about hype videos, and you're the best in the game."

"That's awesome," Taylor says.

I shoot her a look. "I'll be busy *making* the hype video."

Taylor sets her hands on her hips. "Which more people will watch if ESPN does a story on you."

"Come on, we're friends, right?" he asks. Taylor looks at me expectantly.

This bit of self-promotion will be about as pleasant as my last IUD insertion, but I should do it. I need to keep building my case for sticking around, in case we lose. "Fine," I relent.

"Wonderful!" Taylor claps her hands.

He names a place and time and I don't think any more of

it. But that night, Ben brings it up as we wait for the elevator in the hotel. "The coffee shop where he asked you to meet him is far away. He wants privacy."

That sounds logical. All the teams and most of their fans are clustered in the hotels near Centennial Park, and every restaurant and Starbucks nearby is oozing people in team colors. No privacy to be found.

The doors open. I walk in first and lean against the mirrored wall panel. "He's not going to hit on me, but I appreciate the concern."

He follows me inside and presses two buttons, one for my floor and one for his. The doors shut. "No, what I mean is—I think he's lying. I don't think he's doing a story on hype videos. If he were, he could do it anywhere. I think he wants privacy because he's talking about a job interview. ESPN is going to try to poach you."

I DON'T GIVE a shit about the story JJ is telling about the time he went to Pebble Beach on a golf weekend with his dad and brothers and ran into Phil Mickelson in the clubhouse. But I'm alternating nods and the occasional "wow" every thirty seconds or so, because if he senses my disinterest he might ask me a question, and the only thing worse than continuing to listen to this story would be having to actively participate in this conversation.

It's an endless cycle. He annoys me, and then he senses my irritation and gets agitated, and then guilt sets in so I try to be nice, and then he says something like: "This barista's latte art game is hella on point, man."

Why am I here? He's supposed to be interviewing me and

he hasn't asked a single question yet. I should be back at the hotel, working. We play West Virginia tomorrow, a team that beat us in one tournament game ten years ago. I was splicing together clips from that game early this morning, and I had a rhythm going before a calendar reminder for this meeting popped up to interrupt me.

I work hard to continue to appear interested in whatever JJ is saying while I make a mental to-do list for when I get back to the hotel. Beats I want to hit, effects I want to incorporate—

A face catches my eye. A pale, serious face with dark eyes that does not belong in this coffee shop. I squint past JJ's shoulder. What is Coach Williams doing here?

He slides into a booth across from someone else whose face I can't see. And then the other guy leans forward, resting his elbows on the table, and I realize who it is and what's happening all at once.

I squeeze the gold bar on my necklace. My eyes dart back to JJ. He's still talking, and Jesus Christ, he's so into this pointless story that his eyes are closed. Thank god—he hasn't even realized there's a real story breaking right under his nose.

Ed Daniels is the athletics director at Meagher University. No one in this half-empty café knows who he is. But I do, and so does JJ. There's only one reason for Williams to meet with Ed, especially here, far from the madding crowds. Williams is the assistant head coach of the hottest team in the country. Meagher lost in the first round of the conference tournament and their coach was fired before the team plane touched down in Milwaukee.

This is a job interview for Williams. If JJ finds out, that's going to be the headline tomorrow, and the team can't afford the distraction.

I weigh my options. Under no circumstances can I allow JJ to turn toward the front door. Luckily, the counter is behind me.

I fake a cough. "Hey, JJ?" Cough. "Can you get me a glass of water?"

Thankfully there's a line. I pull my cell phone out of my coat pocket. I'd be less likely to get caught if I texted, but I can't afford the risk that Ben will be in a trance watching film and won't see it until it's too late.

"Pick up, pick up, pick up," I whisper with urgency as it rings.

He answers on the third ring. "I'm at the meeting with JJ, and Williams just walked in and sat down with Ed Daniels," I say quickly. "JJ hasn't seen them yet."

"What's the place called again?" he asks without hesitation.

I tell him. "You have to hurry, I don't know how long I can—"

"I'm on my way."

Breathe in, breathe out. I can't see Williams's face, but he's gesturing with his hands, and Ed Daniels is nodding. *Williams wants to make a move.* It shouldn't be surprising; he's qualified. And if he leaves for Meagher or any other school, a coaching slot will open up at Ardwyn.

Ben can get that job. He can stay, even if his current job gets cut. Which means I can stay too. He can coach, and do what he wants to do without leaving Ardwyn, and especially without going anywhere near Arizona.

First things first, prevent a crisis. I slide out of my seat and head over to JJ. He's still in line, so I squeeze between him and the person in front of him.

"I was tired of sitting," I say. "Anyway, finish your story, I want to know what happened after you got out of the bunker."

The things I do for this team.

When we reach the front of the line, I fumble for ways to stall. I ask for a description of every pastry in the glass case. I scrap the water and order the most elaborate drink ever concocted, even though I have a perfectly good cup of regular coffee back at my seat. The barista sighs and JJ moves to return to the table.

"They'll call you up," he says, confused when I stop him.

"I know, but it's warmer back here. It's freezing by our table. Let's just wait. Have you met any other famous golfers?"

Finally, Ben walks through the door with a purposeful stride. Our eyes connect. I tilt my head toward Williams and Ben veers toward the booth. He puts a hand on Williams's shoulder and bends down, whispering in his ear. Williams rises, and this is the riskiest part because he's so damn tall, and of course JJ turns to scan the room as Williams walks toward the door. Panic flares in my chest and I send a silent apology to the guy behind the counter and let my drink slip through my fingers.

"Oh shit," JJ says, peering down at the splatter on the floor. Droplets of my half-caf-ristretto-syrup-syrup-syrup-syrup-extra-whipped-cream abomination dot his loafers. "Smooth move."

The bell on the door jingles and Williams is gone. I exhale. Ben is still standing by the booth, looking back at me, his eyes triumphant. I want to run to him and jump into his arms for a *Beach House*–style hug.

An employee appears with a mop, and I hold up an inadequate fistful of napkins. He refuses my efforts to wave him off, and I make a mental note to put a twenty in the tip jar before I leave.

When we're back at the table, JJ looks at his phone and winces. "Sorry if it seems like I've been stalling."

I almost laugh out loud. If he only knew.

"It's my bad," he says. "Honestly, I was telling you all those golf stories to try to buy time. My colleague is supposed to meet us, but she's running late. Her flight from New York this morning was delayed. She's the one who wants to talk to you." His face is serious in a way I've never seen before. "Annie, there's no story about hype videos. That's not why we wanted to meet with you."

Oh. Ben was right, after all.

"Who's your colleague?" I ask. If ESPN really wants to offer me a position, it must be someone on the video production side.

"Her name is Lily Sachdev."

My stomach boards an elevator and the cable snaps.

This may not be about hype videos, but it's not a job interview either. *Lily Sachdev* wants to talk to me. Lily Sachdev, who writes about abuses of power in sports, about corruption and misconduct. Who writes about sexual harassment.

She wants to talk to me. There's only one possible reason for that.

I always wondered if this day would come. *What would I do if a journalist came knocking?* I asked myself again and again over the years. Even lately, I've asked myself the question. Other stories like mine have been in the news a lot. Sometimes I thought that if it ever happened, I'd say *No, absolutely not, leave me alone.* Other times I fantasized about it. I knew exactly what I'd say. I practiced in my head.

But now. Now what?

I give him a pained smile. "I don't mind waiting for her."

"HOLY SHIT," BEN says when I walk into the hotel conference room a couple hours later. He's standing by the window, holding his hands to his head. I break into a sweat at the sight of him. He should be getting ready for practice, so I expected the room to be empty.

"I feel like a spy," he continues. "He didn't notice anything, right?"

I set my bag next to my computer and sit down. "Right." My chest is tight and the taste of stale coffee sticks in my mouth. Water. I need water, so I stand back up.

"That was wild." He shakes his head. "Not the smartest decision Williams has ever made. He shouldn't have been there. Is it weird that I'm having an adrenaline rush?"

"Yeah. No," I say, half listening. I open my bag but can't remember what I'm looking for, so I put it back down.

Ben crosses to the table and perches on the edge. I back away, needing time, space to think. He's not supposed to be here.

Lily Sachdev's flight did make it to Atlanta after all. JJ and I met her at her hotel, near the coffee shop. Her handshake was firm, and after she invited me to sit, she thanked me for coming, looked me straight in the eyes, and said, "I'm

working on a story about sexual harassment in college basketball. Specifically about Brent Maynard."

Lily let that information hang in the air for a minute,
watching me through no-nonsense glasses.

"I heard you talking about him after the last game," JJ
explained. "I wondered if maybe you'd want to speak to Lily."

I toyed with the little hotel notepad in front of me, folding
the top piece of paper in half and then in half again. "I see,"
I said quietly.

"You don't look surprised," Lily observed.

I looked up. "I'm not."

Lily's immaculate red lips curved compassionately and
she gave me a brisk nod. "My piece will probably be published shortly after the season is over, regardless of whether
you choose to participate. There are some risks, which we
can talk about. Take the weekend to think about it, and if
you decide to move forward, I'll come to Philly next week to
meet with you."

I want to scream. It's not fair that I have to make this
choice now.

"I have nothing against him for exploring his options,"
Ben is saying. "That's how this works. Although he's been
with Coach Thomas so long, I thought he'd stay forever. I
just can't believe how sloppy he was. He should've waited
until after the season is over, or at least met him somewhere
private."

"You're right," I say.

Ben studies me. "You're quiet."

I shake my head like I'm clearing out the cobwebs and
force a smile. "Sorry. Long morning." The water, I remember. That's what I wanted from my bag. I don't have my

usual bottle with me, so I take a plastic one from the ice bucket on the sideboard.

"It was a different kind of interview, wasn't it." Less a question, more a statement.

My blood freezes in my veins. "What?"

"Like I said last night. It was about a job, right? I bet if you want, they'll have you working on serious stuff, not just game highlights. Those Outside the Lines features on athlete sexual assault cover-ups or steroids or the pay-to-play scandal."

I almost laugh at how close he is to the truth. "It wasn't about a job." The water bottle is cold and the label is damp. I scrape part of it off with my fingernail.

He looks disappointed. "Are you sure?"

Tell him. Part of my brain urges me on, hurling the whole knotted mess at the door, trying to beat it down. But we're still in the snow globe, and if I tell him now, his reaction will be exactly what I'd hope for. Shock at first, remorse where appropriate, exactly the right amount of rage tempered by his cool head. Worse, he'll say things like *I want to support you in whatever way you need,* and *We'll get through it together,* and *What we have is big and real enough for us to handle anything,* and by the end of the conversation I will be hopelessly in love with him.

After that, the final game buzzer will sound, and the snow globe will dissolve into a fine mist. A month or so from now, when each of us is working who knows where, he'll realize that while this has been nice, he's not going to build his life around it. It's easy to believe your feelings can conquer anything when you're slow dancing in a cobblestone piazza or living one of your biggest dreams together. The truth isn't always clear until you're video chatting for the fourth night in a row with nothing left to talk about and no end in sight.

Or worse, the scandal will tank the department's ability to fundraise, and the gymnastics program will be the first to pay the price. He'll say it's not my fault, but the truth will always be that my actions led directly to his sister's dream being crushed. Natalie will go to college somewhere else, and every time she fails a test or gets written up for smuggling booze into her dorm room, we'll be reminded that it could've been different if I had dealt with my past privately.

That's not even the most pessimistic view. In my heart, I'm sure he'll believe me. But it would be irresponsible not to remind myself that it's not guaranteed. I'm not ready to brace myself for that scenario.

I rub the soggy paper between my fingers. "Yes, I'm sure. It was exactly what he said. He's doing a story on hype videos."

He seems to accept this and is quiet, contemplating.

"I better get to work," I say. "And you're going to miss the bus if you don't get downstairs."

He hesitates but thankfully can't pinpoint what's giving him pause. "Yeah," he says. Kisses me once, starts for the door. He stops at the threshold. "I hadn't thought about the possibility of one of our coaches leaving."

Thankfully he doesn't push it further. It takes a while before I can focus on my work. In one morning, everything has changed. Ben has a chance at getting everything he wants at Ardwyn. And I've only recently started to feel confident that I'm cementing my place there, but now—I don't know what's going to happen anymore. Not if I tell the world how Ardwyn basketball failed me.

It's better that I didn't tell him now. There's a safer way to do it. First, I need to clear my head and make a decision about talking to Lily. Then there are games to win, maybe even a face-off with Maynard. After that we'll go home to a quieter normalcy and see how everything shakes out, and I'll tell Ben everything with plenty of time to spare before the story goes public.

It's ten days, at most. I can handle that.

TWENTY-FIVE

ONE BY ONE EACH PLAYER CLIMBS A LADDER TO THE basket, lops off a piece of the net, and passes the scissors to the next guy. It's tradition for the winner of each region to perform this ritual, so we get to do it after beating West Virginia. I'm recording so I can mix the footage with game highlights. If we can get the rights, I'll set it to this catchy hip-hop song Gallimore is always singing, one with a repeating scissor-cutting sound effect.

Snip, snip, boom. Snip, snip, boom. Next Saturday, we'll play top-seeded North Carolina, and Arizona Tech will face Iowa Plains University, a plucky Cinderella school whose practice gym is a converted barn. The winners will compete for the championship.

The players hold the tiny bits of white polyester in their fists like treasure. When the net dangles by the last thread, somebody offers the scissors to Coach Thomas, who shakes his head and points to JGE. He climbs to the top and shears off the rest, and everyone takes turns wearing it around their necks. It's like a lion's mane or a feather boa. A scarf fit for a champion.

This will all be over soon. The thought douses the moment in a cold shower of premature nostalgia. I'm already outside it, like my camera is zooming out even though the scene is still playing out in front of me.

"A-Rad," Andreatti says, bounding up to me. He gazes down to admire the net, the webbing cascading over his shoulders and down his chest. He pets it fondly. "Want to wear it for a minute?"

I tap the camera. "Pretend I'm not here."

My phone won't stop buzzing in my pocket, but I don't check it until I'm on the bus to the airport. **NEW ORLEANS!** Cassie texts me. She declares she won't miss a Final Four in her hometown, even though she has to blow off a committee meeting. **Doesn't matter anyway**, she says. **I'm giving my notice when I get back.**

My family has already booked their flights. **Honestly not that interested in the games**, Kat says. **Mom and I will be there solely for moral support, beignets, and warm weather. And not in that order. Beignets are #1.**

Yay, I respond. I hesitate, and then add, **can you and mom come visit me tomorrow?**

> **Kat: . . . why?**

> **Annie: i need to talk to you guys about something in person**

> **Kat: That sounds ominous . . . ?**

Annie: it's nothing bad. pleaseee

Kat: So secretive. okay, we'll be there

Our flight lands in Philly at two in the morning. Ben and I spent the last five nights bunking with Kyle and Jess, respectively, so we go to his place together. I brush my teeth, change into one of his T-shirts, and climb under the covers. He always showers after he gets off the plane, so I listen to the sound of the water and stare at the wall.

When he walks into the bedroom, I pretend to be asleep. He tries to be quiet as he opens and closes drawers and fumbles to find the outlet in the dark so he can plug in his phone charger. The clean scent of his soap envelops me as he crawls into bed with wet hair and wraps a hand around my waist, tucking himself against me as I lie on my side. He presses a kiss to the back of my shoulder and murmurs, "Good night."

He likes my shoulders, he's told me that. "And you haven't even seen me in tank top season," I responded once, and he laughed.

Maybe he never will.

This will all be over soon. There's that thought again. And then I can't help it, I'm overwhelmed by a need to be close to him. I arch back without saying anything and he makes a little groaning noise. He tries to turn my body toward his and I shake my head. "No, like this." The sex is slow and sleepy, the kind that feels like home. I squeeze his hand when I come and don't let go until he collapses next to me.

The next day is Sunday, but at this point in the season that means nothing. I spend the day clinging to my computer like a buoy in the ocean. I have a vision for the hype video. It's been crystallizing in my mind for days. I get a headache when I've been imagining a video in my head for too long and need to bring it to life, like mental constipation. I'm grateful for it today. It's a relief, to have this thing to shape.

Now that the Final Four is here, all the Philly celebrities are showing up for us. Quinta Brunson *and* Tina Fey are narrating the video together. They'll be talking about teamwork and the bond forged by working toward a common goal. I'm using clips of the guys helping each other up after taking charges and talking each other down when they get flustered. Instead of the most impressive shots from our last game, I'm choosing plays that show them working together: a series of crisp passes, a well-executed pick and roll.

Doing this work is the closest I ever get to understanding this game. Why it has such a hold on so many people. It's the closest I ever get to understanding myself.

I love basketball because it's about the team as a unit as much as it's about individual stars. I love it because it's fast, because the momentum can shift before you realize it's happening, because it feels like no outcome is impossible. I love basketball because I love drama, and it's full of it. I fell in love with basketball because I wanted to share something with Dad.

All most of us want, I think, is to share something joyful with other people. Devotees suffer through the lows side by side to savor the hard-earned highs together. Casual supporters tune in for only the most thrilling moments of the biggest games because they don't want to miss out on what everyone else is watching. No one is a basketball fan alone.

I'm using an amazing song by the Soul Rebels, a New Orleans–based brass band that combines jazz with hip-hop, and I mark a couple spots where I want to add shots of the city after we get there.

I need to leave the office by five to meet Mom and Kat. I hoped Ben would be in the film room, but he's not. "Hey," he says when I peek into his office. "What do you want to do for dinner?"

My phone rings. It's a New York number. "Do you mind if I go back to my place for the night? Kat's coming for a few hours. I haven't seen her in so long, and once we get to New Orleans, things will be too hectic."

"Sounds fun," he says. "I'll be here late anyway. Have a good time."

"We will." I try to smile but it comes out wrong, my mouth twitching weakly.

"Everything okay?" he asks.

"Just tired."

I type out a text message to the New York number—to Lily—in the elevator. In our last conversation, I asked her whether the other person she's interviewing for the story is an Arizona Tech student. She was quiet for a moment. "Annie, there isn't just one other survivor. There are *many*."

My first thought was: Could I have prevented all those people from getting hurt by speaking up earlier? I know, logically, I'm not culpable for any of this, but the question still invades my mind. I've been logging a lot of phone sessions with my old therapist.

My second thought was: He did this to many people. Different people. There was no one trait that made him choose me. I couldn't have stopped him by being less drunk or more emotionally stable, or by responding to one of his texts in a slightly different way. It's messed up, but in a way it's a relief.

In the parking lot I find Cassie waiting for me in the second row, like we agreed. I initially thought Kat and Mom would be enough. But I realized I needed Cassie too, for both friendship and legal counsel.

Later, the three of them sit around the table in my apartment while I'm on the couch, a blanket over my lap. An empty pizza box sits in the middle of the table.

"You don't have to do this," Cassie says. "You're in a good place right now. I want it to stay that way."

"I'm not doing it because I have to," I say. "I'm doing it because I want to."

"Are you sure you want your name to be in it?" Kat asks.

I've been thinking about it a lot. Cassie says there's a chance he'll sue me for defamation, even though I have the text message screenshots. I know I need to go dark on social media. But I need people to know that despite everything, I found my way back to basketball. And if Ardwyn fires me for participating in the story, they need to know that too.

Mom crosses to the couch and rests a hand over mine. Her skin is soft. She's used the same moisturizer for as long as I can remember, a fragrance-free drugstore brand with a lotiony smell I would know anywhere. A smell that makes me feel safe. "Either way, we're proud of you and we love you."

"I keep thinking it means this could be my last week here." I wrap a piece of the blanket's fringe around my finger. "Not to be dramatic about it. I know I haven't been here long. I never even changed my driver's license."

"Oh, shit," Kat says. "That reminds me. You got a jury duty notice in the mail, like, three months ago."

"That's great. After New Orleans I'll head straight for jail."

"You don't know how everything's going to work out," Kat says, hugging her knees. "And either way, the next week is going to be every basketball dream you've ever had come true. Soak in every last bit of it. Make your fucking masterpiece. If this is the end, leave it all out there. Everything you have."

TWENTY-SIX

QUINCY MAY NOT BE VISIBLE IN THE LOCKER ROOM at the Superdome, but he's easy to find. Look for the throng of reporters packed five deep, microphones and recording devices aimed inward at a central point. He's the central point.

Taylor and I slump against the wall in the corner. Taylor is eating trail mix from a reusable silicone pouch. I'm putting all my weight on one foot and then the other in turns, trying to give each one a break from the pinch of my shoes. I let my head tip back against the concrete.

"Should we be filming that?" Taylor asks, her forehead contracting. She examines a raisin and drops it back into the pouch.

I make no move for my camera. "I think those eighty-four journalists have it covered."

In Taylor's defense, I often record this kind of thing. But I've already gotten plenty of footage today, and Quincy's learned enough by now to stick to the same rote answers he's been giving all week. This won't be anything new. Also, it's been a long day, and it's only ten in the morning.

"The semifinal game tonight against UNC will be the biggest game you've ever played in," one reporter says. "How are you handling the pressure?"

"Just trying to concentrate on what we're here to do," Quincy says. "Preparing for the game, staying off my phone, and sticking to our normal routines as much as we can."

During their downtime yesterday, he and JGE convened a meeting of their two-person club to discuss the Super Mario podcast. Sticking to the usual routine hasn't been easy. All week the college basketball marketing machine has taken Coach Thomas's efforts to keep the team insulated from distractions and blown them up like an overproduced pregame fireworks show. Photo shoots, press conferences, open practice for fans and press to observe. It's been fun at times, no doubt, but it's awfully difficult to focus on basketball.

Not even the locker room is a refuge. Dozens of strangers with ID badges around their necks are milling around. The room's cinder block walls have been frosted with banners and signs bearing the Ardwyn name and team colors, the NCAA logo, and the tournament's slogan: *The Road Ends Here.*

The spectacle peaks today and Monday, but it started as soon as our feet touched the ground in New Orleans. When the plane landed, airport employees rolled out a custom carpet in Ardwyn Blue, and a brass band played as we walked into the terminal. Fans in team gear populated the restroom lines, which coiled past the snack kiosk like four-colored snakes. When we walked by, the dark blue parts of the snakes cheered.

It was easier to focus once we arrived at the hotel. It's in an unfortunate location on Canal Street, and outside it smells like hot rum garbage and sugar-dusted spring break. But it's reasonably quiet, and the room I share with Jess overlooks an endless row of palm trees with fronds like waving hands. Every so often a red streetcar moseys by. Between the two big hotels across the street peeks a cluster of colorful buildings with cast-iron balconies, the tiniest glimpse of the French Quarter.

"How is the atmosphere here in New Orleans?" another reporter asks Quincy, stretching his arm to get his tape recorder closer.

"Great," Quincy says. "We haven't had a chance to see much of the city, but the staff here at the stadium is so welcoming, and you can't beat the weather."

His media training has paid off. Every day here has been the same: meals, film, and rest in the hotel, practice and everything else at the stadium. Back and forth, up and down Poydras Street on the bus.

"UNC has no freshmen in their starting lineup," one of the journalists says. "Do you think their experience gives them an advantage?"

"This is the Final Four, so I expect a tough game. All I can say is that my mindset has changed and I've grown a lot this year. The experience I've gained has been priceless for me, and I'm so grateful for it."

It dawns on me that those sound an awful lot like the words of someone reflecting on the looming end of his college career. I guess he's made his choice.

Jess ambles over, tugging on her sagging beanie. "My phone is dead."

Taylor pops an almond into her mouth and chews. "Wall charger or portable charger?"

"Portable, please." Jess holds out her hand.

Taylor pulls one out of her bag. Jess reaches out for it, but Taylor draws her hand back. "You should really carry one of these yourself. You use your phone for work."

Jess takes Taylor's face in her hands. "You are seen, valued, and appreciated," she says.

Taylor emits a tiny, incomprehensible squeak.

As the group of reporters moves from Quincy to JGE like one living organism, the locker room door opens. Eric slips in. He stops to talk to Coach Williams, who holds a clipboard between them and the reporters at mouth level, as if somebody might try to read their lips. When they're done, Eric works his way through the crowd to me.

His eyes brighten when he sees my outfit. "You look like Ms. Weston."

Ms. Weston was an ancient hippie who taught psychology at our high school. The main thing I learned from her—well, from reaching into her car every Monday to help carry a box of books inside—was how to identify the smell of hash. I look down at my floaty skirt and patterned blouse. Hm. Eric may be on to something. "I'm both thrilled and horrified."

He angles his body to cut Taylor and Jess off from the conversation. Not that they're paying attention. Jess has the charger now, but they're talking about how to get a replacement for Jess's headphones, which she left on the plane.

"Arizona Tech just went into their locker room, so we should be fine," Eric says in a low voice. The teams follow a staggered schedule, so if the Rattlers are in the locker room, there's no chance of running into Maynard in the hallway when we head out to the court for shoot-around.

The knot that's occupied my stomach all week loosens for the moment. "Good." I nod once, a wordless *thank you*. Eric offers me a high five, same as he would for a player who needed encouragement.

Every time I think about the prospect of seeing Maynard this week, that knot grows tighter and more twisted. Across the room, across the court, it doesn't matter—he'll be right in front of me, in the flesh. How will I be able to focus on anything else?

Leave it all out there, Kat said. It's become my motto. I won't let him ruin this for me.

"Check this out," Eric says, tilting his phone screen toward me. It's a post from *Beach House* Logan, a photo of an airplane window, captioned: **Final 4 bound, LAX > MSY** ⚜. A goofy giggle bubbles out of his mouth. "Is it weird that I'm nervous? *He's* going to be watching *me* tonight. How the tables have turned!"

"Pull yourself together," I say.

"Five minutes!" Coach Williams's voice booms. Time for the last practice—a relaxed, easy shoot-around—before tonight's game.

I heave my bag over my shoulder and turn to Jess and Taylor. "I'm going ahead to set up." I wind my way through the locker room to the exit, and as my fingers wrap around the handle, the door flies open. Ben stands on the other side. "Hey," I say, touching his arm. "Where'd you come from?"

His mouth is tight, his forehead wrinkled with tension. It's been a stressful week for everyone, but in a good way, and this is not the face of someone experiencing the good kind of stress. Something is wrong. My mouth goes dry, and instead of *I forgot my laptop* or *Kyle screwed up the lunch catering,* my mind immediately flies to the worst possible place. *I just saw Coach Maynard,* it will start.

"I just saw Coach Maynard," Ben says.

A block of ice materializes in the center of my rib cage. "Oh?" I choke out.

He leads me into the corridor, to a spot down the hall. Shifting from foot to foot, he looks around, at the ceiling, the sign for the restroom, the carpet, in a vaguely dissatisfied way. He scrapes a hand along his scalp.

"Uh-oh, not the hair rub," I say, trying to elicit a smile. He gives me nothing, and my heart rate climbs up and up.

Finally his eyes settle on me. "Annie, can I be honest?"

"Okay," I say slowly.

"I'm dying a little." He breathes out a half sigh, half laugh. "I have so much I want to say to you. I know you don't want to talk about us until the season is over. And it's not the ideal moment. But. This is going well, right?"

This is not where I expected this conversation to go. But it's not where I want to go either, not right now. "Ben," I say, twining my index fingers around each other. "Yes, but please."

"I don't need for the season to be over to know how I feel about you," he says.

I'm about to take down your idol, possibly get fired, and doom the school's fundraising efforts all at once, so . . . "Yes, you do. Where is this coming from? What does it have to do with Maynard?"

He rolls his bottom lip between his teeth. "He offered me a job at Arizona Tech for next season. One of his assistants is leaving."

I gawp at him. The universe is supposed to be chaotic, not *diabolical*. I feel as stupefied as a bird that's crashed into a windowpane.

"I see," I manage to say through the rush of alarm swirling through my head.

"He needs me to make a decision by the end of the weekend. A lot of teams are starting to fill slots now that their seasons are over and if I'm not going to take the job, he wants to find someone else."

"What? That makes no sense. It's Final Four weekend. How are you supposed to consider any other options? Tell him you need more time," I say.

"I think he expected it to be a no-brainer for me," Ben says. "He seemed surprised I didn't commit right away. He and I have talked about this for years, but I didn't think it would happen *now*. I don't want to jerk him around."

The ice block in my rib cage turns molten. "He's such an *asshole*," I sputter.

"Please don't say that," he says.

"You need to think about yourself! Not him."

He drags the toe of one shoe along the carpet. "I need to explain something, and maybe it will help you understand where I'm coming from." He swallows. "Coach has always known what my family situation was like. After college, he gave us the most generous gift. It's embarrassing for me to even admit it, but—he paid for my mom to go to nursing school."

"What?" My voice is faint. How much does nursing school cost? I have no idea. But there are enough zeroes for it to matter.

"I owe it to him to take this seriously," he says.

Which is exactly why he gave you something so excessive, I want to say. People who owe him are easier for him to control. "What does this have to do with me, then? Sounds like you've made your decision."

"No," he says. His eyes, wild and pleading, lock onto mine. "If there's a chance Williams is leaving . . ." He exhales an unsteady breath and pauses, clearly turning words over in his mind, trying to figure out which ones he wants to say, which ones he's allowed to say. "I know it hasn't been that long, but I don't want to cut this off if we both think it could go somewhere. And I really want it to go somewhere."

I cover my face with cupped hands and groan. My heart is soaking up his words like a stale cookie in a glass of milk, but damn. There is so much we need to discuss before he makes proclamations like this, and no way we can talk about those things now. My nerves are already shredded, knowing Maynard is in this building as we speak. And practice starts in about ninety seconds.

"Why is that a bad thing?" he cries. A group of reporters exits the locker room, and he waits for it to pass out of earshot. "Do you think in a week I'm going to completely change my mind? I'm not *Oliver.* I'm not a twenty-one-year-old asshole who doesn't understand commitment. And I'm not some guy fucking around on reality TV. This gets more real for me every day. Even if that's not how it is for you. I can't keep trying to guess how you're feeling and what you're thinking about the future, especially when I'm standing here telling you I've been asked to make a decision by tomorrow."

A spiky lump rises in my throat, and I twist the chain of

my necklace around my fingertip. "What are you—do you want me to say okay, you're threatening me so let's do it your way?"

His voice shakes and his cheeks turn red. "I'm not threatening you. This isn't me trying to manipulate anything. I sleep next to you every night at home, and I'm not even allowed to say I *like* you. But I've done it, because you said you needed that boundary, and I respected that. Now I'm telling you what *I* need, and I need you to respect that. Either you want this or you don't. I can't wait in limbo anymore. I can't."

The look on his face is fragile glass, transparent and vulnerable, and I'm terrified of shattering it.

Ben has had enough people waver on whether they want to be part of his life. He deserves someone who can tell him to his face that they're committed to him, and for it to be true.

I need to be that person. There's a throbbing ache in my chest, and the realization flattens me: I already feel all the things I've been trying to hold at bay.

Willful ignorance strikes again. At first, I told myself the flirting was enough, until it wasn't. Then I told myself the kissing was enough, until it wasn't. Finally, I told myself I could have everything except the words, and that would be enough to protect me. But it wasn't. Turns out you don't have to say anything out loud to make a promise. You don't have to name a feeling to experience it. I was trying to control something that couldn't be controlled. It was like trying to catch a wave with a shot glass, and it knocked me on my ass.

Sarcasm, denial, deflection. I've got a lot of well-honed tools in my arsenal for moments like this one. But if there's one thing I've learned during this magnificent, beautiful season of the greatest game ever played, it's that building a shell around myself for the last eight years wasn't an effective way to avoid getting hurt. It was just another way of getting hurt, only with a duller weapon.

Ben is good. He's so good. Inside or outside the snow globe, it doesn't matter. He's trustworthy, and this thing between us is special. What if instead of retreating like always, I . . . don't?

The army inside me drops its defenses, and I catch his hands with mine. "We have a lot to talk about," I say, my voice thick. "Not here."

He nods quickly. "I know, and—"

The locker room door flies open, and the team streams out. We release each other's hands. Williams emerges from the group, looking around, and pivots when he sees Ben. "Callahan," he barks. "With me. Let's review matchups in the paint."

Ben gives me a helpless look.

"Later," I assure him. "We'll make time. I promise."

He disappears with Williams, and I rejoin Taylor and Jess, going through the motions of normal conversation while I'm reeling inside. On our way to the court, we cross paths with some of the North Carolina staff. Coach Thomas and his Tar Heels counterpart greet each other with a firm handshake and an embrace punctuated by a single back slap. Thomas says something in the other coach's ear, and they both laugh.

Work. Right, I should do my job. My equipment is snug in the camera case, so I dig around for my phone. Better than nothing.

314 of JAMIE HARROW

"Excuse me," someone says when I'm done recording, a guy with a crew cut and a powder blue polo shirt. "Are you the one who makes the hype videos?"

He introduces himself as Scott something, from the media office in UNC's athletic department. "We've been watching your stuff all season," he says. I'm not sure who *we* is. He asks if I have a team or work alone, and what my process is like. I reciprocate with polite questions about his department. I'd rather walk barefoot down Bourbon Street than network, but the guy is being especially gracious, and I can't leave anyway.

He glances around as if to gauge how private our conversation is. We're surrounded by coworkers, but he must conclude it doesn't matter, because he offers me his business card anyway. "If you're ever looking to make a move." He walks off with a wave. I stare at the card, then unzip the interior pocket in my bag and slip it inside.

- - - - - - - - - - - -

I PROMISED BEN we'd talk later, but it's easier said than done. The rest of the day is scheduled to the millisecond, like a royal wedding. I can barely find a minute to pee, let alone meet him somewhere private for one of the most important conversations of my life.

The team sits down to an early dinner in one of the smaller hotel ballrooms, with a dark carpet patterned to hide all sins and a large chandelier with gold detailing. The buffet is the same everywhere we go: chicken, steak, pasta, vegetables. Only the most basic sauces and seasonings, to avoid upset stomachs from unfamiliar ingredients. No athlete wants to mainline Pepto-Bismol during warm-ups.

As soon as I sit down with my plate, I realize I forgot utensils. My table was the last to get our food, so the buffet is empty, save for Quincy surveying the row of metal tins on the white tablecloth. He's already back for seconds, piling his plate with a Jenga tower of lean proteins.

"How are you doing?" I ask.

"Just ready to play," he says, looking up from the grilled chicken breast. "Getting antsy."

"You're as prepared as you can possibly be. You'll be great." I pluck a fork and knife from the basket. "I'll see you later."

"Hey, one second," he says. He puts his plate down on the buffet table. "I want you to be one of the first to know. I'm coming back next season."

"What?" I screech, wrapping my arms around as much of him as I can and squeezing hard. "For real?"

He laughs, hugging me back. "For real. I'm not making any promises beyond next year—I'll never be an astrochemical engineer or whatever like JGE—but it's what I want. I want to be a player who can lead, and Ardwyn is helping me become that person. I also want to thank you."

I let go. "Me? For what?"

"The night I hurt my ankle. You were there for me, and it could've gone bad if you weren't. And now look where we are."

I wave my fork at him. "Don't get all sentimental on me."

He makes a dismissive noise. "Don't tell me what to do. That night was a turning point for me, and you helped make it happen."

"You did all that yourself," I say. "I didn't do anything. I just hid your skateboard."

"I don't know. Maybe it didn't seem like anything, but it mattered to me."

Ben's words pop into my head: *Make it better, even in small ways.*

I turn away but whirl back. "I have to thank you for something too. You taught everyone on this freaking team to call me A-Rad."

He grins. "Damn straight."

"Excuse me, guys. Just grabbing a napkin." I turn around, and there's Ben, leaning over the table.

"Benjamin," Quincy says.

He cocks his head, looking Quincy over. "When did you find time to get a haircut?"

He's right. I hadn't noticed before, but Quincy's fade appears refreshed. He pats his head. "Looks good, right? We had a guy come to the hotel earlier."

"TV-ready," Ben says.

Quincy returns to his seat, and Ben gives me a soft, appraising look. "Are you good?" he asks. "I know that was a lot, this morning."

"I'm good," I say. "I want to talk to you about everything. I do. I'm scared, but it doesn't mean I don't want to."

He nods. "I know that. How about tomorrow after dinner? I'll bribe Kyle to stay out of our room for a while."

"That sounds great," I say, and the knot in my stomach eases instead of cinches. A year ago, if someone told me I'd be spending Final Four weekend working for Ardwyn and looking forward to a serious relationship talk with Ben Fucking Callahan, I'd have asked where they got their hallucinogens.

For years I've told everyone I know, including myself, that

certain things weren't for me. But inside me all along has been a stubborn voice, hoping and craving and never dying, even when I tried to suppress it. It whispered, *What if? What if things could be different?*

What if I try to be brave? What if it's worth it?

That voice dragged my heart kicking and screaming all the way here. Tomorrow, I'll be brave and finish the job. In a quiet hotel room, I'll tell him everything exactly the way I want, and we'll deal with it together.

But first we have the game against UNC, our biggest challenge yet. The Tar Heels are well-coached, disciplined, and poised under pressure. They made the semifinals last year too, so most of their team has done this before. It's no surprise, then, when they come out strong, completely unbothered by the magnitude of the moment. They take an early lead by sticking to a sensible if uncreative game plan, focused on getting the ball inside to capitalize on their height advantage. We play jittery at the start, throwing up hasty shots instead of waiting for the right ones. Rosario gets in early foul trouble, and Quincy misses a pair of easy free throws.

We settle down eventually and chip away at their fifteen-point lead. JGE grabs a few clutch rebounds, and Gallimore draws an offensive foul, sending UNC's leading scorer to the bench for most of the second half. Their lead drops to twelve, and then seven, and then two.

With a few seconds left, Quincy threads a pass through two defenders that makes me want to break out a ruler to measure the gap between their bodies. It shouldn't be physically possible, but he gets the ball to Andreatti, who makes an effortless-looking layup to tie the score.

Overtime starts, and it's like a new game. Quincy and Gallimore get hot from three, and nobody in the country can keep up with that. UNC has no idea what hit them. We win by ten. When the buzzer sounds, Andreatti is holding the ball, and he brings it to his mouth and gives it a big, smacking kiss. Our band springs into action, blowing their horns and beating their drums like they're trying to bust a hole in the roof. Taylor's hand digs into my shoulder as she jumps up and down next to me.

We're going to the finals.

Now I can stop pretending I haven't been working on the hype video for the championship game for the last three weeks. I've written the copy, and it's on its way to Michael B. Jordan. An A-list actor with a gorgeous speaking voice and a starring role in the most iconic Philly-set film franchise ever? He's perfect for the job, and I can't believe he agreed to do it.

I don't watch the Arizona Tech game. I don't even follow the score online. It doesn't matter, for my purposes. Despite Taylor's fantasies of a video highlighting long-fermented resentments and intertwined paths leading to a dramatic showdown with Maynard, I chose not to focus on our opponent at all. The video is all about Ardwyn.

It opens on a shot of the players sitting around stretching before practice, filmed last week. No music, just casual conversation, everyone reminiscing about championships they played in as kids or watched on TV. A couple of the guys ragging on Andreatti because he's never made the finals of anything. "It's not only about talent," he says defensively. "It's also about timing and luck. Like that old saying, 'I'd rather be lucky than good.'"

Quincy chimes in, and I swear I didn't script this: "I had a coach who used to say, 'I'd rather be lucky *and* good.' That's how you win a championship. Everything needs to come together at the right moment. It's the only way."

Dad's last championship was Quincy's freshman year, and I remember him saying that, deadpan like always: "I'd rather be lucky *and* good." The game was at Rutgers, in an arena much bigger than any others the team had played in, and the players were nervous. "You can't do much about the luck part," Dad told them. "But you can do a lot about the good. And we have, by putting in the work this season. Being a champion is special and rare. You've worked all season, your whole lives, really, toward the next thirty-two minutes. That work—not whatever happens in this game—has made you into the people you are, the guys I'm proud to coach. Being champions would be icing on the cake. Now go take your shot."

I'm using shots from practice, the players doing drills and conditioning, sweat pouring down their faces. Walking to the weight room before sunrise, snow on the ground. Sitting in the film room, studying tape. These images are interspersed with quick, sudden transitions to the biggest moments of the season, the flashiest dunks, the most impressive three-pointers, the raucous student section. Then I took some old film of Quincy at fourteen staring at the basket, ready to shoot a free throw, and found a similar shot from this season. I morphed the first into the second, so it looks like he's growing up on-camera. JGE and Gallimore gave me some ancient travel ball videos, and I used a similar effect on them.

"Who have you become by playing basketball?" Michael

B. Jordan will ask. "What has this game given you? And with this opportunity, what will you give this game?"

When I finish for the night, I check the result of the Arizona Tech game, even though I know what I'm going to find. Despite their moxie and the fact that most of the country was cheering for them, Iowa Plains's luck has finally run out. And so, it seems, has mine.

We're playing Maynard on Monday.

TWENTY-SEVEN

WHEN THE AUDIO TRACK FOR THE HYPE VIDEO HITS my inbox, I open the file so fast the sender probably hasn't taken his finger off the mouse yet. I've been refreshing my email all morning waiting for it. Of course it couldn't arrive when I was eating a granola bar in the hotel room with Jess this morning, watching hungover UNC fans in powder blue shirts stagger down the street from the window. Or during the bus ride or the team meeting.

It has to land now, when I'm standing in the middle of the concourse at the Superdome, enveloped in chaos. Dozens of reporters surround me, yakking with each other and shouting into their phones, waiting for the doors to the interview room to open. Every so often a golf cart noses its way through the masses, ferrying equipment. A constant stream of people pause by the trash can behind me to chug the remains of the complimentary coffee and toss their empty cups. Not an ideal listening spot.

I scramble for my headphones and press play, struggling to listen as JJ Jones waves at me from a distance, dressed like an Easter egg. I try squeezing them tighter against my head, but it doesn't help. The audio isn't the problem. My headphones are top-of-the-line, supremely noise-canceling. The foam cushions covering my ears are large enough to serve as a pair of flotation devices for a toddler swim class.

The problem is that I need to close my eyes and focus, and I can't do that in this crowd, especially when the guy standing next to me keeps jostling my bag as he squeezes mustard onto his sandwich and spreads it with the empty packet. Damn. I'd like to go back to the hotel, listen to it there, and finish the video right away, but I have to record the press conference first.

In theory I could wait until the press conference is over, but I don't have the self-control for that. I have that Christmas morning feeling, and this email attachment is the biggest present under the tree.

The narration is the last piece of the last video. I imagined Michael B. Jordan's voice in my head while we worked on the script, but hearing it for real—well, it's going to hit differently.

I initially took this job because I had no other options. Now I know: The real reason I took this job was to make this video. Maybe, hopefully, my best video. After the press conference, I'll go back to the hotel and incorporate the audio, breaking it up so it hits the right beats, layering it over the background music. Then it'll be done, ready for Taylor to upload first thing in the morning.

A notification pops up on my screen and I open it without thinking.

Taylor: OMG it's amazing!!!!!

Seriously? It's bad enough that she heard it first, but the last thing I want is spoilers.

The doors to the interview room will open any minute. I need to find a quiet spot nearby. I hurry down the concourse until the voices fade and turn into an alcove near a mechanical closet. It'll do. I take a deep ceremonial breath before pressing play and—

"Of all the gin joints." Scott from the UNC media department stops in his tracks, a broad, clueless smile on his face.

Goddammit. I hope your team loses to Duke every single time you play them for the rest of eternity.

Whoa, rein it in. He did casually offer me a job yesterday. Probably not a great idea to call for a pox on a house I may need to live in next year.

I take my headphones off my ears. "Hi, Scott." My voice is strained with forced politeness. "Sticking around to watch the finals?"

"No, just packing up. We're about to head out. Is it weird that I'm looking forward to seeing what you come up with for tomorrow, even though you just beat us?"

"Little bit," I say, holding my thumb and forefinger a half inch apart.

"You know our program is significantly bigger than Ardwyn's. If you worked for us, you'd have whatever resources you needed. And we're a bigger name nationally with incredible connections, so the potential for working with cool narrators is limitless."

If only he knew. I resist the impulse to wave my phone in his face. "I think we do okay."

"Absolutely. But if you want to go even bigger, give me a call." He cranes his neck. "Looks like the doors are open now."

"Great," I say through gritted teeth.

I give my phone a desperate look before trudging off to the interview room and setting up in my usual spot, near the front and off to the side. The TV cameras get the prime location in the center, but my view isn't bad. Everyone settles in. Normally JJ would swing by at this point to say something ridiculous about swagger or grit, but he's nowhere to be found. Strange. He was just here, wasn't he? Ben, Eric, and Coach Williams stand on the opposite side of the room against the wall, looking as bored as the non-suspects in a police lineup.

It starts with little fanfare. After a week of nonstop press, everyone knows the routine. Coach Thomas climbs the steps onto the platform and sits in front of one of the microphones.

The questions start right away. *What does it mean to you personally to coach your team in a national championship? How important is the three-point shooting game to your prospects for tomorrow? How proud would your father be if he could see you today?*

Halfway through, JGE and Quincy join him at the table. *How do you prepare for a game like this? Have you had a chance to enjoy yourselves here in New Orleans or have you been entirely focused on basketball? What makes this team special? What does it mean to you to be here? What does it mean to your families, who've sacrificed so much? What would it mean to win?*

What does it mean?

What does it mean?

Honestly, once I start recording and make sure everything looks good, I let the camera roll and zone out. I force myself to pay attention to the questions in case somebody asks something interesting, but during the answers I daydream about the audio track. My phone vibrates in my pocket: three or four text messages, then a phone call, then another. At this point Taylor is just rubbing it in. She knows I'm stuck in here. I turn my phone from vibrate to silent.

JGE wraps up a response with two minutes left. The moderator scans the raised hands in the room. This must be the last question, right? Time to get a move on. I tap my foot against the floor.

"In the back, on the left," the moderator says.

The guy recites his name and the name of the publication he works for, and then he asks his question. "Coach, what can you say about the story that broke on ESPN a few minutes ago about Arizona Tech coach Brent Maynard?"

My head goes staticky. No. No, no, not now.

Ben is here, I suddenly remember. Fuck. He's looking at the reporter, his eyebrows furrowed.

Thomas looks mildly irritated. "I've been sitting here with you for thirty minutes, so you know I can't say anything since I have no idea what you're talking about."

"ESPN is reporting the results of an investigation . . ."

This is not supposed to be happening. Not now. A sickening panic floods my entire body, and the room tilts on its axis. I move away from the camera and grab the back of a chair.

". . . pattern of alleged sexual misconduct . . ."

Get the fuck out of here, my body orders, even though I'm not sure where my feet are. I duck my head and charge down the row. It's possible I bump into a chair, but I'm not sure. It's like walking through a fun house full of strobe lights.

". . . at least seven junior female employees and student volunteers . . ."

Seven. That comes through with zinging clarity, like a sucker punch. I had an idea, from my conversations with Lily, but not the exact number. I can't breathe, and I need to get out of here, but I also need to hear this. I hover near the exit.

"Most of the accusers are at Arizona Tech, but at least one has made allegations dating back to Maynard's time as your predecessor at Ardwyn."

A brief silence, and then the room explodes into mayhem. Reporters shout over each other as Thomas holds up his hands. Someone from the university PR department darts into the fray. The moderator says something, but nobody listens. It's all part of the out-of-focus background of a portrait. All I see is Ben.

He looks at the spot I occupied a minute ago. Searches the room when he realizes I'm not there. Finally his eyes, wild and confused, lock onto mine.

I can't even guess what my own face looks like, or if he needs to see my expression to know. But everything clicks into place for him pretty quickly. I can see it happen from all the way over here, his realization that this is not just a story about Maynard. It's also a story about me.

Undiluted devastation.

TWENTY-EIGHT

THIS IS PROBABLY THE WORST POSSIBLE WAY THIS
could have happened. I should be angry. I should be afraid.
Instead, I'm numb.

Ben takes a step toward me. He has to get around the
crowd. I run my hand along the wall behind me until I find
the push bar on the door and slip out of the room. Without
consciously picking a direction, I just walk, out of the interview room, past the mechanical closet, beyond the rest-
rooms. Away.

"Annie."

The story isn't supposed to come out now. What the hell?
A couple weeks after the end of the season, that was the
plan. I'm supposed to tell Ben tonight, on my own terms.
He's supposed to have plenty of time to absorb it before it
goes public.

"Annie!"

I'm still walking. But I can't walk all the way back to the

hotel, or to Philadelphia, and at some point he'll catch up. He's in better shape than I am. When I reach a door labeled VIP LOUNGE I take a chance and try it. Unlocked, and nobody's inside.

Finally I turn around, resigned. "In here."

The room looks like the inside of a bottle of scotch, all wood paneling and leather club chairs. Ben collapses into one. His face is raw, gutted. His body crumples in on itself, his back curved, his elbows barely propped up on his knees. He looks like an open wound. "Tell me."

I can't sit down. "I promise I will," I say. "But first, can you pull up the article while I try to find out what happened? It wasn't supposed to be published today. I need to know what's going on. My *name* is in it."

He starts to make a noise or say something, but it gets caught in his throat. His voice is hoarse when he speaks again. "This is real, then?"

Over the last week, I've had a lot of practice rehashing the worst thing that ever happened to me. Lily Sachdev is an extremely thorough journalist, with her Moleskine notepads and diligent questioning. It was scary, but this is equally terrifying.

"Yes," I whisper. "It's real."

His dark eyes hold on to mine so tightly it's hard to look away. But I need to talk to Lily, and I need to see the article. Maybe they're breaking it into pieces, posting part of it today, with more to come at a later date. Maybe the gory details of my story will be covered in part two.

I pull out my phone. Fourteen missed calls, twenty-two text messages. I ignore most of them.

Lily: Call me ASAP. It's urgent.

Lily: The story is dropping shortly. My editors
feel that we need to publish now, while BM is
most newsworthy. There will be fewer eyeballs
on him and the story after the finals. I wish I had
more time to warn you.

Lily: I'm sorry, Annie.

"Here it is," Ben says.

I lean over his shoulder. "Skip ahead. We probably don't
have much time."

His thumb shakes as he scrolls, first past the introduc-
tion, then through the accounts of some of the Arizona Tech
women.

Annie Radford. Holy shit, there it is. My name. It's so
overwhelming I have to look away, at the light switch, the
crystal glassware on the shelf, the photo of the cathedral in
Jackson Square mounted on the wall.

When I look back, Ben is reading Lily's summary of the
night Maynard drove me home from the bar.

"I was a big believer in the Ardwyn Family." I'm not sure
if Ben is paying closer attention to the words I'm saying or
the words on the screen, but I keep going. "Maynard was
always like . . . a cool uncle, or something. It didn't bother
me that he saw me wasted that night."

"He never acted like a regular boss," Ben says quietly.

"Right. He humored my zaniest video ideas, always asked
what music I was listening to. How much time did we spend

sitting around the office listening to him tell stories about his playing career, his early coaching years?"

"He loves telling stories," Ben says.

"He could tell a story better than anyone else. I don't know about you, but he's still the most charismatic piece of shit I've ever met, to this day."

Ben nods, swallowing thickly. I can't see his face from this angle, looking at the phone over his shoulder. It's better this way.

"His approval was priceless to me back then," I continue. "The way he treated us, like our work mattered?"

"He took us seriously."

"Exactly. You weren't the only one who took that to heart. I wanted to work in basketball so badly. Maynard knew what he was talking about, and he didn't have to tell me I could be successful, but he did it anyway."

Scrolling further, Ben skims the next few paragraphs. When he reaches a picture of Maynard's text messages to me, he freezes.

Metadata confirms that the following screenshots were saved eight years ago, the article says. Thank you, Cassie.

The last thing I need is to read these messages again. I sit in the chair across from Ben, burying my face in my hands. "I don't know which ones they included."

"'What are you dressed as for Halloween?'" Ben reads. "'You're a beautiful girl.'" He pauses, clearing his throat. "'Will you send me a costume picture too?'"

"He texted me a lot. I sent a lot of awkward 'ha-ha' responses. I was already partying too much, trying to forget about Oliver. The stress of the messages only made it worse. I started to develop this Pavlovian stomachache every time my phone buzzed. I drank more. Slept less. Couldn't focus at work."

"Did you tell anyone?" A muscle in his jaw twitches.

I shake my head. "Telling someone would make it seem like a big deal, and I didn't want it to be a big deal. All I wanted was for everything to go back to normal. I was still hoping he'd hire me full time after graduation."

He chews his lip, reading further. "What the *hell*?" His nostrils flare. "He told you to come to his *room* to take notes while he watched film?"

"Yeah."

"That doesn't even make sense," Ben sputters. "Helping with film was my job, not yours."

I stare at him. "That wasn't really why . . ."

"I know. I just don't understand. How, and why." His brows furrow as he continues reading.

My heart aches, watching him wrestle with this. It dredges up memories of what it felt like to have my conceptions of the world and the person I idolized pulverized. It's jarring to see. But then I've had eight years to get used to these facts, and he's had ten minutes. Maynard's picture is sitting on his desk back at home as we speak.

"Can you put the phone down? Let me just tell you." I wring my hands. "It all came to a head when we went to Florida for the holiday tournament."

I'd been dreading it, because I knew it would be a shit show like every year. Four days in a hotel somewhere warm and everyone always acted like it was spring break. I was hoping Maynard would get too drunk at the bar in the lobby with the rest of the coaches to ask me to come to his room, but nope.

"When I got there, he tried to get me to drink a beer with him. He took a sip from the bottle first and then tried to hand it to me, like it was normal for us to share. I said, 'No, thanks,' and he told me, 'It's okay to let loose sometimes. We've been working hard and we deserve to relax.' The next thing I knew he was touching my shoulders, giving me a back rub."

Ben's expression turns from heartbroken to homicidal.

"You're probably sore from the plane," Maynard had said. "I know I am." I froze. Forget fight-or-flight—I sat there and couldn't move. It felt like acid was burning a hole in my stomach and I couldn't process the fact that his hands were *on* me.

My throat closes up. I pull my water bottle from my bag and take a sip.

"After a couple minutes I was able to move away and a ridiculous story came out of my mouth, about how I hated massages and once got a spa gift card for my birthday but gave it to my sister, and I told him I wasn't feeling well and left. The following night I went straight to my room after the game even though he told me to come by. I was climbing into bed when he sent me a text. It was a picture, the outline of an erection through his pants."

My voice breaks. Ben leans forward on his elbows and picks up my hands, dropping his forehead to rest against them. I give myself a few breaths to regain my composure before continuing, but the memory of that night is vivid in my mind.

After I got the text, I went to the bathroom and threw up. Then I called Cassie and woke her up and told her everything, finally. We cried together, and then she went into

Cassie mode and started talking through all the options, but none of the options seemed viable. What was I going to do? He was like a religious figure on campus. Even though I had proof, going up against him was unfathomable.

A little while later he texted again. **I apologize. That was meant for Kelly.** I knew he was full of shit, and I didn't feel safe. I was sharing a room with Daria, the student athletic trainer, and thank god she came back to the room at that moment, because I was worried if he knew she was at the bar he would come to find me. But in the morning Daria had to leave early to tape ankles.

I squeeze Ben's hands. "He came to see me the next morning. I shouldn't have let him in, I knew that, but what was I going to do, make a scene in the hallway?"

As if all the people whose futures and livelihoods depended on his success would save me. No, my plan was to tell him I didn't see him like that, but no hard feelings, and that we could pretend it never happened. No big deal. I kept thinking about the fucking video I had to finish editing to send to the recruits, how I needed footage from the game that day. How I needed to deal with this—him—to get to that. I was in that stage of shock where you go on with your daily routine because you can't bear to accept that everything has changed. But he didn't give me time to say what I wanted.

Ben's face is hidden, resting against my hands, but my knuckles are wet with his tears.

"He told me he couldn't stop thinking about me." My voice wobbles. "That we had a connection, and he'd been trying to deny it, but he couldn't anymore. That he wanted me so badly, and he knew I felt the same way. He told me I'd been dropping hints for months with my texts and the way I always made an effort to dress up. That I was constantly hanging around that spring, making excuses to spend time with him. Pretending it was all about the internship I wanted. The internship he'd gotten for me."

The internship that, maybe, Ben would've gotten instead of me, if Maynard hadn't had ulterior motives.

Ben's head snaps up and he releases my hands. "Like you said earlier," he says. "He's a talented storyteller."

I fiddle with the lid on my water bottle. "He told me I was sexy. And I said, 'I'm sorry if I gave you the wrong impression.' When I think about that, I want to rip my hair out."

I finally got to say something and I *apologized*. Afterward I fantasized about what would have happened if I'd told him he was delusional and needed to fuck off. Nothing different, I know that now. In the moment I wanted to de-escalate the situation, and honestly, part of me felt bad for him. I was worried about his feelings, which was a total joke, because he'd never given a single thought to mine.

I close my eyes. "Then he looked down at himself and said, 'So, what, you're going to leave me like this?' I didn't look. I walked right past him, out the door and down the hall, and sprinted to one of the team buses outside."

Every sympathetic feeling I had for him, every remnant of admiration—it all went poof. I just felt bitter. This was the guy I thought was so capable, so supportive? That I looked up to? I went to the game. My hands wouldn't stop shaking. The footage was crap. I called Cassie at halftime, and she booked me a flight home.

"I left in the third quarter, packed, and was through airport security before anyone else left the arena. I never heard from him again. I got some texts from other people—you included—asking what happened, and I ignored everyone. I told my family, and Eric, and I begged them all not to tell anyone else. I wanted to forget it, and forget basketball."

I just wanted it to be over. A system where a person like that has so much power, enough power to fool most people and control the rest, can't be healthy, I decided. The whole thing was corrupt, rotten, top to bottom. I believed that for a long time.

I open my eyes. "I always thought—hoped—I was the only one. But I recently learned there were others. As soon as he left for Arizona Tech, he started pursuing a student manager there. No one before me has come forward, but Lily—the ESPN reporter—doubts I was the first. There's always been at least one at any given time. There's probably one right now."

I fall silent, and relief seeps into my body. I'm done. I told him everything.

Ben sits up and exhales a jagged breath, red eyes blinking rapidly. I watch him try to gather himself to speak, but he's not doing so hot.

I offer a weak smile. "On the bright side, you can never again accuse me of being a bandwagon fan."

He ignores the joke. It's probably time to retire it for good.

"I didn't know," he says. "How could I not have known?"

I shrug. "You couldn't have."

"Shouldn't I have been able to tell something wasn't right? I spent all that time with him, I worshipped him. Shouldn't there have been signs?"

"It's not like he walked around wearing a pin that said 'Serial Sexual Harasser.' He fooled a lot of people for many years," I say. Well, not everyone. Lily told me there have been rumors on certain message boards for some time, but it wasn't until a woman at Arizona Tech approached her that she had enough for a story.

I had a fleeting suspicion my first day back. What did Verona say when I accidentally recorded his conversation with Ben and Lufton? Something about Coach Thomas: *At least he's not a sexual predator.*

Both our phones light up. My missed calls and texts have doubled since I last checked, and Coach Williams's name appears on Ben's screen. He glances down but ignores it.

"What was it like for you, after you left?"

I have to wipe my eyes before I answer. Now we're both crying. "I went numb for a while. Then Oliver moved to Boston, and I thought, well, our relationship was the first domino in the chain reaction that led to my life being ruined, so maybe I should try to salvage it so I have something to show for this entire mess."

Ben opens his mouth to speak.

I hold up my hands. "Ass-backward, I know. But that's why I forced it so many times. And he was good to me, about what happened. I had panic attacks, and he was so supportive. He's the one who convinced me to go to therapy, and it helped. He probably didn't anticipate that therapy would also help me realize that our relationship wasn't working, but it did that too."

He rubs his face. "I can't believe this. All I do is tell people how great he is. My mom loves him. We took his *money.*" His voice breaks. "Annie, you didn't tell me. I get why you would've stayed quiet back then, but we're close now. At least I thought we were. *Why* didn't you tell me?"

"I wanted to. I was scared, and it was complicated. I was planning to tell you tonight."

"This is why JJ wanted to meet with you." He blinks as it sinks in. "Deciding to do this article was probably the biggest decision of your life. You must've been thinking about it nonstop the past few weeks. And you didn't say a word to me. I must be the least observant person on the planet."

I'm trying to be patient, but it's becoming difficult. "I get it, Ben, but this isn't about you. Right now I'm stuck in this room, with Maynard somewhere in the building, and a bunch of reporters who know who I am right outside the door. It's not ideal."

The rumble of something heavy being wheeled down the concourse interrupts the silence that follows, and a walkie-talkie beeps from somewhere nearby. Ben's jaw tightens as he gives the door a dirty look. "You're right," he says. "We shouldn't be talking about this."

Here, he means. We shouldn't be talking about this here.

"What do you want to do?" he asks.

Maybe I should say *take a quiet moment alone,* or *call my therapist,* but neither of those comes to mind.

I take a deep breath. "I need to get out of here." I stand, and he follows my lead. "I need to get my computer from the hotel. I spoke to the press about things that make Ardwyn look bad. I have no idea what that means for my future. But I have to finish the video, do you understand?"

I need to hide out somewhere no university administrator can find me. Cassie has told me the school won't fire me right away. If they want to get rid of me, they'll let a few months float by and blame the budget or tank my performance reviews. But I have visions of some HR person cutting off my access to the network, telling me to take some time for myself, a paid leave of absence, effective immediately. I need to work on the video, because no matter how this ends, I'm not leaving my story unfinished. I need the rest of the day.

He doesn't question whether it's the right thing to focus on right now. Because he does understand. That's why, when he inevitably tries to leave with me so we can finish our conversation in private, I need to convince him to go to shootaround instead. Because he deserves a chance to concentrate on basketball right now too.

He grabs a handful of tissues from the table in the corner and hands me one. "Let's go, then."

I dab my eyes and fan my hot, swollen face. I'm completely drained. Too drained to contemplate whether our tiny baby bird of a relationship and my future at Ardwyn can survive this.

All I can do is try to find the exit.

TWENTY-NINE

THE REPORTERS ARE GATHERING ON THE CON-
course. Not right outside the door, but down toward the interview room. The hallway curves so it's impossible to see,
but their chatter carries toward Ben and me.

Damn. I hoped they'd still be behind closed doors at the
press conference. Or better yet, that they'd already be gone,
leaving a clear path for my escape. The longer I wait, the
more likely it is that someone will wander in our direction,
but I linger anyway. Is it my imagination or do they sound
louder? Energized? More frenetic than usual? How could
they not be, after a bombshell like that?

They know. They know, and they're going to write about
it. My pulse picks up, like the world's most twisted slow clap
accelerating in my veins. This is frightening and unfair, and
I feel so exposed, especially here.

Despite all that, there's also this: I'm going to exit the stadium today and leave my story with these reporters and their

readers. It's no longer trapped inside me, and for the next few hours at least, I'm walking away from it completely. In that sense, I'm free.

Meanwhile, Ben looks like he wants to lie down on the floor and tell me to go on without him. My heart hurts, seeing him like this. How many emotions can one person possibly feel at once? I'm at, like, seven, and it seems like too many.

I didn't make the decision to participate in the story on impulse. For once I thought through the pros and cons first, consulting Cassie and Kat and Mom and my therapist. I had valid reasons for saying no, of course. The pain of reliving my worst memories; the disappointment, if he weasels his way out of any consequences; the risk of doxxing and harassment from angry Arizona Tech fans and garden-variety misogynists. The million ways the Internet might grasp onto the truth, twist it into something unrecognizable, and run with it screaming, like a streaker zigzagging across a football field with his hair on fire and the words *Flat Earth* painted on his ass.

But the reasons for saying yes won out. Yes, because maybe he'll lose his job. Yes, because there's a woman out there he's going to hurt next, and maybe this article will stop him. But I can't count on either of those things happening. So yes, most of all, for a more selfish reason: because he never fucking listened.

What I said to him never mattered. What I wanted was irrelevant. He never listened, but he'll be forced to hear me now. Over these past few months, I've finally accepted that by leaving basketball, I lost something good for a long time. A dormant red rage crackled to life inside me and I had nowhere to put it, until I poured it into the article like molten steel. Inner peace, acceptance, healing: all well and good. Maybe a smidge overrated. Anger, though. Sometimes anger is the best you've got. I don't know if I have the power to change anything, but I'm sure as hell pissed enough to try.

Like Dad always said: *Don't be afraid to take up space in the paint.*

Maybe Maynard will stick his fingers in his ears, close his eyes, and shout denials. Even so, my words will be there. His friends and family, his employees, his players and recruits, his bosses—they'll hear them. The uncontrollable beast of the Internet will absorb them and pass them on. And my voice will be louder and stronger because it won't be alone. It'll be joined with the voices of many brave women from Arizona Tech. Maybe he'll emerge with minimal damage, but these women won't make it easy for him. Our words will chase him, stick to him, haunt him everywhere he goes.

Boo, motherfucker.

"Let me think about how we're going to do this," Ben says. In one direction are the reporters. In the other direction a tall metal security gate looms, stretching across the width of the concourse.

Reality crashes in. I have to walk past all those people, and they know *everything*. My bravado crumbles. I blink away tears and hug myself, pulling the cuffs of my sweater down over my thumbs.

"Hey." Ben squeezes my shoulders. "It's going to be okay. We'll walk fast, heads down, stick close to the wall. I know it seems like everyone will be paying attention to us, but they won't. I'll walk in front of you."

His eyes are red and his cheeks are splotchy. Not exactly

inconspicuous himself. But he doesn't seem to care about that.

I make a hideous, wet sniffling sound. "Okay. Let's get this over with."

We inch through the crowd along the wall. My nose is touching his spine.

I hold on to his belt loop with one hand and thrust the other into my bag, casting around for my sunglasses so I can cover my puffy eyes. They must be all the way at the bottom. I dig in farther.

It's a sturdy tote, but not a miracle worker. With one strap in the crook of my elbow and the other dangling free, the mouth of the bag opens too wide and the heaviest item inside topples to the floor: my water bottle. The lid detaches with a loud popping sound. The bottle's contents spill everywhere.

"Shit!"

"So much water," Ben says, dumbfounded. Eight hours' worth, to be precise.

People are staring now, and not just in my imagination. They're coming over with napkins, and someone's looking for a janitor.

Somehow, across the throng I make eye contact with Quincy. I'm lucky this is basketball, because he can see me over everyone's heads. He's standing with Coach Thomas and Coach Williams next to a pair of golf carts, the ones that are supposed to ferry them off to the locker room in time for shoot-around. His eyes scan my tragic face and the commotion around me.

Quincy raises his hands in the air. "Attention, everyone!" His voice reverberates, and the crowd stills. The guys with the napkins turn away from the puddle.

Out of nowhere, Eric is there, picking up my water bottle. "You okay?"

I stuff it back into my bag. "Peachy."

"I have a major announcement to make!" Quincy says.

"Time to go," I say. But then through the open doors of the interview room, I see—"Wait, my camera."

"I'll tell Jess to take care of it," Eric says. "Go."

"The announcement is about my future after tomorrow's game!" Quincy shouts.

"Come on," Ben says, tugging me gently by the wrist.

On the other side of the crowd, Thomas and Williams wait with one of the golf carts. "You take it," Thomas says. "This is James. He'll get you out of here." The man behind the wheel raises a hand in acknowledgment.

Quincy is still going: "As of next week, I will be taking my talents . . . drumroll please . . ."

Somebody, somewhere, starts banging a series of beats on a trash can. Thomas squats down next to me as I climb into the golf cart.

"We'll see you tomorrow, okay?" He looks me straight in the eyes, waiting for me to acknowledge him in the affirmative.

A lump swells in my throat but I manage to nod. The room is spinning, but his message is clear: *I still want you here.* On the other side of the golf cart, Williams is saying something to Ben, but I can't discern his words.

I brace myself for an argument with Ben about whether he should come with me. I need to convince him not to let Maynard ruin this experience for him. It's the Final Four, and he deserves to participate every step of the way.

But Ben doesn't climb into the golf cart. Instead, he flags

down Eric, who hops in next to me. My eyes connect with Ben's. His expression is blank, and I don't know what it means. An uneasy feeling washes over me. He can't possibly be that angry with me for not telling him.

As James accelerates, Quincy finishes his declaration. ". . . I will be taking my talents back to Twitch, hopping on stream for the first time all month!"

The reporters groan in unison.

The stadium whizzes by as James expertly maneuvers toward the exit. Despite my confusion about Ben, relief washes over me when it comes into view. I leap out before the cart stops completely and run for the door, Eric's footsteps trailing mine.

We're outside and alone. "Holy shit," I say, stretching my arms out as if to hug the brilliant blue sky. I let go of the cuffs of my sweater, finally. The right one has a hole in it where my thumb worked its way through.

We're near the loading docks where the bus drops us off every day. I have no clue how to get back to the hotel from here, so I pull up a ride-hailing app on my phone. It's a long wait, with everyone in town for the game. When I finally get a car, I'll have to pack up everything at the hotel, wait for another car, and go—where? My family's Airbnb, maybe?

Once I'm somewhere safe I'll finish the video. Thomas acted like the events of the day won't change anything, but I don't want to bank on that when the fallout isn't over yet.

"You don't need a Lyft," Eric says. "I called in reinforcements."

"My family? I don't even know where they're supposed to be right now."

But wait. Their plans for the day are irrelevant, because

they're not at a restaurant or museum or botanical garden. They're here, walking through the parking lot toward Eric and me. Even at a distance, I'd recognize Kat's riot of sunshine hair and Mom's vacation capris anywhere.

I fall into Kat's arms. "I have never been so happy to see you."

Mom puts a hand on my back. "We came as soon as we heard."

With horror, I remember Mom's plans for the day. "You're missing your tarot reading!" She's only been talking about it for a week straight. I shoo Eric back toward the building. "Get to practice," I say. "We're good."

He squeezes me like a near-empty tube of toothpaste. "I'm proud of you."

I do my best to explain to Mom and Kat what happened: the press conference, my conversation with Ben, our escape, the long wait for a car, and my half-baked plan for finishing the video.

"It took us forever to get here," Kat says. "The city is mobbed right now."

"It's true," Mom agrees. "Some strange people too. I asked this guy to take a photo of me in front of Lafitte's Blacksmith Shop this morning and instead he did a selfie of the two of us together."

"Cassie will know what we should do," Kat says.

"Good idea. I'll call her." I pull my phone out of my pocket.

"You don't need to call her," Mom says. "She's right there."

I spin around.

There she is, jogging toward us, arms flapping and curls bouncing. She wraps me in a hug so forceful we almost fall to the ground. "Eric told me," she says, huffing and puffing. "I'm so sorry. I was at my aunt's barbecue. I got here as fast as I could."

"I feel awful for making you miss a family party," I say.

"I feel awful that this is happening right now," Cassie says. "What's the plan?"

We fill her in on what I need to do, and our transportation troubles.

Cassie's got a strange, tense look on her face, and she keeps nodding aggressively. "We can go to my parents' house," she says. She's standing very still. Like she doesn't trust herself to move.

"Are you sure?" I ask.

"Sure as shit." She claps a hand over her mouth.

"I've never heard you curse," Kat remarks.

That's when it dawns on me. "You're drunk!"

Cassie steps to the side, swaying a little. "A *little* bit." There it is, a hint of a slur. "All the relatives were there. Uncle Henry made his special red punch. I get drunk maybe twice a year, how was I supposed to know my friendship services would be needed today?"

I laugh, and Cassie raises a finger. "Joke's on you because I am extremely useful, even when intoxicated," she says. "My cousin went to her office after she dropped me here to do some work. Workaholic lawyer, sound familiar? Her office is on Poydras. We can take her car to the hotel and then to the house."

She holds her hand up for a high five. Kat obliges.

"Only problem is, my BAC is way too high. Obviously. Whoever drives has to be careful. Traffic normally isn't too bad here, but with the tournament it's pretty chaotic today, especially near the hotel. And watch out for streetcars."

Kat and I exchange a look. All those rides to and from school, the mall, the movies. The hours of sitting in strangers' driveways, at houses with FOR SALE signs on the front lawns. Unnecessary lifts to train stations and airports when public transportation or rideshares would suffice. Mom can't help it; it's her love language.

She's already pushing up her sleeves. Her jaw is set. This is the moment she's been training for her entire life. "I'll drive."

THIRTY

IT'S DARK WHEN I FINISH THE VIDEO. IT ENDS ON A shot from practice, the camera zooming out as the players stretch on the court like they do every single day. "This is your moment," Michael B. Jordan says. "Go take your shot."

I send it to Taylor. While I wait for a response, I lean on the windowsill in the second-floor office and peer outside. The patio behind Cassie's parents' house is weathered stone, illuminated by bronze lanterns. A thick swath of ivy climbs the back fence, and creamy white flowers bloom on the magnolia tree below the window. It's only a few miles from the hotel, but it's a different world.

It's seven thirty. The last team dinner of the season probably just wrapped up. A twinge of anxious longing hits me, the feeling that my life is happening elsewhere. I should be eating bland chicken and listening to motivational speeches with everyone else.

Taylor: It's AMAZING.

Taylor: I'm crying!

Taylor: Posting at 9am.

Peace settles in. That's it, then. The best thing I've ever made is done. Ben was right, I couldn't have created something like this five years ago.

Taylor: We missed you tonight.

Jess: 🖤

A heart emoji? From Jess? Things are truly dire. Maybe it's best I'm not with the team. The last thing I need is people fumbling for how to treat me.

I take my time descending the creaky wood stairs, making the transition from my editing cocoon back to the real world. Not that this version of the real world is a hardship to endure. Cassie's parents' house is a gorgeous Greek revival, with original moldings, towering ceilings, and an eclectic art collection. I find her sitting at the kitchen table in the dark, hugging a bottle of coconut water like it's a life raft. A bag of ice sits nearby, melting.

"How are you feeling?" I ask.

Cassie groans. "Day drinking is fun, they said. You're starting your own practice, let's do shots, they said." She rubs her forehead. "Nobody mentioned the seven P.M. hangover."

"Oh, you sweet, innocent girl." I pick up the ice and hold it against Cassie's temple. "On the bright side, you'll be fully recovered by the morning."

"On the bright side, even if I'm not, I don't have any work to do tomorrow before the game."

"What's the next step, after you give your notice?"

"A trip somewhere nice, since we didn't take a honeymoon. I'm not thinking about anything else until after that." She takes a sip of coconut water and makes a face. "So. How was Ben?"

I trace a crack in the old table with my finger. "Pretty sure 'shattered' about covers it. I think he's mad at me for not telling him."

"It's all going to work out. I know it will."

"I don't know," I say. "A lot has happened. A lot is happening. The Maynard stuff, and work—I have no clue how it's going to turn out for either of us. We've never even had an honest conversation about what we want from each other. Our relationship is so new I don't know if it can take all this. You think . . . he believes me, right?"

Cassie sits up straight. She looks horrified that I'm even asking. "I'm *sure* he does."

She's right. He believes me, of course. It's just . . . I haven't heard from him all evening. And I keep going over some of the things he said, his facial expressions, the fact that he didn't try to leave with me. What if, when he asked *How could I not have known?*, he meant *I don't believe this could've happened without my knowing*? What if, when he said *I can't believe this,* he meant it literally?

I force a smile. "I'm sure you're right."

"Well, I'm rooting for you guys," Cassie says. She takes

the bag of ice from me. "I think my eyeballs are sweating. Is that normal?"

In the living room I find Mom watching *Jeopardy!* while Kat lies on the couch frowning at her phone. "I'm updating Fuckwaffle's Wikipedia page," she says without looking up.

"Is that wise?" I ask.

"Well, I could go back to fighting with trolls. This seems better, doesn't it?"

"She sent pictures of one guy's rude comments to his employer," Mom says.

I cringe. "Oh, god. Please don't tell me what they're saying on the Internet about this. I don't want to know."

Cassie's thumbs fly across the screen. "Most of the response is good. But the rest need to pay."

"They'll drag you down to their level, you know that, right?"

Kat offers a cheery smile. "We're past that point. I'll be down here in hell for another couple hours. See you on the other side."

Mom pats the seat next to her. "Come over here." I sit. "I don't want you doing anything basketball-related from now until you leave for the game tomorrow. You need to decompress."

I look at the TV. "If I even go to the game," I say, a bitter taste flooding my mouth.

"Annie, it's the national championship."

"I don't know if I'll be allowed. I may be blacklisted by now."

"I don't think they're going to be that harsh. And lucky for you, your lawyer is in the other room."

A loud banging sound echoes from the kitchen. "I'm fine!" Cassie shouts.

"She'll be sober by tomorrow," Mom adds, wrapping a reassuring arm around my shoulder.

"I don't want to be a distraction. I don't want to see Maynard. And I especially don't want him to see me. It's better if I stay away." I try to say it with confidence, but my bottom lip trembles.

Mom mutes the TV and studies the remote. She turns it over, opens the battery compartment with her thumbnail, clicks it back into place. She sets it on the coffee table. "You were my bold child," she says. "You threw yourself into everything from a young age. It terrified me. I was always afraid of you getting hurt. And then you did get hurt, and you stopped being bold, and that was worse.

"But your fearlessness still came through when it was for other people. It wasn't gone, you just reserved it for the rest of us, not for yourself. You've always shown up for the people who matter. I think it's so important to do that. I don't really like basketball, do you know that? But I've been to more games than most people who love it passionately."

I open my mouth, but Mom holds up her hand. "Don't look so surprised. I don't like shopping all that much either."

"Mom!"

"But I love my family, so I went to basketball games, and I take my daughters to the mall so I can spend time with them," she says. "I still remember the way you yelled at that guy who was criticizing your father's coaching from the bleachers a few years ago. And when you marched into that frat party to confront that kid who was spreading rumors that he had nude pictures of Kat on his phone.

"Lately, you've been my bold girl again, more and more, just older and wiser. Don't stop now. You have to show up for the people who matter, and this time the person who matters is you. This is the national championship, and you should be there."

Fine. After this trip I'll sit down and help her figure out that ancestry website once and for all. I rest my head on Mom's shoulder, wiping my eyes with the poor beat-up sleeve of my sweater. "Ah, god, Mom. You're such a Pisces."

She laughs and wraps an arm around me. On the other couch, Kat is still poking feverishly at her phone, her eyes alight with mischief. It's almost a perfect moment.

I swallow. "I miss Dad."

Mom squeezes me closer. "Me too. Always."

"It's weird," I say. "I didn't go to a single basketball game from the day Dad died until the day this season started. I was afraid it would make me miss him too much. But I've realized it does the opposite. When I'm at a basketball game, for a little while, he's *there*. Not in a religious way, obviously, and I know Kat's full of crap when she tries to convince us there's a ghost in your attic—"

"Rude!" Kat objects.

"—but it feels like, if I turn around, he'll be standing behind me. Just . . . the sound of dribbling, the smell of popcorn and pretzels, the rhythm of the game. It's what he was made of. It makes me feel so close to him."

Mom smiles. "Basketball connected the two of you for your whole life. Why would it be any different now?"

We watch TV in a comfortable silence until Cassie shouts from the kitchen. "Dinner's ready!"

The three of us exchange puzzled looks.

"You should not have cooked," I say when I enter the kitchen. "I'm surprised the fire department isn't here. You should have gone to bed instead."

"Relax," Cassie says, depositing a pan in the sink. "Even in my current state I can handle this."

I follow her gaze to the four grilled cheese sandwiches laid out on the table.

"I wanted to make something better, but when I opened the fridge I rested my head on the orange juice carton for a minute and almost fell asleep. I decided not to push it."

"This is amazing," Kat says, busting into the kitchen.

"It's perfect," I agree.

When we're all sitting around the table, Cassie picks a gooey string of cheese off the edge of her sandwich and turns to Mom. "How are you liking New Orleans, Mrs. Radford?"

"I love it here. I've never been any place like this. I don't think there *is* any other place like this," she says. "I took some photos this morning." She pulls out her phone and puts on her reading glasses. "Let's see. Tons of beautiful buildings in the French Quarter. Oh, here's the one with the weirdo selfie guy. He was actually pretty cute."

"Ooh-la-la, Mother," Kat says. "Let's see him."

She flips the phone around and the three of us lean in. *Holy shit.* Cassie shrieks and her chair tips forward. She barely catches herself on the table. I laugh, and Kat sits back with a bemused smile.

I rip the phone from Mom's hands to get a better look. "Mom, he wasn't a weirdo! People probably ask for photos with him all the time. He misunderstood what you wanted."

"What? Why would they ask for photos with him all the time?"

Now Cassie grabs the phone. "Because," she gasps. "That's Logan. From *The Beach House*."

I GO TO the game. Probably I always intended to go to the game, if I'm being honest. But sometimes it's easier to say you don't want something when someone else controls whether you get it or not. When I board the bus, I half expect a stranger in a suit to rip my access pass from around my neck and shove me out the door.

It doesn't happen.

Another thing that doesn't happen, despite my wishes: Arizona Tech suspending Maynard for the finals. They release a gutless statement about how they take the allegations seriously and will conduct and release the results of a thorough investigation in due course. Blah, blah. They want to squeeze in a national title before dealing with any consequences.

"Glad you're here," Eric says during shoot-around.

"Me too," I agree. Last night I asked him to tell people not to say a word to me about the article, and so far they've all obeyed. Except Taylor, who checks on me every five minutes and keeps offering me snacks. It helps that the team has the biggest game of their lives to focus on.

Ben shuffles past with his hands in his pockets and does a weird eyebrow-raise-chin-jerk-acknowledgment-thing. "You okay?" he croaks, not quite making eye contact. I didn't know my stomach could sink any lower, but somehow it does.

I look for Maynard as soon as his team files onto the court. Better to get it over with. When my eyes settle on him, the shrill wail of a danger alarm jolts to life in my head. I want to limit myself to a quick glance, but I can't look away.

His hair is starting to gray. He still wears his jacket too long in the sleeves and wide in the shoulders, like he's trying to look disarming. Despite the last twenty-four hours, he's carrying himself like he belongs here, with complete ease, even in front of all these people.

I won't have to speak to him. I've planned out how to do my job tonight while giving him a wide berth, and if he approaches me there are a dozen people here who will body-slam him to the ground, starting with Taylor.

I'm on the opposite corner of the court filming warm-ups when Ben approaches Maynard. The camera falls to my side, their interaction commanding my full attention. Ben leans in to speak directly into his ear. The conversation lasts for at least three years, each of them taking turns speaking. Both of their expressions are unreadable. Unfortunately, most coaches are good at maintaining a poker face when an entire arena is watching their every move. Then Maynard nods, claps Ben on the back once, and walks back to his bench. When Ben turns around, his face is neutral, but I know him well enough to spot the tension in his jaw. He doesn't look at me.

I'm pretty sure Ben just asked Maynard for his side of the story. I need to accept what's happening right in front of my face: Ben is, at minimum, hearing him out. He's distancing himself from me. And it's possible he's aligning himself with the enemy.

The stadium vibrates with anticipation as the teams gather at center court for tip-off, amped-up fans screaming louder and louder. I feel dead inside.

Arizona Tech wins the tip-off. Their small forward drives aggressively to the basket and makes a layup, drawing a foul and making the free throw. On the next possession, we run the length of the court, and Quincy sinks a picture-perfect three-pointer. Fifteen seconds into the game and both teams have set the tone.

Mercifully, basketball does what it does best for me. It takes over, and I mostly stop thinking about Ben. The Rattlers are rough near the basket, not shying away from contact. Elbows dig into abdomens, but we give it back as best we can.

With a few seconds left in the half, their point guard floats a miraculous alley-oop pass to the rim as he's falling over, and their center slams it home to give them a four-point lead. Oof. It's a killer play, and it sets them up to take command after halftime.

On the first possession of the second half, Andreatti catches their point guard flat-footed. He lunges toward him and swipes the ball away as smoothly as a pickpocket, then passes to JGE, who makes an easy layup.

Okay, then. No need to worry about us giving away the momentum. It's a close game the rest of the way, both teams making impossible shots out of sheer will, playing at an unrelenting pace. The lead changes hands more times than I can count. I knew our team could play at this level, but I've never seen them do it for forty minutes straight. Based on how loudly Arizona Tech's fans are cheering, I'm guessing they feel the same about their own team.

With seven seconds left we're down by one point. It's time for Tiger, the play we run at the end of every practice to prepare for situations exactly like this one. Only no matter how many times we practice it, it's impossible to know how it'll turn out in a game. There are endless permutations, all hinging on snap judgments. That's the point.

Quincy waits for the inbound pass from Gallimore, eyes locked on the ball. JGE wipes the bottom of his shoes with his palms for traction. Gallimore completes the pass without issue and Quincy dribbles down the court calmly, like this is any old play and not the most important seven seconds of their careers.

JGE sets a textbook ball screen. When Quincy crosses half-court and reaches the three-point line, he has a shot. Not a perfect shot, but he's made dicier ones. But then Gallimore is on his right, trailing him by a couple feet. He's wide open, his defender lost in the paint somewhere near the basket. And he's standing in one of his favorite spots on the court, a spot Ben would say—has said, many times—gives him the best chance of scoring.

Quincy tosses him the ball, easy. Gallimore flicks his wrists and releases a perfect arc and the ball swishes through the net as the buzzer sounds.

Thousands scream in joy and agony. The rest of the team rushes the court, jumping on top of each other until the whole pile gives way and they collapse. Streamers rain down from the heavens and Quincy lies in them, moving his arms and legs like he's making a snow angel. It's an ending fans will relive for generations. When an Ardwyn die-hard has a bad day or is in a nostalgic mood, they can go to YouTube and press play, again and again.

For me the ending is like the final moment of a good dream, right before you wake up and remember that your life is in shambles. Ben and I should be hugging in the middle of the chaos right now. Eric should be running over to us, his eyes bright and gleeful as he yells, "Mom and Dad!" and tackles us to the floor.

Instead, it's like my heart has been carved out of my body. I search the crowd for Ben automatically, but he's completely disappeared. My camera is like a brick wall. I capture everyone on the other side shaking with adrenaline, roaring in triumph, crying with joy. But on my side of the lens, the volume is muted and I can't seem to locate any sort of feeling whatsoever.

By the time I put down my camera, Arizona Tech has left for the locker room, and Coach Thomas is doing a postgame interview at center court. Dozens of people are still milling around, soaking in the atmosphere. Quincy bounds up to me with his hands full of streamers and ties one around my ponytail. Taylor and Jess grab me for a three-way hug like the one I thought I'd have with Ben and Eric.

I feel a little better.

Where were you when we won it all? Ardwyn fans will ask each other years from now. *I was buzzed at a bar,* some will say. *I was at the campus watch party. I was with my family, watching at home.*

Me? I was heartbroken. I was spiraling. But I was here. I was part of it, and no one can take that away. That's going to have to be enough.

THIRTY-ONE

TEN MINUTES A DAY. TEN MINUTES TO CHECK THE news, and that's it. Next week, five minutes a day. After that, I'll cancel my Google Alert and mute Maynard's name on social media. My friends and family can let me know if there's anything I should see.

I sit cross-legged on my bed, laptop resting on my knees, and click on the first article.

SPECULATION RUNS RAMPANT AS AZ TECH BEGINS SEARCH FOR NEW COACH.

I smile; the headline gives me the warm fuzzies, like a video about interspecies friendships at wildlife rehabilitation centers. Rumor has it Maynard tried the sex addict angle behind the scenes, pleading with the university to let him check into rehab so he can beg for another chance when he inevitably bursts out in a month calling himself a changed man.

Rumor also has it he knew the story was coming and

scrambled to upgrade his staff to tempt Arizona Tech to keep him around. Which is probably how Ben found himself with a job offer on a ridiculously short deadline.

Regardless, Arizona Tech didn't bite. They fired him the day after the finals, and a bunch of the other women are filing a lawsuit against him and the university. Sometimes people get what they deserve, after all. That doesn't mean I'll be surprised to see him quietly hired as an assistant coach at a smaller school in a year or two. Memories are short, but I've done my part.

I couldn't blow the whole thing up, but I contributed to incremental change. The lasting impact remains to be seen. The institution of college sports is severely flawed, maybe fatally so. I still believe that. But it's less messed up than it was a month ago, and there's enough good in it for me to try sticking around for a while.

I scroll through the rest of the new articles. Arizona Tech, Arizona Tech, Arizona Tech. The part of the story that took place at Ardwyn is almost a footnote.

Ardwyn has survived this scandal unblemished so far. Maybe I should've predicted this. Most of the obvious individual targets for blame—Maynard himself, the former athletics director, even the head of the Title IX office responsible for sex discrimination complaints—are long gone, since so much time has passed. Condemning institutions and structures isn't sexy when there are real people with names and faces to blame instead.

Also, the team just won a championship, which bought the school a gold mine of goodwill. When people talk about Ardwyn now, our win dominates the discussion. A couple days ago, Reddit latched onto a ridiculous thread speculating that Maynard left Ardwyn because he was quietly fired for his misbehavior. It's not true. He left of his own volition, for a pay increase and a job at a school with lower academic standards, where admissions and academic requirements would be laxer. But many people want to believe it, and it's not like Ardwyn is going to correct them.

Donors are happy, the NCAA is about to throw a mountain of cash at us for winning the title, and tons of high school juniors have added Ardwyn to their college application list. The school's piggy bank is overflowing. Nobody's job is going anywhere, and every other sport—including gymnastics—is safe.

That's why I spent most of the week after the championship lugging my furniture and other belongings from Kat's place to my apartment. It's time to settle in for real. I even hung pictures on the walls, although I'm keeping Mona Lisa Vito right where she is.

I have mixed feelings about how the story has (not) affected Ardwyn. Thankfully, at the bottom of the list of recent articles is this, from a Philly paper: ARDWYN TO COMMENCE MAYNARD INVESTIGATION, REVIEW TITLE IX PROCEDURES.

I heard about it yesterday, and I'm cautiously hopeful. I never expected Ardwyn to engage in much self-reflection. The university president is a Catholic priest. The precedent doesn't instill optimism.

It's possible the investigation is just for appearances, because they're obligated to send a message that they take harassment seriously, or because they want to stay a step ahead of Arizona Tech and win the head-to-head PR battle in the headlines. But they hired an investigator who's known for not messing around. She's from a firm in D.C., and magazine profiles rave about how she's led the charge for anti-harassment reform at multiple Fortune 500 companies. Change isn't guaranteed, but it seems possible.

And with that, my ten minutes of news consumption are up. It's time to go anyway. I close my laptop, grab a coat, and wind a scarf around my neck. It's a chilly day, and I'll be outside for hours.

The route for the championship parade runs through Center City Philadelphia, down Market Street to City Hall and back toward campus. The cheerleaders lead the way, carrying a banner and waving flags and pom-poms, trailed by a pair of double-decker buses full of players and staff. Blue confetti floats through the air like lazy butterflies. People pack the sidewalks, kids sitting on their parents' shoulders. All the voices shouting "wooooo" harmonize into a never-ending exuberant droning sound.

I sit near the front of the second bus so I can film the players, most of whom claim the upper deck of the bus in front. When I'm done, I plop onto a seat next to Taylor, Jess, and Donna.

"Let's take a picture together," Taylor says, handing Donna her phone. She leans in closer to me. "Jess, come on."

Taylor pushes Jess's beanie off her forehead so her entire face is visible, and Jess squeezes in. Donna holds the phone away from herself and squints. She taps the shutter button. "Good," she declares, looking at the photo.

As we gathered in the parking lot to board the buses this

morning, I saw Donna for the first time since the story broke. She didn't say a word, just wrapped me in an uncharacter-istic hug, long and tight enough to make me wonder.

My phone vibrates in my pocket. **Aww you have work friends!** Kat says, with a picture of her computer screen. She's watching the parade online, and the camera panned past us as Donna took the photo. I send back an eye-roll emoji, even though she's right. They may be a ragtag crew of people I never would've bonded with otherwise, but yeah, they're my friends.

When we reach the park outside City Hall, Coach Thomas gives a speech. Then we pile back onto the buses, which wind through the streets back toward the Main Line.

I haven't spoken to Ben today, but it's impossible to be unaware of his presence. He's on the front bus, sitting with Eric. He looks happy, his posture relaxed as he leans back to hear Verona say something into his ear, his smile easy as he points out a fan in the crowd to Eric. He got a haircut, I no-tice. Just a trim, but it makes my chest ache, that I didn't know about it until I saw him. Maybe he's preparing to in-terview for coaching jobs.

We haven't spoken since we returned from New Orleans. I've avoided the office, waiting for things to calm down. He called me once, last night, but I was too afraid to answer.

This is how it ends, I guess. It was worth the risk. I've survived awful things. I can do it again.

Cassie is somewhere on this block with her law school friends. I scan the crowd, find her, and wave. On the bus ahead, Eric is waving at Cassie too. But Ben is gone. Maybe he went downstairs to the lower level when I wasn't looking.

No, he didn't. He's still on the bus ahead of me, but he's

not sitting in the same spot. He's standing at the back, facing the bus I'm on, looking down toward the road in deep concentration. For a moment his bus brakes, and mine gets close to it, and then—what the hell?—he's climbing over the railing at the back of his bus, and the one at the front of mine. As he swings his leg over, his bus accelerates.

"Oh my god!" a parade-goer shrieks from the sidewalk.

"What is he doing?" someone else yells.

That about covers my own thoughts. I jump up from my seat, as if that will help. If he falls and gets flattened under a tire, I'm never going to be able to look at my pasta roller the same way again.

Fortunately, he manages to land on the bus, albeit with a total lack of grace, stumbling forward and collapsing on one knee. He stands and brushes off his chinos without embarrassment, as if bus-hopping is a normal activity. "Hey."

I sink back into my seat and cross my arms. "I thought you were supposed to be an athlete."

"Hurdles were never my thing." He steps closer, his expression cautious, like a zookeeper wondering if it's safe to approach a lion. Not that I feel much like a lion.

Donna clears her throat and picks up her handbag, rising and moving a few rows back. Jess stands too.

"What's going on?" says Taylor. "Oh—is this . . . ? But coworkers aren't supposed to . . . Isn't there a rule . . . ?"

"Who cares?" Jess grabs her hand and pulls her up. "It's not a big deal."

"It's not?" Taylor's entire face turns pink and she looks down at their joined hands as Jess drags her away. Jess was right. Taylor's freckles do look ridiculous when she blushes.

Ben takes the seat next to me. "How are you?"

Now that the panic has subsided, annoyance and confusion take over. "What is this? What are you doing here?"

"I was hoping we could talk after we get back to campus."

I huff. "You've been ignoring me completely for days, and now you want to talk?"

He tilts his head toward mine. "I've wanted to talk to you every single minute of every single day, Annie."

My heart rate ratchets up a notch at the softness in his voice. Talking. I don't know if that's a good or bad thing. I want to jump into his lap and never leave, or maybe into the street, where I can crowd-surf all the way back to New Jersey. I want to know how the conversation is going to go, or maybe never find out so I can live off the best version of it in my imagination for the rest of my life.

Whatever mixed emotions I'm experiencing will have to go unresolved a bit longer. "Not today. I'm going away for a few days. My flight is this afternoon, but I'll be back on Thursday."

"Okay," he says with an easy nod, like maybe Eric already told him where I'm going. "Good. But there are a few things I need to say now." He moves to rest a hand on my knee, then thinks better of it and grabs the railing. "First, I can't stop watching your last video, and thinking about how lucky we all are that you came back here. I've also started talking to a therapist. I met with her this week. I think I need to work through . . . everything, with a professional."

"That's good," I say stiffly. "I'm a big fan of therapy."

"Second." He turns his knees toward me, so he's looking me square in the eyes. "I need you to know that I turned down Maynard's job offer on Saturday night. Before the press conference, before I knew anything."

My mouth falls open. "Why?"

"I thought about waiting, so I could see how things went when you and I talked. If you wanted me, I could've turned it down then. If you didn't, I could've gone. But I knew how uneasy you were about the possibility of me working with him, even though I obviously didn't understand why. I knew it would be lurking over our heads. And I didn't want to waste another second talking to you about him when we could be talking about us instead." He lets out an anemic laugh. "Funny how that worked out."

"I know that was big for you," I say, my throat burning.

"Also, someone once told me that I spend too much time worrying about what I'm supposed to do for other people. At the end of the day, I didn't want the job. There are no Wawas in the state of Arizona."

A snotty laugh escapes my mouth. I dig through my pocket for a tissue.

"I'm so sorry he did what he did to you." His voice is coarse with emotion. "I'm sorry he made basketball feel like an unsafe place for you. I'm sorry for the things I did this year that hurt you. I'm sorry they published the story early. You deserve so much more than what you've gotten. I hate that I made you miserable when you came back, when it took so much courage for you to do that."

"I can get past all of that," I say. "But, Ben, you abandoned me when I needed you most. I thought you didn't believe me."

His mouth freezes in an O-shape. "I never doubted you for a second."

"You couldn't even look at me!"

"I was so ashamed," he says. His hand finds my knee, and

I allow it. "I was ashamed of how oblivious I was, of how I made things worse for you. I was sick over the fact that Maynard thought I was someone he could hire and make complicit in what he was doing at Arizona Tech—that I almost let it happen. I didn't know how to make any of it right. I needed to think after you told me everything, and I kept sticking my foot in my mouth the whole time we were talking, so I figured you'd be better off if I gave you space until I got my shit together."

I bite back the urge to ask why he didn't just communicate with me about how he was feeling. It's not like I'm an expert on that front myself. "I should've told you everything earlier," I admit. "My self-protective instincts are too strong. I'm working on it."

The corner of his mouth lifts.

"I saw you talking to Maynard at the game," I say. "You weren't asking him if it was true?"

Ben squeezes my knee. "No. I told him how disgusted I was, and that our relationship was over. I told him I'm paying him back the money he gave my family for my mom's tuition. I don't want to owe him anything, even symbolically."

"And you're not mad at me for the article? Our boosters could've run for the hills. No jobs. No gymnastics program."

"I'm proud of you. I wish I could've been there to support you from the beginning. Jesus, Annie, do you not understand how I feel about you?"

"You never wanted to talk about your feelings," I say, barely maintaining a straight face.

He shakes his head. "Speaking of which, one more thing." Quiet falls over us as he turns his gaze away from me, toward the bus in front of us. I take the opportunity to study him: the dent in his bottom lip where he's biting it, the cold-reddened tip of his nose. He looks more focused on the road ahead than the guy driving the bus, probably. His face glows in the watercolor April sunshine. It never fails. The perfect light always finds him.

The silence continues. Maybe I misheard him. Maybe he changed his mind.

"Ben?" I ask.

"Just—wait a minute." He cranes his neck. "Two minutes. Give me two minutes."

I wipe my nose again, put the tissue away. When he finally looks back at me, his eyes are so soft it's not fair. Those eyes feel like he's holding me.

And then he does reach out for me, his thumb tracing my jaw, his warm hand settling on the back of my neck.

"You are so brilliant and so brave. You are the funniest person I know. We won a national championship and it was only the second-best thing to happen to me this year, because the best thing was you. You are the best thing. I would walk across town on the coldest night in January just to laugh with you. I would sweat my face off in the office day in and day out if it meant you stayed warm. If this was the last time I ever saw you, fifty years from now I'd still never be able to taste Funfetti cake or look at Marisa Tomei without missing you."

He scans the road one more time. The crowd has thinned out to nothing, the cheerleaders are gone. The bus is cruising at a faster pace. "I love you," he says. "The parade's over. I can say that now."

I fall back in my seat and blink, stunned. He's right. There's not a single piece of confetti left in the sky, and the last cluster of fans is half a block behind us. *Not until the last piece of confetti hits the ground after the ticker tape parade.* He followed my rule to the letter.

My heart is so full, brimming in my chest. He said those words, knowing everything I'd been terrified to tell him. He said those words, even after the real world came crashing in on us.

"Have a nice trip." He stands. "I'll see you when you get back."

THIRTY-TWO

I'VE NEVER BEEN TO ARIZONA BEFORE. I SHOW UP AT
the low-slung stucco ranch house bearing a veggie-and-dip
platter and an apology. The celery is browning at the edges
and the plastic lid is dented.

"I went to the grocery store near my hotel," I say. "Clearly
the wrong choice."

"Oh, please." Monica wears purple glasses and a high,
curly bun that bobbles when she talks. "I'm glad you could
make it."

Monica emailed me the day after the finals.

Dear Annie,

Subject: Raise your hand if you've ever been
personally victimized by . . .
      Sorry, bad joke? My name is Monica Valenzuela. My
story: When I worked for the Arizona Tech basketball

team as an admin a couple years ago, I had the displeasure of catching Brent Maynard's eye. I reported him through the proper channels and nothing happened. Then I came across a story Lily wrote about the harassment of pro football cheerleaders, sent her an email, and here we are.

Anyway, not too long ago I started meeting up with a couple of others here who went through the same thing we did. The group got bigger and bigger and then I thought, why not try to get as many of us together as possible?

Next Tuesday about a dozen of us will be meeting at my house in Phoenix for lunch. Nothing too formal, we'll just be hanging out and eating good food and chatting. No one is obligated to talk about anything they don't want to, but some of us have found it helpful to unpack everything with others who understand.

It's the friend group you never wanted to join, but once you're in, you're glad to be there, I promise.

Maybe this is a ridiculous idea because of the distance and short notice, but we'd love to have you join us if you can make it. If not, please let me know if you'd like to talk via email or phone or anything, any time.

I booked my flight before I even responded to the email. At Monica's house the women gather in small groups throughout the kitchen and living room. The mood is upbeat. Someone who doesn't know any better might mistake the gathering for a bridal shower, except instead of playing the Newlywed Game we're bonding over feminist revenge.

Some of the conversations are about Maynard. Others discuss work and family and television. One woman says she wishes she still worked in basketball, and another offers to help her get her foot in the door at a school in Tucson. As things wind down, a latecomer walks in. A tall woman with a pixie cut and freckles and a face I've seen before.

Her name is Lauren. She was a junior at Ardwyn during Maynard's first season as head coach, two years before I started. Her picture is on the wall in the office kitchen, a shot of all the student managers from that year on Senior Night.

I wasn't first.

Lauren is sharp and no-nonsense and I like her immediately. She invites me on a hike for the following day. "Something easy," I request, not confident in my footwear and uncertain whether I have the constitution to survive the desert. Lauren obliges, and we walk together along a mostly flat path surrounded by sandstone formations and alien-looking cacti.

Lauren is a dentist in L.A. She declined to be interviewed for the ESPN story, but she reached out to Monica anyway. "I didn't trust that my name would stay out of it, and I wasn't willing to open myself up to scrutiny—and probably harassment—by die-hard basketball fans," she explains.

We meander along the path, sipping water and talking about life. When you bond instantly with someone over shared trauma and are unlikely to ever see them again, you can skip the small talk.

Lauren tells me about her fertility treatments, her foster

dogs, and her narcissistic mother-in-law. I spill my guts about Ben.

"I'm going back tomorrow, and I'm scared," I say. "We've both hurt each other. I've only been in love one other time, and it wasn't good for me. It was exhausting, draining. I was out of control. The rest of my life suffered because all my energy was sucked up by our relationship."

"Does this guy make you feel that way too?" Lauren asks. "Don't think about the other guy. Think about this guy."

Think about Ben. Okay. When I think about Ben, I think about . . . snack-sized bags of pretzels appearing next to my computer. Laughing in a dark office. Long, unnecessary walks that fly by despite the cold. A painstakingly earnest debrief after every episode of *The Beach House*. The look on his face as he watches each of my videos for the first time, how fast he talks when he's trying to convince somebody he's right about strategy. The way he holds my body, the way he respects my needs, the way he walked in front of me through the throng of reporters at the Superdome even though he'd been crying more than I had. He owns up to his mistakes. He says what he means. He does what he says he's going to do.

"No," I say. "He makes me feel grounded. More sure. Of him, of us, of everything. Being with him makes the rest of my life better."

"Well, then," Lauren says. "Get your ass on that plane."

THIRTY-THREE

WHEN BEN OPENS THE DOOR AND I SET MY EYES ON his familiar face and his familiar body in his familiar joggers and familiar gray T-shirt, I want to launch myself into his arms. But it's not the moment for that, so I resist. He must have the same impulse, because he leans in but aborts and sticks a hand in his hair instead. His face does go from blank to Christmas-light-bright when he sees me, which is so nice I'd like to bottle the feeling and hoard it in bulk in a dooms-day bunker. I smile back, just as goofily.

"Hey."

"Hey."

Poets, the two of us.

"It's good to see you," I say. My heart is bouncing off the walls of my chest. I thought it was beating at top speed on the walk over to his apartment, but apparently that was just the warm-up.

"You too." He leans against the doorframe and looks down at me with dark, curious eyes. "What's in the bag?"

The duffel bag at my feet that I lugged here, set on the step next to me, and promptly forgot. "Right," I say. I pull out a covered baking dish and thrust it at him. "This is for you."

He peels back the foil slowly and scans the contents. "Uh-oh."

"It's not stress lasagna," I assure him. "I swear. It's regular lasagna. You haven't had it yet, so."

"Thanks." He puts the foil back in place and rubs the back of his head. "Do you want to come in?"

I bite my lip. I could say yes and do this the straightforward way. But I create narratives for a living, and I'm a sucker for a cinematic moment. I can do better than the straightforward way. Which means there's something else burning a hole in my bag.

"I have a better idea." I reach down and pull out the basketball. "Let's play a game."

The park near Ben's apartment is most popular with the toddler set, for whom the primary attraction is the new, state-of-the-art jungle gym. But next to that is a green field dotted with picnic tables, and behind it is an old basketball court that's rarely in use, the lines sun-bleached and the nets frayed.

"You remember the rules?" I shift the ball from one hand to the other and back again. "If I make a shot, I get to ask you a question. If I miss, you can ask me something."

"Oh, I remember," he says. "I remember you shooting eighty percent from the free throw line. But please, go right ahead." He leans back against the chain-link fence, folding his hands in front of him, and watches me expectantly.

After I make the first shot, I turn to find him standing near the three-point line in the corner. The sun is behind him; I squint and lift a hand so I can see his face.

"How are you?" I ask.

"Pretty good." He drags a toe across the line on the court. "I've missed you."

I may never get used to the way he's unafraid to be straight with me. Honest. It's like jumping into the ocean the first week of summer, when the water is bracing cold. Unable to resist, I jog to him, give him one quick crushing hug, and sprint back before I'm too tempted to abandon the game. He laughs.

"Is Williams taking the Meagher job?" I ask after the second shot.

"Yes. He leaves next week."

The third one sails right through the net, easy. "What about you? Are you applying for the open coaching job here, then?"

His hands rest on his hips. "Depends on how this conversation goes. If I apply, I may not get it. Kyle wants it too, and I'm sure they'll consider outsiders."

I snort. "Kyle will be lucky if he doesn't get demoted to water boy. It'll be you."

I get set in my position again, take my usual dribbles, square up to shoot. The ball starts off arcing toward the basket like it should. But then out of nowhere a hand appears, flicking the ball off course, redirecting its trajectory to send it sailing sideways until it clangs against the fence.

"Hey!" He's standing in front of me now. How did he even move so fast? "It's like you used to be a basketball player or something," I say.

"You never said I wasn't allowed to play defense."

"That's goaltending. It's different."

"Yeah, yeah. How was your trip?" He ambles toward the sideline to grab the ball.

"Cathartic," I say. "I went to Arizona."

"I heard. I'm glad you got to do that."

I reach to take the ball from him, but he pulls it back. "Nope, my shot." He nudges me out of the way at the free throw line. Even the brief contact with his elbow makes my stomach flip. The shot goes up and in, his form textbook. "Are you staying at Ardwyn?" he asks.

"Yes," I say. "Tentatively, but optimistically. I want to see how the investigation goes and what happens when the dust settles. JJ did reach out to me a couple days ago about a potential opportunity at ESPN, so that's my backup plan, but I want to work here if I can."

I can't promise that I'll want to stay forever. I don't even know if I'll want to stay past next year. It won't be the same. Williams is leaving, JGE and Gallimore are graduating. There are rumors that Thomas has had NBA offers, although I don't think he'll take one—at least not yet. Even Eric's name is starting to circulate on lists for head coaching candidates at smaller schools.

I got a perfect season, and I'll always have that. Even if next year is different, even if it's never as good as this.

"ESPN. I *knew* it," he says.

"It's in Connecticut. That's two hundred miles away."

"Numbers aren't real, Annie," Ben says. He gestures between the two of us. "But this is."

Before I can respond, he raises the ball, and I hold up my arms, jumping up and down to defend the shot. He dribbles, backs up a couple steps, and makes a tidy basket from the three-point line.

"Show-off," I grumble.

"Okay," he says. "While I thoroughly enjoy trying to keep up with you while you put on a clinic out here, let's hear it, because I'm dying a little. What's it going to be?"

He's been patient for long enough. The little shrieks of toddlers float over from the playground. I draw in a breath, and the fresh air smells like warm grass.

"Well," I start. "The first time I saw myself falling for you was Valentine's Day, when you wrote a thesis about a reality show on a napkin and gave me the best hug of my life. Then, I saw your throw pillows for the first time, and I actually *started* to fall for you."

His head tilts. "You like my throw pillows?"

"No."

He breathes out half a laugh.

I go on. "I fell for you, for sure, on Selection Sunday."

"Great night," he says softly.

My teeth find my bottom lip, worrying it between them. "I knew I was falling in *love* with you when I had to decide whether to do the story, and I realized how shattered I'd be if you hated me for it. It only took hundreds of hours of working together and walking together and staying up late talking in bed for me to appreciate that you're the best person I've ever known. For me to make it through every stage of the *Beach House* flow chart."

His mouth edges up at the corner. "All of them?"

"All of them," I confirm. "I don't know what's next, but now we're here, and I don't want to be anywhere else. Because I love you."

His smile cracks wide open. "Wow," he says. "The whole journey, and you're speaking my language." He presses his fingertips to his eyes for a breath. When he looks at me, his eyes are shining. "That settles it. If I don't get the coaching job, I'll stay in my current position for another year. My sources in the finance office have only good things to say about the budget."

His current position. My heart sinks. "What? Ben, no. You need to be coaching. I'm sure you have a ton of options right now."

His face is serene. "One year," he says. "And then we'll figure it out together. You had to wait long enough to get what you deserved. I can wait a year."

Guilt pricks at my conscience. "I was supposed to be encouraging you to put yourself first more."

"It's not entirely unselfish," he says, collecting the ball from where it's settled behind the basket. "I'll get to see Natalie's meets. And what I want most is to be with you. I love you so much."

His smile is obnoxiously moony, and I can't get enough of it. I'm at risk of turning as mushy as an environmentally friendly straw right here if I don't put a stop to this.

"Enough of that, Callahan," I bark. "You can't undress me with your eyes within fifty yards of a public playground."

He shakes his head and shoots the ball. "Are we having that lasagna for dinner or do you want to go out?"

My smile feels like it's going to break my face. "Are we still playing this game?"

"I'm sorry, that's a question. You'll have to earn my answer." He tosses me the ball.

I shake my head, reposition myself, make the shot. The ball rolls toward him and he picks it up.

"Will you get over here, already?" I ask.

He walks toward me, chucking the ball over his shoulder. I follow it up with my eyes. I can't help it; it's instinct. But the sun is too bright and I lose it in the glare. I look back at him, at his messy hair haloed by light and his brilliant smile with the lazy corners. The closer he gets, the easier it becomes to see every detail of his face, the way he can already see me. And then his arms are solid around me and my eyes are closing and all I hear is the sound of the ball landing, bouncing, a sound that feels so natural and right to me that it might as well be the sound of my own heart.

ACKNOWLEDGMENTS

I'm allowed one sports metaphor in these acknowledgments, and I'm using it now: I am so grateful for the dream team of MVPs that made this book happen.

Thank you to my wonderful agent, Allison Hunter, for your tenacious support, instincts, and vision for what this story could be. You'd get my fan vote on *The Beach House* every single time. At Trellis, Natalie Edwards contributed invaluable feedback and guided me through this process from start to finish, and Allison Malecha and Khalid McCalla provided excellent advocacy and direction on foreign rights. I'm also fortunate to have had Maddalena Cavaciuti in my corner.

My incredible editor, Cassidy Sachs, understood this book from the beginning. Cassidy, I am in awe of the care you've taken in shepherding it along, together with your enthusiasm, kindness, and probably your jump shot, though I haven't seen it (yet). Working with the rest of the team at

Dutton has been a dream: many thanks to Christine Ball, John Parsley, Caroline Payne, Hannah Poole, Erika Semprun, Tiffany Estreicher, Melissa Solis, and Ryan Richardson. Much appreciation also to Emma Capron and Frini Georgakopoulos for championing this project.

I would not have attempted to write a book if it weren't for the educators whose words of encouragement have stuck with me for years. Thank you especially to Jeff Silverman for believing in me, making me a better writer, and introducing me to the best sports journalism there is. I'm also forever grateful for what I learned from Rick Eckstein and Karyn Hollis.

To Karen Petrillo and the teachers who've helped care for my children during the years I've been working on this book: thank you, thank you, thank you.

My online writing communities, including SF 2.0 and the 2024-ever Slack, have been a great source of knowledge and friendship. To the members of those groups: You and your work inspire me.

Early readers of some or all of this book were generous with their time and thoughtful with their feedback. Thank you to Sarah Maclean, Ava Wilder, Ruby Barrett, Rawles, Shika, Emily, Nicole, Melanie, Samantha, Gennifer, and Kate.

I am so lucky to have the support of my family and friends. Thank you to my Villanova crew for the many adventures without which this story wouldn't exist; to Sara, the best hype woman, whom I am grateful to know; to the aunts, uncles, and cousins who let me run off with a book whenever I wanted as a child; and to Harry and Otis, my best boys, who kept me company throughout the writing process. Meredith, there were many days I wouldn't have been able to write without you. Thanks for letting me slither off.

Mom, you've been there for me every step of the way, tirelessly and with love, and it means everything. Eddie, I'm proud to be your sister and grateful for your help with my questions.

Jeremy, throughout this process you've given me your humor, unwavering confidence, and terrible fan-casting. I love you and our family.

Dad: Thank you for letting me sit on the bench during JSBL games, for teaching me how to bunt and spit sunflower seeds, for taking me to my first Sweet Sixteen (the sporting event, not the birthday party). Many of my best memories involve sports, and part of the reason they're the best is that I experienced them with you. Except the time you fed a wonky ball into the pitching machine and it broke my nose.

Maybe you dreamed you were training me to become a professional athlete. Well, it turns out you were training me to write this book. I love you.

ABOUT THE AUTHOR

Jamie Harrow lives and writes at the Jersey Shore. She is a graduate of Villanova University, where she wrote a sports column for *The Villanovan*, and Harvard Law School. *One on One* is her first novel.